Behold
the Reaper

To Elaine and Mark, Jack and Joe,
for all their support along the way

Behold the Reaper

BEN BEAZLEY

First published in the United Kingdom in 2011 by Bank House Books.

This paperback edition published in Great Britain in 2014 by DB Publishing,
an imprint of JMD Media Ltd

British Library Cataloguing in Publication Data
A catalogue record for this book is available from the
British Library

ISBN 978-1-78091-413-8

Typesetting and origination by Chandler Book Design

Printed and bound in the UK by Copytech (UK) Ltd Peterborough

Prelude

'Got him this time!'

Detective Superintendent William Mardlin pushed his hands deep into the pockets of his heavy overcoat and stamped his feet against the damp of the cold December morning, which was inexorably seeping through the thin soles of his shoes. Standing on the bank of the River Kell, he watched as the two constables took up the long rope's slack and began hauling in its weighty burden.

'What the hell was he doing down here, Will?'

Mardlin kept his eyes on the taut line. The leading prong of the drag hook had caught securely in the greatcoat belt; the body would be out of the water in a matter of minutes. He turned to his companion. 'Your guess is as good as mine, Webster. We're going to have to find out, though – and quickly.'

Webster Pemberton scrubbed a large hand across his stubbled jaw. As senior divisional officer he had been turned out of bed three hours ago at half past six, to be told that one of his officers on night shift was missing. Constable Thomas Weldon on beat fifteen had not been seen since just after four o'clock, and had failed to come back into the station at Long Street to sign off at six. The duty inspector, having initiated a search as a matter of course, alerted Pemberton.

At nine o'clock Weldon's helmet, bearing the number 82 on its ornate laurel wreath badge, had been found in the Kell, trapped among some weeds near Eastgate Bridge. The implication was clear, and a team of officers armed with drags were set to work. The body was spotted almost a mile downstream, caught on the guardrail of the top weir where the river flowed through Priory Park.

Will knew that, as the force's senior detective, the responsibility for finding out exactly how PC Weldon came to be in the river was going to fall squarely upon his shoulders. Side by side, he and Superintendent Pemberton walked the few yards to where the body was being pulled from the water.

It was impossible for the men on the line, now joined by two others, to work with any degree of delicacy: the weight of the corpse, dressed in full uniform and hampered by the addition of a waterlogged greatcoat, made the job extremely difficult. While the first pair held the body close to the bank, one of the other men, leaning over, fixed a second hook into Weldon's leather belt.

Hauling and grunting like a tug-of-war team, the four policemen heaved the body onto the river bank. Lying flat on his back, water pouring from his sodden clothing, Thomas Weldon was not a pretty sight. He had either suffered an injury when he first fell into the river or, more likely, had collided with an obstacle in the water while he was swept along by the current. His face had a livid bruise across the left cheek, and from its unnatural angle his nose appeared to have been broken. As if to hide the smashed teeth, a length of slimy green vegetation protruded from his slack mouth.

'I think your first job is going to be telling his wife, Webster.'

Nodding morosely, Pemberton turned and walked off along the bank to perform his unpleasant errand. The constables, now that their grisly work was completed, had moved away from the body. Visibly shaken, they stood to one side, talking in low tones.

Detective Inspector Harry North, the third member of the small group, stared down dispassionately at the heavy gold wedding band on Weldon's left hand. Like Webster, he was still wondering how Weldon's wife would take the news when a voice further along the river bank broke into his train of thought. 'Doctor's here, Sir.'

Will raised a hand briefly in acknowledgement and watched the sprightly figure of the Divisional Police Surgeon, Arthur Mallard, striding briskly along the footpath.

Courtesies exchanged, Mallard went down on one knee next to the prone figure and made a cursory examination. Standing up a moment or two later, he brushed the mud from his trousers and turned his attention to the two detectives.

'Any opinions?' Will had met Dr Mallard several times in the year and a half since he had taken over as head of Kelsford Borough Detective Department, and quite liked the old boy. Somewhere in his early sixties, Mallard had been the police surgeon for approaching thirty years. Unlike many practitioners of his age, he still showed a keen interest in his work and had a reputation for both accuracy and reliability.

'Not yet.' Mallard's clear grey eyes were almost on a level with the detective's. 'He hasn't been in the water for very long – a few hours at the most. The injuries at this stage are difficult to assess. At a guess I'd say that some are *ante mortem*, probably caused when he first entered the water, others *post-mortem*, because he was battered about in the river. There's one wound that's interesting: a heavy blow on the back of the head has fractured his skull. That could have been caused when he fell, or inflicted by a blunt instrument before he went into the water.' Retrieving his medical bag and cane from the path, Mallard prepared to leave. 'You can have the body removed as soon as you wish.' He glanced across to the other side of the swiftly flowing river, where a crowd of spectators was gathering as news of the incident spread. 'I'll inform the coroner, and if you talk to me later in the day when I've made a full examination I'll be able to tell you more.'

Once the doctor had left, Will Mardlin and Harry North followed the path upstream towards Eastgates Bridge. The December rain that had fallen during the night, replacing the previous day's snow, had become a cold, penetrating drizzle, turning the ground beneath their feet to a thick slush. Lost in their own thoughts, neither man said very much until they came to the spot where Weldon's helmet had been found.

Harry North, at fifty-one the older of the two men, stared speculatively at the wrought-iron structure twenty feet above them. A motor car and a horse-drawn delivery van bearing the legend 'Nesbitt's Bakery, 3–5 Selvidge Lane' were crossing the bridge. Tom Weldon, he reflected, had been a popular, outgoing young man, good at his job and well liked by the majority of his colleagues. There were, however, as with most people, one or two dark corners.

'I think we're on the wrong side of the bridge,' Will murmured speculatively. 'If this is where he went in it was on the other side.'

'What makes you think that?'

'There was a tear on the front of his greatcoat. I think it was probably made by one of the stanchions on the far side. I'll show you.'

As they passed under the bridge, Harry saw what Will was referring to. Sticking out of the ironwork about three feet below the parapet were a series of long metal bars, across which boards could be placed for maintenance workers to stand on.

'If you're right, then he went over the bridge just here,' Harry surmised. 'His coat must have caught on the ironwork, then ripped as he dropped into the water.'

Will considered the fast-moving current for a moment. 'But how and why? If the fractured skull was the result of his fall, then it was an accident. If he was hit from behind and dumped over the bridge, it's murder.'

His colleague's next words took him by surprise. 'There's another question to be answered. He was off his beat.' Harry had Will's full attention. 'Weldon was working the fifteen beat; this is on the sixteen. So what was he doing here?'

Ten minutes later, alone on the roadway that ran across the bridge into the town centre, Will leaned on the broad cast-ironwork and peered into the swollen current below. After a while he straightened up and, turning round, leaned his back against the parapet. His hands were frozen after holding onto the metalwork.

The rain had almost stopped now. On the opposite footway a middle-aged woman in a wide-brimmed crêpe hat and ankle-length black overcoat, the hem of which was trailing in the slushy snow, was shaking out a large dark blue umbrella before closing it. They were the only people on the bridge. Without apparently noticing him, the woman glared up at the sky as if defying the rain to start again, and, bunching the folds of the umbrella together, took up her solitary vigil next to a tramcar stop.

Like so many other things, resolving the cause of the officer's death was not going to be simple, Will reflected, and if it followed the pattern of recent events he could well have a murder to deal with.

The rattle of an electric tramcar coming past the barracks from the direction of Leaminster Gardens caught his attention. Gliding sedately down the middle of the road, shiny brass bell clanking to warn pedestrians and cyclists of its approach, the double-decker came to an abrupt halt opposite the woman in the crêpe hat. Along its upper deck an advertisement in foot high letters commended to those who suffered from bilious attacks the efficacious remedies wrought by 'Sea Breezes Headache and Nausea Cures'.

Deciding not to board the tram, Will sighed and, pushing his hands back into the pockets of his overcoat, shrugged into its enfolding warmth. On the far side of the road his eye caught a notice in the window of Mason's Grocery and provisions shop pledging that, with the second Christmas of the war approaching, 'there will be no unavoidable increase in the price of our commodities during the forthcoming run up to Christmas 1915' and that 'the management have every confidence in the ability of the British Fleet to keep our Trade Routes open, thus ensuring the free passage of sugar to this country'.

At the moment Christmas was the furthest thing from his mind. Too many things had happened lately for comfort – or coincidence – than he cared for. Perhaps the walk back to the station would help him to think.

Part One

Chapter One

Captain Samuel Norton laid down his pen and picked up the clean white handkerchief which lay next to the report that he had just finished writing. He mopped the perspiration from his face. Despite the open window the atmosphere in the room was oppressive, but the hint of a breeze stirred the pile of papers next to the young officer's elbow. Replacing the damp handkerchief, Sam appended his signature to the top sheet, before adding beneath it in a small clear hand, 'Thursday, 22nd April 1915'.

Deep in thought, he replaced the cap on the Mont Blanc fountain pen that his mother had given to him as his twenty-third birthday present in August 1913, almost a year to the day before he joined up. Stretching his arms above his head to ease the cramped muscles in his shoulders and neck, he pushed his chair back and walked over to the open farmhouse door.

Staring out across the Belgian countryside at the once carefully tended fields, now shell-scarred and barren, his eyes travelled over the rooftops of the red brick cottages of St Jean half a mile away to the rising ground to the north of the tiny village. At the foot of the first ridge was a large copse. He did not know its real name: on the battle maps it was simply shown as Kitchener's Wood. Behind was Pilckem Ridge, which from his interrogation of German prisoners he knew to be a prime objective for von Deimling's troops, dug into their trenches less than a mile further back. It was one such interview which was the source of the report that he had been labouring over for the past hour.

Sam's gaze moved nearer to home. In the field at the bottom of the lane the tents of the 2nd Buffs, set out in orderly lines as if waiting for a visiting general to inspect them, stretched out. After days and nights of living in the squalor and danger of the trenches, the soldiers welcomed – however short the break – clean bedding, cooked food and some degree of normality. The Buffs, he knew, were due that night to relieve the men of the 3rd Middlesex Regiment at Zonnebeke, near Polygon Wood.

Far enough from the front line to avoid anything more than the odd stray shell, St Jean was regarded as a relatively safe area in the middle of the cauldron of the Ypres Salient.

Twenty feet away the piercing scream of a man in agony came from the back of a horse-drawn ambulance, which stood outside the canvas marquee that served as a field operating theatre. The two tired horses in the shafts waited patiently, their heads held firmly by a young RAMC soldier while what looked like a bloody bundle of rags was lifted gently down on a stretcher. Sam reflected that the wagon, apart from the great red crosses emblazoned on its sides, was identical to that in which Louis Santine used to deliver bread to his parents' château in the Haute-Loire before the war. He could see now that the injured man was stripped to the waist, the rags which enveloped his chest and abdomen a series of hastily tied field dressings. Sam watched as he was carefully carried into the tent. Chest or belly wounds, he mused; probably shrapnel from the earlier barrage. Poor bastard was conscious enough to know what was going to happen to him in the operating theatre.

Going back into the house, Sam sat down at the heavy mahogany dining table that served as his desk. He needed to read through what he had written before sending it off to Corps Headquarters. Settling back, he picked up the closely written sheets of paper.

> . . . of the German prisoners interviewed during the last two days, each has stated unequivocally that preparations are being made by the German High Command to launch a major attack against Allied troops in this sector.
>
> The testimony of one such prisoner is I feel worthy of special note:
>
> Private Joachim Dolman; No. 2 Company, 172nd Infantry Regiment, XV Corps. This man was taken prisoner during the action to capture Hill 60 on 17th April by a unit of the 1st Royal West Kent's. Dolman was held in the 27th Division prisoner compound at Zillebeke until yesterday pending interrogation, after which he was transferred back to the main Second Army Prisoner Reception Centre.
>
> At 6.45 p.m. yesterday evening (21st April), I interviewed the prisoner and report as follows.
>
> He states that it is common knowledge amongst the German soldiers manning the line between Steenstraat and Langemarck that dug in along the northernmost sector of the German held lines (roughly opposite to the French 45th Algerian and the 87th Territorial Divisions) is a network of canisters containing asphyxiating gas. These devices are distributed amongst the infantry at a rate of four batteries of per company, each battery holding twenty canisters. Special Pioneer Troops have been

stationed with these canisters in order to release the gases at the appropriate moment.

The prisoner has given a detailed description of these containers which he alleges are each four and a half feet in length and are activated by using a spanner to turn the release valve. German infantry stationed along the northernmost part of the sector have been issued with fabric pads which they have been instructed are to be dipped in a chemical solution. These, they are assured, will give them protection against the fumes. Rumour in the German trenches is that the use of this gas is imminent. Orders have been passed down the lines of the German XXIII and XXVI Reserve Corps that following a standard artillery barrage, on the signal of three red artillery flares, the gas is to be released against the French lines. Troops of the 46th, 51st and 52nd Divisions have been told by their officers that following release of the gas they will be able to walk over unopposed and occupy the trenches presently held by the French troops.

Dolman is a native of the German occupied territory of Alsace and as such is a conscripted soldier rather than a volunteer. As the officer for intelligence gathering in this sector I feel that a high level of credence should be given to the information supplied by this man.

Two further paragraphs outlined Sam's assessments of the strength of the German Landwehr units in the area, before closing with the inevitable 'submitted for your information and evaluation . . .'

The intelligence officer knew that in emphasising his concern over the information about these gas canisters he was running a serious risk of drawing a sharp rebuke from his superiors.

Restless, Sam returned to the doorway of the farmhouse and stood listening to the sound of the heavy guns firing four miles away to the north. German howitzers, he thought. The British gunners did not have enough shells to open up such a sustained barrage at this time of day.

For at least a fortnight word had been filtering back from prisoners concerning a new chemical weapon that the Germans were planning to use. The problem over this latest information was that the allied commanders had already made up their minds. As part of General Smith-Dorrien's staff, Sam knew that over the last two weeks the old man had reviewed several reports similar to the one he had just written, and decided that they were mistaken. It was very much a matter of judgement, he reflected. Horace Smith-Dorrien, along with other senior officers, had concluded that because the information supplied by German prisoners was so specific it must be false. Sam did not agree: too many of the prisoners and deserters were saying exactly the same thing. He was worried that if the Germans had manufactured a new secret weapon the chances were that the Allies were going to be caught wrong-footed when it was deployed.

A sound in the lane, mixed with distant shellfire, came to his ears: the deep rhythmic throb of a Douglas motorcycle engine. Turning back into the room, he slid the envelope containing his report into a leather transit pouch, and was back out in the cobbled farmyard at the moment the motorcyclist drew his machine to a halt.

The dispatch rider, who wore the single stripe of a lance corporal, pushed up his dust-filmed goggles. Similar in looks to Sam, although thinner in the face, the man was fair haired, the thick stubble covering his cheeks an almost white blonde. He had removed the wires from his uniform cap, Sam noticed, so that it could be pulled back flat on his head and not blown off when he accelerated the powerful machine along country roads.

'Do you want a drink, Corporal?' Sam asked, handing over the bulky pouch.

'Thank you, but no, sir, I need to keep going.' The broad Birmingham accent was temporarily muffled as the rider bent down to shove the pouch into his pannier, along with two others. 'Bastards are putting down a new pattern on the road between Kitchener's Wood and Mousetrap Farm. They don't usually lay a barrage on this near to dusk. They must be planning something.'

Sam gave the man his full attention. Dispatch riding was, he knew, an extremely skilful and dangerous occupation. The men became adept at working out the timings and fall of shot along the routes that they rode. It was practice to hide until a pattern of shells had fallen along the road they had to negotiate, then, knowing it would take the enemy gunners a certain time to reload, use the temporary respite to hurtle through the danger area at full throttle.

'What's different?' he asked, offering the corporal a Life Guard from his gun metal cigarette case.

Carefully the man broke off the cork tip and, pushing the other end into his mouth, fished in his pocket for a match. The corporal looked tired, Sam thought. His tunic was smeared with oil and dust and his pale grey eyes were bloodshot from peering out through the thick goggles. They were probably much of an age, Sam reflected briefly. How much longer would the Brummie last, dodging shells and snipers on his motorcycle rather than sheltering beneath the fire step of a crowded trench?

The corporal inhaled deeply. 'Wrong time of day, sir. They're absolutely plastering the road between Keerelare and Kitchener's. They hit the church in St Julien just as I was coming through. Some stretcher bearers and a load of wounded were sheltering in front of it. Poor sods must have been taken out to a man. I only cleared it because I was travelling fast.' The loose tobacco, where he had snapped off the end, was burning unevenly. Taking the cigarette from his mouth, he pinched it out and blew on the end. 'If you don't' mind, I should move on. I've got to get through to Steenstraat yet.'

Sam nodded. He did not envy the corporal the next leg of his run – across country round by Pilckem Ridge and up to the front line trenches, before returning along the canal to Second Army Headquarters.

Watching the Douglas disappearing past the field ambulance tent, Sam realised that the artillery fire to the north had ceased. This meant that the Germans were about to make an attack on the lines in the sector the dispatch rider was heading for.

Looking back over his shoulder he saw in the doorway the other occupant of the farmhouse.

Commandant André Tessier, despite the mandatory uniform changes recently imposed upon the French army, still persisted in wearing the blue trousers with a distinctive yellow stripe down the side that proclaimed him to be an officer of the Chasseurs à Pied. It would not be long, he knew, before General Ferry insisted that all of his staff officers complied with the recent regulations, and in common with the front line troops he would be forced to wear the new anonymous light blue-grey field uniform.

Tessier extended a hand holding two glasses of milky pastis towards his companion. He regarded Captain Norton as being different from the other English staff officers whom he had encountered, no doubt because he had been brought up in France.

Unlike André Tessier, Sam Norton was not a professional soldier. His parents, although English, were major shareholders in the Kosminski jewellery empire. This was based in France, and as a consequence they had moved from England to the Haute-Loire before Sam or his sister Irene were born. To be more correct, thought Tessier, Sam's mother Ruth was the one who owned the Kosminski chain. She was known throughout France as 'la belle Kosminski'. Tessier realised that he knew nothing at all about Sam's father. Sam's posting to the Second Army General Staff was entirely thanks to his background. Given his upbringing he was in reality more French than English. When war was declared in August the previous year Sam had been working at the London branch of Kosminski's, and had enlisted in the Queen Victoria's Rifles as a territorial officer. Had he been working in Paris, he would doubtless have joined an elite French regiment.

During the previous month in St Jean, assessing information and interrogating enemy prisoners, the two men had come to know each other well.

'Ricard?' Tessier asked, as Sam approached across the cobbles. The mixture of morphine and ether having taken effect, the injured man in the operating tent was now quiet. It was his thin screams that had woken Tessier from his afternoon doze in the back bedroom of the farmhouse. By mutual agreement Sam used the dining room as his office, while André worked in the master bedroom.

Tessier had arrived on the Staff of XX Corps by a somewhat circuitous route. Coming from an army family, he had joined as a Chasseur à Pied twenty years before. Having seen service in various parts of the empire's colonies, for a short while he had served under 'Papa Joffre' as a young officer in Madagascar. The outbreak of war had seen his regiment stationed in the Pas de Calais. Famous for his prodigious memory, Joffre – by now army commander-in-chief – had spotted him when visiting the region, and had stopped to speak to him. Two days later, as his company was being ordered up into the area of the Mons canal, Capitaine Tessier was summoned to Army Headquarters at Chantilly. There he was informed by a rather supercilious aide that he was being promoted with immediate effect to the rank of commandant and should report forthwith to the headquarters of General Balfourier at 11th Division.

Thus it was that Tessier found himself sharing a farmhouse in the Ypres Salient with a British officer, both of them attempting to convince their commanders that the unpalatable information they were passing back was at best accurate and at worst feasible. Along with Sam, Tessier was convinced that prisoners such as Dolman were telling the truth. Nine days before, a prisoner taken by 4th Chasseurs at Langemarck in the sector held by the 11th Division had told an almost identical story to the one that was the subject of Sam's report. The commander of the division, General Ferry, had passed the information to the units either side of his own, and been severely criticised by Balfourier for listening to such nonsense. With Balfourier gone, his replacement – General Putz – was equally sceptical.

Sam interrupted his train of thought. 'Penny for them, André.'

'I was wondering when we're going to get some generals who are young enough to understand that the future's not necessarily a continuation of the past.' Tessier was well aware that at thirty-nine, should he be fortunate enough to survive the war and remain a staff officer, his future would be bright.

'We'll have to wait a long time, my friend,' sighed the young Englishman. 'I heard the other day that an RFC observer plane reported a large concentration of enemy troops in front of Haig's sector. Field Marshal French dismissed the information because one of his cavalry patrols in the same area had come back and said they'd seen nothing.'

Like Sam, Tessier was in his shirt sleeves and braces. Standing companionably in the late afternoon sunshine, they sipped at their drinks and enjoyed the cooling breeze that was starting to blow in from the north. Now that the guns had ceased there was welcome peace.

Pulling a gold hunter from the watch pocket of his trousers, Sam Norton checked the time. It was exactly half past five.

The tranquillity of the moment was suddenly shattered by the sound of shouting from the Buffs lines a hundred yards away. At first neither of the officers could make out what the cause of the commotion was. Soldiers who seconds before, like themselves, had been enjoying the late sunshine while waiting to be called to the cookhouse for their evening meal, were running towards the far side of the encampment. Shading their eyes against the bright light, Sam and André sought anxiously to see what was happening.

Tessier gave a horrified gasp and pointed to the left of the tents. 'Mother of God – Tourcos – what's happened?'

Sam followed the Frenchman's gaze. Streaming across the fields in total disarray, their weapons and packs discarded, were dozens of Algerian soldiers, known throughout the French army as 'Tourcos'.

'To the left, André!' Close on the heels of the Algerians, also in full flight, were a dozen more baggy trousered French Zouaves.

Of one accord Sam and André pelted across the farmyard and into the field. Already British soldiers were bringing groups of the men into the lines of tents. They halted next to a thick-set middle-aged soldier, wearing the stripes and crown of a company quartermaster sergeant, who was kneeling beside an Algerian who had collapsed on the grass. Others were helping exhausted and apparently half-blinded men towards the ambulance tent.

Crouching down next to the man, Tessier demanded, 'Qu'est-ce qui c'est passé?'

The Algerian, wracked with a fit of coughing, was unable to answer. His eyes were tight closed, tears streaming down his cheeks and his face a deep purple. Only just conscious, and in extreme agony, it was obvious that he had little idea of what was going on around him. Blood flecked the spittle which his next bout of coughing brought forth. The sergeant signalled to a soldier nearby, and together they heaved the Frenchman onto his side as he began to vomit.

'Go and get a stretcher, Hutchins. Come on, move it!' The sergeant was a regular and had been in France since the beginning. He knew that whatever happened at the Front must not be allowed to spread and cause panic among his men.

Hutchins got to his feet and backed away slowly, his eyes on the casualty, before turning to run across the farmyard. Some RAMC men were pulling stretchers from a stable.

Along with Quartermaster Sergeant Borthwick and the two officers, Private Hutchins had not failed to notice that the brass buttons on the Frenchman's tunic had turned from burnished gold to the dark green of a piece of rotten meat.

That their predictions had come true was obvious. There was absolutely no doubt that the soldiers pouring back into the lines at St Jean had been gassed. After a hurried conference Sam and Tessier decided to split up and make their way towards the front lines, in the hope of finding out what had happened. Returning to the farmhouse, they swiftly saddled up their horses. Sam set off through Wiltje towards the point where the Canadian and French lines joined, while André headed in the opposite direction for the canal and Steenstraat.

The sight that greeted Sam as he made his way along the road was appalling. Most of the walking wounded had by now reached relative safety at the rear of the lines, but strewn along the roadside were those who were less fortunate: men who had collapsed and fallen while fleeing for their lives. Many of them, some dressed in the distinctive baggy trousers and waistcoats of the Zouaves, others wearing the collar flashes of the 87th Territorials, were already dead. The remainder, blue faces contorted in agony, blinded by the effects of the gas, were coughing their lives away in desperate agony.

As he pushed on through the ruins of the little village of St Julien, Sam's attention was caught by the sound of heavy fighting away to his left. The harsh chatter of machine gun and rifle fire from somewhere in the direction of Langemarck signalled that the entire Front had not been overrun. The absence of Canadians among the casualties indicated that their sector of the line had not yet been subjected to the gas.

The air was suddenly filled with the whine of an approaching shell. Throwing himself from his horse, Sam dived into what was left of a farm building, dragging the mare with him. Seconds later the ground shook with the impact of a series of high explosive shells. Part of the wall next to him collapsed, covering him in dust and rubble.

Sam waited a few moments to ensure that the battery had stopped firing before emerging from cover. The German shelling was now directed well behind the lines, which meant that their advancing infantry could not be far away. Pulling his Lee Enfield free from the saddle scabbard, he checked the magazine and worked a round into the breech before setting the safety catch. Above him he heard the dull drone of an aircraft engine. Looking up, he saw a bright yellow German Aviatik B1, the black crosses that adorned the underside of its wings standing out clearly against the blue sky. Bastards, he thought: the enemy were using an aircraft to spot the fall of the shells and direct the gunners. Deep down he knew that was exactly what he would have done in the circumstances. All that the men on the ground could hope was that a British fighter would show up soon, to drive the spotter away.

Approaching round the bend of the road just in front of Sam were two Algerian Tirrailleurs. One, a tall black-bearded sergeant with a bloody dressing covering the upper part of his face, was holding onto a smaller man – a private- who was dragging his leg. The stock tucked into his armpit, he was using his long-barrelled Lebel rifle as a crutch. Their progress was slow and painful. The sergeant supported the smaller man, who was acting as the eyes for the pair of them. Such was their exhaustion that neither seemed aware of Sam until he grabbed at the private's tunic and pushed the mare's reins into his hands. It was a purely practical decision. Sam could not go further forward with the horse, and the men were not going to make it to safety on foot.

There was no time for conversation. The sound of renewed shellfire filled the air as gunners, under the tutelage of the circling airman, opened up again.

Pushing and heaving, Sam helped the two men onto the horse's back. To the private he said, 'Go back up the road past the next village. About three kilometres further on there are some British lines and a field ambulance. They'll look after you.'

Blindly, the sergeant reached down from the back of the horse and, finding Sam's head, pulled his face in against his thigh in a gesture of thanks.

'A la prochaine, Capitaine,' muttered his companion, holding out a calloused fist.

'Go with God.' Sam shook hands briefly and, picking up his rifle, started off down the road in the direction from which the men had come.

Darkness was beginning to fall before Sam finally found his way into the Canadian lines. His assessment that the gas attack had been limited to the French trenches was confirmed by the men to whom he spoke as he made his way forward through the communication trenches to the firing line.

Taking shelter for the night in a command post dugout of the 8th Winnipeg Rifles, Sam gratefully accepted a tin of hot mutton stew served from a billy can that was bubbling away over a large iron pot-bellied stove in one corner. How the bizarre cooking appliance came to be there he neither knew nor cared. Until he smelled the aroma drifting out of the shored-up timber entrance to the dugout Sam had not realised how hungry he was.

Dipping a piece of hard tack biscuit into the steaming liquor he took stock of his surroundings. The dugout, a cross between a hole in the ground and a tiny half-finished room, was identical to every other one that he had been in during the last eight months: two unmade truckle beds for the officers whose turn it was to get some sleep, a sturdy kitchen table brought in from an abandoned village house, and a couple of chairs, doubtless from the same source.

The Canadian major seated on one of the beds opposite to him was unshaven and looked as if he had not slept for some time. 'I guess you know that now you're here you're staying, bud.'

Sam nodded. As he worked his way to the Front he had become aware that the fighting was closing in around him, and any thought of return to St Jean was impossible. At least he had found out what was happening.

The Canadian officer, whose name was Tom Merrick, took up his story again. 'The Jerries laid down the usual bombardment during the morning. "Jack Johnson's" – "Coal Boxes" as you call them.' He was talking about the seventeen inch howitzer shells that the Germans sent over: their English name derived from the pall of thick black smoke that erupted from them. 'They let up for a time during the afternoon, then wham! Spot on five o'clock off they went again. Not for long, mind you. They stopped as quick as they started. Next thing, down on the Frog lines to the left there, God-damned great clouds of yellow smoke. Least that's what it looked like at first, then of course we realised what was happening. Jesus, I've never seen anything like it. Men dying like flies. Twenty minutes later over they came, all wearing great big pads of cloth over their faces, like something from fuckin' Mars. We held them here, no problem, but they just walked into the Frog trenches.'

Merrick was a big unimaginative-looking man, aged about thirty-five, Sam judged. He wondered what his profession was before the war. Sam was worried. If reinforcements did not get through quickly then getting his report to Corps Headquarters was going to be the least of his worries. The Germans would make a sweep through the broken line and come round behind them. It was possible that they had already done so. He wondered if André had fared any better than he had.

The Canadian stretched. 'I'm going to get a couple of hours' sleep. If you're staying I could do with you taking command of C Company at the far end.' His voice was resigned. 'Jeb Struthers, their lieutenant, was killed yesterday. I could certainly do with you.'

Sam Norton spent all the next day and most of the night in the trenches at the far end of the Canadian line near the Poelcapelle road. The Germans kept up constant pressure, alternating between interminable barrages and a hail of machine gun fire across the hundred yards of no-man's-land that separated them from C Company.

The men he had unexpectedly taken command of regarded the Englishman philosophically. Almost to a man they had enlisted in the Canadian Expeditionary Force to see some adventure overseas. The reality was not what they had been promised. Arriving in the north-east sector of the Ypres Salient a week previously, they had found that the trenches they had taken over from the departing French troops were in dire need of repair. Digging trenches while under fire from an enemy who was within shouting distance was a costly business, and casualties had been high. Lieutenant Struthers was the second officer they had lost in four days, and there was little likelihood that this latest one would last much longer.

Although the gap created by the rout of the Algerians had been plugged by a battalion of Northumbrians, it was obvious to all of the officers in the sector that they were being pinned down while the enemy made gains elsewhere.

During the second night that Sam spent with the Canadians a divisional runner brought the alarming news that despite heavy fighting around Mauser and Pilckem Ridges the Germans were in control of most of the area. Leaning back against the trench wall, Sam looked up at the night sky and mentally pictured a map of the salient. Without a doubt they would have to withdraw or suffer a crushing defeat. He wondered if the two Frenchmen to whom he had given his horse ever made it to the field ambulance. Even if they had, they were more than likely prisoners now.

A light tug at his sleeve made him realise he had dozed off for a few minutes. The sky was beginning to lighten, and he knew without looking at his watch that it must be around four o'clock.

'Rum ration, sir.' Sergeant Evans, like most men of his rank, was in his middle years, probably nearer fifty than forty: a regular soldier who in normal circumstances would have been looking forward to a peaceful retirement when war broke out.

Sam grunted and, leaning on his rifle, levered himself to his feet. Rum ration was the company commander and senior NCO's perk of the day. Every morning at daybreak the senior sergeant and duty officer passed among the men with a gallon stone jug filled with Navy rum, doling out a tot into each man's drinking pannikin. As they passed into a new section and the men lined up, the sergeant would casually ask the officer if they were going to take their tot then or later. It was an unusual morning when they did not have four or five tots each.

'Fine, Sar'nt. Do you think we should test first?'

The older man's face split into a grin, and he brushed the ends of his heavy grey moustache with the back of his forefinger: in better days they would have been waxed into needle-sharp four inch points. He had not been sure about this new addition to the company, however temporary he might be. Like most of the officers now he appeared too young for the job, and the red General Staff tabs on his tunic were ominous.

A generous measure of the fiery liquid burning through his empty stomach, Sam set off with Sergeant Evans. They were in the third bay of the zig-zagging trench about to sample their second tot of the morning when the lookout on the fire-step whispered hoarsely. 'Sir, I think you should look at this.' Climbing up next to him, Sam took the long periscope and peered through it into the barbed wire wasteland between themselves and the enemy trenches. At first he could not make out what the sentry had seen in the half light; then, as his eyes gradually adjusted, he saw a series of pipes projecting above the German trenches at five yard intervals. From the nozzle of each one the beginnings of a thin trail of vapour was pumping out into the clear morning air.

Pushing the periscope across to Sergeant Evans, Sam turned to face the expectant soldiers and bellowed at the top of his voice, 'Gas! Cover your faces. Pass the word down the line. Gas attack!' He grabbed the periscope from Evans who, leaping down into the trench, was already shouting at the crew of the nearest Maxim gun to open fire. All along the adjacent bays men were climbing up to the trench parapet and firing as fast as they could at the enemy trenches.

Sam knew that it was a wasted effort. In fascinated horror he watched as dense white clouds belched from the mouths of the narrow pipes a hundred yards away. Slowly rising into the air before beginning to vaporise, they merged into a single dense fog – the bottom of which was beginning to turn a dirty greenish yellow colour. As if it had completed its own inevitable preparations, the fifteen foot high pall began to roll inexorably towards them, obscuring all view of the intervening barbed wire and dragging with it on the breeze the pungent odour of chlorine. The gently rolling gas began to envelope the Canadian trench.

Sergeant Evans was down on one knee, bellowing at the top of his voice for the men to get down as low as they could as the gas began to drift lazily into the trench. At the top of the fire step Sam was still trying to make out whether enemy troops were coming in behind the gas cloud when, gasping and choking, his lungs on fire and his head splitting from the pain that was forcing his eyes tight shut, he slumped forward unconscious, supported in a standing position by the arms of the trench periscope. Further along the line beyond the reach of the gas cloud, the busy clatter of machine guns rent the early morning stillness as they hosed fire back and forth across no man's land.

Chapter Two

Two old ladies glared disapprovingly at the smartly dressed young woman seated at the next table and reading a copy of the morning's *Daily Telegraph*. Young women, reading newspapers and smoking cigarettes in public – what was the world coming to?'

Conscious of the disapproval attracted by her breach of feminine etiquette, Irene Deladier deliberately lowered the newspaper to stare coldly at the elderly matrons, and was quietly satisfied at the confusion that her challenge effected. Dropping their eyes, the pair busied themselves rearranging the empty tea cups in front of them and engaging in a hurried discussion about the effects of this 'dreadful war' on the escalating costs of living. Their discomfort was heightened when, having made her point, the young woman continued to gaze pointedly in their direction for several seconds more. Finally, faces red with embarrassment, they pushed back their chairs and left the coffee room to continue their morning's shopping expedition.

Returning to the newspaper, Irene continued her study of Philip Gibbs's dispatch from the Western Front. According to his half-page report the Germans had achieved much success in an attack on the British and French troops in an area of Belgium that she had never heard of: Ypres. The crucial factor in a recent battle had been the use by the Germans of poisoned gas, which according to Gibbs's report had killed hundreds of Allied troops. Frowning, Irene wondered where her brother Sam was – she hoped as far away from this latest outrage as possible.

The heavily built man seated across the table asked, 'What's happening in the papers?' James Simmonds's deep, well-modulated tones carried an air of polite concern. News reports nowadays were seldom cheerful, and from his cousin's expression today's item was no different from usual.

'It looks as if "les Boches" have unleashed a secret weapon. Some form of gas. They've used it against our men in Belgium. Casualties are pretty high.'

'If the War Office is admitting to a high casualty count, then you can bet the real figures are much higher,' Simmonds replied knowledgeably. Despite Irene's flawless English her French background was constantly reflected in her choice of words, such as an insistence on referring to the Germans as 'les Boches'.

The dark-haired woman inclined her head sombrely. 'The problem is of course that things will escalate. We'll loudly denounce the Kaiser as a war criminal while doing our best to devise something more deadly in retaliation.' Folding the paper with an air of finality she placed it on the table and picked up her coffee cup. Unlike the two recently departed ladies, she found herself unable to acquire the English taste for tea. The coffee itself tasted insipid to her palate, accustomed as it was to the dark aromatic brews served in French cafés and bistros.

Irene Deladier cradled the warm cup in both hands and gazed idly round. The main room of Phipps's Coffee House was large and accommodating, each of the polished tables covered with a crisply starched white linen tablecloth. The red leather-bound menus informed their clients that morning rolls, cakes and pastries were available until midday, after which time a three-course luncheon could be obtained for one shilling and sixpence. If she was honest, Phipps's was the nearest thing to a French café that she had encountered since her arrival in Kelsford four months ago. Sitting here of a morning, sipping coffee and reading the papers, was now part of her daily routine; part of rebuilding her life.

Irene's mind wandered back over the events of the recent months, since she had received the telegram informing her that Jean-Claude had been killed. It felt as if she was remembering a bad dream.

Although brought up in an extremely affluent environment, the young woman had never been a pampered or spoilt child. Her parents, having married relatively late in life, had ensured that. When Irene was born her mother was in her late thirties and her father forty-one. They had married and moved to France in 1889, the year in which her father, Thomas Norton, had resigned as head of Kelsford Detective Department. The hint of a frown creased her forehead. She and her older brother Samuel had always been unclear about the course of events that had led to their parents forsaking England. It had never been a secret, rather something that was not a matter for discussion.

Irene knew that her parents had both been married before and widowed. Ruth's first husband had been a wealthy banker, and upon his death his interest in the bank had passed to his widow. Tom Norton's wife Kathleen had died in a smallpox epidemic a year or two before he met Ruth. Her father had been shot and badly wounded in the course of duty, resulting in him being invalided out of the police force. Tom's face, with its sweeping white moustache and piercing blue eyes, floated into her mind. Irene Deladier might have inherited her mother's dark good looks, but it was her beloved father's fathomless blue eyes that had been turned so devastatingly on the two women who had censured her.

While Irene and her brother Sam, both born in the tiny village of St Martin, were brought up as the children of affluent parents, they were neither of them indulged. Irene was taught home and business management, while her brother became versed in the intricacies of the huge jewellery empire that their mother's unerring business acumen had successfully built up.

A year and a half before, while studying business management in Paris, Irene Norton had met and fallen in love with Jean-Claude Deladier. Like herself Jean-Claude came from a wealthy background: his father was a successful financier. Within a few months of meeting, and with the storm clouds gathering across Europe, the couple were married in the summer of 1914 by the mayor of St Martin. Two months later, along with every other young Frenchman who had completed his compulsory military service, Jean-Claude was recalled to join his regiment.

While she was visiting one of her mother's diamond merchants in Cherbourg three weeks later, a telegram arrived at Irene's hotel informing her that Lieutenant Jean-Claude Deladier of the 11th Regiment of Chasseurs à Cheval had been killed in action at Neufchâteau on 22 August. The following day, with Paris under threat from the advancing German armies and return to her parents' home in central France too dangerous to attempt, the grieving widow took passage on a Cornish fishing boat which was refuelling in Cherbourg, and made her way across the Channel to England.

Kelsford wasn't so bad, she thought, looking out of the large picture window at the busy street outside. Her aunt Anne – her father's sister – and Reuben, her husband, had given Irene a warm welcome. Initially she took a room at the pub they kept in the town – the Rifleman – before finding the spacious accommodation that she was renting at 26 Kingsbury Lane, which was more than adequate for her needs.

Fortunately Irene was not a stranger to her English relatives. Both she and her brother had spent several holidays with them while growing up, while Sam was a regular visitor to Kelsford during business trips to Kosminski's offices in London.

Lost in her thoughts, Irene wondered where Stefan was. The three of them had grown up together: Irene, Sam and Stefan Capewell. When Irene's mother moved from Kelsford to St Martin, Stefan's mother Mirka and her husband moved with them, she to become housekeeper and he the estate manager. That was before Stefan was born. Mirka Sloboda, like Ruth Norton born of Jewish parents on the borders of the Romanov Empire, had come to England from the Ukraine as a child. Of an age with Ruth, she worked for her as a personal maid, and before leaving Kelsford had married Ruth's coachman, Daniel. Irene smiled quietly to herself. When she was a little girl, wrapped in the cosy warmth of the château's kitchen, Tante Mirka would tell her dark and sinister tales of things that she and Irene's mother had done in their youth. Silly impossible stories of adventures in the cold and forbidding Carpathian mountains . . . stories about midnight train rides across Austria, and killing German officers before escaping back to England.

Whenever the little girl asked her mother about the stories Ruth laughed and gave her a kiss, saying that she should not believe anything that the housekeeper told her. Irene remembered how angry her mother would become afterwards with Mirka. Listening outside the door to the kitchen while they argued, how frightened she was by the sound of their raised voices as they shouted at each other in a mixture of Russian and Yiddish. As she grew older, it often occurred to Irene that the two women seemed to argue as equals, not as mistress and servant. The outcome was always the same. Deathly silence, followed by her mother stalking out of the room her face set in an angry mask, and the dumpy little housekeeper sulking in her kitchen for days afterwards, refusing to speak to anyone in anything other than Russian. Eventually Irene would see her mother go down to the kitchens with a bottle of Wyborowa vodka under her arm and two square tumblers in her hand. Listening once more at the door, Irene would catch the sound of quiet conversation and the chink of glasses. Half an hour later the scraping of a chair being pulled back signalled the need to dive for cover behind a laundry basket or under the stairs before Ruth reappeared, an enigmatic smile on her face. After this life would return to normal, until the next time that Tante Mirka began telling her foolish stories.

Where, she wondered, was Stefan now? Having finished his military service, when war broke out he was studying economics at Vienna University to prepare himself to take over management of the Norton estate when his father retired. Being a foreigner, half English and half Ukrainian, Stefan would have been interned by the Austrians as an enemy alien when war was declared, and sent to a detention camp.

'You look worried, my dear.' James broke into her train of thought. 'Can I help?'

Irene shook her head slowly. She liked James. The senior partner in a flourishing law firm, he was solid and reliable. Since her arrival in Kelsford Jamie had been very good to her. 'Just thinking.'

'Are you doing anything this morning?' he asked, anxious to bring his cousin out of the mood that was beginning to envelop her. He had made a special effort to take the young woman under his wing.

'Yes,' she said brightly. 'I'm going down to the refugee centre to meet Father Mullahy. He's got a family there who arrived a couple of days ago and have now been found a home. They're from a place between Liège and Brussels called Louvain. Apparently the Germans gave them a particularly bad time. They've been on the road for months and arrived here last night from London. Father Mullahy would like me to explain to them where they're going, what's happening with finding work and that sort of thing. It'll keep me busy for the rest of the day.'

Simmonds nodded. Irene was good at dealing with the refugees who were pouring into Father Mullahy's dispersal centre from the offices of the Belgian Legation, and the work was giving her something to focus on.

When refugees had begun to arrive in Kelsford just before Christmas 1914, it was the Catholic community of the town who had undertaken responsibility for finding them homes. Now, however, with the newly established War Refugees Committee at Aldwych in London operating a more structured system, the workload was easing considerably. A clothing depot, run by the Kelsford Ladies' Temperance Committee in Welbeck Street, was giving out clothing and footwear donated by many of the local manufacturers. Other items of clothing came in from charity bazaars or bring and buy sales, and these were augmented with gifts collected by local schools. Notice boards in churches and chapels carried pleas for members of their congregations with a spare bedroom or space in the front parlour to accept families into their homes while more permanent accommodation was sought. In an effort to persuade landlords and property owners to make accommodation available, Kelsford Town Council agreed to waive rates and subsidise rents on any houses let to refugees. On the direction of the finance committee the manager of the gas department was supplying gas at cost price, and free use of the corporation baths was provided on the production of the necessary vouchers.

Nine months into the war not everyone remained quite so enthusiastic about the newcomers, Simmonds reflected.

Every factory and workshop in the district was operating at full capacity, in order to supply the ever increasing demands of the war effort. Situated as it was in the North Midlands, Kelsford's fortunes had improved considerably with the rapid industrialisation of the region, and the town manufactured everything from boots and shoes to light machinery. Straddling the main rail route from London to Edinburgh and the canal network running up into Lancashire and Manchester, the town was a natural centre. The production of munitions, as every businessman in the town had quickly discovered, was not limited to uniforms and shells. Every item that found its way into the storehouses of the War Office, from a pair of socks to an enamel drinking mug, came under the same heading. As far as local enterprise was concerned, business was booming. Men who had previously worked for a pittance in the town's factories and workshops were now being paid overtime and substantial war bonuses, and were earning more money than they could ever have dreamed of. With the talk that conscription would be brought in towards the end of the year, they were becoming every day more dedicated to their jobs, all seeking to have their employment classified as a reserved occupation – unwilling to volunteer for Kitchener's New Army at a shilling a day.

An influx of refugees flooding the labour market was the last thing that many of the working people wanted. Sympathy for their plight did not necessarily extend to relinquishing of job opportunities. If, as James Simmonds suspected, a prolonged war brought about food and fuel shortages, then the situation was likely to deteriorate dramatically.

He idly ran the forefinger of his left hand across the ends of his upturned cavalry moustache. 'Have you thought any more about the hospital project?'

A thoughtful look came over the woman's face, her attention drawn firmly back to the present. 'I don't know. If I were involved it would have to be as an organiser. I don't enjoy fund raising and charity events.'

Simmonds beamed expansively. This was the reply that he knew he would receive. Irene's wealthy background was more directed towards giving to worthy causes than to soliciting donations. 'Don't worry. There's a group of businessmen organising that side of things. They deal with the financial arrangements, while I ensure that all the legal matters are taken care of. What I need is someone who's capable and can handle the practicalities of organising staff – you know, square pegs into square holes, that sort of thing.'

Pursing her lips, Irene sat back to consider her answer. Jamie had asked her some time ago if she would be willing to play a part in the management of the new Kelsford War Hospital, which was being set up in the property of the old lunatic asylum on the outskirts of the town.

Unoccupied for the last six years, the asylum was perfect as a hospital for the treatment of sick and wounded men who were returning from France – the site being surveyed and earmarked for the purpose as early as 1912, as part of Lord Haldane's army reforms. Byron Carstairs, a Sheffield architect, had been commissioned to draw up and lodge with the War Office a set of plans to allow speedy conversion of the buildings. Within days of the embodiment of the Territorial Force Nursing Service, a matron – Kathleen Doyle – had been appointed, along with a Commanding Officer for the RAMC personnel, and amid an army of builders and carpenters Kelsford War Hospital was declared ready to receive its first patients.

By now the majority of the construction work was completed, and with its first patients admitted some months earlier the hospital was up and running. Irene was not certain that the offer to become part of the management committee was what she wanted. In reality she was not certain what she wanted to do – other than return to France and attempt to rebuild her life there.

Their conversation was interrupted by the tinkling of the brass bell over the front door, announcing the arrival of two new customers. The older of them was a thin and dapper man in his late fifties stylishly dressed in a lightweight dove grey suit and silk waistcoat. His companion was younger, not more than forty she judged, of a stockier and more powerful build. Like the thin man he wore a smart suit, although not quite as expensively cut, and was clean shaven.

James waved a friendly greeting and indicated to the newcomers to join them. Standing up, he extended his left hand to the thickset man. In a practised motion he reversed it so that the palm faced outwards, thumb down. His gloved right hand remained motionless at his side.

'Nice to see you.' Will Mardlin took the proffered hand in his right and shook it awkwardly. 'Madam.' He touched the brim of his bowler hat politely to Irene.

'May I introduce Madame Deladier – my cousin. Irene, this is an old friend of mine, Superintendent Will Mardlin.' Irene nodded. 'And of course Detective Inspector North,' continued Simmonds, his hand sweeping round to include Will's companion.

Harry removed his bowler hat and took Irene's hand lightly, giving a half bow in the French style. 'Enchanté, Madame.' Irene smiled politely. It was a long while since she had received any courtesies in French. Along with his impeccable dress sense the inspector had a charming manner, she noted. On second glance she decided he was probably not as old as she had first thought. The impression was to an extent created by his old-fashioned side whiskers, and the fact that his hair and moustache were prematurely snow white. In his younger days he would, Irene suspected, have been something of a ladies' man.

'Would you care to join us?' Simmonds indicated the two free chairs at the table. Will was mildly amused to see that the solicitor appeared a little disconcerted by Harry North's easy manner with the young woman. Both he and Harry were perfectly aware who James Simmonds's wealthy cousin was – a fact that Will knew would not ruffle his colleague in the least. In her assessment of Harry North, Irene was absolutely correct. A lifelong bachelor, Harry had never found a woman in whose company he was not completely at ease.

'Thank you – another time perhaps,' replied the detective. 'We only dropped in as we were passing, to see Henry Phipps. Someone tried to break in during the night, and we need to speak to him.'

Having excused themselves, the two men made their way through to the rear of the premises, where they spent the next ten minutes in conversation with the coffee house proprietor before taking their leave through the back door.

'Enchanté, Madame,' mimicked Will as they strolled back along the High Street towards Long Street Police Station. 'You smooth old sod! Where did you learn to speak French?'

'I had a French nanny once,' Harry retorted primly.

Will let out a guffaw of raucous laughter, which drew a glare of disapproval from a well-dressed lady who was passing. Harry's childhood would definitely not have included a nanny, so there was only one other interpretation that could be put upon his statement.

Will was, he knew, extremely fortunate in having the likeable old reprobate as his deputy. Brought up in India the son of a serving soldier, he had first seen England as a fifteen year old when his father was posted back to Blighty as recruiting sergeant at Kelsford's military depot, Sevastopol Barracks. Following their arrival in the town, the Mardlin family lodged for two years with Mrs Holloway in Wordsworth Lane, and the young William took employment as a booking clerk at the Midland railway station. When Will was nineteen the assistant stationmaster at Kelsford, Wilfred Ashcroft, was promoted to stationmaster at Leicester, and suggested that Will should go along with him as senior booking clerk.

Shortly afterwards Will and Ashcroft's daughter Susan became engaged and were married. With a new wife to support, Will soon began looking for better opportunities than those presented by the railways, and joined Leicester Borough Police Force, where he remained for the next nineteen years – rising to the rank of detective inspector. In July 1914 he applied for the job as head of the Detective Department at Kelsford, and at the outbreak of war returned to the place that so many years before had been his home.

'I've never asked you – didn't you want the Superintendent's job yourself?'

Harry shook his head. 'I might have when Jesse Squires retired in '09. I'd worked for him for nearly twenty years. He was good, taught me a lot. While I was thinking about it Dan Chote put his name forward, and I knew that it wasn't worth my while bothering.' He grinned wryly at the unspoken question on Will's face. 'Dan and I came up through the ranks together. He was a decent fellow. More importantly he spoke nicely and had all the right connections. When he went, I was almost due to retire. If it wasn't for the Kaiser I'd be sitting at home now with my feet up the chimney.'

Will grinned back. What Harry was not saying was that he knew too much about too many people for them to be comfortable with him as head of the detective force. He also knew that if Harry had wanted to he could have made Will's position untenable. As it was, the older man had been nothing but helpful to him.

They paused while North put a light to a cigarette, and their discussion was interrupted by a thin reedy voice from the doorway of a nearby milliner's shop. 'Penny for a bun, sir, or tuppence would be nice.'

Will peered into the shadows. The shop was closed, its blinds rendering the deep entrance dark and cool in the bright morning sunlight. After a second or two he made out a diminutive figure clad, in spite of the warm weather, in an old army greatcoat and wearing an incongruous balaclava helmet, under which he could just see the whites of a pair of eyes shining brightly. Seated on a wooden box, surrounded by the brown paper bags and parcels that comprised his worldly possessions, the old vagrant bore an uncanny resemblance to an attentive rodent.

Harry pulled a second cigarette from his packet and dropped it into the little man's tin. There you go, Tuppenny. Now bugger off before I send someone to nick you for begging.' His voice conveyed a mixture of benevolence and authority.

'Thank you, sir,' the squeaky voice rang out. 'Penny buys a bun, sir, tuppence gets some rice!'

'Who's he?' asked Mardlin as they continued on their way, turning off the main thoroughfare towards Long Street.

'Tuppenny Rice,' replied North, holding open the door of the police station. 'Arrived in town a year or so ago – don't ask me where from. He's completely harmless. Always chants the same lines: "Penny for a bun, sir, or tuppence would be nice. Penny buys a bun, sir, tuppence gets some rice."

26

Doesn't matter what you give him – he never says anything different.

Will knew why he had never seen the tramp in the cells. Not even the keenest of young constables would want to bring him in and then have to search him, working through the layers of verminous clothing in which the little man was undoubtedly swathed beneath his greatcoat. Even if one of them did, he thought, the exercise would not be repeated. The duty charge sergeant would see to that.

Before Will could fit his key into the door at 23 Lyndon Terrace, Edith, the maid, had opened it, and with a small curtsey admitted him into the hallway. Although he appreciated that employing a maidservant was in keeping with his status as a senior police officer, Will could not get used to the idea. He always felt slightly embarrassed when, as now, the young girl – she would be about fifteen, he supposed – politely took his hat and gloves, helped him off with his coat and announced that the mistress was out. 'She's out shopping for the morning, sir.'

'Thank you.' Seeing the enquiry in the girl's bright eyes, Will continued. 'I'll be working for a couple of hours, Edith. I'd prefer not to be disturbed unless it's urgent.'

Edith Renshaw smoothed down the back of the overcoat as she hung it up tidily on the hall stand, then made her way back to the kitchen to inform cook that Mr Mardlin was home and would welcome a pot of tea. The Mardlins were nice people to work for, the girl decided, as she clattered noisily down the stairs. Some of her friends employed nearby were not so fortunate. Ada Manners, who worked for Mrs Sutton at number seventeen, had a miserable time – and Mr Sutton was always 'doing things'. Ada told her that he liked putting his hand on her bottom or brushing past her in the hallway so that he touched her chest. Eliza Craxford who worked at the park-keeper's house across the road said that Mr and Mrs Bennett were horrible to her, and Mrs Bennett was always making her do jobs twice because she said they weren't done properly the first time. Mind you, thought Edith, that might be about right. Eliza's dad was a cowherd. She had come into service from the farm – and she was as thick as a board.

No, as far as Edith was concerned, working for Mr and Mrs Mardlin was all right. Madam was a bit flighty, and Mrs Lynam the cook reckoned that she had got a bit on the side, but Edith didn't believe that. Mrs Mardlin treated her nicely and Mr Mardlin was a gentleman. He was never anything but polite and he always asked her to do things rather than telling her.

Will laid out the court papers that he had to familiarise himself with in readiness for the next day's magistrates court, and walking to the bay window he looked out across the road to the park opposite. It was a beautiful view, across Cranley Park. According to a report in the *Gazette* the previous week the park, 'comprising seventy acres of rolling grassland and previously forming part of the estate owned by the late Eustace Cranley', was presently being given over to the war effort. Ten acres at the furthest side would become small allotment gardens, upon which local residents could cultivate their own produce, while in common with other similar areas of open ground the central slopes would be given over to grazing land for sheep, to ensure a continuing supply of meat to the town.

Will watched as a squad of army recruits, still dressed incongruously in civilian clothes and carrying army rifles, were drilled by a moustachioed corporal just inside the tall black wrought-iron gates. The measured beat of a drum, slung around the neck of the private who was standing to one side of the group and marking out the time, floated across the road, carried on the light summer breeze. He wondered if the bandstand near the pavilion would continue to host the fortnightly concerts of which he was so fond. Already the head constable, Sydney Hall-Johnson, was talking about discontinuing the borough police band until the end of the war. He was probably right, thought Will. With thirty per cent of his manpower away serving with the Colours, it was going to be difficult to justify time off for band practice.

The young maid's words came back into his mind: that his wife was out shopping.

It was twenty-two years since Will had moved to Leicester as a lodger with the Ashcrofts. Susan, their only daughter, had been twenty at the time, a year older than Will. With her green eyes and trim figure he had thought her the most beautiful girl he had ever seen. Late at night after he came home from an evening shift at the railway station he would lie awake in the bedroom next to hers, listening to her getting ready to go to bed, and fantasising about her.

He recalled with absolute clarity how their affair had begun. It was the middle of the summer. He had been living with the family for about three months when he tripped over an uneven board in the station booking hall. He sprained his ankle and was confined to bed for a week while it healed. One afternoon towards the end of the week he was lying on his bed reading a novel – Charles Dickens's *Martin Chuzzlewit* – and dozing, when Susan softly knocked at the door and came into the room with a tray of tea for them both. Will remembered his confused embarrassment. Clad only in a thin nightshirt, he had no opportunity to climb under the bedclothes and make himself decent. Susan waved aside his stammered apologies and placed the tea tray on his dressing table before settling down comfortably on the foot of the bed. There was hardly any conversation. Susan asked how his ankle was progressing, and then in a sisterly manner placed her hand on his shin, just above the swollen joint, as if testing to see how far the injury extended. Mardlin flushed slightly as he thought about the sudden hard erection that had thrust up under his nightshirt, and the look that came into her dark green eyes. Deeply ashamed, Will had expected her to berate him or flee from the room. Instead her hand moved up his leg, pushing the nightshirt back until the offending member was fully exposed to her view. He could still see the fire burning in the back of her eyes as she caressed him into a swift climax.

After this their affair quickly became the main focus of their lives. They met during the warm summer afternoons at nearby Western Park, strolling casually across the wooden bridge over the little stream up the hill to the small spinney at the top, then checked round carefully to ensure that they were not observed, and crept into the shelter of the trees to make love. With the onset of autumn and a chill creeping into the air, the pair became more daring – waiting each night until Susan's parents were asleep before slipping like silent wraiths into one or the other's bedroom.

In February Susan broke the news to him that she had missed her last two periods and was pregnant. Terrified of the consequences of their folly, Will offered to go immediately to her father and confess all. Susan proposed what she called 'a more practical solution'. If Will could get his hands on five pounds the matter could be resolved without anyone being any the wiser. With few outgoings other than his weekly rent, the young man readily admitted that he had over twenty pounds put away, and safe in that knowledge Susan undertook to remedy matters. Will never knew how it was that Susan came to be put in contact with the woman who procured her abortion, other than that she lived nearby in one of the streets off the Hinckley Road, and that Susan's friend Clementine Farrar had accompanied her.

In one respect fate was with the couple, as Susan's parents were away visiting some friends at Hinckley, and had rather naively arranged for Clementine to stay with their daughter to act as a chaperone. Susan, looked after by Clementine and Will, had sufficiently recovered from her ordeal by the time her parents returned home for them not to notice that anything was amiss.

The fright was sufficient, however, for the lovers to call a halt to their activities. Informing Susan's mother and father that they were desperately in love, they persuaded the Ashcrofts to allow them to marry after a short courtship. Whether or not his in-laws had any suspicions that all was not quite above board, Will was never certain. The newlyweds rented a terraced house in Clarendon Park, and Will left the railways to become a policeman.

It was only as time went by that two things became apparent that were to have far-reaching effects on their marriage. The first was that the clumsy ministrations with an adapted knitting needle to resolve their early problem had rendered Susan sterile. The second was that Susan's voracious appetite for sex extended to the need for more than one partner.

At first, when Will realised that Susan was seeing someone else, there had been tremendous rows. Her first lover was a young medical practitioner who was acting as their GP. Will threatened him with being struck off the medical register, and the liaison ceased forthwith. After that it was a bank clerk whom she met while discussing a problem over unpaid interest on their account. Next was a solicitor, to whom Mardlin was introduced when he first became a detective. By now Will neither knew nor particularly cared who figured in his wife's convoluted extramarital activities.

The ironic thing, he mused, watching the would-be soldiers parading in the park, was that in every other way Susan was not a bad wife. Always discreet in her activities she never sought to embarrass him, and while he was fairly certain that there were those with whom he worked in Leicester who suspected that his wife was readily available, as far as he was aware she had never involved herself with any of his colleagues. Susan was a likeable woman, at forty two still attractive, with a trim figure and pleasing – if inviting – smile. It was her eyes that were her downfall, he thought. Those dark green cat-like eyes that lit up and started to burn slowly with deep desire when she became excited. The strange thing was that, although inevitably they had grown apart over the years and no longer loved each other, they remained friends – and on the odd occasion still had sex together. From time to time she came to him in his room, her green eyes smouldering like a predatory tiger, and they would make love as they had twenty years ago in the back room at Bismarck Street. At other times, answering to his own needs, Mardlin went to her, slipping quietly into bed by her side; and she seldom refused him.

Will hoped that now, embarking on their new life in Kelsford, things would change. They never discussed the problem but simply lived with it – an unspoken shadow lurking in the wings of their existence.

A hansom cab drew up outside, and he watched as the door opened and his wife descended. She straightened her skirts and adjusted her hat before paying the cabbie. Turning towards the house, she made her way to the front door, smiling pleasantly at an old gentleman who tipped his hat to her in passing.

Mardlin gave a long sigh before turning to pick up his paperwork. She was not carrying any shopping: just a parasol to protect her against the summer sun.

Chapter Three

'Y ou've got a visitor.'

Startled out of his reverie, Sam Norton looked up at the portly middle-aged nurse in surprise – not because someone was paying him a visit (since he had been admitted to the field hospital at Béthune seldom a day had passed without someone from either the General Staff or his old regiment dropping by to see how he was getting along) but because a visitor had arrived while he was waiting to be discharged.

Rising from his chair, Sam stared through the open ward door into the passageway. As he did so a tall dark-haired major wearing the red collar tabs of a staff officer strolled in. Sam had never seen the man before. Perhaps he had come to give him a lift back to Divisional Headquarters, or to brief him about the sector he was to be posted to. Sam had to admit that it would be good to get back to work. It was going to take him a while to pick up what was happening again, so he could make sense of the intelligence that was coming in.

With the deference that people always seem to extend to the sick, the tall major held out his hand with an amiable smile. 'Captain Norton. Pleased to meet you.'

Sam took the proffered hand and shook it politely. 'Nice to meet you, sir. I hadn't expected Division to send an officer along with the transport.'

'I was passing, and they asked me to pick you up along the way. Got your orders here in my bag.' The major tapped the worn leather briefcase at his side. 'Sort them out later, old chap. If you're ready we could do with moving.'

'This is very good of you, sir, but I've not been officially discharged yet. I'm still waiting for the doctor to make his rounds.'

'Not a problem, Captain Norton. I cornered him on the way in – while Nurse Nightingale out there was packing your kitbag. I've got your discharge papers here, all signed up and ready. Perhaps if you'd like to grab your kitbag we could be on our way. Time, if I might say so, is of the essence.'

Sam paused a moment; he found the man's proprietary attitude mildly irritating. He had been waiting all morning for the duty RAMC doctor to make his rounds, and it was irksome that this officer had seen fit to walk into the hospital and, using his rank, take matters into his own hands. Apart from anything else, Sam wanted to say goodbye to the other officers on the ward and to the medical staff who had cared for him so attentively for six weeks.

Looking back, they had been the longest six weeks of his life. The only men in the Canadian trench apart from Sam who had survived the gas attack were the machine gun crews on either side of him. With the gas rolling in across the wire they had remained at their posts until the cloud overcame them, firing over the parapet at the German lines. When he lost consciousness Sam had been held up by the trench periscope, which supported his inert body, but Sergeant Evans and the soldiers huddled at the bottom of the trench, seeking protection against the cloud, were asphyxiated as the chlorine, finding the lowest level, choked them to death.

After the gas cloud was released the Germans had to wait for a short time while the fumes dispersed before launching an attack across no man's land, giving the Allied troops on either side sufficient time to mount an adequate defence and prevent them from overrunning the stricken trenches. When the action was finished Sam Norton and six other men were the only survivors in the Canadian line.

'If you don't mind, sir, I'd appreciate a few minutes to speak to the staff and to say goodbye to one or two of the other patients.' Sam's tone had lost any hint of warmth. He had already noted that the visitor's staff flashes were brand new, and that his unit badges identified him as a sapper from the Royal Engineers. The crown on the cuff of his tunic and the third of the three lines of braid above it were recent additions. Light catching his wrist as he tapped the briefcase clearly showed the pale patches where three captain's stars had been removed, before being replaced by the crown.

So, the major was new to the Front, Sam concluded. Fresh out from England – probably during the previous month – and promoted directly into a nice cosy job on the General Staff. Well, major or not, he was going to have to wait until Sam Norton was ready to leave.

Without waiting for a reply, he took hold of the walking stick on his bed and turned to make his way along the row of beds in which lay the bandaged and damaged men who had been his companions for the last few weeks.

The major picked up the kitbag from the side of the bed, the initial good humour replaced by a long hard stare directed at Sam's back. 'I'd appreciate it if you did not prolong matters, Captain Norton. As I said, time is of the essence.'

Ignoring him, Sam made his way down the ward.

Deliberately taking his time, Sam spent the next fifteen minutes saying his farewells before sauntering out to the waiting open topped Darracq motor car which, engine running was pulled to one side in the roadway outside of the makeshift hospital. A convoy of field ambulances loaded with fresh casualties from the Front was pulled up alongside it.

The major, his short toothbrush moustache bristling, was in less than a good humour. As Sam climbed into the back seat of the Darracq, the senior officer leaned forward and spoke quietly to the driver. With a brisk nod the lance corporal engaged first gear, and set off with a jolt that threw Sam back into his seat.

'When I said that time was of the essence, Captain, I was not studying social niceties.' The voice contained suppressed fury, and his next words took the smugness from Sam's face. 'On our way to collect you, a group of German aircraft flew over heading for the coast. As that's the direction in which we're heading it's reasonable to anticipate that we'll be directly on their return flight path. It's the habit of German gunners to expend any unused ammunition on vehicles or troops that they pass over.' The acid tones were those of a schoolmaster addressing a backward pupil. 'If you've never been shot at by an aeroplane while travelling along an exposed road in an open motor car I suggest that you're in for an extremely unhappy experience.'

Sam felt a deep pang of unease and shuffled about in the upholstered back seat. The driver he noticed was fumbling for something at his waist, steering the vehicle one handed. A second or two later he produced a pistol from the holster at his side, placing it within easy reach on the passenger seat.

With a sudden flush of embarrassment it occurred to Sam that he had not collected his service revolver from the hospital administrator's office before leaving. As a matter of routine it had been taken out of his kitbag on his admission to the ward and held for safety by the almoner. He was relieved to see that there were two Lee Enfield rifles clipped into a rack which ran lengthways across the back of the front seats.

Reaching into his briefcase, the major wordlessly handed him a leather holster containing a .455 Smith and Wesson. Sam did not need to look for the initials branded onto the back of the holster to know that it was his. Head down, face burning, he fixed it onto his Sam Brown belt and slipped the lanyard round his neck.

Travelling in silence, Sam realised that he didn't know the major's name, or for that matter where they were going. The other officer, he saw, was alternately scanning the countryside around them and checking the sky. Sam began to do likewise, peering into the hedgerows and fields that they were passing at a steady twenty miles an hour. Aware that his companion was now keeping a lookout as well, the major confined his observations to the fields on the nearside, while Sam searched those on the offside. Why the coast, Sam wondered. Why were they heading west for the coast? From Béthune to Calais was a good three hours over pavé roads, but at least he now knew that the port was still in British hands.

After a further half an hour, in an attempt to break the oppressive silence, he said, 'Look, sir, I'm sorry for the delay. I really did have people to see before

I left, it was . . .'

The major cut across him with a sudden bellow. 'Aircraft!' The warning was not directed at Sam but at the driver, who brought the car to a slithering halt and in one swift movement pulled on the handbrake and leapt onto the road.

As Sam sprang over the side of the car he saw the major throwing one of the rifles to the lance corporal, who caught it deftly. All three men dived into the irrigation ditch which ran alongside the road.

The drone of aircraft engines came nearer, approaching from the west. Sam could see them now silhouetted against the cloudless blue sky: two Albatros biplanes, one bright red, the other with a cream fuselage and dark green wings. It looked as if they had already been in a fight, with long strips of crimson canvas like torn shreds of skin fluttering from beneath the observer's cockpit of the first aircraft. From the erratic manner in which it was being flown, he presumed that the control wires had been damaged and the pilot was having difficulty holding the aircraft on a steady course. Listening carefully, he could hear its engine misfiring badly. The other machine was flying a couple of hundred feet above its partner, shepherding the damaged plane back to their airfield, or at least to the safety of the German lines.

As they watched, the escort peeled off and started to make a run, as if having spotted the abandoned vehicle it was about to make a pass over the road. Instead of dropping down, however, the pilot pulled his machine into a tight circle and began to climb, gaining height and distancing himself from his damaged charge. Shielding their eyes, the three men in the ditch began to search the sky to their left.

It did not take long to spot why the German was manoeuvring. Three hundred feet below him, in hot pursuit of the disabled Albatros, was a British BE8 reconnaissance plane. It was eleven thirty, the blazing sun, high in the sky was full in the eyes of the two men in the pursuing scout plane. Concentrating on overtaking his prey, the British pilot had not yet seen the green-winged Albatros waiting patiently above him.

The first indication the men in the BE8 had of the impending ambush was when, having allowed them to pass underneath him, the German swooped down in a steep dive, his observer raking the British plane from tail to nose with a prolonged burst of machine gun fire. The BE8 fell away to the right, its starboard wing drooping down alarmingly, before the startled pilot regained control and took evasive action. It was too late. Sam listened to the engine of the BE8 coughing out its last few revolutions before lapsing into silence.

The abrupt movements of the British plane, along with its sudden loss of momentum, caused the German pilot to overshoot his target, and as the BE8 started to glide lazily down towards them he made a tight turn to bring his aircraft back into line with his adversary. By now both machines had lost a great deal of height, and it was obvious that the English pilot was going to attempt to crash-land in the field next to the road.

It was not unusual in these circumstances for the victor to follow his opponent almost to the ground in order to prevent any attempt at escape. In the very early days of the war it was quite common for a pilot to land and take the enemy flyer prisoner. Nowadays that rarely happened: it was merely a question of logging where the landing had taken place and sending a detachment of soldiers to round up the stranded aircrew.

To their horror another burst of machine gun fire reached their ears as the observer of the Albatros, once more above the British machine, raked it again with bullets before the pilot pulled away in a steep bank.

'Bastard!' exclaimed the major. Holding out a restraining hand, he said to the corporal, 'Hold your fire. You'll never hit him – and if he knows we're here he'll come looking for us.'

Sam knew he was right. Although aircraft were occasionally brought down by ground fire from the trenches it was more often down to good luck than marksmanship if a random shot found its way into the cockpit of an aeroplane several hundred feet above the ground.

With a sudden shock he realised that the stricken BE8 was heading directly for them. A fine spray of oil splattering its engine cowling and blowing back over the occupants of the plane, it came gliding in slowly at a height that would barely allow it to clear the gully in which they were lying. Whether or not the pilot spotted them at the last second he could not tell, but the nose of the aircraft was suddenly dragged up and it skimmed by, wheels brushing the hedgerow. As it passed them Sam had time to glimpse the observer slumped across his Lewis gun, killed in the attack.

Watching, Sam saw the plane, as if in slow motion, touch lightly onto the ploughed soil before rising up again, its momentum carrying it a few more yards further. Then it dropped like a stone. The undercarriage dug into the earth and collapsed like a child's toy, pitching the machine onto its nose. In the ensuing silence there was no sign of any movement in the cockpit.

Once more the sound of an aircraft engine reached their ears, this time becoming louder by the second: the cream-fuselaged plane was following an identical path to the BE8. The German pilot was coming in at a height of about twenty feet to finish off the British crew.

Sam intercepted the quick glance which his two companions exchanged: the corporal enquiring, the major nodding. Rolling to one side in order to free their weapons, they waited until the exact second that the cream fuselage was overhead. The German had throttled back almost to stalling speed in order to allow his observer to aim the heavy parabellum machine gun accurately. Catching sight at the last moment of the three men in the ditch as they passed slowly over, the startled gunner attempted to swing his weapon around to open fire on them. Working the bolt of his rifle with swift precision, the major put three rounds into the unsuspecting pilot, who, oblivious of their presence, never knew what it was that killed him. The corporal put a burst of rapid fire into the observer's cockpit, while for good measure Sam emptied his pistol at the man.

The Albatros, completely out of control, wallowed drunkenly for a few seconds before its wing dipped down to touch the ground. Cartwheeling, it buried its still churning propeller into the soft earth. Once again an eerie silence descended. The silence was, Sam knew, illusory, a relief from the tensions of the last few minutes. Within seconds the sounds of distant gunfire echoing from the Front again imposed itself on their senses. A motorised tractor towing an 18 pounder field gun pulled to a halt in the roadway, unable to pass the Darracq, and the crew dismounted, eager to satisfy their curiosity.

Having reloaded their weapons, Sam and the major made their way over to the BE8, while the corporal cautiously approached the German plane, the black and white cross on its shattered port wing pointing accusingly skywards.

Both the pilot and the observer of the BE8 were dead. The observer was some years older than the ashen-faced young man in the pilot's seat, whose head was thrown back, blood trickling from the corner of his mouth. The impact of the crash had thrown the observer clear of the plane, and he was lying in a crumpled heap several yards away. Crumpled, Sam thought, because having taken the full force of the heavy machine gun bullets when the Albatros made its second deadly pass, there would be little left of him under the tattered flying suit. He had been standing up when it happened, waving his arms at the German gunner to indicate that the fight was over and they were going down. It was the face of a man in his forties. A dark moustache, weather-beaten face pallid now in death, dark unseeing eyes staring up at the sky.

The tall major was gazing down at the dead man, a sad and distant expression on his face. The two were quite alike, Sam realised, much of an age and not dissimilar in looks.

Away to his right, the corporal was busily engaged in puncturing the fuel tank of the Albatros before setting light to it. With a huge whooshing noise the flames from the match which he hurled into the steadily dripping fuel turned the aircraft frame into a blazing funeral pyre of wood and canvas. Picking up his rifle, he made his way back to rejoin the two officers. Grim-faced, he halted in front of the major. 'That's sorted those buggers out, sir,' he said solemnly.

'Yes, that's sorted those buggers out, Percy,' replied the officer. 'And now, if we could get moving . . . as I keep trying to impress upon you, time is of the essence.'

'I owe you an apology.'

Under way once more, the further they travelled from the Front the better time the Darracq was able to make. There were fewer shell holes in the road to negotiate, and the likelihood of a sniper taking a shot at them was no longer relevant. The sound of artillery fire was diminishing rapidly.

From the moment they had spotted the aeroplane it had been obvious to Sam that his assumptions about the major were wrong. The smoothly rehearsed manner in which he and the driver had taken cover. The two rifles snatched from the seat rack before abandoning the vehicle, the spare one being thrown not to Sam but the man he could rely on – the corporal. It was Sam who had allowed himself to appear amateur. He had even forgotten to collect his sidearm before leaving the hospital, and had been handed it in the car like a raw recruit. That alone should have told him that the other man was experienced.

The dark moustache twisted in a small grimace as the side of the officer's mouth pulled down in an involuntary muscle spasm. Sam hadn't noticed the twitch before. Reaching into his tunic pocket, the major pulled out a cigarette case and, pressing the catch with the thumb of his right hand, offered one to his companion.

'Ralph Gresham,' he said amiably.

Sam took the proffered cigarette and, holding a match between them, cupped it against the slipstream. 'I do really owe you an apology,' he repeated. 'I shouldn't have held us up at Béthune. It was stupid of me.'

'No harm done – as it happens.' Gresham was not going to allow him to get away with it entirely. He was busy lighting a third cigarette from the glowing end of his own. Satisfied that it was burning properly, he leaned forward and passed it to the driver. A muffled 'Sir' and a raised hand signified the driver's acknowledgment. Strange, thought Sam: on the other side of the Channel in a different world it would be inconceivable for a commissioned officer even to pass a cigarette to a lance corporal, let alone light it for him first.

'We're making for the coast, sir,' he said. 'Has General Smith-Dorrien moved his headquarters west?' The reply to his question startled him.

'Sadly, in the words of the poet, "'Orace has gorn 'ome". Or to be more precise, following a dispute with Sir John French he has been replaced by General Plumer.' The words were heavy with irony. It was apparent that Major Gresham held Sir Horace Smith-Dorrien in a great deal of respect.

'I see . . .' Sam was puzzled. Smith-Dorrien was a good soldier and a competent general. Why, he wondered, had he been replaced?

His travelling companion took a pull at his cigarette. 'Donkeys, you see. We're led by donkeys. At least Christ had the sense to ride on one.'

Sam was prevented from replying by the fit of coughing which overtook him. Since being gassed he had been advised by the hospital to stop smoking, and if he was honest he knew that they were right. Each morning when he awoke his chest felt as if bands of steel were being tightened around it. A cigarette as soon as he got up threw him into a violent and painful bout of coughing, after which, for a short while, he gained some respite and felt much better. He knew that the habit was not really helping, and his shortness of breath was not improving. Recently he had found that even with the aid of a stick he could not walk far or undertake any strenuous exercise. The dash from the car to the ditch had left him tired and debilitated, which was why the cigarette was affecting his inflamed lungs so badly.

Gresham's next pronouncement provided a further shock. 'We're going to Calais. There's a supply ship leaving on the evening tide for Dover.

We're supposed to be on it, and if we're not there'll be all hell to pay.'

'England . . . what on earth are we going back to England for? If it's a question of recuperation then I can manage very well here in France.'

The amiable smile with which he had first greeted Sam at Béthune returned to Gresham's face. 'Do you think I'd have come all the way from London simply to drive you to a base hospital for a spot of relaxation?' The smile was now one of genuine amusement. 'You're to be involved in a rather important project. By the way,' he added almost as an afterthought, 'you've been promoted to major.'

Chapter Four

As he waited for a builder's cart to pass before crossing over the High Street, Will Mardlin watched the little man in an old-fashioned curly brimmed bowler hat who was selling lemonade on the opposite pavement. Standing no more than five feet tall, 'Sherbet Billy's' tiny hunchbacked figure was a regular sight on the streets of Kelsford during the summer months. He must, Will thought, be in his late seventies. He wondered idly what the old man did during the winter when the cold sherbet drinks that he sold from his polished churn were not required.

As Will looked on, Billy fished in the pocket of his greasy frock coat for some change to give to a woman of about his own age who was wearing a black crêpe bonnet tied with ribbon under her chin. Even at this distance he could see the toothless grin as the little street trader politely tipped his bowler and took the housewife's ha'penny before turning to his next client, a younger woman in a dark shawl and a white apron who was proffering a large white milk jug to be filled. Not a bad way to earn a living, thought Will: no worries and few overheads, just selling the home-made drink round the streets during the week and at the cattle market on a Wednesday, when the farmers came in to trade.

There was the sound of an engine and the rumble of solid tyres on the cobbled road surface. An army lorry approached along the High Street, and as it drew level with Will he saw two more trundling round the corner behind it. He paused to allow them to pass before crossing. At first he thought they were military ambulances, but as they passed it was obvious from the absence of red crosses and their panelled sides that they were converted hauliers' trucks. There were four in all, and as the last disappeared round the bend at Beggars Lane he gave a puzzled frown. Usually lorries were going to or coming from Sevastopol Barracks, but these were on the other side of town, and in the back of the last were six armed soldiers.

When the road was clear Will walked slowly over towards the diminutive street trader.

'Drink, sir? Ha'penny a time.' The soft Edinburgh burr had not been diminished by the man's years away from his native home.

'Thank you, Billy.' Handing over a penny, Will lifted a glass from one of the metal rings round the side of the three foot high container. 'Keep the change. Where would you say the "sodgers" were going?'

Sherbet Billy turned on the tap to fill Will's glass, grinning at the music hall Scots accent. The thickset detective was well known by most of the street traders in Kelsford, and if you caught him in the pub he was usually good for a pint. 'I think that you'll find, Mr Mardlin, they're away to the Old Watermill upon the Mere. Lilian Crookshank was telling me that the army's taken the mill over as a recuperation home for soldiers who've been gassed.'

Downing the cold drink in one long swallow, Will handed back the glass and, nodding absently, took his leave of the lemonade seller. As he walked along the High Street he was deep in thought. Rumours abounded in the town about the sudden military interest in the land around the Watermill. Everyone you spoke to had a different story. Some said that it was going to be a Royal Flying Corps base, others an ordnance depot for the storage of artillery shells, while one current in the Prince Albert was that the mill was to become an observation post for the tracking of incoming Zeppelins. Whatever was being set up, Will very much doubted the latest convalescent home theory. The lorries had been laden with equipment, and the soldiers were armed.

Strolling along the High Street, enjoying the summer sunshine, he continued to turn the matter over. Will decided that it was unlikely the old mill was going to be used as storage. The warehouse complex that had been built soon after he and his parents moved to Kelsford was far better suited, and required none of the construction work that was obviously going on at the mill. Similarly an RFC base required a runway, and what was the point of clearing woodland when there were plenty of properties around the district with open fields suitable for landing strips. An observation post for the detection of incoming raiders required no alterations to existing buildings, and the Kelsford War Hospital ruled out the need for a convalescent home.

One point, though, was relevant. The Old Watermill was within the town boundary, and therefore within his area of responsibility. Coming to a decision, Will quickened his pace as he decided that a few official enquiries would not go amiss.

At the Old Watermill Sam Norton was busy organising his new office while waiting for the arrival of more equipment and supplies. Although he had visited his relatives in Kelsford, Sam was not particularly familiar with the town's environs, and was both surprised and pleased with his new quarters.

The mill had been a going concern when it had quietly been bought from Tobias Sutledge. Sutledge's son Eldred, who before the war had worked the mill with him, had recently been killed in France, and with no further incentive to run the business the old man had been content to accept the more than generous offer made to him by the man who had arrived unannounced from the War Office.

For the purposes of the project that Sam was to manage, the premises were ideal, he decided. During his journey back to England with Ralph Gresham, and later in a series of meetings at the War Office, an exciting and highly confidential venture had been revealed to him.

Codenamed Project 19, the scheme – authorised at the highest level – was being implemented to produce an antidote to the effects of chlorine gas used by the Germans. While units in other parts of the country and in France were working to enhance the retaliatory potential of gas used by the Allies, the task of Project 19 was to neutralise the effects of the new weapon entirely. If such a result could be achieved, the stocks held by the Germans would be worthless, and the British would have no need to pursue any further research.

The need for secrecy concerning the work to be conducted at Kelsford was stressed both by Gresham and by the senior member of the Civil Service who Sam had met in London. In accordance with the adage that 'he who lives by the sword shall die by the sword', there were those both in government and military circles who were dedicated to the elimination of all German resistance by developing another toxic gas. If the existence of the Kelsford establishment, working in opposition to such an aim, were to become known, all funding for Project 19 would be withdrawn immediately. Having suffered the effects of being gassed, Sam subscribed wholeheartedly to this latest proposal, and apart from his recent promotion to major he was immensely pleased to be involved in something which, if successful, would have a huge impact on the outcome of the war.

The mill itself was a large six-roomed stone house with a tightly thatched roof, resembling the home of an affluent farmer rather than that of a working miller. The fast-flowing stream known locally as the Mere (once clear of the mill it ran into a quiet open stretch of water before joining the Union Canal on the north side of town) had years ago been diverted to run beneath the premises, so an internal waterwheel could be used to grind corn.

A newly arrived construction team was about to start work on converting the spacious living area into quarters for the small group of scientists who would soon be arriving. The separate grain and flour store on the opposite side of the courtyard was being made ready for occupation by the soldiers who were to guard the site, while a secluded part of the mill's woodland was being cleared in order to build the laboratories where, away from prying eyes, the crucial research work would be conducted. In order to store the materials eventually produced, an underground bunker lined with concrete and steel was to be excavated near the laboratories. It was now early June, and Sam had been promised that the work would be completed within a matter of weeks.

An added bonus was that his sister was in the town, only a mile or so away. Irene had written to him soon after his arrival in Belgium, telling him of Jean-Claude's death during the first few days of war and of her escape to England. He was aware of their aunt's kindness to her when she first arrived and of the assistance that their cousin James had given her in finding a place of her own. Although he had met James a couple of times since his arrival in Kelsford, Sam had not warmed to the man who, while close to Irene, seemed to want to distance himself from her brother. Perhaps it was the loss of his hand, he thought. An ardent patriot, James, an officer in the Kelsford Yeomanry, had been badly wounded in the early fighting around Mons, and this had resulted in the amputation of his right hand. Awarded the DSO, he was invalided out of the army and sent back home to England. Perhaps, thought Sam, it was this that was the basis of his cousin's antipathy.

All in all, the young man concluded, as he leaned on the wooden rail of the narrow curved bridge, smoking a Life Guard and listening to the restful murmur of the stream bubbling out from under the mill, this was going to be a most enjoyable posting. If nothing else, his experiences in France had taught him to 'enjoy life while ye may'. Circumstances could, should the fortunes of the war alter, have him back at the Front before he knew it. Checking his pocket watch, Sam wondered how much longer it would be before the rest of the lorries carrying scientific apparatus arrived.

Chapter Five

S am Norton would have been less content with his new situation had he been party to a meeting that was taking place in a secluded office in Whitehall at the very moment he was taking stock of his new domain.

Sir Rowland Leigh-Hunt folded his hands in front of him on the polished rosewood table and cast a speculative eye around the room. Although the décor was extremely conservative, it was overly ornate for his taste. Like so many of the large conference rooms discreetly hidden around Whitehall it vastly overstated its purpose. The room must, he estimated, be at least forty feet long, the walls hung with a small fortune in original oil paintings depicting various military leaders from around the world both past and present. Glaring down on him from the far wall in full regalia was the epitome of Teutonic might: Otto von Bismarck. Obviously the Master of the Pictures had missed this particular room when clearing from the building everything un-British. There was, he noticed, not a portrait anywhere of Napoleon Bonaparte.

Coughing delicately, Leigh-Hunt decided it was time for the meeting to begin. 'Gentlemen, may I first thank you for taking the time from your busy schedules to be here this afternoon.'

The other men responded politely. Each had received a hand-delivered note with their correspondence that morning, requesting 'that they be so good as to make themselves available', and 'regretting any inconvenience caused to the recipient in advance for any other engagement which he may have to cancel'. The neatly penned signature left no option but to comply.

Sir Rowland smiled distantly. A thick mane of silver hair, parted in the middle of his forehead, topped a long beaky nose on which perched precariously a tiny set of pince-nez. The pale watery eyes that peered out from behind the gold-rimmed glasses and his urbane manner could have been mistaken by anyone who did not know him for those of an elderly solicitor or bank manager.

The men seated along the other three sides of the conference table did know him, and were not about to be fooled by his appearance. Sir Rowland Leigh-Hunt was, they were aware, a diplomat with over forty years' experience and a reputation, both at the negotiating table and away from it, as a man not to be underestimated. Those who chose to presume otherwise did so at their cost. Not for nothing was the elderly diplomat known as the smiling assassin in the corridors of Whitehall.

'The matter which we are gathered here to discuss is, I must emphasise, of the utmost secrecy.' He paused long enough to ensure nods of assent round the table. The fact that there was no secretary present to take minutes would, he knew, not have been lost on the small group. 'During recent weeks there has been a development in the war which cannot be allowed to go unchallenged. I refer of course to the use by the Germans of poisoned gas.'

To his right he saw the soldier's mouth set. General Sir Hedley Thompson was one of the sabre and lance brigade, who while being appalled at the latest turn of events would be violently opposed to replying in similar fashion. Unfortunately his school of thought was shared by Field Marshal Sir John French, and so long as French commanded the British armies on the Continent the implementation of any new tactics was going to prove difficult. That was soon to alter, however, Leigh-Hunt thought with grim satisfaction. The bellicose field marshal – although he alone appeared sublimely oblivious to the fact – was soon to be replaced as commander of the British Expeditionary Force. His performance to date had been abysmal, and even Kitchener no longer supported him. As long as Haig doesn't get the job we may have a chance to move things forward, Leigh-Hunt mused.

Returning to the matter in hand, he continued, with a small gesture to the man in the Royal Engineers uniform seated on his left. 'First I'm going to ask Major Gresham to outline the situation.'

Ralph Gresham repositioned the notepad and pencil neatly in front of him, and clasped his hands together on the table. Of those gathered in the room only he and Leigh-Hunt knew exactly why the meeting had been convened. For many years Gresham had worked for Sir Rowland, and while others knew the man as a career diplomat who beneath the veneer of sophistication was a shrewd and ruthless politician, Gresham also realised that when occasion demanded – as now – the old man was a highly competent controller of intelligence agents, ideally suited to further the best interests of Project 19.

Gresham's assessment of General Thompson, seated opposite him, coincided with Leigh-Hunt's. Middle sixties, overdue for retirement, Thompson had made his way up the army list through a series of colonial policing actions and a good family background. In relation to the proposals which were about to be put forward he would bluster and procrastinate, but eventually accede to the inevitable, albeit with a notable lack of grace.

The fourth man, who was wearing the three rings of a naval commander on the cuffs of his dark blue uniform jacket, was an unknown quantity. He was, suspected Gresham, a member of Admiral Hall's staff in Naval Intelligence.

Leigh-Hunt noted the involuntary spasm of the major's jaw muscles, the twitch momentarily jerking at the side of his mouth.

'As you are aware, gentlemen, six weeks ago on the afternoon of 22nd April the Germans launched a poisoned gas attack on the Allied positions along part of the Ypres Salient in Belgium.' Gresham had no need of any notes; the details were imprinted on his mind. 'It is estimated that in a period of five minutes along a four mile stretch of Front, something like one hundred and sixty tons of poisoned gas was released from between five and six thousand cylinders dug in along the German lines. Further attacks in later days caused severe disruption to our forces, particularly to the sector held by the Canadians. Out of some fifteen thousand casualties around a third – five thousand – proved fatal.'

Gresham paused to look round. The naval officer was studiously playing with his pencil, listening carefully, not for something new but mentally checking against his own information the accuracy of what the Sapper was saying. General Thompson's face had taken on the frozen aspect of someone preparing to distance himself from what might be to come.

'The substance used was a lachrymatory gas with a chlorine base. Because it's heavier than air this substance can be released through nozzles directed over the parapet of a trench and allowed to roll across the ground, carried on the breeze until it reaches the enemy lines. There, searching for the lowest level, it settles into the bottom of the trench. The effects upon a person exposed to the gas are extremely uncomfortable. The irritant effect causes temporary blindness, combined with a bronchial condition similar to acute pneumonia and it is this that usually proves fatal. As yet we've been unable to develop a completely suitable face mask to protect our troops against the gas's effects.' Gresham paused again. Time to ruffle some feathers. 'There were very clear early intelligence reports about the impending danger, which unfortunately were dismissed out of hand by General Staff officers along the sector involved. Had these reports been acted upon, a large number of the casualties could have been avoided, and the overall psychological effects of the gas significantly reduced.' Sitting back in his chair, he indicated to the chairman that for the moment he had nothing further to say.

'Thank you, Major Gresham.' Leigh-Hunt indicated to the far end of the table. 'Commander Bayliss . . .'

Edward Bayliss leaned forward, hands clasped. He was wondering who exactly Gresham was. That he was a regular soldier was not in question, but despite the uniform Bayliss doubted that he was in the Royal Engineers. Glancing quickly at his notes, the commander put the matter to the back of his mind. 'We've been monitoring the German chemicals industry for some time.' Bayliss did not say who 'we' were. 'In October of last year the German

General Staff under Erich von Falkenhayn set up a committee to explore the possibility of using gas as a weapon of offence. One of his officers, Gerhard Tappen, has a brother – a civilian called Hans – who is a chemist. Under his direction their technicians experimented with some chemicals which were loaded into shrapnel shells for use by the artillery. The indications are that they were not successful. Our contact within the General Staff tells us that they actually tested these at Neuve-Chapelle, but they had so little effect that we would never had known.'

Gresham almost burst out laughing at the expression of perplexity and outrage that this information brought to Sir Hedley Thompson's face. More soberly, he ruminated upon the very real possibility that the Germans also had their own agents deep within the War Office in London. His attention returned to the naval officer.

'Then they developed a lachrymatory or tear gas, which contained a chemical that we think is a mixture of xylyl bromide and bromacetone. How successful this has been we're not certain, as it was tested on the Eastern Front.' Bayliss gave a wry smile. 'Ironically, the use of Bromacetone as a tear gas was pioneered before the war by our friends the French, for use by their police.' Picking up his pencil, he examined its sharp point while ordering his thoughts. 'The suggested addition of chlorine to the gas was made by a man named Haber. Our researchers have traced him quite easily. Herr Doktor Fritz Jacob Haber. Before the war he was director of the Wilhelm Chemical Institute in Berlin. Along with a team of scientists he's now responsible for developing the gas which is presently being used against our men in France.'

Ralph Gresham made a slight gesture to attract the commander's attention. 'How long ago is it since the first lot of shells were sent to the Russian Front?'

'Around last Christmas, according to our man.' Bayliss could see where the conversation was leading. 'I think it's safe to discount any serious developments in that direction. If they'd been successful I can assure you that we'd know. Our scientists think that the xylyl bromide and bromacetone mixture – the Germans have called it T-Stoff – would have been adversely affected by the intense cold.' Bayliss gave Gresham an appraising look. He hoped he would find out who the dark-haired man was before the meeting ended. 'Although we've established a small unit on the French side of the Channel to research and further our own development of gas, at the moment we've got a distinct problem with the availability of materials.'

'Why are we working on this in France and not here in London?' General Thompson interrupted.

Leigh-Hunt took off his pince-nez and, using a large white pocket handkerchief, began to polish them, deliberately not looking at the general. He thought that Sir Hedley, with his bulbous eyes and pudgy overhanging jowls, bore a striking resemblance to a large bullfrog in uniform – and he wondered if more intelligent members of the armed forces found men like Thompson as irritating as he did.

Ralph Gresham was tempted to answer the question, then decided to leave it for the navy man rather than further interrupt his flow.

Clearing his throat, Bayliss replied patiently. 'The research, Sir Hedley, is heavily reliant on the early identification of the effects of any new gas upon our men at the Front. While we have access to the medical reports on casualties it's more important to know precisely how, in the more extreme cases, death is caused. This means we need to be in a position to carry out post-mortems on men near the battlefield.'

General Thompson gave a curt acknowledgement, as if to signify that the explanation confirmed something of which he was already aware.

Commander Bayliss glanced down at his notes before resuming. 'The research establishment in Northern France – at Helfault – is under the direct command of Colonel Foulkes of the Royal Engineers, who's been appointed Senior Gas Advisor to the British Expeditionary Force.' He glanced enquiringly at the man in the Sapper's uniform, but Gresham, with a slight shake of his head, signified that he did not wish to make any comment. 'Our main problem, as I've said, lies in the supply of materials. At the moment, here in Britain, we have the capability of manufacturing one ton of liquid chlorine per day. At Ypres the enemy released 160 tons in five minutes. The reason for this is that for some years now the Germans have dominated the world's chemicals industry. They have factories capable of producing vast amounts of chlorine at Ludwigshafen, Hochst-am-main, Leverkusen and many other similar sites. We, on the other hand, have only one factory with any capability: at Runcorn in Cheshire. The one area of difficulty shared by the Germans and ourselves is how best to store and then deliver the gas.'

Gresham shot a sidelong glance across the table. General Thompson was suddenly interested. Whatever was to be discussed in relation to supply and delivery would involve his branch of the Ordnance Department. Leigh-Hunt was idly studying the portrait of Bismarck.

'The Germans have evolved two methods of storage and delivery. The first involves one hundred and thirty pound iron cylinders, and the gas is released through long metal pipes which are elevated over the top of a trench and pointed in the general direction of the enemy. The drawback is that distribution of the gas is dependent upon the weather. A dry day with a light breeze blowing from behind constitutes the optimum conditions. Too much wind and it's blown away ineffectively. If there's a change in wind direction the cloud is delivered back to those releasing it. The second method is to put lead canisters of gas into highly explosive artillery shells, the gas being released when the shell explodes. There are logistical problems with this, the primary one being that the munitions industry can't supply sufficient high explosive shells for bombardment purposes – so gas shells are therefore very low priority. Secondly, delivery is totally dependent upon the accuracy of the gunners. Unless the shell explodes directly on target the effort is wasted.'

Hedley Thompson could contain himself no longer. 'My feelings are that we shouldn't involve ourselves in this game of dirty tricks. One good push while we've got the weather will resolve matters.'

Commander Bayliss, his briefing almost complete, was not to be deflected. 'The assessment of the Naval Intelligence Service is that Great Britain has two matters which need to be addressed as a matter of urgency. First, how to develop our potential for the use of poison gas in a quantity equivalent to that which the Germans have already achieved. Second, to determine an effective means of delivery which will allow us to realise maximum physical and psychological effect.' Looking round the table, he added with an air of finality, 'If we don't succeed in those two areas our chances of winning the war are very slim.'

Replacing the eyeglasses on his nose, Sir Rowland Leigh-Hunt carefully smoothed out the length of black ribbon that attached them to the lapel of his dark jacket. 'Thank you, gentlemen.' For a man of his age he had a strong clear voice, Gresham noted. 'It remains for me to bring things together, and to discuss certain matters that will under no circumstances be repeated outside this room. First, General, unfortunately "dirty tricks" are what will eventually win this war – and whatever our personal feelings we'll not only be involved in them but will of necessity have to initiate them.'

Sir Hedley Thompson had relapsed into what Gresham took to be his version of a sulky silence.

'The government has, despite reservations among certain members, agreed to the use by this country of poisoned gas as a weapon of war. The gas unit in Northern France is looking into the properties of chlorine. Discreet advertisements have been placed in various periodicals inviting chemistry graduates to volunteer for a Special Pioneer Unit, which will be dedicated to the production and use of gas as a weapon.' He paused, removing his glasses as if a slight blurring of his surroundings would help him to concentrate. 'In addition to the factory mentioned by Commander Bayliss, an industrial firm at Lancaster has been contracted to explore the possibilities of using a chemical called phosgene, which I'm told will have a far more potent effect than chlorine. A gas warfare unit has been created by the War Office under the overall command of Colonel Charles Foulkes, who'll be responsible for overseeing all future developments. We, however, have been charged with a most secret endeavour, codenamed Project 19.' Leigh-Hunt had the undivided attention of his audience. 'Among a group of refugees who've recently come to this country from Belgium is a chemist named Paul Kändler. The son of a German father and Belgium mother, Kändler has for some years been employed in the German chemicals industry by the Badische Anilin und Sodafabrik of Ludwigshafen. Having served his period of conscription several years ago, under the complicated German military system, when war broke out our man was still on the army reserve list. He was recalled to be part of a technical unit, and in January of this year was seconded to the military's chemical laboratories to work on the development of their chlorine gas weapon.' Sir Rowland's gaze settled upon the stout figure of the German chancellor. 'Kändler was from the outset unsympathetic to the Kaiser's military aspirations, and disturbed at the direction in which his career was being directed. When the posting to work on the gas project came through, he was on holiday with his mother's family in Antwerp and took the opportunity to escape to England, where he offered his services to the British government. For a while in civilian life Kändler has been involved privately on research aimed at dealing with pain relief by using muscle relaxants which operate through the body's nervous system. It's something of an understatement to say that his arrival here has come at a critical time for this country's development of chemical weaponry. His work ties in with similar research being conducted here by a biologist called Herbert Duggan. Since the beginning of the year Dr Duggan has – at the behest of the War Office – been looking into the possibility of producing a chemical that would be capable of incapacitating an enemy by attacking his nervous system.'

The fact that the British government must have been working on a gas weapon since the beginning of the year at least, and well before Ypres, was not lost on his listeners.

'Given time, Duggan and Kändler are confident that they will be able to produce a liquid gas capable of attacking the human nervous system with fatal results. Most importantly – and in answer to your second point concerning delivery, Commander – if they are correct in their calculations it can be dropped from an aeroplane over a specifically targeted area, and would be capable of wiping out immense numbers of enemy troops without a shot being fired.'

Weighing the politician's words, Bayliss noted the major's lack of reaction: he already knew about the project. Gresham was working directly for Leigh-Hunt.

The sudden draining of colour from General Thompson's pudgy features confirmed that this was the first he had heard of what was being planned. 'My department will have no part in this!' Thompson was unable to conceal the anxiety in his voice.

Bayliss studied the signet ring on the little finger of his left hand. It was too late – and Sir Hedley knew it. The general could do nothing to stop the project, and from this moment the army could not deny knowledge of its existence. Nicely done, he thought.

Leigh-Hunt separated a single sheet of paper from the thin folder in front of him and passed it over to the general without bothering to look up. 'You'll see, Sir Hedley, that you already are a part.' His thin and wintry smile was devoid of any humour. 'That document is a copy of one which was delivered by hand to the Master of Ordnance an hour ago. You'll see from the signature that this project is authorised at the highest level.'

Thompson stared blankly for a moment before finding his voice. 'Winston is involved in this!' he exclaimed hoarsely.

'We're all involved in beating the Kaiser.' The bleak smile was gone, replaced by the bland, inscrutable expression of the professional diplomat. 'The feelings of the First Lord about furthering England's prospects of winning the war are well known.'

Choosing his words carefully, Commander Bayliss asked, 'How does this project fit in with the work of Colonel Foulkes's unit?'

'Totally separate matter.' Leigh-Hunt's tone was incisive. 'This research is independent. Foulkes knows nothing at present, and will be told nothing until we know whether or not this Belgian can do what he says.'

Edward Bayliss looked across at Gresham, who returned his gaze steadily. By God, you'd better be good, he thought. Even with the signature on the document in front of Thompson this was a house of cards. One false move and the whole lot would crash down around their ears. If on the other hand it worked, then the results would probably end the war at a stroke.

Once again toying with his pince-nez, Sir Rowland smiled at the faces of the men around the table. This time a hint of warmth touched the edges of his mouth. 'There is, of course, a need to ensure the security of this affair. Premises have been acquired and an adequate cover provided to ensure that the work be allowed to proceed unhindered. Major, would you be so good as to explain the arrangements.'

Outlining the 'arrangements' took Gresham some considerable time. Over the next half hour, as the briefing progressed, Bayliss posed a few relevant questions and General Thompson lapsed into a sullen silence. Leigh-Hunt, as Gresham's controller, was fully aware of every detail of the plan that his subordinate was meticulously unfolding. Releasing the Iron Chancellor from his scrutiny, Sir Rowland spent some time examining a different painting, this time of the Duke of Wellington, as he vaguely listened to Ralph Gresham's voice.

During the weeks that had elapsed since the middle of April a small and select group of highly placed civil servants, politicians and army officers had been charged with finding some way of countering the latest German threat. An unbelievable piece of good fortune had come their way when an officer routinely screening refugees had identified Paul Kändler in a settlement camp near Dover. Once the newcomer's credentials had been verified things moved swiftly.

Kändler's arrival coincided with a donation to the war effort of almost one million pounds in cash by an international firm of jewellers: Kosminiski's. Fortuitously, administration of the donation – which was intended to assist in the financing of Field Marshal Lord Kitchener's 'New Army' – fell solely to Sir Rowland Leigh-Hunt. The results of enquiries into Kosminski's stimulated Leigh Hunt's active mind.

Based in France and massively wealthy, the company rested in the hands of a single family – or more precisely the matriarch of the family, Ruth Norton. Discreet enquiries revealed that as a young woman Mrs Norton, born Ruth

Kosminski and of East European Jewish descent, had lived in Kelsford. It was there, through marriage to an older man named Isaac Samuels that the foundations of her wealth had been laid: her husband was part owner of the Kelsford Bank of Commerce. What particularly interested Leigh-Hunt was Ruth Norton's later days in the town.

Widowed at an early age, it was fairly certain that during the 1880s she had become involved in a Jewish underground movement that helped Russian and East European dissidents to escape from the Tsarist regime and travel to England and America. There was also a strong suggestion that she had been involved, during the latter part of 1888, in the smuggling to America of a diamond necklace stolen from the Tsarina of Russia. This last particularly interested Leigh-Hunt, as it was only a matter of months after this that she remarried, sold her interest in the bank and moved to France – where, he pondered speculatively, she had become extremely wealthy.

The potential for the Kosminski donation to fund a clandestine weapons project was not lost on Sir Rowland. It had been an easy matter to purchase suitable premises on the outskirts of Kelsford and have them equipped as a research centre – so far as the military establishment was concerned for the furtherance of current gas production – while for the benefit of the citizens of Kelsford it was alleged to be manufacturing anaesthetics for use in French field hospitals. Shrouded in a double cloak of secrecy, and funded by money that was not traceable in Treasury or War Office budgets, the future of Project 19 was secured. Should things go well, the new weapon would be put into production and the research centre quietly closed down – with all credit passing to the official government teams working under Foulkes. If it went disastrously wrong then the source of funding would be quietly revealed and responsibility could be shifted to Kosminski's, which would be identified as an independent private concern based in France.

'We've acquired a watermill on the outskirts of the town,' Gresham explained. 'At a rough estimate we can house a team of around ten scientists and twenty soldiers. The research facility is being constructed in nearby woods, which were purchased along with the mill. Because it's supposed to be a government establishment a number of soldiers billeted at the site won't be questioned by the locals. A further advantage is that because there's a warehousing complex on the edge of town, on the canal and with excellent rail links, we'll be able to move materials in and out quite easily without arousing any suspicions.'

'Who's responsible for running things at the watermill?' asked Bayliss.

'Now that', replied Gresham, flashing his opposite number a disarming smile, 'is the *pièce de résistance*. The officer who's been appointed – and has taken command today – is Major Samuel Norton, son of Mrs Ruth Norton, and a minor director of Kosminski's.'

Edward Bayliss returned the grin. Like Gresham he was in his late thirties and a professional intelligence officer, and he was impressed by the finesse that the major was bringing to the operation. 'Where did you find him?' He could not resist the question.

'Béthune Military Hospital, recovering from being gassed at Ypres – which in view of what we had in mind is a rather nice touch. We arranged for his discharge date to coincide with the premises being ready, and I simply went over and fetched him. He's under the impression that the object of Project 19 is to develop an antidote to chlorine gas.'

'And presumably there was an immediate promotion for him – something to occupy his mind so he didn't focus too closely on the cover story?' Bayliss speculated.

'Correct.' Again the slight spasm of his jaw, as Gresham acknowledged a fellow spirit. 'He's a silver spoon job: affluent background, well educated, not overly bright. I'd say he's ideal for what we need.' Gresham watched with amusement the look of distaste that passed momentarily across the face of the fat general. Intelligence work was still considered by such men as an occupation for cads and bounders – those unable to succeed in life honourably. The major had used the term 'silver spoon' deliberately, to offend Thompson personally. Thirty years spent in comfortable postings across the Empire, a commission guaranteed by birth and position, he would be even more affronted if he knew Gresham's own background – which he never would.

Born in 1877, the son of a Manchester grocer, Ralph Gresham had joined the 5th Dragoon Guards as a boy soldier at the age of fifteen, and by the time his regiment left for the South African War in 1899 he was a full sergeant. An aptitude for languages enabled him to quickly pick up the strange mixture of Dutch, English, Javanese and African, known as Afrikaans, which was spoken by the Boer farmers; and he was soon interviewing Boer prisoners as they were brought into the British camp. It was not long before he progressed to more clandestine work. Sent off alone on horseback into the veldt, Gresham spied on Boer encampments, returning days later with invaluable information. After the war he returned home as a senior warrant officer wearing the Queen's and King's South African campaign medals, as did almost every soldier who had fought in the war. Ralph Gresham learned early in his career a lesson that sat easily with him. The dangerous work of spying on the enemy did not carry with it many decorations, but – far more importantly – it resulted in rapid promotion.

During the first decade of the new century Gresham spent little time in Britain. When Russia went to war with Japan in 1904, as a lieutenant temporarily posted to the General Staff he was one of the select group of officers sent by the British government to observe as events unfolded. The fall of Port Arthur to the Japanese, followed by the further Russian loss of Mukden in Manchuria, enabled Gresham to prepare a scathing appraisal of Russian military defences. Similarly, four years later, and now a captain, he was in Turkey to witness the revolution of Enver Pasha and his Young Turks.

During the two years before 1914 Gresham, out of uniform and in the guise of a pharmaceuticals representative, spent most of his time travelling around Eastern France and across the German border into Alsace and Lorraine. He, and others of his profession employed in Germany itself, soon came to a disturbing conclusion: the French Army's Plan 17, dedicated to repelling any future German acts of aggression at the point of a bayonet, was doomed to failure.

A mixture of arrogance and disdain for those involved in clandestine intelligence work led certain members of the British War Office – and consequently the government – to fatally disregard the German military build-up. The result was that when Kaiser Wilhelm's troops marched through Belgium and into France in August 1914, it was only thanks to the German high command's disastrous last minute tinkering with the meticulously prepared blueprint for the invasion of France, the Schlieffen Plan, that a catastrophic Allied defeat was averted.

In his presumption that Gresham was no stranger to active duty in the present conflict, Sam Norton was correct. Returned with the rank of captain to uniform duty as soon as war was declared, he had first seen action at Nery before being seconded to the 1st Royal Dragoons, who were in need of battle-experienced officers. As part of the 3rd Cavalry Division, Gresham's unit fought at the Battle of Langemarck a month later, earning him the Military Medal and a field promotion to major. In the early summer of 1915, while Gresham's unit was resting behind the lines, he received orders to report immediately to the Army Headquarters at Hazebrouck. Three days later he was in London, once again immersed in the cloak and dagger world of military intelligence.

The meeting concluded, Leigh-Hunt sat alone. Taking out a slim gold pocket watch, he noted that ten minutes had elapsed since the others had left. He replaced it in his waistcoat pocket, got to his feet and walked slowly round the room, checking that no trace had been left of their presence.

Closing and locking the door behind him, Leigh-Hunt walked along the corridor, his footfalls deadened by the expensive deep-pile carpet, to another door at the far end. He unlocked and opened it. The young grenadier lieutenant seated by the window and reading through some papers on his lap stood up hurriedly, pushing a file into the leather dispatch bag next to him on the floor.

'John, would you be so good as to lock this door behind you and take the key back to reception.' Leigh-Hunt's thin-lipped smile was one of polite instruction.

As the lieutenant secured the strap on his case, Leigh-Hunt moved aside a tapestried curtain at the far side of the room and disappeared down a narrow staircase.

The elderly pensioner seated behind the wide reception desk on the ground floor looked up from his newspaper as the young lieutenant leaned over to return the key for room 109. With a nod and a polite 'Thank you, sir,' he replaced the key on the hook behind him and entered the time in his ledger.

Not very tall for a guardsman, he thought, as he attempted to make out the illegible signature that the young man had scribbled when collecting the key earlier in the day. 'About time some of them learned to write,' he muttered, watching the back of the uniformed figure as it disappeared through the revolving door into the street.

Fifteen minutes later the young man, minus his moustache and wearing a sober grey suit and public school tie, tapped gently on the door of Sir Rowland Leigh-Hunt's office. 'No problems, Sir Rowland,' he said quietly.

'Thank you, John.' Leigh-Hunt did not raise his head from the paper that he was studying.

Chapter Six

Will Mardlin's intention to find out what was going on at the Old Watermill suffered a setback the following day, when shortly before six o'clock in the evening the station messenger boy, Eric Broughton, knocked timidly on his office door and handed him an urgent message from Harry North. Handwritten on a page torn from the back of a police notebook, it was brief and to the point. '42 Devonshire Gardens. Body found. Suggest that you may wish to attend. H.N.'

'Run back and tell Mr North I'll be there in twenty minutes,' he said to the waiting boy, before returning to the file of evidence that he was examining. It related to the theft by a servant girl of a half guinea from her mistress's dressing table, and Will was not completely convinced with the case against the young woman. Her name was Ada Manners, and he noted that she was employed at a house only three doors from his own home.

Other than an admission of guilt at the police station to Detective Constable Cleaver, the officer who had arrested her, there was no other evidence to substantiate the allegation. It bothered him that when charged with the theft she had said to the desk sergeant, 'No, sir. I've stolen nothing.' Putting the file to one side without signing it, Will resolved to have a word with Nathan Cleaver.

It was a few minutes before a quarter to seven when Will turned into Devonshire Gardens from Collington Road. The warm sunshine of the day had been replaced by ominous black clouds, which promised one of the sudden downpours characteristic of June and August – and as Will paused to check the house numbers a large cold raindrop fell on his face. Number forty-two was further on, halfway down the street. If he needed confirmation it was provided by the presence of a uniformed constable and half a dozen people standing by the front gate.

Built twenty years ago as part of the redevelopment of the Downe Street area, the houses in Devonshire Gardens were already beginning to slip into genteel disrepair. They were, however, an immeasurable improvement on the old back-to-backs that made up the district he remembered as a lad. From the outset, though, they had fallen just short of their intended purpose, which was to provide housing for office managers and middle-class artisans. Now, behind the rows of bay windows and peeling paintwork, there were the same itinerant building labourers and poorer families who had inhabited Downe Street for generations, having to a large extent reclaimed the properties as their own.

Outside number forty-two the small group of curious onlookers was speculating on the police presence, and trying to steal a glimpse through the open front door. A man in a cloth cap with a muffler knotted around his throat caught hold of the superintendent's sleeve. 'What's 'appening, mister?' he demanded as Will pushed open the gate to the tiny front garden.

'You're going to get off home – that's what's happening,' Will answered shortly. 'Get rid of this lot,' he hissed over his shoulder as he pushed past the spare figure of the elderly constable who had positioned himself in the doorway of the house to shelter from the now steadily falling rain.

In the narrow hallway Will paused to get his bearings. A movement to his right caught his attention, and he saw a small slimly built woman of about forty, wearing a long grey dress and white apron, watching him apprehensively. Seconds later a dark-haired man with a waxed moustache and neatly trimmed beard appeared from the room behind her. He wore long green detachable cuffs over the white sleeves of his collarless shirt, as if he were engaged in polishing silverware or blacking a fire-grate.

'Good evening to you,' Will said politely, at the same time looking round for a police officer who could show him where to find Inspector North. The woman remained silent, obviously frightened.

'Bonsoir, monsieur,' the man murmured, placing his hands on her shoulders in a protective gesture obviously intended to reassure her, although he also appeared ill at ease.

'Frogs, sir. No parley Anglais.' The dour voice of Detective Sergeant Bertram Conway floated out from the room. It was followed a moment later by the sergeant's portly figure, a pencil and notebook in his hand.

Will continued to appraise the couple in the doorway. First impressions were important, and in his experience usually accurate. It was a dilapidated house in a run-down area, yet these people, albeit shabbily dressed, were clean and neat. He recollected the white net curtains at the front room window, and the fact that the brass doorknocker, already spattered with rain was freshly polished. Belgian refugees ... the town was teaming with them.

'Mr North's in the back bedroom with the doctor, sir.'

The superintendent nodded briefly before making his way up the stairs and along the dimly lit landing to the rear of the house, where he could see a gaslight burning and hear muted voices.

In the doorway of the tiny bedroom Will stood perfectly still, absorbing every detail. To his left, immediately inside, was a narrow single bed, the covers thrown back in disarray as if it had recently been vacated. In front of him a cheap deal wardrobe with a full length mirror screwed onto its single door was positioned at an angle to the wall ,thereby giving anyone on the bed a clear view of themselves. The small iron grate, not required during the warm summer months, had been cleaned of ashes and tidily stuffed with newspaper. Under the window stood a dressing table with a mirror, hinged to allow it to be tilted. Beneath the mirror on a white doily was a glass tray on which was neatly arranged a set of women's hairbrushes. A grey shawl was thrown over the upright chair in front of it.

The gathering storm clouds had robbed the room of what little light was admitted through a narrow sash window, and someone had lit the gas mantle on the wall over the fireplace to give some illumination. Dr Arthur Mallard was kneeling in the cramped space between the bed and the far wall, his medical bag open beside him, carefully examining in the flickering light the body of a woman. Harry North stepped back from behind the doctor in order to allow Will to move in and look over Mallard's shoulder.

The woman, in a vain attempt to escape from her attacker, had retreated to the furthest corner of the room, where her body was, legs spread, back pushed against the wall, her head – what was left of it – slumped forward onto her chest.

Even without the benefit of a medical opinion it was obvious that death had been caused by a beating around the head with a heavy instrument. The left side of the face was almost unrecognisable, and was smeared into a bloody mask. The flesh had been stripped away from the cheekbone down to the edge of the mouth, leaving the macabre spectacle of a splintered jawbone with a serried row of broken and discoloured teeth. The woman's left eye had been torn from its socket and lay on the exposed white cheekbone, still attached by a length of grisly tissue. Thrown back behind the shattered head, the corpse's left arm was bent at an unnatural angle, causing the splayed fingers of her hand to point accusingly into the centre of the room. The fingers were badly lacerated, where she had attempted to ward off the fatal blow.

Fighting back the urge to vomit, Will forced himself to take a careful look at the hideous sight. Later it might be critical for him to recall every detail. The right side of the face was that of a woman in her late thirties, thin but not unattractive. Her remaining eye was a pale washed-out blue colour. The shoulder of her dark blue dress had been torn away during the struggle, exposing a small sagging breast. Beginning at her armpit, a deep gash, the blood from which stained the entire left side of her clothing, ran down towards her stomach, exposing white ribs.

'A girl called Rose Dunford found her,' Harry said. 'Came up to see if she was ready to go out for a drink, found the door open and walked in.'

'Where is she now?' asked Will quietly, not taking his eyes from the body.

'I had her taken down to the station at Long Street, before she could disappear or spread the story around the local pubs.'

Will grunted his approval. 'What do we know about her, Harry?'

Harry pulled a packet of Players Navy Cut from his pocket and lit one. Even in a small town like Kelsford murders were not uncommon, and in the last thirty years he had been involved in the investigation of most of them. According to his reckoning he should not be here now: he should be retired and sitting at home in the digs where he had lived for the past fifteen years, dozing comfortably in his armchair and reading about this sort of thing in the late edition of the *Kelsford Gazette*. As it was, either Will would take over the case and use him as his deputy, or – as Will's predecessor Daniel Chote would have done – would walk to the door and ask to be kept informed on the progress of the investigation. He took a deep draw on his cigarette. 'According to Rose Dunford, her name was Charlotte Groves. She was a working girl. Often did clients here of an afternoon rather than take the risk of trawling the streets at night.'

Will took a final look at the body, satisfied that he could recall every detail. He looked around the room again. The street women whom he had encountered usually existed at subsistence level – unkempt and dishevelled, their rooms dirty and reeking. The majority spent the larger part of their earnings on gin and ale, with little need for further nourishment. That stereotype certainly did not fit with the woman lying in the corner. She was reasonably well nourished and clean. Her room was neat and orderly, even down to the clean grate. Avoiding the ruined face, he stole another glance at her ripped blue dress: the lower part, which had escaped a lot of the bloodstaining, was pressed and of reasonably good quality. Mardlin sniffed the air in the room. It was clean, not, as he might have expected, dank and stale.

'Unless the killer springcleaned the place before he left she's got to have been more than your average working girl.'

Picking a strand of loose tobacco from his tongue, Harry indicated the tall wardrobe with his free hand. 'There's a nurse's uniform in the cupboard.'

The grey dress was hanging neatly on a rail, along with two plain black skirts such as any housewife might wear. An apron and nurse's cap along with two white blouses were folded in tissue paper in the top drawer of the dressing table.

In the bottom drawer was a small shoebox containing three buttons from a long-discarded coat, a four inch steel hatpin, the point of which could have taken a man's eye out, a newspaper cutting, an old music hall programme and half a dozen coloured beads strung along a piece of fine cord. Will discarded the buttons and the remains of the bead necklace. Picking up the hatpin, he held it up speculatively to the gaslight. It was shaped into a small metal rosebud, its petals tightly closed.

'That was for protection, no doubt,' Harry surmised. 'Most of the girls keep something like that about their person. A hatpin's ideal – easy to use, and it won't attract attention if she gets arrested.'

Will replaced the pin and took out the news cutting. Underneath it was a photograph and a small enamelled lapel badge. The picture was of the dead woman, probably when she was in her late twenties, wearing the white headdress and pinafore apron of a nurse. The badge bore the letters VA D in its centre, and around the outer edge were stamped the words 'Voluntary Aid Detachment'. This Will returned to the box with the hatpin. The music hall programme was two months old: a souvenir of a visit to London when the dead woman had apparently gone to the Tivoli Palace, to see Wee Georgie Wood in his new sketch, 'Winkles', and Hayden Coffin, Elsie Spain and Mrs Sam Walsh in the musical farce *The Best Man*. Will wondered if she had enjoyed the show.

The final item, the news cutting, was simply a recent advertisement placed by the War Office in every daily paper up and down the country, encouraging women to volunteer as nurses to serve in France with the British Expeditionary Force: 'Your Country and Sir John French need you! Enrol now in the territorial Force Nursing Service and ensure a place for your name on the roll of honour of those who served their country in its time of need.' In smaller type underneath was the address of Kelsford's Army Recruiting Office. Will sighed inwardly: the halcyon days of men volunteering to fight the good fight were a thing of the past. Disillusionment, and the sight of those who ten months earlier had marched out behind pipe bands being pushed through the streets in spinal carriages or limping along on crutches had tolled the knell for volunteering. If this woman had been considering working in a field hospital in France then she must have had a good reason.

Harry had already been through the meagre contents of the shoebox. He was gazing out of the window into the paved yard below. 'Whoever killed her couldn't have climbed up here without being seen. He must either have come into the house with her or already have been here waiting.'

Will joined him at the window. 'Who've we actually got here at the moment?'

The inspector flicked his cigarette stub out of the half-open sash window. 'Bert Conway's downstairs sorting out the family who are living on the ground floor. Up to now he's not got very far. They're refugees and don't speak much English. Father Mullahy, the local priest, is on his way with an interpreter. Once he's here we might find out who's been in the house this afternoon. Bernard Ashe is going round the neighbours to see if anyone saw or heard anything suspicious.'

Will stroked his jaw thoughtfully. Young Ashe was new in the department. It would be good for him to be involved in a major enquiry. 'Find out who owns the house, Harry. Start with the Corporation offices: they'll be paying the landlord for the Belgians downstairs. Then we can begin to find out about her background. If she's been a serving nurse we ought to be able to come up with something.' The question that he was asking himself was why a nurse was working as a prostitute.

Moving away from the window, Will made space for Dr Mallard to join them, his examination now finished. Once out of the confined space the doctor stretched to ease his aching back and turned to face the two detectives. 'Nasty one.' As a police surgeon he had seen a great number of dead bodies. There were in his experience only two sorts of corpses: those that were clean and those that were messy. This one definitely fell into the latter group.

'I know it's very early, but is there anything you can give us to make a start on, doctor?' asked Will hopefully. Like the other two men, he had seen his fair share of bodies, and did not expect to be told anything that was not glaringly apparent.

'She's been killed by a heavy instrument that also has a sharp edge.' The doctor chose his words carefully. 'I'd say that the first blow was to the body, and knocked her back into the corner. It looks as if she threw her left arm up to protect herself. A subsequent blow or blows to the head and arm probably killed her outright. That's where most of the blood on her clothing has come from.' Mallard paused, then pre-empted Will's next question. 'She's not been dead long. Not more than a couple of hours. Three at the most.'

A discreet tap on the door drew Will's attention to the plain clothes officer who had appeared from downstairs. 'Mr Ingram from Saunt's is here, sir. Mr North asked me to arrange for him to take some pictures before the body is removed.'

The detective looked young and nervous. Whether it was because of a reluctance to be in the room with the body, or because of the detective superintendent's presence, Will was unable to judge. The aura surrounding his rank was something that he could not readily accept, and he knew that he never would.

His unease was based on a childhood spent in army camps and barracks in India. As the child of a senior NCO he had been part of a class system that he came to detest. Commissioned officers and their families existed in a privileged world where rank and social training were paramount. For the gentlemen, uniforms and equipment were maintained by a servant in the form of a private British soldier or an Indian sepoy. An officer's wife led an indolent existence. During the summer months, when temperatures soared and cholera stalked the cantonments, bags were packed and officers' families took themselves away up to the hill country around Simla to luxuriate in the cool breezes and clean water. As a child Will had compared this lifestyle with that of his parents. His father, as a senior sergeant, commanded a level of respect just below that of an officer. They lived in married quarters and enjoyed a life of relative comfort and ease, away from the families of the rank and file. There were significant differences, however. Will's father, a professional soldier and holder of the Distinguished Conduct Medal, was regarded as little more than a servant by the officer class. Will along with the rest of the other ranks children attended a tiny single-room school in the cantonments of whichever base they happened to be stationed at. The schools were, he remembered, monotonously similar: an airless stone-built room, usually a converted storehouse, presided over by the wife of one or other of the non-commissioned officers, who taught them reading, writing and simple arithmetic. Officers' children had private tutors who visited them in their homes.

The single great leveller was India itself. No matter how well born one was, the heat and the flies were the same for all. Everyone's day began in the cool of the early morning at about five and ended when the sun reached its zenith at noon. Everyone ate the same ripe food, the taste of corruption masked by hot spices, and everyone, their bowels in a perpetual state of flux, was consigned to the stinking dry earth latrines.

In the years just before his father was posted back to England, Will, his perceptions honed by impending maturity, came to appreciate one other factor in the social structure of his environment. From time to time he overheard his parents discussing the philandering of certain of the wives in the camp. Occasionally a fight took place between two of the men from the lower ranks, which usually resulted in those involved being posted up country and the offending wife being sent back to Blighty in disgrace. The wives of certain officers, he noticed, also seemed to fall into this mysterious group of miscreants. The difference was that they were rarely openly censured, a fact which young Will found difficult to understand.

The result of all this was that as a senior police officer he never felt comfortable with the barriers that rank inevitably imposed on his working life. A line from one of Rudyard Kipling's poems came unbidden into his mind: 'for the Colonel's Lady an' Judy O'Grady are sisters under their skins . . .' Strange, in view of his own marital situation, how life's parallels were drawn, he thought. Unable to prevent himself, he felt his eyes drawn once more to the pitiful bundle slumped in the corner.

Will turned his attention back to the young man. 'Thank you, Bernard. Bring the photographer up, and stay with him while he takes the photographs. When he's finished go back with him to his studio, stay until he's developed them, then bring them directly to Inspector North or myself.' Will had no intention of any unauthorised copies being kept by the photographer to be sold later to the press.

As the young detective was turning to leave Harry said, 'Is Sergeant Conway still downstairs?'

Ash nodded. 'Yes, sir.'

North looked across at the superintendent. At least he appeared to have the answer to his question about who would be conducting the investigation. 'I'll go and tell Bert to arrange for the removal of the body as soon as Ingram has finished – unless you have anything else to do.'

Will shook his head wearily. There was nothing else now other than to discover who was responsible for killing the woman.

Out in the street the rain had diminished to a fine drizzle. Turning up his overcoat collar Will paused long enough for Harry to light another cigarette before they began the stroll back to Long Street Police Station. Despite the weather they needed the walk to clear their heads and to distance themselves from the scene they had just left.

'What do you think, Harry?' Will spoke quietly so as not to be overheard by passers-by.

'From the severity of the injuries I'd say that the killer is almost definitely going to be a man. So that rules out a dispute with another prostitute.' Harry had been turning the matter over while the surgeon was performing his initial examination. 'Given that it's probably a man then it's going to be someone she knew.'

'She'd been with a client recently, we know that from the unmade bed, but I don't think he was necessarily the murderer,' said Will. 'There was no blood on the bed linen, and if she were killed by a client he'd either have brained her in a sexual frenzy during intercourse or afterwards, as the result of some sort of dispute.'

'Either way she wouldn't have been dressed,' agreed Harry. 'If they'd already had sex she wouldn't have bothered to put her clothes back on until after he left – just in case he wanted to do it again. No, this is premeditated. He came with the intention of killing her. We need to find out what the bloody hell he used. Those injuries are among the worst I've ever seen.'

'I think we're looking for a soldier,' Will murmured softly, pausing at the edge of the pavement to allow a cab to pass.

'Why so?' Harry was looking hard at him.

'Because I think I know what he used. First thing tomorrow morning, while you go down to Ducky Mallard's surgery to collect the post-mortem report, I'll visit the barracks.'

The two men walked in silence through the gathering gloom, each lost in his own thoughts. Thunder rolling overhead presaged another downpour.

Next morning at half past nine, Harry North, Bert Conway and Bernard Ashe gathered in Harry's office to await the arrival of the detective superintendent. They had only been there for five minutes when Will entered the room, a brown paper parcel tucked under his arm. After a quick good morning he invited everyone to take a seat. 'I don't want this meeting to take long,' he began. 'There's not a huge amount to discuss, but what we've got is important.'

Conway and Ashe stole surreptitious glances at the parcel, which Will had deposited near to his elbow. Harry already knew what it contained, as Will had taken time to show him before going upstairs to brief the chief constable.

'I'll be the officer in overall charge of the enquiry, Inspector North will be responsible for the day to day running.'

Will shot Conway and Ashe a quick look, giving them the opportunity to raise any initial points. Bert Conway was, he knew, a steady reliable sergeant with a lot of experience as a detective, and despite his gloomy demeanour possessed of a sharp and active mind. His previous partner, Joseph Rowell, had left to join the Colours two months before, and was presently serving somewhere in Turkey. Rowell's replacement, Bernard Ashe, was something of an unknown quantity. Still relatively young, at twenty-six, he had been in the Force for five years, and seemed slightly unsure of himself. Will hoped that this was only in the presence of senior officers and did not carry over into his dealings with the criminal classes. Harry seemed to be satisfied with the lad, and if Will was perfectly honest it was only going to be a matter of time before Ashe also disappeared into the ranks of His Majesty's Forces.

'We know who the woman is,' Will continued. 'We know roughly when she was killed, and we now have a good idea what she was killed with.' Conway's eyes went automatically to the brown paper parcel. Will smiled grimly. 'All in good time, Bert, all in good time.'

He signalled to Harry to continue with the briefing. Harry shifted in his chair. He would dearly have liked a cigarette, but the superintendent had not given permission to smoke. 'Her name's Charlotte Groves. I've checked the staff records at the War Hospital. She was employed there for seven months from September last year until March this year – which accounts for the nurse's uniform and VAD badge. They've got her date of birth as 12th August 1881, which makes her thirty-four. Before working here she was a nurse at the 5th Northern General War Hospital in Leicester.' Pausing for a moment, he slipped his hand into his jacket pocket, wondering whether or not to give Mardlin a hint by getting out his cigarettes but not lighting one. He decided against it. 'The reason she left both jobs was because she was a drug addict.'

A sharp look of surprise passed over Ashe's face. Conway's paunchy visage remained unmoved.

'Kathleen Doyle, the matron at the War Hospital here, says that Groves was addicted to morphine. Apparently it happens from time to time with nurses. They picked her up when supplies started to go missing from the drug cupboard on the ward she worked. It was simpler all round – as far as the hospital was concerned – to quietly dismiss her. Apparently she was also at it in Leicester, but left and moved up here before they got onto her.'

Will interrupted. 'The post-mortem confirms that she was an addict. There are several needle marks in her arms and the top of her thighs. It also accounts for her keeping the advert for nurses with the BEF. I'd think that if she were working in a casualty clearing station at the Front it would be quite easy to steal morphine. In the meantime she appears to have been making some money turning a few tricks.'

Harry picked up the thread again, this time addressing Will. 'The house letting is managed by Shannon and Waites in Argyle Street, who are agents for all sorts of absentee landlords. Bernard and Bert spoke to them first thing this morning. The dead woman's been renting the back bedroom of the house for six months. As one might expect they firmly deny knowing that she was a prostitute.' He glanced at Sergeant Conway. 'Bert, you talked to the girl who found her. What's her story?'

Conway rubbed a meaty fist across his jowls and cleared his throat noisily. 'Rose Dunford's another whore. She and Groves had been out drinking at lunchtime in the Prince of Wales. They got to the pub at about eleven thirty and left soon after half past one. I've got to check that with the licensee, but I don't think she's lying.' Conway was well known among Kelsford's criminal fraternity as a man it was extremely dangerous to lie to. 'When they left the pub Lottie Groves went off with a soldier who she'd met in the bar. Dunford walked with them to the corner of Collington Road. She says he was one of Lottie's regulars, so it shouldn't be too difficult to find him. Apparently Groves hadn't had much to drink and certainly wasn't drunk. They'd arranged to go back to the pub early in the evening before Dunford started working her patch. On her way back to the Prince of Wales, Dunford went around to Groves's lodgings, and found her in the bedroom.'

Harry pulled a box of Bell's Royal Vestas from his jacket pocket and began turning them over in his fingers before prompting the sergeant to continue. 'The downstairs of the house is occupied by a family of Belgian refugees. What do we know about them?'

'The Palmaerts family.' Conway pronounced the name 'Pal-mee-urts'. 'Father, mother, two children. Each of them was out all day until early evening.' He ran a hand through his thinning hair and consulted the hardback notebook in his hand. 'Very difficult to talk to because they hardly speak any English. Father Mullahy brought a lady by the name of Madame Deladier to interpret for us. The husband, Matthias, and the son, Philippe, are working as labourers at Winstocks Brewery in Salmon Lane, and the mother's doing some domestic cleaning for an accountant in Bassett Walk. She was there all day.' Conway ran a finger down the page of his notebook. 'And the daughter, who's twelve, was with another Belgian family over in Gray Street. They all got back home at about five o'clock, and didn't know anything was amiss until Rosie Dunford arrived half an hour later, went upstairs and started screaming.'

Will turned over what the sergeant had said. He remembered the frightened woman in her crisp white apron and the man's reassuring hand on her shoulder. Bert Conway was a good detective, but the Belgians would have been ill at ease with his heavy-handed approach. 'Any signs of a break-in, Bert?' he asked.

'Not exactly. When the Palmaertses got back into the house the front door was still locked, but the kitchen was unlocked – with the key still in the door.'

Will glanced at Harry. 'Looks like whoever killed her let himself out through the back door and slipped away.' Not the actions of a man who was running away in a panic, Will thought. Reaching over, he laid his hand on the brown paper package. 'Although his written report isn't ready yet, Dr Mallard has done the post-mortem. Lottie died sometime late yesterday afternoon, probably around four o'clock, from a single massive blow to the head. As we already presumed, the one to the body that tore her clothes and damaged the upper torso wasn't fatal. Again Mallard thinks that was a single blow. Those two facts tell us a lot. We're not looking at the repeated blows of a frenzied killer. Whoever murdered her first knocked her off her feet, then hit her again with sufficient force to break her arm, smash one side of her face to a pulp and knock her eye out.' Each man's mind went back to the tiny bedroom and the corpse of Charlotte Groves. 'One other thing.' Mardlin drummed lightly on the desktop with his fingers. 'She was suffering from gonorrhoea. We haven't yet established a motive for the killing. When the body was searched at the mortuary she had three and sixpence in the pocket of her dress, so we can rule out robbery. It's a long shot, but it's possible to speculate that a client – possibly the soldier – whom she's infected came back to take a spot of retribution.' It was, he knew, a tenuous theory, but at present he could offer nothing else. 'This morning I went into the barracks and saw Company Sergeant Major Cluley. He gave me this.' Will pulled the parcel towards him and undid the knot. The other three leaned forward to get a better view of the evil-looking instrument that he laid on the desk. 'For those of you who've never seen one before, it's a trench knife.'

Fitted into a bayonet handle was a gleaming five inch long steel blade. Honed to a razor sharpness, the blade curved wickedly towards the end in the shape of a fishmonger's gutting knife. The unpolished wooden bayonet haft was set into what they all knew from experience to be a knuckleduster, along the top of which were five serrated brass spikes. It was easy to imagine this weapon causing the injuries that had been inflicted on Lottie Groves.

Will handed the weapon to Bert Conway, who weighed it in his beefy fist and gave a low appreciative whistle.

'A seventeen inch bayonet fixed to the end of a short Lee-Enfield service rifle is an excellent weapon for close hand to hand fighting out in the open, but in the confined spaces of a trench it has limited capabilities. The soldiers in France are existing in conditions which we cannot even begin to imagine.' Will's voice had dropped, as if he did not want his explanation overheard by an unseen listener to whom the inhumanity of man to man was an incomprehensible thing. 'Someone – an engineer, a blacksmith, a streetfighter from the Gorbals, I don't know who – came up with this. Most of them fit onto the belt in a scabbard and are used in a trench or a dugout where there's insufficient room to wield a rifle and bayonet. They are, I'm told, in common use both by our troops and the enemy. In fact, some of the smaller local units are being issued with them by private benefactors before leaving for France. This one was taken as a souvenir from a captured German infantryman.'

Bernard Ashe now had the heavy knife. He slipped the brass knuckle over the back of his hand and stared down in fascination at the glinting metal spines. Glancing up quickly at the others, the expression on his face mirrored what was in all their minds. A terrified woman, her eyes fixed on the sharp blade and deadly spiked knuckle, arm thrown up trying to protect her head and face, knowing what was about to happen to her. The first single slash of the blade knocking her off her feet, ripping away the flesh and staving in her ribs. The second blow breaking her arm like a matchstick before shredding the flesh from her face and cracking her skull like an eggshell. Even Bert Conway's features had lost their customary deadpan expression, the muscles along his pouchy jawline clenching and unclenching.

Will filled the empty silence. 'On arrival at the War Hospital from the Front, patients have their kit and weapons taken away for the duration of their stay. Likewise they're given a blue uniform suit to wear in place of their regimentals. The soldier with whom Groves left the Prince of Wales was in khaki – so presumably he isn't a casualty at the hospital who was out for the day.' The men in transit at Sevastopol Barracks all keep their weapons. Although officially they're not allowed to take them outside the camp gates, a lot of them still carry something for protection. We know that Charlotte Groves picked up a soldier in uniform just before she died, so presumably he falls into the latter category.'

'The first thing we need to know is what the dead woman's movements were in the two and a half hours between leaving the pub with Tommy Atkins at half past one and being killed at four o'clock.' Solemnly the others nodded. Will closed his eyes and reviewed the small pieces of information that had been gleaned. A major difficulty was that few of the local residents were at home during the day, and around Devonshire Gardens those that were would not be overly inclined to talk to the police. 'Groves left the Prince of Wales with the soldier at half past one. It's a five minute walk back to the house, which if they went directly up to her room puts them there at about twenty-five to two. If she had sex with her client and then he killed her it's a fairly simple matter. He'd have quietly let himself out of the back door from the kitchen, walked up the entry, checked there was no one about and slipped off down the road.'

'Who was the beat man working that area?' asked Ashe.

'82 Weldon,' replied Harry. 'He was on the day shift until six. I've spoken to him. He was at the opposite end of the beat at the time she'd have been killed, so that's no help.'

Will exhaled his breath in a long sigh. 'We need to talk to the soldier today – before he's spirited away to another army camp or gets his mates to confirm some alibi that it'll take us weeks to pull apart.' He scrutinised the faces of the two older men – like himself experienced detectives – and knew that they were assessing him, waiting to see if he would leave it at that. 'On the other hand, of course, the soldier may not be the man that we're looking for at all. There may well be a factor that we know nothing about yet. So let's not decide what must have happened and then set out to prove it . . .'

A further twenty minutes were spent discussing details and allocating each man's responsibilities. Conway and Ashe were given the job of making enquiries at the Prince of Wales and Sevastopol Barracks. Harry was to go back and re-interview Rose Dunford. Will was to return to Devonshire Gardens to speak to the Belgian family.

As the meeting was about to break up Conway said suddenly, 'There were no pawn tickets.'

Ashe looked at him enquiringly, while Will and Harry's eyes lit up in startled comprehension.

'Very good, Bert . . . we shouldn't have missed that.' Will's appreciation was genuine. Conway's bloodhound features remained impassive, although there was a small gleam in his eyes which seemed to be the nearest he ever got to smiling. 'Very good indeed. I've never yet seen a working girl who didn't pawn her trinkets, bed linen or some other little treasure in times of need. Our Lottie may not have been a big drinker, but she had a much more expensive habit. You've just got yourself another job. Check out every pawnbroker in town.'

After the other two had left, Will pulled on his coat and gave Harry a satisfied grin. 'We might be on a winner with this one,' he said.

'Let's see what the hoteliers come up with first,' Harry replied cautiously.

'The hoteliers?' Mardlin's voice carried a note of puzzlement.

It was Inspector North's turn to grin. 'Bernard and Bertie. B and B – Bed and Breakfast. The lads downstairs have taken to calling them the hoteliers. Neither of them seem to think it's very funny.'

Chapter Seven

Watching the handcart laden with Matthias and Béatrice Palmaerts's meagre possessions being hauled away, Irene Deladier, with a pang of deep loneliness, wondered if she, or they, would ever see their homelands again. During the six weeks since their arrival in Kelsford she had come to know the Palmaerts family quite well, and felt a strong desire to help them in their present situation.

Irene, summoned to Devonshire Gardens the previous evening, was deeply shocked at what had happened. Her concerns for the welfare of the family were in no less way lessened by the large and surly detective who before her arrival, unable to communicate with the Belgians, appeared to have spent his time poking through their meagre possessions. Even with her assistance it had taken almost two hours before the policeman, with a parting declaration that someone would be back tomorrow, could be persuaded to leave.

That they would not want to live in the house any longer was obvious, and Irene had offered Matthias, Béatrice and their children accommodation at her house in Kingsbury Lane – an offer they had readily accepted. Béatrice could work for her as a cook-housekeeper, and she was certain that James would be able to find a place somewhere for Matthias, either as a clerk or possibly in an accountant's office. She decided to wait at the house, speak to whoever visited from the police station, and arrange for the family to be re-registered at their new address.

Shivering despite the warm morning sunshine outside, Irene gazed around the dark and depressing room. Now devoid of any personal possessions, the heavy green floral wallpaper and cold linoleum floor lent the room an air of depression that was accentuated by the cheap furniture, supplied by the Kelsford Corporation Emergency Refugee Fund.

As she looked out of the bay window at the deserted street Irene, alone in the house, found herself becoming very nervous. While it was unlikely that the murderer would return, a sinister atmosphere pervaded the place, and as the minutes ticked by she became increasingly aware of an inexplicable feeling of panic.

Just as she had made the decision to lock up and leave, the stocky figure of the detective superintendent, whom she had met in Phipps's Coffee House, pushed open the garden gate and made his way up the path. Opening the front door to admit him, Irene's relief at being joined by someone was palpable.

'Come in, Mr Mardlin.' Her apprehension began to drain away and she showed him to the empty sitting room, relieved that she had at least remembered his name.

Will took off his hat and stared around the empty room. 'I'm a bit confused, Madame Deladier. Where have the people gone who were living here?'

'Their name's Palmaerts. I'd have hoped that if nothing else your sergeant would have taken that away with him. I've moved them out of here to my house.' From the change in the detective's expression, Irene realised that she had made a mistake. The tension of being alone in the house combined with her dislike for the other policeman had made her waspish retort unnecessarily rude.

'You shouldn't have done that, Madame.'

Will struggled to control his irritation. Conway had already complained that the young woman appeared to have ideas above her station. The previous evening, rather than confining herself to the task of interpreting, she had persisted in either answering on behalf of the Belgians or demanding to know the purpose of each question. Along with everyone else who had come into contact with Irene Deladier since her arrival in Kelsford, Will was aware that she was reputed to be very wealthy, and it appeared she had the arrogance that often accompanied this. Consequently he was taken off guard by her next remark.

'I'm sorry. I shouldn't have said that. I'm afraid that what happened upstairs has unsettled me.' She gave an embarrassed smile. 'I was about to lock up and make my escape.' With a sweeping gesture of her hand, Irene drew his attention to the dismal room. 'Look at it. Would you want to stay here?' She spoke quietly, the tension building within her again.

Will noticed for the first time that the woman had a naturally soft, slightly throaty voice, and, unbidden, a sudden vivid recollection of her mother came back to him from his younger days. She was Mrs Samuels then. Will's father and Tom Norton – Ruth Samuels's future husband – had been close friends, and Will remembered being introduced to her at the wedding of Norton's sister Anne. A lad of fifteen, Will had been entranced by the tall dark-haired woman with a deep sensual voice and smiling eyes. Irene was not as tall as her mother, but she certainly had her sultry good looks and captivating way of speaking.

'When the Palmaertses arrived here in April I helped them to settle in,' she continued. 'They're a very respectable family, Matthias is – or was – an accountant. When the Germans overran Belgium their town was sacked.'

The pain in her eyes was real. The German occupation of Louvain had occurred only a matter of days after Jean-Claude had been killed, and she was suddenly finding difficulty in separating the incidents in her mind. 'I visited Louvain when I was at finishing school. That's one of the reasons I can relate to what happened to Matthias and Béatrice. When the Germans first arrived everyone thought that it would be all right, that they would simply pass through on their way into France. At first they behaved in quite a restrained fashion. Then some fool shot one of the soldiers in the leg. After that the burgomaster and a group of officials were taken as hostages. Others were simply put up against a wall behind the railway station and shot.'

Will stood in silence, puzzled at the unexpected change of mood, and not fully understanding the real cause of the woman's outpourings.

'Those of the officers who weren't actively encouraging their men did nothing to stop them. People were killed, houses and shops were looted, then set on fire. The library in the Clothworkers Hall was gutted: more than two hundred and thirty thousand books were destroyed. The Palmaerts family was turned out onto the street, and their house was ransacked then set on fire. It took them three months to make their way on foot to a Channel port, then they spent five months in an internment camp near Dover before being sent up here.'

'And you?' Will asked quietly.

'Me? Oh, I was part of the great Kosminski empire. A wealthy Parisienne who simply upped sticks when the first shots were fired, and slipped back across La Manche to the safety of England.' The bitterness in her voice hung in the oppressive atmosphere of the empty room like the echo of a hollow bell. Will waited, sensing that what had happened in the house had somehow resulted in the breaching of her emotional defences, and that however unwilling a witness he should not attempt to prevent it. Tears welled up in her eyes and began to trickle unheeded down Irene's cheeks. 'I loved my husband, Mr Mardlin. He was kind and handsome and so *French*. He laughed a lot, and he loved life so much. Every Sunday after we were married we went out to lunch at one of the restaurants, then took a stroll, just walking and talking, planning what we were going to do with our lives. It lasted a year and a half from the time we first met. We were married for eight weeks before he was called up. Two weeks later he was dead. Just like Matthias and Béatrice Palmaerts I'd like to see every one of those bâtards Boches cold and dead in a grave alongside my husband.'

Will was tempted for a second to move towards the woman, to touch her, attempt to give her some sort of comfort. Instinctively he knew that it would be a mistake. Instead he said gently, 'Don't worry about moving the Palmaerts family. I'll sort that out. What I came to see them about can wait. I'll talk to them later. For now I think we should leave.'

Nodding resignedly, Irene gave him a tired smile and, accepting the proffered handkerchief, began to wipe her eyes.

When Will arrived at Long Street he found Harry waiting for him in the main detective office, along with Conway and Ashe.

'Things are beginning to come together,' Harry said, as Will, dropping his high-crowned bowler on an unoccupied desk, pulled up a chair and sat down.

'We've got the soldier downstairs in the cells. Frank Kempin – a little gutter rat from Manchester. He was easy to find. The landlord at the Prince of Wales loaned him ten shillings a week ago and has got a signed IOU. He's among the sick and lame who've been sent back from France. On his army file it says that he's got chronic chilblains, which in the middle of summer one would think shouldn't trouble him too much. His real problem is that the sound of gunfire affects his bowels. Anyway, at the moment he's employed in the barracks cookhouse.'

'Any trouble bringing him in?' asked Will.

'None at all. The CO at Sevastopol is quite happy for us to interview him, and if we decide to press any charges an officer will attend the police court to speak on his behalf. Colonel Redfern appeared quite pleased to be rid of him for a while.'

Will gave a satisfied smile. At least he was not going to have some pompous second lieutenant interfering with his enquiry. 'What else have we got?'

Harry delved into the bottom of a large brown paper bag and produced a short-bladed trench knife, almost identical to the one that Will had borrowed from the barracks. The blade and knuckle spikes were crusted in a thick brownish-black substance which could only be dried blood. 'Found under the upstairs back seat of the number fifteen tram yesterday afternoon when it went in for cleaning at the end of its run. The number fifteen goes from the town centre to Leaminster Gardens, stopping at Sevastopol Barracks.' Turning the weapon over, he showed Mardlin the initials FK cut into the wooden haft. 'But there's a small problem.' Harry paused, and gave Will a searching look.

The superintendent was turning the weapon over speculatively in his hands. 'Go on,' he said.

Harry cleared his throat and, twisting an unlit cigarette in his fingers, tapped the end of it on the table. 'I sent Bert and Nathan Cleaver out first thing this morning to knock on a few more doors – try and find anyone in the street who might have seen something. Nathan's come up with a knife grinder, Jeremiah Boam, who was in Devonshire Gardens yesterday afternoon. He says that he saw Charlotte Groves going into the house at about twenty to four.'

Will's frown deepened. 'That doesn't fit in. If this man Kempin went to her room with her before two o'clock and killed her, she can't have been going back in at the time Boam says he saw her.'

'Unless', suggested Harry, 'Kempin stayed on in the house while she went out for something, then killed her when she got back. Boam says that he was in the street with his sharpening cart for about ten minutes. He had no customers, so he was moving away when he noticed Groves going through the front door of number forty-two. He knows Lottie by sight because he's done some knives for her recently. He didn't see her face, but he recognised the navy blue dress and shawl.'

Will glowered at the cigarette in Harry's hand, hoping that he would stop tapping it and light it. Pushing back his chair, he got to his feet. 'I think you and I better talk to our soldier before we go any further.'

'My name's Mardlin. Detective Superintendent Mardlin. And this is Detective Inspector North. We're investigating the death of a woman named Charlotte Groves who was, I think, quite well known to you.'

The thin-faced man seated on the opposite side of the interview table stared at him in silence, a truculent expression on his narrow pockmarked face. Will picked up the single typed sheet and glanced at the details of the man's background.

> *Private 835942 Francis Selwyn Kempin*
> *Born: 5th March 1889, at Ancoats, Manchester*
> *2nd Battalion, South Lancashire Regiment.*
> *Joined: 10th January 1915 at Salford.*
> *16th April 1915 posted:- ll Corps. 7th Infantry Brigade, France.*
> *24th May 1915: posted:- Medically unfit, return to Britain.*
> *28th May 1915:-posted:- Sevastopol Barracks Kelsford.*
> *Cookhouse duties while awaiting medical reports.*

Replacing the paper face down on top of the documents spread across the table in front of him, Will stared at the soldier in silence and decided that he did not like him.

Private Kempin looked more than his twenty-six years, his gaunt features accentuated by hollow sunken cheeks and small shifty eyes over a long pointed nose. A wispy moustache served to accentuate his thin lips and receding chin. One thing was certain, thought Will, he was no stranger to the inside of a police station. He wondered what the incentive was in Ancoats that had prompted the man to volunteer for the army.

The silence lasted for what seemed like an eternity – although it was only a couple of minutes – before it was broken by Kempin. 'I want an officer here to speak for me.' The flat Lancashire accent cracked with uncertainty.

'All in good time.' Mardlin decided not to tell him yet of his commanding officer's decision to withhold the services of an officer.

'No, not all in good time – right now. I know my rights. You've got nothing on me. I'm a serving soldier, subject to military law.'

Harry exhaled a thin plume of cigarette smoke before leaning forward in his chair. 'Listen to me carefully.' His voice was soft and menacing. 'You're in deep shit, and the only rights that you've got at this moment are us. Yesterday afternoon somebody went to Lottie Groves's room and beat her to death with a trench knife. Now that person was you. The only question we need answering is why did you kill her?

'I never went to her room. I left her outside the pub and she went off on her own.' Kempin's voice had lost what little self assurance it had previously carried.

'I don't think so.' Will picked up another sheet of paper, handwritten this time, with a scratchy signature at the bottom. Turning it towards Kempin, he allowed him to look at the statement. 'Rose Dunford, who knows you from previous occasions when you've been with her and the dead woman, walked with you and Lottie from the Prince of Wales to the bottom of Devonshire Gardens. You then went off up to the house at number forty-two with Charlotte Groves.'

'All right, so I went back with her.' The soldier threw a wary glance in Harry's direction. 'We did it a couple of times, then I left. I certainly didn't kill her.'

Will looked at him speculatively, 'Did you not? Have you ever seen this before?' He glanced across at Harry who, bending down under his chair, pulled out the trench knife. Wordlessly he turned the weapon over in his hand, showing Kempin the damning initials on the haft.

The colour drained from the soldier's face as he stared at the offending item. His Adam's apple worked up and down in his scrawny throat as he tried to pump saliva into his dry mouth. 'You bastards, this is a sort-out. I've never seen that thing before in my life.' Springing to his feet he pointed accusingly at Harry, his voice rising to a shout. 'You'll never get away with this, you . . . you . . .'

'Did you do this, Frank?' asked Will very quietly.

Kempin, caught unawares, turned to see what it was that the detective was showing him. For a second the policemen thought that he was going to pass out, then, turning abruptly, he doubled up in the corner of the tiny room and vomited. Will carefully returned the sepia photograph of what remained of Charlotte Grove's head to its place among the documents on his desk.

After a few moments Kempin straightened up and turned to look at the men, wiping his mouth with the back of his hand and silently mouthing words that refused to come out.

'Now come and sit down and we'll talk sensibly about this.' Will's voice, still pitched low, was commanding, like a teacher speaking to a difficult child. The stench of vomit was overpowering in the confined space.

'I've not killed her.' The sullen manner was now replaced by an overwhelming need to convince the policemen of his innocence.

'So tell me what you know.'

The Adam's apple bobbed again, and Kempin ran a finger around the neck of his collarless khaki shirt which, far too big for his skinny body, was wet with perspiration.

'I met Lottie in the pub for a drink. I often see her on a Tuesday afternoon, and we – well, you know . . .' The voice became confidential, man to man. 'After that I left. It was about a quarter past three. I went back to the barracks and the next thing I knew it was all over the papers.'

Will glanced at his colleague for confirmation. Harry nodded imperceptibly. Private Kempin had been logged back in by the guardhouse at five to four, which would just have given him time to walk into town and catch a number fifteen tram out to the barracks.

'Look, I've never owned a trench knife, not even when I was in France. Christ, I wasn't there long enough. I got sent back. I've got bad feet. Couldn't cope with the trenches.'

'How much did you give her?'

Momentarily a shifty look flickered across Frank Kempin's narrow face. 'Two bob,' he replied slowly, back on his guard.

'You're lying again.' Will's voice had developed a dangerous edge.

'You had a freebee, didn't you?'

'I hadn't got any money. It happened before. I pay her next time I see her in the pub.' Kempin was evasive: it was not a question that he had been expecting.

'Let me tell you what I think has been happening, Frank.' Will's tone was less than friendly. 'You're working as a cook at the barracks, and part of your job is to go out with a wagon each day and bring in supplies. Once, perhaps even twice a week you go out late and when you come back with the supplies Lottie Groves is in the back – probably under some sacks. The gate guard knows you, so the wagon doesn't get checked. Am I right so far?' The mixture of apprehension and malice in the soldier's eyes told him all that he needed to know. 'Then after dark a select few of your mates – those who can be trusted – get to share a few pleasures down by the stables with Lottie in the back of the wagon. Next morning you ensure an early run out, and good old Charlotte gets dropped off round the corner. Tuesday afternoons are your personal pay-off sessions, aren't they?'

'I want an officer. What are you after?' The arrogance engendered by fear was back. 'You can't prove a thing and you know it. You're going to have to release me right now.'

For the first time since they had sat down a smile lit up Will's face. 'Release you?' he laughed. 'No, I don't think so. You were the last person to see Charlotte Groves alive, you were sharing her earnings, and I've got a bloody great knife with your name on it.'

'Anyway, why do you want to be released? So you can be sent off to get killed at the Front, or face a court martial here for immoral conduct? And then, of course, there are your mates who've been getting two bob shags and a dose of the clap for a bonus.' You did know about that, didn't you? That Lottie was suffering from gonorrhoea? Once half of the barracks start pissing razor blades you'll be far safer here with us.'

Kempin swung his gaze desperately in Harry's direction. Scraping a match into life , the inspector applied it to a new cigarette, and watched him quizzically through a cloud of blue smoke, saying nothing.

Twenty minutes later Harry walked into the bar of the Pack Horse Hotel and spotted Will in a secluded alcove at the back of the room. The old place had changed over the recent years, he thought. When he was a young man the clientele at this hour would have comprised businessmen and solicitors discreetly closing transactions over a lunchtime drink. Now the room was packed with farmers who had come in from the outlying districts for the weekly market day, along with the odd soldier from the depot who had slipped into town for a pint. Threading his way through the crowd to the alcove he settled himself on the upholstered bench seat next to Will, and gratefully took a pull at the pint of bitter which was waiting for him.

With the low hubbub of noise in the saloon bar ensuring that their conversation would not be overheard, the Pack Horse was a good choice for a relaxing half hour in which to review the situation.

Will picked up his own pint and stared out across the bar. 'There's going to be a lot more to this one than we thought, Harry,' he said.

As a habit rather than a need to smoke, Harry pulled a packet of Players from his pocket and tapped it gently on the edge of the table. 'It's a crock of shit.' Despite the fact that he was Will's deputy and they had worked closely for some time, he never called him by his first name, nor did he ever call him sir. Neither fact was lost on the superintendent, who appreciated the easy way in which Harry handled their difference in rank. 'This Tommy Atkins hasn't killed her. We both know that.' He opened the packet and took out a cigarette.

Will raised his hand in acknowledgement to a short stout farmer in a hacking jacket and leather gaiters. About to come over to join them, the man changed his mind and moved to sit with three men who were playing cards at a table near the door. 'So what have we got?'

'We've got an obvious suspect who can't have done it,' the older man replied testily. 'If you were going to murder a woman whom you met on the same day every week for sex in her room, would you choose that to be the time and place to kill her? No, of course not. You might as well leave a signed note saying "I did it"!' Harry lit his cigarette, contributing to the heavy pall of tobacco smoke hanging across the room. 'There's no blood on Kempin's uniform, not even a spot where he might have cut himself shaving; and if it was him how would he get something like a trench knife past the guard on the barracks' gates?'

'The trench knife is central to everything,' Will cut in. 'I believe him when he says that he's never been issued with or owned one. And his reaction to the photograph. He was a failure as a front line soldier, and now he's back here as a cook. So if it's not his, whoever used it to kill Lottie Groves took it away with him and then planted it on the back seat of a tram to implicate Kempin.'

'Having first carved Kempin's initials on the haft,' grunted Harry.

'The clincher is this sighting of Groves going back into the house at a quarter to four. Kempin was booked back through Sevastopol gates at five to four, which means that it can't possibly be him.'

Mardlin broke off as the slim figure of Bernard Ashe came in through the door. After a quick glance round he spotted the two men and joined them at their table. 'We've found the pawnbroker.' Ashe kept his voice low. 'Groves popped three ornaments last month at Israel Feinemann's shop in Thomas Street.'

'Have you got them?'

'No, sir.' North's flash of annoyance brought a flustered look to the young detective's face. 'They were pawned on the 3rd of May for twenty-eight days. If they aren't claimed after that time the pawnbroker can legally sell them. The time expired a week last Monday on the 31st. Feinemann sold them, he thinks within a couple of days.'

'Who to?' asked Will.

'He doesn't know. Problem is they were booked in by the lad who worked in the shop for him, and Feinemann never saw them himself. The same lad sold them on after the redemption date, which was the day before he went into the army. As he's now somewhere in France we don't know exactly what we're looking for. But a young lad, who Feinemann thinks is local, came in late yesterday afternoon with a pawn ticket trying to redeem them. When he found out that they'd been sold he just left the shop with the ticket.'

Mardlin sucked in a deep breath and said slowly, 'Go back and see Izzy Feinemann. Tell him that unless he comes up with that boy's name and address before the end of today I'll have policemen swarming all over that midden he calls a shop like a pack of dockyard rats. There must be enough stolen property in that place to finance the war for the next six months.'

Ashe gave a quick smile. The instruction was, he explained, unnecessary. Sergeant Conway had already taken a pocket watch and two rings from the pawnbroker's back room 'to check on, in case some unscrupulous customer had duped Mr Feinemann'. Bert had told the pawnbroker to send someone round to Long Street within the hour to find out if the items could be returned, and at the same time give him the boy's name.

As the young detective picked his way back through the throng around the bar Will said, 'Is he going to be good?'

'Probably,' replied Harry. 'Bert will either make or break him. I prefer him to young Cleaver. He's a bit too flash for me – too clever by half.'

Will finished his beer and made a mental note to mark Cleaver's file against the maidservant 'no action', and have the charges withdrawn. Unfortunately, by now the girl would already have been dismissed.

In less than an hour Bert Conway and Bernard Ashe were picking their way through the accumulated rubbish that carpeted the broken concrete surface of Wendell Court. Named after the contractor who fifty years before had erected the two-up two-down hovels in one of the few remaining areas of what had once been the Downe Street district. Ashe wondered if it had been the long-dead builder's intention from the outset to put up slums, or had he, in common with the town fathers of the day, thought that he was solving the problem of poverty and deprivation. If such was his vision he had been sadly mistaken. Never from the outset adequate for the families that were to occupy them, the tiny houses were now overcrowded insanitary rat-holes which the unfortunate occupants had little hope of escaping. It was in hovels such as these that deadly summer diarrhoea and typhoid, which continued to plague the town each year, invariably occurred.

Taking a deep breath against the stink emanating from an outside toilet, its door left open to indicate to residents that it was free, they made their way to number seven at the far end. Glancing in as he passed, Ashe noted with curiosity the four wooden seats side by side in the privy, and the nails knocked into the brickwork at each side, from which sheaves of newspaper cut into rough four inch squares were hanging from loops of string.

Before becoming a policeman at the age of twenty-one, Bernard Ashe, the son of a Kelsford newsagent, had been brought up in what he had always considered to be a normal middle-class environment. Now, five years later, he was still amazed and often appalled at the conditions in which so many of the town's occupants lived. A bright young man, he was initially dismayed at being partnered with Sergeant Conway when he was offered a place in the Detective Department after Joe Rowell left for the army. Conway had a reputation for getting things done in his own way. Old enough to be Bernard's father, he was at best a rough diamond. Although abrasive and often uncouth, he was – as Bernard quickly discovered – a highly efficient and intuitive detective. He was also, to the young man's surprise, a very willing teacher.

'We're not going to get much fucking joy here,' muttered Conway, glaring around.

'Look at it: they even go for a shit together. This lot aren't going to be telling us much. Foxy knew what he was doing when he gave us this job,' he grumbled, picking his way over the broken cobbles. His prematurely white hair and the devious ploys he adopted when dealing with the criminal fraternity had earned Harry North the nickname of 'Silver Fox' many years before, although it would have been a brave man who allowed himself to be caught referring to the detective inspector as 'Foxy'.

When repeated knocking on the peeling paintwork of the flimsy front door at number seven drew no results, Sergeant Conway picked up a twelve inch length of gaspipe from among the debris littering the courtyard and struck the cast-iron drainpipe which ran down by the side of the door frame from the leaky guttering above their heads a series of resounding blows. The resulting cacophony reverberated around the enclosed area like the crashing of a steam hammer in a foundry.

The front door of the house at number five opened suddenly to reveal a stout woman in her late fifties wearing a dirty apron and smoking a clay pipe. Glaring coldly at the two men, she removed the pipe from her mouth before spitting unerringly onto the broken ground a matter of inches from Ashe's right shoe. Having satisfied her curiosity, she wordlessly turned her back and disappeared into the house, slamming the door behind her.

With a sharp scraping sound, the front door of number seven was dragged open by a thin slatternly woman, aged about forty. 'What do you want?' she demanded.

'Police,' growled Conway. 'Is Alfred Belcher in?'

'No. He doesn't live here any more.'

'And you are?' enquired the detective, pushing past her into the tiny front room. The odour of dirty washing and stale humanity assailed their nostrils.

'You can't just walk in like this,' exclaimed the woman in a thin rasping voice. 'Piss off! You have no business here.'

'Wrong on both counts,' declared Conway. Striding across the room, he pulled open the staircase door and stood with his head cocked, listening for any sounds of movement on the floor above. With a sharp inclination of his head he sent Ashe up the stairs to check that there was no one hiding there. Two minutes later Ashe confirmed that there was no one else in the house.

The sergeant turned his attention back to the woman.

'Now I asked who you are . . .'

'I'm Mrs Belcher, and he doesn't live here now, so you can bugger off.'

'Right. Listen to me.' Conway's lugubrious face looked as if it had been hewn from a block of granite. 'First, you're not Mrs Belcher. There's no Mrs Belcher. You're Sarah Jane Foulds: five previous convictions for prostitution, the last one for indecency in a alleyway which got you thirty days. You've lived with Alf Belcher for the last fourteen years . . . and you're not currently wanted.' Reaching into his inside pocket Conway pulled out a folded sheet of paper, which he held up for her inspection. It had the coat of arms of Kelsford Magistrates Court across the top. 'Now your Alf's a different matter. This is a warrant to commit him to prison for non-payment of rates for sixty days, or until such time as he settles the debt.' The big man's jowls lifted in a semblance of a smile as he paused long enough for the information to register. He had, Ashe realised, paid a visit to the summoning department before setting out from Long Street, and checked if anyone who lived at the address was currently wanted.

'I've told you, he isn't here,' the woman replied sourly. 'He's ill and he's gone for a walk.'

'He's bone idle and he's down the pub,' retorted Conway. Folding the warrant, he returned it to his pocket. 'If we resolve what I want to talk to you about before he comes through that door, then this piece of paper can go back to Long Street until next time.'

'Go on then.' Whatever her feelings towards the two men, Sadie Belcher did not want her common law husband arrested. It was what the detectives were really there for that worried her. The reason when it came was unexpected.

'Your youngest lad, Leonard, where is he?'

'I don't know, that's the truth. He's a little bleeder. First he's here, then he's not. Went off yesterday morning and I haven't seen him since. Didn't come home last night, but that's not unusual.'

'How old is he?' Ashe spoke for the first time.

'Twelve. I've got two. The other one, Albert, works down at the goods yard.'

'I want to talk to him, Sadie.' Conway was scribbling in his notebook. He tore the page out and handed it to her.

'He's not in trouble, but he's seen something that I've got to talk to him about urgently. When he comes home he's to go straight to Long Street and give the man on the desk this paper with my name on it. If that happens before the end of today, then this warrant', he tapped his pocket significantly, 'disappears for ever. Understand?'

Puzzled, but relieved to be rid of her visitors, the woman pushed the scrap of paper into her apron as she watched them pick their way back across the yard.

Back out in the warm sunshine and away from Wendell Court, Conway, paused to light a cigarette. 'I just hope this doesn't go sour,' he said thoughtfully.

'In what way?' Ashe had discovered early that the other man did not make idle comments or assumptions.

'I just find it worrying that the lad chose last night to stay out – not that there's much to go home for. All we can do is wait and see.'

Bernard gave the sergeant a quizzical look. The remark seemed out of character. 'Have you ever been married?' he asked curiously. What sort of woman, he wondered, would choose to spend her life with Bert Conway?

'Years ago. All in the past now.'

'What happened?' asked Ashe curiously.

Conway took a deep pull on his cigarette before replying. 'She fell down a wishing well.'

Ashe grinned. He was pleased to see that his partner had not completely lost his sense of humour.

At five o'clock that afternoon Will Mardlin gathered his small team together in the main detective office. Leonard Belcher had not yet come into the police station, and Will was going to have to move the enquiry in another direction until the boy was traced. As soon as Harry joined the group he would put the matter up for discussion.

A few minutes later the detective inspector walked in through the door from the first-floor corridor. It was apparent to everyone that something was wrong. Without bothering to pull up a chair he sat on the corner of a desk and said in a resigned voice, 'We found the boy.'

Will held his gaze. 'Where?'

'Body of a young lad washed out through the bottom chamber of the Town Locks about an hour ago. Not been formally identified as yet, but there's no doubt it's him.'

'I bet the poor little sod didn't have a pawn ticket on him,' muttered Bert Conway grimly.

Chapter Eight

A hundred miles from Kelsford the darkness was lifting as the cold grey dawn began to show along the distant horizon. An early morning breeze raised a slight swell on the North Sea, lapping gently against the hull of the submarine. On the bridge Siegfried Keppler was beginning to shiver, despite his warm seaman's jacket and muffler. Although he was never a good sailor, he was glad to be up in the fresh air, out of the claustrophobic atmosphere of the submarine's hull.

Standing beside him, Kapitänleutnant zur See Klaus Diessbacher touched his sleeve and indicated with his binoculars to a point out in the darkness. 'Also, da drüben.'

Peering into the gloom, his eyes adjusting to the dim light, Keppler made out the shadowy form of a motorised trawler about a mile away.

U39 was hove to some twenty miles off the English coast. To have arranged his transfer to the fishing boat during darkness could have resulted in a collision between the two vessels. Now, with the sky growing lighter by the minute, it was imperative that the U-boat should submerge as soon as possible, before it was spotted by one of the ever vigilant patrol boats that cruised up and down the coastal waters off Alnmouth.

'How long before you can get under way?' Keppler asked.

'He's already heaving-to. We'll steer for him while he lowers a boat. The transfer should be in about fifteen minutes.' Kapitän Diessbacher's voice was tense. During the last month, since the U20 had sunk the *Lusitania* off the Irish coast, English waters had become extremely hazardous, and in fifteen minutes it would be fully daylight. It was only a fortnight since another German U-boat had been trapped by a French patrol boat on the surface in the Channel while charging its batteries. The sub had gone down in seconds with all hands, the only remaining trace a small slick of oil.

Nodding, Keppler drew his pea jacket closer around him. The sooner he was aboard the *Viking Tun* the better he would like it. Backtracking and zigzagging to avoid Royal Navy patrol boats meant that it had taken the U39 five days to make the journey from its base at Wilhelmshaven to the rendezvous point. Although the seas had been relatively calm Siegfried Keppler knew he would be more than grateful to escape the uncomfortable diesel-laden air and the incessant drone of the boat's twin engines. Less than a week of sharing the sixty metres of cramped living space with the boat's thirty-five man crew had convinced him that he never wanted to see the inside of a submarine again.

Twenty minutes later, clinging to his sailor's duffle bag, Keppler was in the stern of the other boat's dinghy, watching as the conning tower of the U39 slid gracefully beneath the waves.

Safely aboard the *Viking Tun*, he stowed his bag in the space below deck which served the four man crew of the vessel as both galley and sleeping quarters. The captain, a thick-set grey-haired man who looked as if he shaved once a week, and then only if it was necessary, greeted him with a grunt and a brusque nod. He had given his name simply as Tam. Despite an excellent knowledge of the English language, Keppler found great difficulty in understanding the broad Scots accent with which the man spoke. The vessel, he was told, originated from a fishing village up the coast from Uig on the Isle of Skye, and had spent the last week trawling along the Northumbrian coastline. He was to remain below decks until they put into the port of Whitby later in the day.

As soon as the captain had returned to the bridge, Keppler dropped onto an empty bunk and attempted to sleep. Being virtually alone for the first time in five days, and sufficient space to stretch out, were luxuries that he had been anticipating since the moment he had spotted the trawler from the conning tower of the submarine. For the hundredth time he ran over the arrangements that had been made for his arrival in Whitby.

Over the past twenty years German High Command had slowly and carefully built up in every country across Europe, including England, a 'fixed post' system of intelligence agents, whose role it was to blend in with the local population. Once established, other than passing information to High Command, these agents were only 'activated' in circumstances of extreme importance, as now. In most instances an agent was given sufficient funds on his arrival to set up a small business, and progressively become an established member of local society. Sometimes it was possible to suborn a national of the country that was being infiltrated, which made things easier in some ways, despite being fraught with difficulties. What if the person were a double agent acting for the British Intelligence Services, or betrayed his contacts? On the whole, the intelligence arm of the General Staff preferred to use German nationals.

When the *Viking Tun* berthed in Whitby later in the day, ostensibly to pick up supplies, he would slip ashore undetected in his guise as a Swedish sailor. From that moment he would be on his own. He would make his way to the address of a French polisher just off Flower Gate, where he would be given the keys to a safe house in the town. Here he would live for the next few months, until Operation Nemesis was successfully completed.

The polisher, he was assured, had carried on his business for several years without arousing the slightest suspicion, and the safe house had not been used before. Even so, Keppler resolved to keep his contact with the man to a minimum: the less he knew about this present mission the better.

It was mid-morning when the *Viking Tun* pushed into the choppy waters of the River Esk at the mouth of Whitby Harbour. Leaning on the rail of the trawler, Keppler gazed over the starboard bow at the fishing boats and cobbles tied up along St Anne's Staith, and the busy traffic passing back and forth along Pier Road. As the vessel nudged its way against the tidal water past Tate Hill Pier, on the opposite beam he saw for the first time the impressive ruins of the eleventh-century Benedictine abbey set high above the town.

Easing back on the throttle, the skipper took the boat towards the stone wall of the Fish Pier. As he used the engine to hold the bows against the harbour wall, Tam bellowed instructions through the door of the tiny wheelhouse to the crewman who had leapt onto the dockside to secure the mooring rope around a stout bollard.

'There'll be no customs or harbourmaster bothering us. We're going to be tied up for an hour at most.' Keppler had to listen carefully to the man's heavily accented tones. 'Leave your gear here and come ashore with me an' Angus. When we go away into the chandler's you slip off. Your bag will be down there for ye at the shop when you arrive.' Without waiting for a reply, the Scotsman climbed the three steps onto the trawler's deck.

So much for security, thought Keppler, strengthening his resolve to act independently once he had made his initial contact.

On the harbour pier, his feet on firm ground for the first time in several days, he had to fight down a slightly nauseous sensation as he adjusted once more to terra firma. He had to hurry to catch up with the shambling figure of Captain Tam, who was already disappearing past the buildings at the end of the dock.

Just beyond the first corner, Tam and Angus went through the narrow front door of Marchmant's Chandlery and Marine Stores. Keppler waited patiently for two or three minutes before following them. Inside, Tam was in deep conversation with the storekeeper, a narrow-faced individual aged about sixty, whose thin body was almost buried in a light-brown smock, tied around the middle with a length of baling twine.

Standing patiently in the doorway, Keppler ignored the trawlermen, waiting until he caught the eye of a delivery boy in an enormous cloth cap and a clean white apron. Having just made a delivery, his baker's basket over his arm, the lad was preparing to leave the shop. 'Excuse me, please.' Siegfried put on his best Swedish accent. It had been decided from the outset that he would assume the guise of a Scandinavian sailor, who was between ships and looking around the fishing port for work. 'Could you please direct me to Flower Gate?'

The boy eased the basket into a more comfortable position on his arm before answering. 'Go right out of here, down past Coffee End as far as the swing-bridge. At the bridge follow the road round to the right and you're on Flower Gate.'

Thanking the lad, and nonchalantly picking up the sailor's bag leaning against the doorpost, Keppler took his leave, and five minutes later was turning down the narrow alley that housed the French polisher's workshop.

The polisher was a slightly built man in his late fifties whose closely cropped receding white hair was matched by a carefully trimmed moustache of the same colour. Looking up from his task as a shadow cast through the stable door of the workshop fell across his bench, he smiled politely and asked, 'Can I help you, sir?'

'I was looking for a present to take home to my wife. I was told that you might have something of interest,' replied Keppler.

The little man eyed him speculatively. 'Anything is possible in this world.'

Keppler gave him a slow smile before supplying the third part of the identification code. 'Only for those who know where to seek it.'

Putting down the piece of rag with which he had been applying a coat of stain to the leg of an antique chair, the polisher wiped his hands on a square of clean cloth and indicated for Keppler to follow him through into a small kitchen at the rear of the premises. 'Ludwig Heitmann,' he introduced himself. 'Would you like some tea? I'm afraid that with this war on I can't get any decent coffee.'

Reaching into the pocket of his pea jacket, the visitor handed him a blue paper packet full of coffee beans.

Heitmann's expressive eyes lit up in delight. 'Rechts vielen dank.' He went to a small cupboard and took out a wooden coffee grinder and a tall metal coffee percolator.

Keppler examined his surroundings. The place was spotless. The kitchen and workshop were clean and tidy; and under his brown apron the little man wore a white shirt with a stiff wing collar and carefully knotted tie. Even his hands, Keppler noted, watching him spoon coffee into the jug, were small and neat, almost like a woman's. Placing the percolator on a single gas ring near to the sink, the little man watched with satisfaction as the thick brown liquid gurgled up into the pan at the top and drained off down to repeat the process. 'Even after eight years I still miss good coffee and German beer, Herr . . . ?'

'Schmidt,' replied his companion, giving him a conspiratorial smile.

Drawing aside the low curtain under the sink, Heitmann dived in and came up with a shoebox wrapped in brown paper, which he handed to Keppler.

Inside, wrapped in oiled cloth, was a 9mm, Parabellum Luger of the type issued to the German army, along with three clips of ammunition. Having checked the action of the weapon, Keppler deftly inserted one of the eight round magazines into the butt and, ensuring that the safety catch was on, slipped the gun into the back of his belt. The spare magazines he dropped into the pocket of his heavy sea coat, which served admirably to conceal the Luger. The remaining items in the box were a leather wallet containing two hundred pounds in English currency and a ring holding three keys. 'I sincerely hope that this money isn't forged,' he said pointedly.

The other man gave a quiet chuckle, poured two steaming cups of black coffee and handed one to his guest. 'Nein, mein Herr. I can assure you that this is all genuine Bank of England sterling.' Both men were aware that one of the less practical schemes to have been proposed by a staff officer in Potsdam, bent on ingratiating himself with the Kaiser, was to flood the British and French economies with millions of forged banknotes.

Keppler smiled back thinly; he was not joking. It was not beyond the bounds of possibility that some fool might have decided to finance his mission with forged money. Sipping the coffee appreciatively, he studied the polisher. Heitmann had been living quietly in Whitby for the last eight years, noting what shipping went up and down the coast and reporting on the economy of the town, along with any information that might be useful for military action. How careful he had been remained to be seen. It was likely that his role was completely unsuspected, but alternatively the workshop could even now be under surveillance. The arrest in London less than a year ago of a barber, Karl Gustav Ernst, one of the General Staff's most trusted and deeply buried agents, had shaken German Intelligence to its foundations. Deciding to leave the shop as soon as possible, Keppler held up the keys enquiringly.

'The small key is to a left luggage locker at the railway station. I thought that you might have need of somewhere secure to keep documents.' The little man seemed to be inordinately pleased with his forethought. 'The others are to the rooms that I've rented at a house off Church Street. Although they're not particularly luxurious it's secluded and out of the way, at the back of Mission Yard. The neighbours down there aren't of a curious nature – nor are they interested in helping the authorities.'

Draining his coffee cup, Keppler slipped the keys into his pocket with the ammunition clips. He had been there long enough and was anxious to be on his way.

After a few more minutes of conversation, during which he was given directions to the safe house, the agent took his leave and slipped out of the kitchen door and down a series of alleys, which brought him once more into Flower Gate. Crossing the iron swing-bridge that spanned the River Esk, he was soon on the other side of the town among the tall warehouses and buildings of Church Street that backed onto the river. As he walked, Keppler turned over in his mind the resolve that he had formed. He would have a quick look at the rooms that Heitmann had rented for him, before moving on and finding accommodation of his own nearby. Once he was satisfied that his presence in the port had not attracted notice he would use Heitmann's rooms as a store or hideout in an emergency; until then it was safer to make his own arrangements. The most pressing matter was to establish contact with the agent in Kelsford upon whom the success of the entire mission depended.

The British, he thought grimly, believed with their typical complacency that the true purpose of their latest venture – Project 19 – was known only to themselves, but from this point the results of all their experiments would be fed back to him. Codenamed Nemesis, the German agent in Kelsford would ensure that whatever progress the British scientists made in relation to the gas experiments would be known in Berlin within days. Keppler was based at a seaport within the patrol area of the North Sea U-boat flotilla to facilitate direct contact with German High Command.

Following the directions given to him by Heitmann, Keppler found himself walking past a row of tall warehouses on his right. Through the narrow alleyways which pierced them he could see the murky waters of the estuary. On his left were a series of courtyards. The one he was looking for was about halfway down Church Street, and appeared to be even more run down and bleak than those he had already passed. Mission Yard opened into a square of loose ground ten feet wide and twenty deep. At present baked hard by the summer heat, during the winter months the loose earth would be reduced to a quagmire. At the far end stood a three-storey tenement, an old-fashioned plank door giving access to the ground-floor rooms that Heitmann had rented for him. Next to the door, on the right, a dozen badly worn stone steps led up to an archway, which gave access to buildings beyond. Halfway up the steps a broken boardwalk ran off sharply to the left, leading to rooms on the first and second floors.

A weaselly woman, her grey hair tied back in a bun, was dragging a pail of water along the boardwalk towards what looked like a first-floor kitchen door. Pausing to rest, she placed her hands on the rickety wooden banister and watched Keppler in silence as he crossed the area and, reaching the door beneath her, disappeared from view.

Fitting the key he had been given into the lock, Keppler was not surprised to find that it turned easily and the door swung back on its hinges without a sound. Herr Heitmann appeared to know his job. The room was no more inviting than the tenement's exterior promised. A table, two chairs and a truckle bed made up the room's furniture. Keppler noted that the place was clean, and that although the weather was warm the stove in the corner had recently been lit to keep the bed from becoming damp.

Locking the door behind him, he went over to the window and spent the next five minutes studying the courtyard through the flimsy curtains. Satisfied that he had not been followed, Keppler returned to the bed and, feeling about underneath, located and removed two loose floorboards. He pulled out a wireless set and Morse tapper, and spent a short time assuring himself that it was in full working order before replacing it in its hiding place.

Reaching around behind him, he drew the pistol from his belt and pushed it into the compartment on top of the radio, along with the spare ammunition clips. Before replacing the floorboards Keppler felt about in the cavity until his hand closed over the cover of a thin book tucked away at the back. He pushed himself onto his feet once more, dusted down his trousers and slipped the code book into his inside pocket.

Unlocking a second door in the far corner of the room, he entered a tiny communal scullery, with a sink and a bucket for drawing water from a nearby well. This must, he decided, have been where the woman upstairs was coming from. Locking the door behind him, Keppler let himself out through the scullery door to find himself in a narrow enclosed alley. A tall man, the passage was barely high enough for him to stand straight in. It was almost pitch black. Stooping low, he followed it towards a patch of light ten yards away. Here the alley turned at a right angle, and he found himself in an open courtyard – where a set of precipitous steps took him back down to the main street.

Hefting his duffel bag onto his shoulder, Siegfried Keppler turned right, and walked back along the road towards the town centre.

Edward Bayliss sipped tentatively at his pint of bitter before, folding his newspaper, he fished a packet of cigarettes out of his jacket pocket. Casually he checked his surroundings. Other than himself and a couple of railwaymen, who from their conversation were night workers taking a mid-morning drink before returning to their beds, the taproom was empty. The long glass mirror behind the bar gave him a view of the traffic passing along Gray's Inn Road, while through the two tall windows on the other side he could see the heads of people going about their business in Calthorpe Street.

Opening the packet of Passing Clouds, Bayliss took out one of the oval cigarettes and lit it. Not for the first time he wondered why the manufacturers had chosen to depict a seventeenth-century cavalier seated comfortably in his chair, a book at his elbow, luxuriously exhaling a plume of cigarette smoke. A churchwarden pipe clasped elegantly between his fingers would have been appropriate, but puffing away at a cigarette he had just lit, with a box of fifty more close to hand, was decidedly unauthentic.

The commander's contemplation was interrupted by the reflection in the bar mirror of a tall figure, wearing a light grey Homburg hat and matching suit, crossing the road. Seconds later Ralph Gresham appeared through the doorway. With a wave of acknowledgement Gresham walked over to the long bar and asked for a pint of stout, before joining Bayliss at his table. 'I'm sorry this place isn't ideal,' he murmured, 'but it's only ten minutes from St Pancras, and I've got a train to catch at eleven thirty.'

He was, Bayliss realised, referring to the fact that there were only two entrances to the pub, in easy view of each other. Both men would have preferred another exit at the back, probably via the toilets and a yard, to afford a discreet means of escape.

Bayliss pushed his cigarette packet towards the soldier. In spite of the civilian suit, he noted that Gresham was wearing a Royal Engineers tie. 'I thought it might be to our mutual benefit to have an informal chat.' His voice was low enough that only his companion could hear him.

Gresham smiled pleasantly and picked up his Guinness. Having checked him out, Naval Intelligence had decided that he could be trusted, he mused. 'I think that's eminently sensible. The question is, who goes first?'

Bayliss stubbed out his cigarette. 'How much do your people know about the Kosminski set-up, or, to be precise, Madame Norton?'

'She's a Russian Jew. Exceptionally clever, and a self-made millionairess. Her company is, to use her own word, kosher. No dark corners and no skeletons in the well-stocked vaults. Ideal for our present purposes.'

Gresham was no fool. In the days that had elapsed since the Whitehall meeting Bayliss had been digging, finding out about himself and about Project 19. The navy man had undoubtedly discovered something significant, which as a token of good faith he was about to divulge.

'You're now going to tell me differently, are you not?'

The commander moved his pint to one side and lit another cigarette. For Edward Bayliss the week had been a busy one.

After a series of telephone calls and an expensive lunch (paid for by the Admiralty) at the Savoy, Bayliss could claim to have been reasonably successful. The telephone calls were to Service colleagues who had connections at the War Office, or more exactly with the Committee of Imperial Defence. The lunch had been with a well-known senior member of the Civil Service, who was appalled to discover that his recent peccadillo with a willowy young officer of the Household Cavalry was not the closely preserved secret he had supposed it to be. During the morning he had been closeted in the office of Captain Eustace Cummings, a senior assistant to the Director of Naval Intelligence, briefing the captain on his findings.

Officially Gresham was, according to Bayliss's enquiries, one of a select handful of operatives employed by the MI5 branch of the British Secret Service Bureau. A lengthy career in clandestine activities had ensured Major Gresham a place in the intelligence organisation upon its discreet inception in 1909. All of Bayliss's instincts militated against this. While MI5 operatives came under the specific control of the department's director, Vernon Kell, or K as he was better known, Ralph Gresham had for some unspecified reason been put under the wing of Sir Rowland Leigh-Hunt, ostensibly with responsibility for the nerve gas project in Kelsford. The commander had a shrewd suspicion that something much deeper was happening. He suspected that Leigh-Hunt was running a separate 'special operations unit' of his own, and that the MI5 director was not even aware of Gresham's existence.

According to Bayliss's civil servant, very little was known by his department about Project 19, other than that it was a top secret military matter. However, he divulged that Sir Rowland Leigh-Hunt had been given a discreet watching brief over the activities of the Secret Service on behalf of the government.

'What does he mean by watching brief, Ted?', asked Cummings. The closely trimmed white beard and balding head, Bayliss realised, gave him a striking resemblance to the king.

'That's the interesting point, sir. My man, who's very near to Sir Rowland-hence his nervousness – doesn't know. My instinct is that MI5 know nothing at all about Project 19. I think it's an operation that Rowland Leigh-Hunt has set up independently. Ralph Gresham isn't, and never has been, an MI5 operative. He's part of some very deeply buried department run by Leigh-Hunt that takes on jobs that never officially exist.

Eustace Cummings's brow furrowed. 'Extremely clever. By making it look as if Gresham is one of Kell's men, Leigh-Hunt can quietly disappear into the background and leave MI5 to pick up the bill for something they know nothing about if things go wrong.'

'If he weren't so tied up with this Gallipoli thing, I'd have said that this has Winston's stamp about it. As it is, Leigh-Hunt's ensuring that later on nobody who's involved will be able to deny knowledge. Your soldier, Major Gresham, is going to be the crucial factor. He's the field man, with the Smiling Assassin as the controller. The fact that they're both professionals is the one thing in all of this that can work to our advantage. Stick close to Gresham. Let's face it, history definitely won't applaud Project 19. If Gresham and Leigh-Hunt are successful we'll quietly withdraw at the first opportunity. If they fail we'll need to extricate ourselves well before it happens.'

Commander Bayliss nodded slowly in agreement. 'As you say, Ralph Gresham's a professional. Can I tell him about Ruth Norton?'

The captain pursed his lips and stared at the ceiling while he pondered the question. 'Yes. But under no circumstances must he know about "Zeus".'

A small thin man in workmen's clothes at the bar glanced across the room at the men seated in the corner. Deciding that they were simply a pair of businessmen taking a quick drink before walking down to the railway station, he turned his attention to ordering a pint of mixed.

'There is, or more correctly was, more to "la belle Kosminski" than you may be aware of,' said Bayliss quietly. 'Have you ever heard of an organisation known as the Pipeline?'

Gresham pondered for a moment. 'A long while ago, in '04, during the war between Russia and Japan, there was talk among the Russki officers of an organisation called the Pipeline which filtered refugees out of Russia into Western Europe and the States.'

Bayliss watched the men at the bar. They were intent on their own conversations and well out of earshot. 'The Pipeline was, and still is, a Jewish organisation. It was set up fifty years ago by a group of first generation Russian

Jews who'd escaped to England and America from the Tsarist pogroms, and decided to help others do the same. As time went by more and more money found its way into the coffers of the Pipeline, until by the 1870s it was running one of the most effective covert operations in Europe.' He paused to take a fresh cigarette from his packet. 'Ruth Norton's first husband and her father were both founder members – and she was quickly recruited. We know she made several visits to Vienna in the mid- and late '80s. Her contact there was a man named Joachim Schallmeier.'

Breaking off to touch a match to his cigarette, Bayliss took the opportunity to marshal his thoughts. He needed to be careful. Gresham must be wondering how he had such detailed information. The truth was that Ruth Norton's controller in the Pipeline, Manfred Issitt, was now an agent of the British government. Operating under the codename Zeus, he was one of the most important men in the Jewish organisation, and since August 1914 had been using his network exclusively on behalf of British naval intelligence. Not only were his operatives active within the German administration, but they were also closely monitoring conditions in Russia.

'Inevitably as the organisation grew, so it diversified. Passage to America for those wishing to emigrate, goods and valuables converted into hard cash . . . you know the sort of thing. For a while they had dealings with the Fenians and one or two Anarchist cells. By the outbreak of the South African War they'd gone back to working in isolation. In the meantime Ruth Samuels had married a Kelsford policeman, and had taken herself off to build the Kosminski empire in France.

For the next quarter of an hour, over a second round of drinks, the two men quietly discussed the more mundane aspects of the war and its possible consequences. The business for which they had met was dealt with. By the offering and acceptance of the navy's information, both had made a tacit agreement that their respective departments would cooperate. Their opinions about the morality of Project 19 were not discussed, nor were they relevant.

Consulting his wristwatch, Ralph Gresham saw that it was a quarter past eleven, just sufficient time for him to stroll across to St Pancras and catch his train for Kelsford. He pulled the cuff of his white shirt back over the watch – widely advertised as 'the luminous variety, easily read in the dark and worn by night patrols in France'. He wondered if the fad for wristwatches would die out when there were no more 'night patrols in France'. 'I need to be going,' he said. 'Will you be hanging on?'

'Yes, I might have another,' replied Bayliss, as Gresham picked up his Homburg.

Bayliss made no move towards the bar to renew his drink as Gresham disappeared into the busy street. Resuming his perusal of *The Times*, he waited a further five minutes before, satisfied that Gresham had not been followed out by any of the men at the bar, making his way out into Gray's Inn Road.

Chapter Nine

Pursing his lips, Matthias Palmaerts put down the invoice that he had been studying, and looked at the large-scale plan of Kelsford War Hospital which was pinned to the wall of his cramped office. Deep in thought, he failed to notice the presence of Irene Deladier at the small glass partition opposite his desk.

'I'll give you a sou for them, Matthias,' she said brightly.

'Ah, bonjour, Madame,' he replied. 'Just sorting out some invoices before the guests arrive.'

Matthias reached into his desk drawer, took out a thin exercise book and made a note in it. Picking up the docket, he placed it carefully in a folder marked 'invoices – processed', and replaced it on the shelf behind him, along with a stack of others. Pushing his chair back, he reached for his jacket. It would, the Belgian reflected, require more than a sou to purchase his thoughts at present.

'You look very much at home in your new office,' Irene continued as he searched in a second drawer for his keys.

'Thank you, Madame. It's far better than working at the brewery.' The waxed moustache lifted as he gave her a grateful smile.

It was two months since Matthias and his family had moved from Devonshire Gardens to become part of Irene Deladier's household in Kingsbury Lane. Since that time their fortunes had improved immensely. Béatrice now cooked and kept house for Madame Deladier, while he had been found regular employment as a clerk at the Kelsford War Hospital. Initially he was given responsibility for logging in and keeping track of the equipment in the packstore. Upon arrival, every man who was admitted to the hospital had his kit and any weapon in his possession tagged and sent to the store, where it was retained until he was declared fit for duty and released. It was an easy job for the Belgian. Once the man's rifle had been stored away safely, it was merely a matter of listing all of his personal items of kit, sending them through the Manilove Alliott Steam Disinfector, and storing them in readiness for the day when he was discharged from the hospital.

Once James Simmonds, whose tireless efforts to make the Kelsford War Hospital into one of the biggest and most efficient in the North Midlands, had realised the potential of Palmaerts's accounting background, the Belgian's duties had been rapidly expanded. Tucked away in a tiny office on the first floor of the administration block, Matthias was now responsible, in addition to the pack store, for the hospital's day to day accounts. His tasks included collating and filing all incoming documents and bills relating to the construction work that was taking place around the complex, and it was an invoice relating to this that he had been puzzling over. A consignment of slabs, made from an extremely expensive stone and to be used for surfacing a quadrangle at the rear of the hospital, had recently arrived. According to the plan on Matthias's wall, the contractor appeared to have delivered about three times the amount needed.

Still preoccupied, Matthias locked the office and, slipping the keys into his coat pocket, politely offered Irene his arm. Together they made their way down the stairs and into the reception hall.

Today was a red letter day. Exactly a year since the declaration of war, the refurbished hospital now had a fully equipped operating theatre. Until now the Royal Army Medical Corps doctors had only been able to perform routine surgery in the converted first aid room of the old building. The new facility, funded partly by the War Office and partly by donations from local citizens, and to be opened by the consulting architect Byron Carstairs, would enhance the hospital's surgical capabilities dramatically.

Local dignitaries from the town and county had been invited to witness the opening and partake of a buffet luncheon which, despite the growing wartime shortages, was to follow. Among the guests who were being shown around, Irene Deladier spotted Superintendent Mardlin, accompanied by a small good-looking woman in her early forties. Irene had not seen Mardlin since the morning at Devonshire Gardens and felt a little embarrassed by her emotional behaviour on that occasion. She decided that the best way to deal with matters was to go over and speak to him.

When Irene saw that the woman whom she presumed to be Mardlin's wife had become involved in a deep conversation with her brother Sam, leaving the superintendent standing alone to one side of the group, sipping a glass of red wine, she went over to him. 'Mr Mardlin, it's nice to meet you again.'

Will had been preoccupied with his wife. That Susan had a new lover he had little doubt. Working out who it might be had for many years been a purely academic exercise, and in truth he knew it was best that he remained in ignorance. Recently she had been out on 'shopping trips' twice and sometimes three times a week, usually after lunch, returning in the mid- to late afternoon. He looked speculatively at the fair haired young major wearing the uniform of the Queen Victoria's Rifles with whom she was sharing a joke. There were no tell-tale signs that he could detect: no whispered exchanges, heads close together to avoid being overheard, no surreptitious touches on the arm or hand. Giving up, he turned towards the voice. 'Madame Deladier, it's good to see you.' Will realised he meant it. From time to time since their last meeting thoughts of the young woman had crossed his mind. She seemed brighter and less careworn now, he thought. Elegantly attired in a navy dress skirt and embroidered voile blouse, topped off with a stylish silk tulle hat, she was, it occurred to him not for the first time, an extremely attractive woman.

'Has your enquiry progressed any further?' she asked.

Will shook his head resignedly. 'Charlotte Groves? I'm afraid not. We thought we had a strong lead – a soldier the dead woman was associating with. But she was seen alive after he returned to barracks, so we need to keep going. If we keep on with the enquiry for long enough something will turn up.'

The something that Will needed to turn up was a pawn ticket. Once that, or the items to which it related, could be found, he would be able to make some progress. For the time being, although all of those involved in the Groves enquiry knew differently, the death of Leonard Belcher had been recorded as an accident. There would be time enough to deal with it as murder when a genuine suspect was found for the Charlotte Groves killing.

'I couldn't help overhearing what you were saying. The whole thing seems to have been completely motiveless.' Will heard Jamie Simmonds's deep fruity voice over his shoulder. Turning to greet the solicitor, Will saw that he was accompanied by a well-built woman in her late thirties, wearing a nurse's uniform. 'Have you met Kathleen?' Simmonds continued, indicating his companion.

Will smiled politely and extended his hand, while Simmonds introduced the hospital's matron, Kathleen Doyle.

'Is it Charlotte Groves that you're talking about?' If the chestnut hair and sea grey eyes had not given them away, the thick brogue would have confirmed her Irish origins. 'She was a strange woman, that one. Not a bad nurse, mind you, but once I found out she had her hands in the drugs cabinet she had to go.'

'Didn't you think of prosecuting her, Miss Doyle?' Will enquired.

'Bad for the image of the hospital,' cut in Simmonds. 'It isn't uncommon, so Kathleen tells me. Normally they just let the woman go.'

Will was not impressed. 'The same thing happened when she was at Leicester, though. Had she not been killed, and no one had ever prosecuted her, she could have kept moving to different hospitals indefinitely.'

The solicitor's reply was cut off by the announcement that Mr Carstairs was ready to declare the operating theatre open.

After twenty minutes of interminable speeches, first by the guest of honour extolling the virtues of modern medicine and then by Simmonds exhorting those present to press on with the war effort, it was suggested by Miss Doyle that the guests might like to adjourn to the buffet.

The tables of food and drink had been set out in a newly completed and so far unoccupied ward adjacent to the operating theatre, and as people drifted in Will found himself once more in the company of Irene Deladier and James Simmonds. They were joined almost immediately by his wife and the young major who, Will noted with a degree of satisfaction, appeared to be attempting to politely disengage himself from the older woman.

Introductions over, and Will having discovered that the major was in fact Irene's brother, his interest was aroused when the conversation revealed that Major Norton was in charge at the Old Watermill. 'What's the nature of your project, Major?' he asked.

'I'm not at liberty to disclose that. It involves research into improving the anaesthetics that are given to casualties at the Front.'

'I wouldn't have thought it required a full major to supervise a few technicians and test tube boilers.' Will picked up the rancour in James Simmonds's voice.

'Hardly technicians and test tube boilers, James. This is work of vital importance to the war effort,' Sam replied evenly.

'I'm sure it is,' retorted Simmonds. 'But I still fail to see why a major, and one from the General Staff at that, needs to manage it. Even if the accommodation is most conducive,' he added pointedly.

Before Sam could reply, Simmonds spotted the architect on the other side of the room and abruptly excused himself. Susan Mardlin and Irene began to chat amiably about the steadily increasing cost of living, while Sam signalled a waitress to bring over more wine. Mardlin was intrigued. Apparently Simmonds, while having a close relationship with Irene Deladier, did not like her brother.

Sam sipped his wine. 'Sorry about that, Superintendent. Jamie was all set for a good war, but within days of arriving in France he lost his hand at Mons. Decoration for bravery above and beyond, all that sort of thing, but he's never quite accepted that it was over so soon for him.'

Will nodded. And meanwhile you came back to a safe billet, being promoted into the bargain, he reflected.

Sitting on the edge of his bed in shirt and braces, James Simmonds began to carefully undo the buckles on the straps that clamped his artificial hand in place. Over the last few days the warm summer weather had been causing his stump to sweat and chafe against the cup of his prosthesis. Once the gloved hand was removed he saw that what remained of his right wrist was raw and bleeding. This had happened several times before, and he knew that the only remedy was to leave the stump open until it was completely healed. Simmonds's mood since the conversation with his cousin had deteriorated into one of smouldering anger. This latest circumstance meant that his legal files would have to be sent to his house for him to work on, which only served to darken his mood.

Reaching into his dressing table drawer, Simmonds withdrew a presentation box, five inches long and half as wide. Manipulating the hinged lid with his left hand, he gazed down at the gold and white cross of the Distinguished Service Order, with the king's crown and laurel wreath in its centre. Picking it up by its crimson and blue ribbon, he weighed the heavy medal in his hand.

Sam's assertion that for Jamie Simmonds the war had been a short if eventful one was correct. Thirteen years ago, at the age of twenty-three, following the return of the troops from South Africa, Jamie had joined the Kelsford Yeomanry as a Territorial Force officer. In the intervening years, by dint of assiduously attending all the evening parades and participating in weekend mounted drills, he had risen to the rank of captain in command of B Squadron. The day after England went to war with Germany, Captain Simmonds and the rest of the Kelsford Yeomanry entrained for France, cheered on by crowds of enthusiastic citizens and preceded by a marching band.

In less than three weeks they found themselves at Maubeuge, just south of Mons. On the night of Saturday 22 August, amid rumours that the French were withdrawing to cover an area south of the River Sambre, the Yeomanry moved up to assist in the defence of the Mons Canal. During the early hours of Sunday morning the British commander, Horace Smith-Dorrien, ordered that the bridges along the canal be destroyed. When day broke the Yeomanry were dispatched as unmounted cavalry to the loop in the canal between Mons and Condé, where the fighting was at its heaviest. Simmonds's squadron was detailed to support a unit of the City of London Regiment of the Royal Fusiliers, defending the bridge at Nimy which had escaped demolition. As the fighting progressed, and they were in imminent danger of losing control of the bridge, two of the Fusiliers volunteered to go forward and set charges, in order to destroy the structure and prevent the enemy crossing. Volunteering to provide covering fire for the operation, James, with a sergeant and four men, set off with them. Their effort was in vain. Enemy troops were already on the bridge, and delivered murderous fire onto the exposed men. Both of the Fusiliers, along with most of Simmonds's men, were killed in minutes, and the sergeant, a Scotsman by the name of Billie Auld, was severely wounded in the legs by machine gun fire. Slinging Auld across his shoulders, Simmonds began to crawl back towards his own position. Although a general retreat was taking place, a single machine gun was giving him cover and holding back the Germans, who were now pouring across the bridge. He and Sergeant Auld almost made it. They were only yards from the lone machine gunner when a howitzer shell exploded a few feet from them. The force of the blast was absorbed by the man on Simmonds's back, killing him outright, while shrapnel tore the fingers from Simmonds's right hand, stripping what was left of it to the bone. The fact that he was alive at all was, he knew, down to the bravery of the Fusilier who had stayed with his machine gun.

Against all the odds the German advance was held, and Simmonds was evacuated to a nearby regimental aid post. For his actions in attempting to carry Sergeant Auld to safety under heavy fire, he was awarded the DSO.

James turned the medal over in his hand. There were many other acts of equal bravery that had remained unacknowledged. A decoration for gallantry was something to be proud of, but at what cost, he reflected.

After Nimy Bridge it had been a long hard road. During the retreat from Mons the entire work of caring for the wounded between the front lines and the nearest base hospital, had been carried out by field ambulance units. Temporary dressings were applied to his damaged hand, and within days he had been moved by train to the casualty clearing hospital at St Omer. It was there that the decision to amputate his hand was taken. Despite the warm afternoon, Simmonds felt a cold chill run through his body at the thought of it. He clearly remembered being wheeled into the busy operating theatre, in desperate pain and sedated by morphine. Five days after being wounded, Captain James Simmonds was administered chloroform, followed by nitrous oxide and oxygen, and his right hand was removed.

Closing his eyes, Simmonds could remember word for word the neatly written notes on the board that was hanging at the foot of his bed when, two days later he recovered sufficiently to be aware of what was happening around him.

James Simmonds/Captain/Kelsford Yeomanry
Amputation of right hand
St Joseph Cas. Clng Hospital, St Omer. 27th August 1914
Surgeon: Walter Trethowan. Col. RAMC
Amputation carried out through right wrist joint. Preservation
of the inferior radio-ulnar joint appears to have been successful.
Full pronation and supination anticipated. As the styloid
processes remain, the site should be suitable to accept the fitting
of an artificial appliance at a later date after a suitable period of
hospitalisation.

Unfortunately a nerve left exposed by the surgeon gave Simmonds intense pain and a constant twitching in the weeks following the operation. After being returned to England, in order to remedy the problem, the stump was encased in plaster of paris at the military hospital at Ampthill before he was finally sent to the 5th Northern General at Leicester. There for the next two months, as autumn eased its way towards winter, he spent his days in one of the officers' wards, waiting patiently for the pain to ease and the plaster to be removed. Eventually, just before Christmas, he was discharged from both the hospital and the army as permanently disabled, and returned home to resume his law practice in Kelsford.

Simmonds sat for several minutes, holding the medal loosely in his left hand before replacing it in its case. Getting up from the bed, he went to the night stand by the bedroom window. He lifted a pitcher of water from the floor, filled the deep porcelain bowl standing on the table and plunged his swollen limb into it. For a few seconds the icy water brought sublime relief.

Drying the damaged scar tissue carefully on a clean towel, he opened a jar of greenish salve that stood next to his shaving kit. Since he had lost his hand, he had learned to deal with most of the mechanical functions that two handed people take for granted. Shaving was one of many. He had long ago given up attempting to use his open cut throat in favour of the smaller Gillette safety razor that had become so popular over the last few years.

Gently Simmonds began to massage the ointment into his stump. It would be several days before he could strap his artificial hand back on and reappear in public.

His mind returned to the object of his annoyance. Almost without exception men who had been gassed at the Front spent some time recuperating, then returned to their units in France. His well-placed cousin, however, had successfully ensured for himself a safe posting in England. It had taken all of Simmonds's self-control to remain silent while listening to Sam expounding upon 'the necessity of progressive experimentation on the Home Front'. Easing his arm into a more comfortable position, he felt his anger rising again. Doubtless some highly effective string-pulling had taken place while the young prig had been in hospital. Even before Ypres Sam had been removed from the firing line into a supposedly safe job on the General Staff. The fact that he had been gassed must have been seen as an ideal opportunity to remove him from the firing line altogether. It would, after all, be unthinkable for the heir to the Kosminski fortune to be lying dead in a ditch somewhere in France.

Opening the lower drawer of his dressing table, Simmonds took out a small medicine bottle and a hypodermic syringe. Removing the cork stopper from the bottle with his teeth, he carefully drew off a measured dose of the clear liquid. As morphine-induced euphoria began to envelop him, he lay back on the bed and drifted off into a dream-filled world where pain did not exist.

The day's fine weather had by mid-afternoon become overcast and thundery with the promise of an imminent heavy downpour. Claude Biddles stroked the head of the heavy carthorse as it stirred in the shafts of the dray. The animal, sensing the changing atmospheric pressure, was becoming uneasy. 'Come on, get that barrel off before it starts to rain,' he called to the well-made young man on the back of the wagon.

Philippe Palmaerts raised a hand and threw his weight against the huge beer barrel. It began to roll slowly towards the dropped tailboard and ramp. He took hold of the stout rope wrapped around it and pulled back hard, to control its descent.

He enjoyed working for Winstock's Brewery. Fit and strong and just turned sixteen, Philippe was too young to volunteer for the British army, and was quite happy in his present occupation. In another twenty months he could go and take revenge on the Boches.

'Watch it now, keep a hold on that rope . . .'

Perhaps if you came and helped me it would be easier, thought the lad: there should be two of us working this barrel. But that was not Biddles's way. As the old drayman was constantly telling his workmates back at the yard in Salmon Lane, 'There's no point in having a frog and croaking.' Working with the drayman and making daily deliveries round Kelsford's pubs had enabled Philippe to develop his English to the point where he was almost fluent. When chatting with the other labourers he could even slip the odd 'bloody' into their conversation.

Hauling back on the rope, Philippe halted the barrel's slow passage at the edge of the tailboard and, taking the strain, waited for his mate to come to the back of the dray to help him lower it down.

Biddles rubbed his hand soothingly along the horse's flank and moved back towards the driver's seat, automatically running his eye over the harness as he did so. Get this delivery at the Pack Horse done, one more drop at the Cattle Market Hotel, then he would be away home. Pausing next to the animal's rump, he felt around on the driver's footboard above his head to find his tobacco pouch and pipe. Unhurriedly he shovelled the dark black shag into the heavily carbonated bowl.

A deep rumble of thunder caused the horse to move uneasily, stamping its massive hind hoof an inch from the drayman's boot. 'Easy Kitchener, easy.' His voice was soothing, and quietened the animal. Turning into the shelter of the wagon's front board Biddles struck a match and ran it back and forth across the bowl of the pipe before tamping down the contents with a calloused forefinger.

Without warning, a massive clap of thunder broke with a tremendous crash immediately overhead. The cart horse whinnied loudly in sudden fright and began to push back anxiously against the traces, making it almost impossible for the lad on the tailboard to hold onto the taut rope. Biddles, between the wagon boards and the backing shire, was caught off balance. His pipe, knocked from his hand, sent a shower of burning embers onto the horse's rump. Rearing up in pain, the startled animal bolted. Trapped between the shafts and the wagon, Biddles was knocked from his feet beneath the wheels of the catapulting dray. The front offside wheel passed over his legs and the rear over his chest. Philippe Palmaerts, finally losing his grip on the rope, was thrown headfirst off the wagon, and lay stunned on the pavement a foot away from the open cellar door.

The barrel that Philippe had been holding onto careered into the roadway and smashed against the pub wall as the frantic horse bolted along the High Street, scattering pedestrians and traffic to left and right. Loose on the back of the dray, the three remaining seventy-two gallon beer barrels, released from their lashings, began to roll precariously towards the open tailgate. The first two hit the roadway almost together, shattering on impact and showering beer and timber over a hundred yards of High Street. The third, having gained more momentum in its travel along the length of the flat wagon, struck the surface of the road before rising ten feet into the air, spinning crazily, like a child's top suddenly released from its string, and hurtling towards an oncoming Siddeley-Deasy army lorry. The driver was transfixed. Even had he not been paralysed with fear, there was nothing he could have done. His passenger gave a strangled scream and threw up his arms in a vain effort to protect himself.

The barrel, weighing just under half a ton, struck the lorry's windscreen with the force of an artillery shell exploding. The metal frame buckled and the glass shattered, driving shards into the bodies of both men and decapitating the driver. The impact of the barrel reduced the cab to matchwood, crushing the two occupants beyond recognition. The lorry hit the kerb, rolled onto its side and slid across the pavement into the window of Vernon's Clothing Stores.

In the silence that followed, broken only by hissing steam escaping from the lorry's punctured radiator, the horrified onlookers hardly registered the half dozen metal canisters that spilled untidily from the rear of the canvas-covered truck onto the pavement.

Ten minutes later the Kelsford fire engine clattered down the street, brass bell clanging, to assist the two constables who had been summoned from the nearby police station. While the policemen moved back the growing crowd of spectators to the far side of the road, two of the firemen fixed a chain onto the shattered lorry to pull it back onto its wheels. Taking a set of spanners from the fire engine's tool box, Fireman Anselm Griffin checked that none of the small canisters that he had carefully recovered and stacked by the side of the vehicle were leaking. Painted a dirty orange colour, they weighed about twenty pounds each. A nozzle at the top was held closed by a brass nut. The buffeting that they had undergone did not seem to have affected most of them, but the last one he checked seemed to have a slightly loose release valve. Putting a spanner onto the nut, Griffin gave it a quarter turn. The sharp hiss of gas told him that he was turning the wrong way, and he quickly reversed his action, securing the nut tightly in place.

Fifteen minutes later, Fireman Anselm Griffin became the fourth person to die that afternoon as a result of a brewer's dray horse bolting through Kelsford town centre.

Chapter Ten

What you must understand is that the use of poisons carried on the air is as old as warfare itself. The Greeks and the Romans used burning faggots soaked in pitch as a siege weapon. In medieval times stink pots containing all manner of noxious materials – including dead bodies and plague victims – were catapulted over the walls of besieged cities in the hope of causing panic and spreading infection.' Ralph Gresham paused in his quiet exposition to rummage around in the open briefcase by his chair. Sam Norton presumed that he was searching for some paperwork to back up his calm explanation of the horrific situation into which the young man found himself thrust. Instead, with a grunt of satisfaction, he produced a bottle of Jameson's Irish Whiskey. Holding it out, he said, 'You do have some glasses, I presume?'

Nodding, Sam got to his feet and opened a cupboard behind his desk. He produced two tumblers, into which Gresham poured liberal measures of the amber liquid before replacing the bottle in his case. Sitting back in his chair, he took a swallow and peered speculatively at Sam over the rim of the glass.

Sam could still not fully comprehend what was happening. The news the previous afternoon that a driver and one of the mill's technicians had been killed in a road accident had come as a tremendous shock. That a fireman who had opened one of the canisters they were carrying had also been killed, apparently by its contents, was appalling. His subsequent row with the head of Kelsford's Detective Department had not helped the situation.

The reception that Sam received from Will Mardlin and a stout uniformed superintendent on his arrival in the High Street was glacial. Initially he was at a loss to understand what was happening. It was he who had lost members of his staff in the accident, after all. Only when he was shown the body of the fireman, and was told how he had died, did he begin to comprehend their antagonism.

'Where . . . where are the canisters now?' he asked, glancing hurriedly around.

'I've had them removed for the safety of everyone concerned. They're at the police station,' Will replied coldly. 'I suggest you leave some of your men here to assist Superintendent Pemberton's officers, and the rest of the firemen who aren't dead yet, while we adjourn to the station for an explanation.' Without waiting for a reply, he turned on his heel and walked away.

At the police station matters deteriorated rapidly. Once both men were alone in the privacy of Mardlin's office, Sam found the time to gather his thoughts. He needed to regain control of the situation and recover the canisters.

'Superintendent, whatever's happened out there, those containers are War Department property, and must be returned to my care.'

'Whatever's happened out there,' Will hissed, his anger bubbling up. 'Whatever's happened out there! I'll tell you what's happened out there, Major Norton. Two of your men have brought into town something deadly – concocted by you and your confederates at the Old Watermill, and an innocent man's died.' Barely able to suppress his anger, he pointed an accusing finger at the army officer. 'Yes, you'll get your containers back, we both know that. But exactly when, and how difficult I make it, depends on what you tell me. What's going on at the mill? Just what the hell are you making out there, that one whiff will kill a man stone dead?'

This was precisely the same question that Sam posed to Ralph Gresham the following morning, when in answer to the flurry of telegrams between Kelsford and London, once more wearing the uniform of the Royal Engineers, he descended from the train at the Midland railway station.

Gresham paused to sip appreciatively at the whiskey before continuing. 'In more modern times, just over a hundred years ago, a naval officer named Thomas Cochrane came across a peculiar phenomenon in Sicily. He noticed that the locals produced sulphur in kilns, and that the fumes given off killed any animals in the surrounding area. Not unreasonably he presumed that the fumes would have the same effect on human beings. Once back in England he suggested to the government that the sulphur gas had a significant military potential. HM Government toyed with the possibilities on and off for years, but nothing ever came of it.' He smiled brightly. It was the same open smile that Sam remembered from their first encounter in the hospital at Béthune. 'Not, that is, until this present conflict forced upon us the need to re-examine our consciences and explore the outer reaches of our imagination.'

Ralph Gresham had known from the outset that this moment would come sooner or later. Sam's realisation that the chemistry laboratory in the mill's outbuildings, guarded twenty-four hours a day by what amounted to a small garrison of soldiers, was not for the simple production of anaesthetics had been inevitable. If it had not come through overheard snatches of conversation between the two scientists, Herbert Duggan and Paul Kändler, it would have been something else.

Gresham was intensely annoyed that the situation had arisen, and that he would have to reconcile matters with the local police. Perhaps from the outset he should have laid down rules for the transportation of materials instead of leaving it to be dealt with by the young man who was pacing nervously up and down in front of him; but to have done so would have prematurely alerted Sam Norton to the fact that Project 19 involved more than he was aware of. No one could have envisaged that a truck taking canisters to the railway station for onward transmission to the Rosyth naval base would be hit by a flying beer barrel. 'What's this superintendent like?' he asked.

'He's a stupid, pig-ignorant bastard who doesn't know his place,' Sam burst out, his frustrations overcoming his judgement. Not only had Mardlin refused point blank to hand over the containers the previous afternoon, but he had also told Sam that from now on any military vehicle driving through the town would be stopped and searched. If it was found to be carrying dangerous materials of any sort it would be impounded. In the ensuing heated row, Sam had declared loudly that any such action would not be tolerated, to which Will had coldly demanded how he intended to prevent it – 'by shooting people, or gassing them?'

Gresham looked out of the office window, watching two soldiers who were walking across the grass towards the meal hut. It was time to see what he could do to repair the damage that had been done with the local police, but there was something else he needed to address. 'I suppose you're examining your conscience now, and deciding on the best course of action,' he said softly.

Sam sat down behind his desk. 'I've already reached my decision. I want no more involvement in this. I want to be returned as soon as possible to my unit in France.'

'There's a problem with that.' Gresham's gaze had become steely; his voice was flat and full of menace. 'Something we neglected to tell you at the outset is that the entire project is being funded by your mother. She made a huge cash donation to the War Office, which has been used exclusively to finance this venture. The research, the buildings equipment, scientists, transport facilities – everything – Kosminski's have paid for it. Why else do you think you're here? You're going nowhere, young man. You're going to remain in this office – the heir to the Kosminski empire safeguarding the interests of the family's latest investment. Should anything detrimental happen, any adverse publicity for instance, anything at all that compromises the project, the government will withdraw, declaring that it's been the subject of an horrendous conspiracy, and publicly naming Kosminski's as the perpetrators.' The stunned look on Sam's face told Gresham that he would have no further problems with ensuring the young man's compliance. Pulling back the cuff of his shirt he consulted his wristwatch. It was eleven o'clock. 'I've arranged an appointment with Superintendent Mardlin at half past eleven. I take it that you've arranged for a truck and a driver to take me to town.'

'It'll be by the bridge in ten minutes.' Sam walked over to the window and looked out at the picturesque view. What, he wondered, had he allowed himself to become involved in? He was genuinely appalled at the horrific deaths of his staff, to say nothing of the mysterious manner in which the fireman had died. Then there were the two scientists to consider. For weeks now he had shared the living quarters of the Old Watermill with them: eating meals together, sharing a quiet glass of whisky in the evening while chatting about the war and exchanging experiences. All the while they had been deceiving him. Each time he had asked about the progress of their experiments, they talked to him about the properties of morphine and chlorine, nitrous oxide and oxygen, while all the time, in their secret laboratory, they were creating a monster of which he knew nothing.

The revelation that Project 19 was dedicated to the production of an advanced form of poison gas had still not really sunk in. If this ever became known to the people of Kelsford, the consequences would, he knew, be dire. Superintendent Mardlin would ensure that.

Gresham stood up and placed his empty glass on the desk. Sam, he noticed, had not touched his drink. Carefully adjusting his cap, he tucked his leather-covered swagger cane under his arm and walked to the door. 'Better get going then. See you later.'

Still looking out of the window, his back to the room, Sam said slowly, 'Who are you, Ralph?'

'I'm your guardian angel. Now drink your whiskey, laddie.'

'Major Gresham's here to see you, sir.' Frank Broughton ushered the dark-haired army officer into Mardlin's office.

'Please sit down, Major. I think we have things to discuss.' Looking up from the file of evidence that he was studying, Will indicated the seat opposite. Sitting back in his chair, he pushed the light card folder to one side and said, with studied politeness, 'Would you care for a cup of coffee?'

'Thank you, no. I'd prefer to resolve the matter in hand if you don't mind.' Gresham replied equally politely.

'In which case, perhaps you'd like to open the discussion.' Will leaned forward. He was under no illusions as to the purpose of the major's visit: it was to recover the canisters that were securely locked away in the spacious property safe at the back of the charge office at Long Street police station. He knew perfectly well that he would not be allowed to keep the offending items until the inquest upon Anselm Griffin. Whatever those heavy metal tubes contained, the army was desperate to recover them. The previous afternoon it had been relatively easy to deal with the young officer from the Old Watermill: Will's genuine outrage, combined with a display of absolute intransigence, had given him the opportunity to retain possession long enough to have the containers photographed by Saunt's photographer, Ben Ingram. This morning he was reconciled to handing them over to the man in front of him, after some verbal fencing.

'The discussion's quite simple, Superintendent,' Gresham said smoothly. 'I have some documents here which you should read.' Reaching into his briefcase, he handed over two stiff buff envelopes.

Opening the first, Will noted the bold War Department header at the top of the sheet before casting his eyes over the neatly typed bright blue text. As he had expected it was a directive, signed by the Secretary Of State for the Department of War, directing the Chief Constable of Kelsford Borough Police, by virtue of the powers invested in him under the Defence of the Realm Act 1914, to hand over the canisters unexamined. The second envelope contained a similar instruction from the Home Office, confirming that the items were to be returned to the military forthwith.

Setting the papers to one side, Will pursed his lips and looked directly at Gresham. 'The discussion's not that simple, Major. I think we both know that.'

Gresham returned his steady gaze as he evaluated the man. Square face, heavy clean-shaven jaw and pale brown intelligent eyes. Probably mid-forties, he judged. There was a peculiar tiger-like quality to the eyes that he could not quite define. He sensed that this man would make a better ally than enemy. With a conciliatory smile, he gave a slow nod, as if conceding the point. 'Your prime worry, I presume, is that a military operation is being undertaken on your doorstep about which you know absolutely nothing.'

A small movement of the head signified Will's agreement.

'The activities at the Old Watermill are directly linked to the outcome of the war, which there's a strong possibility that England may lose.' Gresham paused for his words to take effect. That at least, he thought, was true. 'An *impasse* has developed along the Western Front, where both sides are dug into trenches and are exchanging shots at a range of a few hundred yards. The campaign that Mr Churchill has engineered in the Dardanelles is about to collapse.'

Registering the frown that had appeared on the policeman's brow, Gresham broke off for a moment, with a pensive expression. 'I'm sorry, but you shouldn't believe all the press releases from people like Douglas Haig and Philip Gibb. It's their job to maintain public morale and to encourage every able-bodied man to volunteer to join the Colours, although, God knows, recruiting's dropped to a trickle in recent months. The Dardanelles expedition has been a total disaster. The Turks have held the vast majority of our troops on the beaches for months. General Hamilton's lost around forty thousand men out there. Submarine warfare's been stepped up in the North Sea and the Mediterranean. To date we've lost over eight hundred thousand tons of shipping.

'At home we've got massive industrial problems as we try to service the war effort. The incompatibility between Lord Kitchener's need for soldiers and Lloyd George's requirement for factory hands has led to a virtual breakdown in production. At present, Mr Mardlin, we're not even in a position to supply sufficient shells to service our artillery in France. In a nutshell, we're being outgunned and outmanoeuvred on all fronts.'

Gresham stared out of the window for a moment. 'And now the Germans have begun to use poisoned gas. It's a situation in which we can't allow them to prevail. Distasteful as it is, we've got to retaliate. Believe me when I say that yesterday's events were as great a disaster for us as they were for you.' He gave the superintendent a hard stare. 'If I assure you that there'll be absolutely no further incidents, will you be prepared to co-operate with me?'

Will considered his position. By rights, Sydney Hall-Johnson, the chief constable, should be a party to this meeting and any subsequent decisions, but he was on holiday. Perhaps that was all to the good, thought Will. This was a decision he was quite happy to take himself, and he was aware that there was only one answer to the army officer's request. 'What do you have in mind?' he asked slowly.

What Ralph Gresham had in mind was that in exchange for his assurance that no more vehicles carrying any form of toxic material would pass through the town, Will would play down the death of the fireman and ensure that the local newspaper received as little information as possible, in the hope that the affair would, with the passage of time, fade into obscurity.

His relief at the outcome of the meeting was considerable. The canisters, while containing the waste material from some of Kändler and Duggan's recent experiments, were not, in the scheme of things, overly toxic. The fact that the contents had been sufficiently deadly to kill a man outright was, he reflected, useful information. What the policeman sitting opposite must never know was that if anything went wrong with the final product, a single canister could wipe out the entire population of Kelsford.

Their discussion ended, Gresham was about to leave when, as an afterthought, he asked, 'Have any photographs been taken?'

'Other than those by the newspaper photographer at the scene of the accident, I've had our local man photograph the canisters at the police station.'

Gresham gave a wintry smile. 'I will of course require those pictures, along with any plates that the photographer has in his possession.'

Will reached into his desk drawer and produced a large envelope, containing three photographs and the same number of glass plates. Sliding them into his briefcase, Gresham gave an inward sigh of relief. The matter was well on the way to being concluded successfully. As a bonus, he now had a contact at senior level in the local police force. Should further problems arise, that could prove extremely useful.

Shaking hands with Will, he handed him a small buff-coloured card. 'If you have any difficulties, or think I may be able to help in any way whatsoever, telephone this number in London. They'll know where to find me. I think we'll need to talk again later . . . and please call me Ralph.'

Releasing his grip, Will took the card and tucked it into his waistcoat pocket. 'Will,' he replied, 'and yes, I suspect we may need to speak again.'

Neither man had any idea of the truth of their polite parting exchange.

After Gresham had left, Will returned once more to his desk and took out the card. He memorised the number before slipping it back into his pocket. Through the office window, in the station yard below, he could see two soldiers loading the heavy canisters onto a small canvas-backed truck, under the watchful eye of Major Gresham.

Setting to one side the government papers requesting the release of the canisters, Will opened the file he had previously been studying, and removed three glossy photographs. He spread them in front of him, took a large magnifying glass from his left-hand drawer and began to examine the images in minute detail.

'Can we afford a motor car?'

Will glanced up from his copy of the *Daily News*. The meeting with Gresham concluded, he had spent the rest of the day working through piles of paperwork, before making his way home at six o'clock. Now, after a particularly enjoyable meal of steak and kidney pie, he was taking a half hour to quietly read his newspaper. He gave his wife an enquiring look.

Carefully folding back the page she was reading in the *Kelsford Gazette*, Susan passed the paper over to him. Down either side of the news columns were a series of advertisements, ranging from the assurances by the makers of Zam-Buk Ointment that a single application of their universal medication was guaranteed to banish piles, pimples, blotches, eczema and spring eruptions for ever, to an illustration of a soldier holding a rifle proclaiming that 'after consuming a nightly cup of Vi-Cocoa not even the sound of enemy gunfire could disturb his night's sleep'. Will was considering whether or not this was actually a good thing when his eye settled upon the left-hand side of the page, where there was an artist's impression of a sleek open-topped motor car. It was being offered for sale by Campbell and Son Ltd of Bell Lane, and according to the text was a brand new 1915 model Morris Oxford.

Susan could read her husband like a book. She knew that Will's initial reaction would be to say no. Afterwards, if she played her cards right and when he had thought the proposal through, she would probably win.

'And who's going to drive it?'

'I telephoned Campbell's, and they send a man along with the car who gives you a morning's tuition – at no extra cost.'

'I don't think so, Susan. We can't afford it, and I can hardly set us up with a motor car when the chief constable hasn't got one.' Privately, he rued the day when, as head of the Detective Department, he had been persuaded to have a telephone installed in the house. It was one thing to be readily available on-call; it was quite another to have his wife telephoning local garages with a view to buying motor cars.

'Ah, but I was talking to Eva Johnson in town yesterday, and Sydney's buying an Austin from Brampton's next month.'

Will folded the newspaper, and with an air of finality handed it back.

'The answer's definitely no.'

Further discussion was forestalled by the sound of the telephone ringing in the hall. A minute later Edith appeared in the doorway. 'Telephone call for you, sir. Sergeant Lyner at Long Street police station.'

The call informed Will that a squadron of Zeppelins had been sighted heading inland over the Norfolk coast, and that a general alert was being sounded. Deciding that as it was a warm summer evening he would dispense with a top coat, Will went outside to wait for George Sutton from number seventeen. As part of the air raid precautions set up several months earlier, members of Kelsford Automobile Owners Club had volunteered their services whenever a state of alert was declared: each car owner picked up an official, such as Will, on their way to standby at either the police station or the town hall.

It would be, Will speculated, another false alarm. In the last five months coastal areas, along with the eastern counties and as far inland as the Midlands, had been subjected to a series of Zeppelin raids. During April and May, London; Ipswich, Bury St Edmunds, Southend and Ramsgate had been attacked. Over the south coast, in one daring daylight raid, a Taube aeroplane had dropped several bombs over Sittingbourne in Kent, causing extensive damage. So far there had been no sightings over Kelsford, but the blackout regulations were being strictly enforced. During the summer this had not greatly affected life in the town.

Further along the road George Sutton backed his small Ford into the road, and turned to head up to where the superintendent was waiting. Climbing into the front seat beside the portly businessman, Will wondered if perhaps Susan was right and that they should purchase a car.

At Long Street the yard at the rear of the police station was a hive of activity, crowded with off-duty policemen who had been summoned to await the impending raid. Several other cars were parked in an orderly line, ready to ferry men out to strategic points. At the far end were two delivery vans, one belonging to Horace Cuttler, a local butcher, the other to Cyril Parker, the baker from nearby Oswin Street. Once clear of the throng, Will let himself in through the back door of the station and made his way to the muster room, where he was greeted by Webster Pemberton – who was briefing a uniformed inspector and two sergeants.

'Sergeant Wheeler, take two men in Mr Cuttler's van and go to the town hall. Sergeant Hawkes, you go down to the tramways depot with another ten in Doughy Parker's van and wait there. You'll be under the command of Inspector King.' Pemberton turned to the inspector. 'Ted Mould, from the Gas Department, is outside. I suggest that you and he share one of the motor cars and take yourselves to somewhere central, probably down by the fire station.' As he was speaking the door opened to admit Harry North, Bernard Ashe and the tall spare figure of Nathan Cleaver. 'Mr North, will you be so good as to keep your men here, and we'll use them as necessary.' Pemberton raised an eye towards the detective superintendent. It was a polite courtesy: these were in fact Will Mardlin's men.

Will gave a quick acknowledgement. He saw a fleeting look of satisfaction cross Cleaver's face. The detective could smell a card school in the offing while the men were sitting about in the muster room.

The briefing over, Will went across to the high desk behind which Webster Pemberton was standing. As he did so, the door at the other end of the room opened. Eric Broughton trotted in holding a piece of paper, which he handed to Mardlin with an excited, 'From the fire brigade, sir.'

The handwritten note was a telephone message received by the fire brigade switchboard: 'Zeppelins sighted in force over Sheffield; e.t.a. Kelsford town 20 minutes.' Will handed the sheet of paper to his colleague. 'I suggest I take Charlie Hawkes and his men and head for the station. When we came past there just now a convoy train of wounded was unloading. If the Jerries spot that we're in for trouble.'

Pemberton nodded, 'Good idea. I'll get the alert sounded on the factory hooters.'

Five minutes later, with the rotund figure of Cyril Parker at the wheel and Will crammed in beside him, the dark green bread van pulled onto the station forecourt. As the back doors swung open to disgorge the blue-uniformed figures, the blaring of a dozen steam hooters around the town suddenly rent the air, their four short and one long blasts proclaiming to the populace the approach of enemy aircraft.

The policemen moved quickly down the wooden stairs which led from the booking hall to the platforms. Some of the men were carrying shotguns over their shoulders on slings, Will noticed. He remembered a Home Office instruction a few weeks previously to the effect that in the event of an air raid any officer who possessed a firearm should bring it with him when he presented himself for duty. Will was not quite sure why this directive had been issued to police forces: there was certainly not the remotest possibility of bringing down an enemy airship with one. Among those who had armed themselves he spotted the bulky figure of PC82 Tom Weldon. It was a pity, he reflected, that fate had placed the man at the opposite end of his beat when Charlotte Groves was murdered. Had he been in Devonshire Gardens the outcome might have been totally different. Last out of the van, brushing down the jacket of his dark suit, was Nathan Cleaver. On the way out of the parade room Will had, on the spur of the moment, instructed the detective to accompany the men in the van. It was a perverse decision on his part, as much to prevent Cleaver from having an easy evening as from needing his presence at the station.

Following his men, Will saw that the platform was a hive of activity. Shunted into a siding was one of the specially adapted passenger trains that delivered casualties from the ports on the south coast to various military hospitals throughout the country. Strewn around the yard were half a dozen motor ambulances, into which casualties on stretchers were being loaded by men and women of the Voluntary Aid Detachment, assisted by RAMC personnel from the war hospital. All were working with a frenzied urgency, driven on by the wailing air raid hooters.

Glancing at his watch, Will saw that it was twenty past eight. Although the daylight was beginning to fade slightly, there was no chance that darkness would give cover to the removal of men from the train.

One of the ambulances, drawing away towards the open double gates that led into the street next to the sidings, pulled up beside him. Behind the wheel in shirt and braces was James Simmonds. 'Glad to see you, Will. We might just do it if your men lend a hand. We have two more carriages to clear – about twenty stretcher cases.' He was out of breath from his exertions. In charge of the town's Voluntary Aid Detachment, Simmonds desperately needed to get the wounded men, along with his ambulance crews, away from the station as soon as possible. Slamming the vehicle into gear and steering with his right forearm on the wheel, he lurched away through the gates before Will had time to reply.

Shouting to his men to help with the unloading of the railway carriages, Will and an elderly RAMC man leaned into the specially widened doorway of the nearest compartment and grabbed at the handles of a stretcher which was being passed out.

As the minutes ticked away, more and more stretcher cases were pulled from the now almost empty train. Once all the ambulances were full, the remaining casualties were carried to the VAD rest room at the end of the platform and made comfortable there. Taking another look at his watch Will realised that twenty minutes had long expired, and the Zeppelins would be over the town at any second. His fears were confirmed by a sudden burst of gunfire from one of the Vickers machine guns that were mounted as anti-aircraft defences at Sevastopol Barracks.

Checking around he saw the figure of Irene Deladier, wearing the long grey dress and white apron of a Volunteer Aid worker, further down the platform. She was hurrying along the train, peering into each carriage as she did so. Incongruously, instead of one of the round straw hats worn by the other women, she was wearing a military-style cap and armlet, denoting her role as an ambulance driver. Will realised that she was checking each carriage was empty, and that none of the wounded had been missed in the rush to clear the train. Running down the platform to catch up with the young woman, he heard an ominous humming in the sky, signalling the approach of an airship. 'Come on, get to cover!' he bellowed, as he caught up with her near the guard's van. Glancing over his shoulder, he saw that people were running in all directions to seek shelter.

'We've got to check!' she shouted back, jerking open the door of the last but one compartment. She climbed in, followed by Will. Quickly they confirmed that each bunk was empty.

A dark shadow fell across the platform outside and the sound of the massive two hundred horsepower Maybach engines that were driving the dirigible grew louder and louder. The hum of the engines was suddenly lost in a series of ear-splitting crashes as the Zeppelin began to make its low level bombing run down the length of the train.

'There's only one more carriage,' she said breathlessly, and evading his hand as it vainly grabbed at the back of her skirts, she plunged on into the next compartment.

The noise of the diesels was immediately overhead. Will caught Irene round the waist and threw her onto the floor, dropping down on top of her. With a rending crash a high explosive bomb pierced the roof of the station buffet alongside them, exploding in the empty restaurant. The blast threw the train about on its tracks like a child's toy, shattering the carriage windows. Bunks and equipment were ripped from their mountings, and a baulk of timber smashed against Will's back with a force that almost winded him. Covering her body with his, he pulled Irene's face into his chest and waited.

The incendiary bomb that followed the first explosion also scored a direct hit, and set what was left of the building on fire. A blast of heat swept across them. Will realised that they had only been saved by the buffet' solid brick walls, which had absorbed the force of the explosions.

After a few seconds, when he was sure the danger had passed, Will eased his position slightly to allow the woman to breathe. They were both covered in broken glass. Without moving her head, Irene looked slowly from left to right, taking in the wreckage surrounding them. Will gazed down with concern, realising that he was still cradling her head in his hands. 'Are you all right?' he asked anxiously, his face inches from hers.

Instead of replying, Irene slowly brought her mouth up to his and kissed him. Gently at first, then, her free arm pulling him onto her, hard and passionately. As the adrenalin flowed through Will's system, his momentary surprise was replaced by an overwhelming sense of relief that they were both still alive. He brought his body back over her and responded equally fervently to her wet lips. The embrace lasted for several seconds before, breathless and confused, they separated.

Lying in each other's arms, they remained quite still for some time, not speaking. Outside the wrecked carriage the sounds of shouting came to their ears. The long piercing single blast of a nearby factory hooter declared that the raid was ended.

Freeing a hand, Will gently brushed a piece of plaster away from Irene's forehead, before leaning forward once more to kiss her on the lips, this time with a gentle brushing motion.

'What do we do now?' he murmured softly, running a finger down her cheek.

'I don't know.' She gave him a small enigmatic smile. 'First of all, we've got to move from here before they come looking for us.'

In bed later that night, sleep eluding him, Will's mind was busy with the events of the evening. The damage caused was extensive, both to the railway building and the shunting yard, but apart from the rearmost carriages the convoy train had escaped serious damage.

In the aftermath of the explosions Will and Irene had climbed out through one of the shattered carriage windows, covered in dust and debris but otherwise unscathed. Having assured those in the vicinity that they were unhurt and that no one else was trapped in the wreckage, Will hurried off to organise his men in assisting with the clearance work, while Irene busied herself with the ambulance crews.

It was not the air raid or its effects that were exercising Will's mind. His reaction to Irene's unexpected emotional outburst had taken him by surprise. Despite Susan's promiscuity, Will had never bothered to look for any relationships outside his marriage, and he was unsure of himself now. He certainly found Irene Deladier an attractive and exciting woman, but had this been a mad reaction to their narrow escape from death or was it the beginning of something much deeper?

Worn out, his mind still in a turmoil, Will was just slipping into a doze when he heard the soft click of the bedroom door being opened. He caught a whiff of expensive perfume as a small figure in a loose nightgown pushed back the covers and slid into bed next to him. Snuggling up close, Susan deftly began to move her fingers across his chest and down towards his stomach.

For the first time since leaving the house several hours earlier, Will recollected that the matter of the motor car was unresolved. Thinking back, he realised that ever since she had shown him the advertisement he had known that this would happen. Despite an earlier resolve he felt his body reacting to her touch. With a dextrous movement of her hips, Susan moved on top of him. Will caught the gleam of those burning dark green eyes that he had never been able to resist, and he was aware that he had lost.

While Will was always a good and considerate partner, Susan was taken by surprise at the ardour of their lovemaking during the next half hour. Later on, curled in a loose embrace, listening to her husband's rhythmic breathing as he slept in her arms, she took a moment to reflect before drifting off to sleep.

If she knew nothing else, Susan Mardlin was well aware that, contrary to the old adage, the way to a man's heart was definitely not through his stomach.

Chapter Eleven

There's definitely something wrong, Will. I've suspected it for some time and now I'm certain.'

Seated in the same secluded alcove in the lounge of the Pack Horse that Will and Harry had favoured for their discussion of the Charlotte Groves case, James Simmonds looked concerned. The superintendent took a sip of beer and waited for him to continue.

'At first I wasn't certain. Where there are large amounts of materials coming onto a site, with numerous contractors involved, it's difficult to keep track of things, but for some time now I've had my suspicions. A couple of weeks ago the fellow who's looking after the accounts at the hospital – a Belgian by the name of Palmaerts – asked to see me about a confidential matter.'

At the word 'confidential' Simmonds stole a glance around the half empty room. He need not have worried: the nearest customers were a group of corn dealers standing at the bar debating the most recent infamy perpetrated upon local trade by the War Office. From the following Monday all corn and animal feed was to be delivered to the nearby Remounts Depot, from where, after military requirements had been met, the remainder would be sold off to the local dealers at a fixed price. Under other circumstances Will would have been interested in the discussion. The men of the Remounts Division – a branch of the Army Service Corps – were universally detested. Accompanied by a local vet, their job was to visit farms and hackmasters in the district with a view to requisitioning horses under a compulsory purchase order for use by the army in France. Apart from the obvious crippling effects upon local horse owners, there were other equally dire consequences for the town's economy. Blacksmiths and saddlers were among those who saw their businesses ruined, as were carriers and other transport services. Without doubt the latest restriction would bring severe hardship to traders, and contribute to a further rise in the already spiralling cost of living. At present, however, more pressing matters required Will's attention.

It was three days since the air raid. The railway station was open again and work had begun on repairing the damaged buildings. When Will had arrived at his office that morning, among the correspondence on his desk was a handwritten note from Simmonds asking that he meet him for a drink at lunchtime to discuss a matter of some gravity. The script, he noted, was large and awkward, indicating that Simmonds was still in the process of mastering the art of writing with his left hand. Waiting for the solicitor to continue, Will wondered what his reaction would be if he knew that the detective was having an affair with his cousin.

The day after the raid Will had telephoned Irene and was surprised how easy the conversation had been. No awkwardness, no embarrassment: he simply asked if he could see her again, and she told him that as it was Saturday and the maidservant's afternoon off he should come round to the house soon after two o'clock.

The detached houses in Kingsbury Lane were large and elegant examples of the mid-Victorian era, built at the time when Kelsford's fortunes were beginning to change, and the growth of industry along with the canal and rail links into the town was bringing a previously unknown prosperity. Number twenty-six stood on the corner of Kingsbury Lane and Wentworth Crescent, and its tradesmen's entrance was at the end of an entry that ran along the rear of the houses. It was ideally situated for anyone making a clandestine visit.

On Will's arrival at the back door it was opened before he knocked by Irene herself. With a finger to her lips, she led him silently through the kitchen and up the staircase to the first floor. Closing the door to the spacious sitting room, Irene turned to him and, putting her arms around his neck, kissed him gently on the mouth. Before Will had time to respond she drew her head back and regarded him carefully. He had not realised how tall she was; their eyes were on a level.

'You probably won't believe me,' she said softly, 'but I've never done this before.'

'Neither have I. The question is, why are we doing it now?'

'I'm lonely, as I suspect you are – it's common knowledge that your wife is unfaithful – and we're attracted to each other. At least,' she added tentatively, 'I'm attracted to you.'

Will brushed his lips lightly across her forehead. 'Oh yes, I find you very attractive, Madame Deladier . . . very attractive indeed.'

Their first lovemaking in the big double bed in the room next door was quiet and gentle, the unhurried coming together of an adult couple exploring each other's bodies for the first time. Afterwards, propped on one elbow, Irene leaned over and looked down into Will's pale brown eyes.

'What are you looking at?' he asked.

'My mother always told me that the eyes are the mirror to the soul.'

'And what do you see?'

'I'm not certain,' she whispered. 'You have kind eyes. I knew that the first time that I saw you. There's something else, though, something deep down that I can't put my finger on. I think that if you were crossed you'd be unforgiving.'

'You have beautiful eyes. You're a beautiful woman.' Gazing up at her, he saw for the first time that her eyes under the dark arched brows were slightly almond shaped, with the tiniest hint of a slant at the outer edges betraying the Russian heritage passed to her by her mother. A long straight nose and broad sensual lips completed an almost perfect face, set in the frame of midnight black hair that fell across her face and shoulders. Will felt his breathing becoming difficult.

With her free hand Irene began to stroke her fingers gently along Will's jaw line, relishing the almost forgotten feeling of closely shaven stubble beneath her fingertips. Will became aware of a renewed musky odour of desire, mixed with the light perspiration of their recent lovemaking, and of her hardening nipples gently brushing his chest. For the next hour they remained together in the bed, alternately making love and lying quietly in each other's arms.

'He showed me a stack of invoices, along with a notebook that he's been keeping for a while, tracking deliveries of materials to the hospital site. Very shrewd man, this Palmaerts fellow, I don't know if you've met him. He was an accountant back in Belgium.'

Will nodded, his attention drawn back to the matter in hand. 'Yes, I've met him,' he replied absently.

Simmonds sipped his whisky and soda, wiping his moustache with the back of his forefinger. 'The paperwork shows quite clearly there's some sort of fraud going on. The quantities purporting to be delivered would be simply impossible to use or store on the site.'

'How much money are we looking at?' asked Will.

'Impossible to say at the moment. I think several thousand pounds. Depends how long it's been going on.'

'Who would have to be involved to make it work?' The detective kept his voice low.

Simmonds stroked the ends of his moustache again. 'Someone at the receiving end who's fairly well placed. One or more of the suppliers – we can figure that out from the invoices. Possibly someone in the hospital management. I honestly don't know for sure about that, but it's a real possibility.'

Will scrubbed a hand across his chin. 'It's not difficult to work out who your first candidate is . . .'

'And that's another thing,' replied Simmonds, the troubled look on his face deepening. Reaching into his briefcase he pulled out an early morning edition of the *Gazette*. Turning to the inside pages he drew Will's attention to a piece concerning a raid during Saturday evening on Sheffield. A short paragraph mentioned that a local architect Mr Byron Carstairs was among those killed when a tramcar in the middle of the town sustained a direct hit. 'The management committee will advertise for someone to replace him, but Byron had to be involved. From the outset he had to authorise every phase of the work. It couldn't have been done without his connivance.'

'This will have to be dealt with carefully. Give me all the evidence that you have, along with the details of all the hauliers and contractors working on the site, and I'll start a very low key investigation. Once we know where we're going we can talk again.'

Simmonds gave him a relieved smile, a huge weight of responsibility lifting from his shoulders. 'Thank you, Will. Can I get us another drink?'

'Yes, that would be good.' An idea coming suddenly into his mind, Will casually asked, 'Is there anywhere I can talk to Palmaerts in private, away from the hospital?'

'That's no problem. He and his family are living with my cousin Irene. His wife is her housekeeper. I'll give you the telephone number. Arrange it with Irene and you can talk to Palmaerts at the house.'

Watching Simmonds at the bar waiting to be served, Will allowed himself a satisfied smile. He had unwittingly taken the bait and provided the detective with a legitimate reason to visit 26 Kingsbury Lane.

He wondered if there was any possible connection, however tenuous, between the newly discovered fraud at the hospital and the murder of Charlotte Groves. There were possible links. Charlotte worked at the hospital as a nurse, she was a drug addict and she shared the house in Devonshire Gardens with the Palmaerts family. Was it remotely possible that he was on the way to discovering a possible motive for the killing?

The atmosphere in the tallow factory was thick and heavy with the rancid stench of animal fats, which during the day had been rendered down in the two huge gas-fired coppers at the far end of the room. Located in a block of converted stables at the back of a butcher's shop in Clipstone Row, the term 'factory' was by any standards generous.

Ivor Rees paused to check that no one had followed him down the entry before securing the outer door behind him. With the door closed, the pitch blackness of the deserted workshop enveloped him like a clammy shroud. Leaning back against the rough brick wall, the little Welshman took a moment to calm his breathing and wait for the pounding of his heart to subside.

What, he mused, had he got himself into? In addition to the tallow factory producing candles, he owned a general haulage business, based at his depot two streets away, in Axe and Compass Yard. When work on Kelsford War Hospital began, he had been quite satisfied to tender for the carting contract to deliver building materials from the barges at the canal basin to the hospital site. Since then his life had become considerably more complicated.

Twenty years before, when he came to Kelsford from his native Rhondda to avoid a life in the coal mines, Rees had begun his business career as a tin man, or rag and bone collector as the trade was now known. From pushing a broken-down handcart round the streets, he had progressed to rag collecting and had then become a general haulier. Over the years he had prospered, and now the war had for Ivor Rees, in common with many others , proved to be a gift from heaven.

Never believing the politicians' transparent lie that the war would be over by Christmas, and too old, in his forties, for army service, the wily little Celt spied out the best business opportunities. While taking on as many government haulage contracts as he could manage, he watched carefully as small businesses in the town, starved of manpower, began to fold. An initial contract to move building materials from barges arriving at the Shires Warehousing basin was lucrative and, at a time when the construction industry was in recession, a source of regular income. Already, with the prospect of conscription becoming a reality in the next twelve months, he was seeking to have his drivers classified as being exempt from military service.

When six months earlier Elias Ragg, who owned the Ardent Candle factory, declared that with five out of his six men now serving in the army anyone who wanted to buy it, could have the business, and good riddance, Ivor made him a minimal offer, and became the owner of the tallow factory. Making the one remaining employee – Lewis Stead – foreman, Rees then recruited half a dozen women who lived in the adjacent streets as workers. It amused him to read the arguments in the *Gazette* against the employment of female labour to cover manpower shortages. The latest furore was over a proposition by Kelsford Transport Committee to employ women as tramcar conductors and drivers. He failed to see the problem. Employ the women at a cut rate until the men came back from the war, then sack them, reinstate the original workforce, and sell the business as a going concern.

The opportunity to take a considerable bonus from the hospital contract seemed at first to be just another commercial opportunity presented by the war. The proposition was simple and lucrative. Each time one of Rees's drivers picked up a wagonload of materials from the barges, he took the load to his employer at Axe and Compass Yard for checking before completing the delivery. Supplied with the necessary blank delivery slips, Rees merely, unseen by his driver, substituted a false docket. At the other end, after the load was tipped, the driver took the invoice to the hospital administration office for payment to be approved by the architect. The supplier would, in due course, be paid the correct amount for the goods delivered, and the difference divided between those involved in the fraud. Rees's share was a fixed ten per cent of the altered paperwork.

The complication was the fact that someone on the hospital committee had become suspicious. Today a young detective had been sniffing around the yard asking to see the delivery records. Rees had deflected the policeman, telling him that they were at his house and that he would let him have them as soon as possible. Something was going to have to be sorted out very quickly if they were to avoid serious trouble. Rees was not sure where the others fitted into the scheme of things, or even who they were. It was obvious that the architect must be making the necessary adjustments between what was being authorised by the hospital management committee and what was being paid to the contractors, but during the time that he had been altering invoices he had only ever met the contact who supplied him with the false receipts. Tonight he hoped he would be told how matters were to be quickly wound up before the police enquiry became a serious threat.

A scrabbling sound a few feet away attracted his attention, and looking down he saw that he was being scrutinised by a pair of tiny brown malevolent eyes. 'Piss off, rat!' Rees muttered, groping his way across the workshop floor to a bench next to the nodding donkey onto which the candle wicks were tied ready for dipping. The sound of his own voice echoing in the darkness gave him a small degree of confidence. There had to be influential people involved in this, he reasoned. If things became too uncomfortable, doubtless one of them would be in a position to buy off the police. Everyone had a price, and coppers were no different to the rest of the world.

Rees reached out, and his hand encountered the brass bowl of the oil lamp that he was searching for. Grasping the base firmly with his free hand, he twisted the glass chimney a quarter of a turn before lifting it off and placing it on the bench. He found a box of matches on the bench, and lit the wick. Replacing the chimney he adjusted the tiny knurled knob to bring up the light. With the illumination from the lamp bathing the area around him in a soft mellow glow, and his eyes not yet adjusted to the light, Rees turned away from the bench.

The sight of the figure standing motionless only feet from him almost gave the little man a heart attack. 'Jesus Christ!' He stumbled back against the workbench, narrowly avoiding knocking over the smoking lamp. Momentarily speechless with fright, Rees gripped the edge of the bench while he regained his wits. The figure remained motionless, merely emitting a small chuckle as if amused at the shock that his silent presence had caused.

'Christ almighty, what a fucking stupid thing to do! How did you get in anyway? You could have killed me!'

The smile broadened, an imperceptible inclination of the head as if in agreement.

It was only at the very last split second that Ivor Rees realised what was about to happen. The long blade appeared as if by magic, and he caught a glimpse of metal flashing in the pale yellow light before it took him under the chin. The powerful upward thrust drove the seven inches of honed steel in one clean motion into the Welshman's mouth, through the soft palate and into his brain. Rees's body, his feet almost off the floor, jerked about like a speared fish, impaled on the trench knife. A sharp acrid stench filled the workshop as his sphincter relaxed, evacuating his bowels.

Satisfied that his victim was dead, the man allowed the body to sink to the floor, then with a quick twist began the task of freeing the heavy blade from the Welshman's cranium. The blade was buried deep in flesh and bone, and it took several savage twists before the killer was able to free it. A huge gash appeared across the corpse's throat as the saw-edged back of the blade was torn free. Carefully wiping the weapon on a piece of cloth that he had brought with him for the purpose, the man checked to ensure that no trace of his presence remained in the room before extinguishing the lamp. It had been a long wait, he reflected: almost an hour of patiently standing in the dark before the little man arrived. A long wait but time well spent. What was it Rees had said? 'You could have killed me . . .' He was still smiling as he closed the door behind him and, leaving it unlocked, slipped out of the gateway into the deserted street.

'Sometime between nine o'clock last night and midnight I would say.' Arthur Mallard closed his medical bag and held out a hand to Harry North. The detective inspector helped the doctor to his feet.

'Old age, Harry,' grunted Mallard as he dusted down his trousers. 'Rheumatics. Once I get down nowadays it's the devil's own job to get back up again. Not', he added, 'a problem which is going to affect our friend here.'

Mallard and North had known each other for nearly thirty years. Harry wondered how many corpses they had stood over together. Listening to the doctor's words of complaint, the inspector took momentary solace in the fact that Mallard was at least ten years older than himself. 'I'm sure he'd swap with you, Arthur,' he replied with a smile.

The police surgeon tugged at the lapels of his old-fashioned frock coat and, moving a brass oil lamp to one side, hefted the bulky Gladstone bag containing his medical kit onto the work bench. Breathing in through his nose, he twisted his mouth in an expression of distaste. 'Damned unhealthy place to work, with those stinking boilers over there polluting the atmosphere.'

Will and Harry briefly followed his gaze. The two reeking brick vats stood in the corner full of congealed fat, while in the centre of the room was a large piece of apparatus that looked like a cross between a Ferris wheel and a clothes horse, the base of which was submerged in a bath of tallow. Once the day's work was begun and the wheel loaded with racks, or hands as they were known in the trade, it would be rotated continually, allowing the wicks to pick up more tallow from the bath then cool in the air before dropping back into it. It was miserable and unhealthy work for the women employed in the sweat shop from six in the morning until seven at night. Today the coppers would not be lit to render down the waste fats brought in from the local butchers' shops, nor would the tallow baths be heated to start dipping the candle wicks.

This morning, just after five, while the cobbled entry outside was still damp with overnight rain, the foreman had arrived to light the gas and heat the vats, ready for the girls to start work when they arrived. The sight of his employer's almost headless body stretched out on the sawdust-covered concrete floor had sent him running terrified into the street to find a patrolling policeman.

'Never mind,' said the doctor resignedly. 'In another ten years everyone will be using electric lights, and these shit heaps will just be a memory.'

Will took out his pocket watch. It was ten past seven: he needed to get things moving. 'Sometime yesterday evening, then. Any ideas about the weapon?' He already knew the answer.

'One straight thrust up under the chin, through the roof of the mouth into the brain.' Mallard waved a hand towards the huge gash in the side of the neck. 'The damage caused to the throat is by the weapon being withdrawn. I'm fairly sure that when I do a PM there won't be much left inside the cranial cavity. The blade's gone in cleanly, killing him instantly. He's a very small, light man: the killer probably held him upright until he was certain that he was dead, then twisted and pulled to release the weapon. I'd say that one edge of the blade was cut into a saw tooth, so that when it came out it ripped the cartilage and soft tissue to ribbons. That's why the jugular and most of the neck on the left side are so badly damaged. The fact that the heart had stopped pumping before he pulled the blade out meant that bleeding was almost non-existent. In answer to your question, a bayonet or something similar.'

'A trench knife.' It was a statement, not a question.

'I'd say so, Superintendent, and before you ask, I wouldn't be surprised to find that the weapon that killed this man is the same as the one that killed Charlotte Groves.'

'You think that he – the killer – is definitely a man?'

'Almost without doubt. The strength required to make a thrust of this nature indicates that your murderer's definitely not a woman. And from the damage to the throat and neck he's got to be right handed.'

As they watched the spare figure of the police surgeon disappearing up the entry towards the street, Harry lit a cigarette before turning back to stare speculatively at the crumpled figure on the factory floor.

'What do we know about him?' asked Will.

'Ivor Morgan Rees, aged forty seven.' Harry consulted a thin cardboard-covered file that Nathan Cleaver had picked up before leaving the police station. 'Native of Merthyr Tydfil, Wales. Came to Kelsford June 1895, worked as an itinerant rag and bone collector. Arrested May 1896 for theft of scrap metal, value seven shillings and sixpence. Served thirty days' hard labour. No convictions since then.' Harry closed the file and dropped it onto the bench. 'I've never had dealings with him, which means that since 1896 either he's led a clean and blameless life, and we can contact the pope to have him canonised, or he decided that one spell inside was enough and got clever.' Pinching out his cigarette end and dropping it into the bath of tallow, Harry stood looking down at the body. 'According to the foreman who found him he's married, no kids, and has another business as a haulier, working from Axe and Compass Yard. Incidentally, young Ashe paid him a routine visit yesterday – majority of the haulage work he's doing at present is for the war hospital.

Will scrubbed a hand across his jaw. 'Yes, that might be interesting.' Like Harry, he was staring down at the body, lost in thought. 'If whoever did this is the same man who killed Lottie Groves, there's a basic difference. The attack on Groves was savage, as if it were personal. This one's a single clean stroke, more like an execution.'

Harry nodded, not taking his eyes off of the mutilated throat and head. 'But in both cases he was careful to avoid getting blood on himself. Knew where and how to strike.'

Will gave a small sigh. One killing was not good; two by the same man definitely boded ill. 'Neither killing was random. On both occasions he brought the weapon with him, and he isn't bothered about concealing the fact that both jobs are his work. It's a military weapon. Are we still looking for a soldier?'

His companion shrugged his shoulders in a non-committal gesture. 'I think we'd better find out where Francis Kempin was last night.'

Walking to the doorway to escape the fetid surroundings of the candle factory, Will took a deep breath of the fresh morning air. 'Who have we got here, Harry?' he asked over his shoulder.

'Clarrie Greasley and Nate Cleaver are talking to the staff. There are six women and the foreman. The butcher who rents the shop at the top of the entry lives over the premises, so we've put them in his living room to talk to. Apart from the foreman, Stead, none of them saw anything. Once he'd found the body none of the others came down here.'

Will gave a grunt of acknowledgement. Clarence Greasley was the other detective sergeant on his staff. A contemporary of Bert Conway, 'Greasy Clarrie' was the exact opposite in nature to the abrasive Conway. According to Harry, as detective constables years ago the pair had made a formidable duo.

'I've sent "B and B" out to knock on a few doors, to see if the neighbours saw or heard anything.'

Both men were aware that in the circumstances the chances of the murderer allowing himself to be seen arriving or leaving the scene of the crime were remote.

Their discussion was interrupted by a young uniformed constable at the workshop door. 'Excuse me, sir, but Mr Bathurst from the *Gazette* is here, asking to speak to you.'

It was, Will knew, inevitable that the editor of the *Kelsford Gazette* would appear sooner or later. 'Ask him to come down, please. But not the photographer with him!'

Less than a minute later the corpulent figure of Gilmour Bathurst appeared in the open doorway. With a cheery 'Good morning' he moved quickly to where he could obtain the best view of the corpse. 'Bad job, Mardlin, bad job.' The man's piggy eyes were darting around the workshop, taking in every detail.

The superintendent supposed that it was the newsman's instinct – see everything before you are thrown out. He made a few polite noises.

Will did not like the editor of the town's sole newspaper, but he was aware of the potential damage involved in refusing to allow him to visit the crime scene. A story of some sort would appear in tomorrow's edition of the *Gazette*, and what the editor did not know he would make up – so it was better that he had an accurate story to write.

Although he had never actually come into conflict with Bathurst, Will did not trust him. The man was too well placed in local society for comfort. Too many stories appeared in the *Gazette* that could only have come from confidential council meetings, or have been the subject of loose gossip at some club or lodge dinner. Such functions were also the source of Bathurst's over-generous figure.

'Similar sort of thing as happened to that nurse, would you say?' The effort of the walk over from the *Gazette* offices in Albert Street had introduced a decided wheeze into the fat man's breathing.

'Too soon to make any assumptions, Mr Bathurst.' Will noted that to avoid being drawn into the conversation Harry had moved to the opposite end of the workshop, and was busying himself peering into one of the stinking coppers. They will need to be drained he decided, just in case the killer had taken the unlikely course of throwing the murder weapon into one of them.

Bathurst treated the body to a long appraising gaze. Like the detectives he was no stranger to death, and in common with them he needed to be able to recall every detail for the story he would be writing. The fact that he referred to Charlotte Groves's former calling as a nurse rather than her latter as a whore was not lost on Will. The murder of a nurse carried far more public sympathy than that of a common prostitute.

'Pity you let that soldier go . . .' The words left a pregnant silence. Will had no intention of falling into the trap.

'You caught us just as we were leaving,' he said, ushering Bathurst towards the workshop door. 'I hope you've got enough for your column tomorrow. So far we've got a completely open mind about how Mr Rees came to die.'

Chapter Twelve

Half an hour later, accompanied by Bernard Ashe, Will knocked gently on the front door of the house in Meadows Road that was occupied by Ivor Rees and his wife. It was on the east side of the town, on the edge of what used to be the Downe Street district: houses with tiny front gardens and bay windows. They were not far from Devonshire Gardens, Will realised, as he knocked for a second time on the door, probably only a five minute walk away. This was one part of the job he hated, breaking the news to a victim's relatives. There was no easy way to do it, and unfortunately once the unpleasant job had been done it was then necessary to intrude upon their grief in order to forward the enquiry. Did the victim have any enemies? Where had he or she been during their last few hours? Would it be possible to have a look round the house for clues.

A movement next door at number fifteen caught their attention. A mousey-haired woman in her early forties, wearing a dark dress that met neat black stockings just above her ankles, came to the low privet hedge that divided the two front gardens.

'Mrs Rees is away and Mr Rees is out at business. Can I help you?'

Mardlin felt a guilty surge of relief. It was going to be easy after all. Raising his hat politely he said, 'Thank you. We're from Long Street police station. Mr Rees has been involved in an accident, and we need to speak to his wife. Do you happen to know where we can contact her?'

The neighbour, whose name was Freda Collins, explained that Mrs Rees was staying with her sister in Wales and was not expected back before the weekend. She hinted that the Reeses were not the happiest of couples, and that Megan Rees seemed to spend a lot of time at her sister's.

Thanking the woman for her help, Will and Ashe walked back through the garden gate, and stood chatting while Mrs Collins closed her front door. As soon as the woman was out of sight, but before she had time to go into the front room and check to see what they were doing, Will tugged at Ashe's coat sleeve and the two detectives slipped back to the front door of number seventeen and stood concealed in the recessed porch.

Will touched Ashe's sleeve again, and pointed at the bay window next to them. Ashe was puzzled for a second, then realised that from their position they could see reflected in the glass the bay window of number fifteen. The lace curtain moved slightly, and was moved aside a few inches. The blurred image of Freda Collins peered out. Satisfied that the two policemen had left, she allowed the curtain to fall back into place. Will gave the young man a knowing wink and, fishing in his pocket, took out the ring of keys that he had removed from Rees's trouser pocket.

Inside the house the chequered black and white tiled hall struck cold beneath their feet, and the dark brown wallpaper was depressing and unwelcoming. A large framed sepia picture of a stag, bearing the legend 'Monarch of the Glen', glared accusingly down at the intruders from the staircase.

'Anybody home?' Will's peremptory demand made Ashe jump.

'Police! Anybody at home?' The repeated question echoed hollowly around the hallway. Satisfied that they were alone, Will went to the stairs and made his way up to the first floor.

The house was surprisingly large. Upstairs there were four bedrooms, while on the ground floor, off the passageway that led to the back kitchen and scullery, were two sitting rooms and a breakfast room. It was in the breakfast room that their search revealed something of interest.

Rees obviously used the room as his office. In one corner near the window, looking out onto an ill-kept back garden, stood a locked roll top desk. Will took a heavy clasp knife from his jacket pocket and inserted the blade under the lid next to the lock, levering it sharply upwards. With a resounding crack that sounded through the empty house, the roll top came undone. Will pushed the shutter back, revealing inside an untidy mass of papers, some of which were letters, the remainder bills and invoices.

Lifting the papers up to make a closer examination, Will saw that they were piled on top of four rectangular grey cardboard boxes, each about eleven inches by eight. They were the sort of box in which a printer would deliver an order.

Watching the superintendent open the first box, Bernard saw a frown crease Will's brow; then he gave a low whistle. Sitting down in the office chair next to the desk, Will stared at the contents of the box for several seconds before reaching out and opening each of the others in turn. The first contained a block of headed notepaper in the name of Weston and Meachin, Building Suppliers, Sheffield. The contents of the second bore the heading of Watson Bros, Plumbers, Swinegate, Leeds, the third that of a firm of tiling contractors in Glasgow. Will pursed his lips. 'Well, well, Bernard,' he murmured. 'We now know who the second man is in the war hospital fraud.'

'Get someone up to the hospital and turn out the medical records of any patient, including officers, who's been treated either for mental problems or who's been discharged and might have a grievance against the staff or the hospital in general.'

Harry nodded. It was a long shot. The soldiers who were treated at the war hospital came from all sorts of disparate units and backgrounds. It was probably best to start with the ones who were suffering from shell shock, what were they called, 'neurasthenic cases'. 'I'll get Clarrie and Nate over there as soon as possible.' He tugged at the ends of his heavy walrus moustache, pondering whether or not to say anything. Despite the fact that he was a heavy smoker there was no trace of nicotine staining in the silver whiskers. A cool autumn sun shone through the windows of the detective office. 'Not strictly my business, but you should watch out for Bathurst.'

Will replaced the trench knife with the damning 'FK' carved on the haft on Harry's desk. If ever its authenticity had been in doubt, in view of the recent incident it was obvious to everyone now that it could not be the weapon used to kill Lottie Groves.

'Tell me about him.'

'Came here from Leeds just after the South African War. He'd been a reporter on one of the northern papers. The word was that they weren't sorry to see him go. The editor of the *Gazette* before him, Charles Kerrigan Kemp, had to retire after a stroke. Charlie wasn't a bad old boy, good news man and fair in his reporting. Died about two years after he retired. Bathurst is different. He makes it up as he goes along. The problem is that he's got more connections than the Midland Railway.'

Listening to the inspector's words, Will gazed idly down onto the narrow street below. A young policeman who had just walked out of the station, notebook in hand, was engaged in conversation with a vagrant sitting on a cardboard box in the shop doorway opposite. Will recognised the diminutive figure of Tuppenny Rice, the oversized greatcoat trailing around his ankles. With a deferential touching of his hand to the tattered balaclava, he picked up his box and trudged off down the road.

A second figure appeared on the police station steps and, with a quick word to the constable, disappeared in the opposite direction.

'Speak of the devil,' Will said. 'He's just leaving the building. Three guesses who he's been to see.'

'Mr Bathurst, the editor of the *Gazette*, has been in to see me this morning, Will. He's somewhat perturbed that we have a multiple killer loose in the town.'

Sydney Hall-Johnson paced across the elegant Wilton carpet of his large office on the first floor of the Long Street building, carefully studying the mirror finish of his highly polished toe caps. Will watched him from the depths of one of the armchairs next to the room's ornate fireplace. The expensive suit hung in baggy folds on the chief constable's tall round-shouldered frame. He had a habit of dipping his head and looking at his shoes when he walked, the less charitable among his staff contending that he had cultivated this practice in order to avoid speaking to people as he passed them in the corridors of the building. Combined with his spare figure and thinning, lank sandy hair, the overall effect was that of a scrawny vulture, Will thought.

'I'd like you to attend the Watch Committee meeting with me in . . .' Hall-Johnson consulted his pocket watch '. . . about half an hour in order to give them a breakdown of what's happening in respect of your enquiries.'

Will grimaced. The fortnightly Watch Committee meetings were held either to pass resolutions in respect of the management of the town's police force, or to initiate a witch hunt when things went badly. It was fairly obvious that today's meeting would be for the latter purpose. What you mean, he thought, is that I can deflect any criticism from you for the lack of police progress. Why has this man not been apprehended, Mr Mardlin? How can you have allowed this man to kill again, Mr Mardlin? Where will he strike next, Mr Mardlin? I should have been a fireman, he thought: no one ever asks the fire chief why he didn't prevent a fire from starting.

The chief constable paused in the middle of his patrol of the Wilton, and in a practised heel and toe movement turned around to walk back towards the superintendent. 'We need to catch this soldier quickly, Will, before he has the chance to kill again. I'm beginning to think that possibly you released the man Kempin a little prematurely. Perhaps if he'd been committed for a while until more enquiries had been made . . . ?'

Will's jaw set in a stubborn line. He could hear Gilmour Bathurst whispering in the chief constable's ear. The speech was almost word for word what the fat newspaper man had said to him in the factory.

'First of all, sir, two killings do not mean that we have a multiple killer. The same man could have killed twice for a specific reason and may never kill again. Alternatively this second murder may be a copycat affair. Someone who wanted Rees dead and decided to try and make it look as if the same person killed him as killed Charlotte Groves. Secondly, we don't know for certain that the killer's a soldier. The fact that he used a trench knife could be a red herring. Personally I'm happy that Kempin didn't kill either Charlotte Groves or Ivor Rees.'

'So what progress have you made?' asked Hall-Johnson pointedly.

'Get that little shit Kempin back in here!' That Superintendent Mardlin was in a foul mood was plain to the detectives gathered in the main office awaiting his return from the Watch Committee meeting. Having spent an hour going over the finer points of how a murder enquiry was conducted, while being careful not to give away any relevant details that he did not wish to become public property on Kelsford Golf Course, Will was totally frustrated. Glaring balefully around the room, his eye settled on Bernard Ashe, watching him apprehensively from the seat behind his desk. 'Bernard, you and Nathan get off of your arses and get down to the barracks. Find Kempin and bring him in here. I want to know where he was last night, and if he knew Ivor Rees. Even if he's got an absolutely cast-iron alibi you lock him up and throw away the key for at least two days. If the chief constable, the Watch Committee, Fat Bastard Bathurst, or the man who delivers the bread to the station canteen want to know why he hasn't been charged, tell them to go and screw themselves.'

Cleaver and Ashe, grabbing their coats, left the office as unobtrusively as possible.

After they had left Will slumped down in a vacant chair, glowering at Harry North and the two detective sergeants. Harry returned his stare. Neither Greasley nor Conway broke the silence. That the superintendent was looking for a fight was obvious. The unspoken thought in both their minds was that he had never seen Harry North lose his temper, which if he started laying into them unjustly was exactly what would happen.

'Has anybody got a drink?' Will's question took them all by surprise. 'Come on, I've never worked in an office before where there wasn't an emergency bottle stashed in somebody's drawer.'

The tension eased out of the room. Clarrie Greasley leaned his chair back precariously on two legs and, reaching into the cupboard behind him, produced a bottle of Ballantine's Scotch Whisky. Harry left the room and returned a minute later with four tumblers. Locking the office door, he poured a stiff measure for each of them.

'So where do we go from here?' asked Will, studying the amber liquid in his glass.

The meeting with the town councillors had been as irritating as it was frustrating. In fairness to Hall-Johnson, the chief constable had spoken up in support of the Detective Department, and Will in particular. It was the inane and patronising attitude of some of those present that irked Will. Rupert Withers, a successful hosiery manufacturer, had insisted on pursuing the question of why a policeman had not been on duty in Clipstone Row to apprehend the murderer as he left the scene of the crime. Amos Painter, a Labour member of the council who owned the coal wharf adjacent to the canal basin, demanded that an 'officer from Scotland Yard be engaged to resolve matters'. This motion was unanimously defeated when Will pointed out that such a course of action would incur huge costs, and mentioned that in his experience Metropolitan officers fared badly in such enquiries as they were inevitably totally dependent upon the cooperation of the local police. Cooperation which, Will privately resolved, would most definitely not be forthcoming.

Harry drew deeply on a newly lit cigarette before throwing the packet to Bert Conway who, taking one, passed it on to Clarrie Greasley. The four of them had spent the last hour examining every detail of the two recent murders in a vain attempt to find some tangible connection. Mardlin rubbed a hand across his temples, waiting for them to light their cigarettes before continuing.

126

They had gone over the same ground time and again until his head was beginning to ache, both with exertion and the effects of the whisky.

'We've got two murders that could be tied together. First we have a similar method of killing and possibly the same weapon. Both Groves and Rees were butchered with a trench knife. Groves was a nurse at the Kelsford War Hospital. Rees was working as a contractor there. We know that Rees, along with Carstairs, was involved in a fraud at the hospital. It remains to be seen how extensive that is.'

'There's another aspect.' Greasley blew on the end of his cigarette. 'All three of them are dead. Not just Groves and Rees but Carstairs as well. It's the one thing that they all have in common. Lottie Groves and Ivor Rees were murdered, Byron Carstairs was killed in an air raid – but they're all dead.'

Will examined the sergeant's statement for a moment before replying. 'It's a valid point, Clarrie. Carstairs was killed in an air raid, but as you rightly say, dead is dead. Question is, if he hadn't been killed would our man have had to eliminate him as well? If the answer's yes, then everything that's gone on is to do with the hospital fraud. For some reason that we need to find out, Lottie had to go, then a fluke took Carstairs out of the equation, which left Rees. Rees wasn't particularly bright. He knew that an enquiry had begun, and had been paid a visit by Bernard, but still didn't have enough oil in his lamp to get rid of the stuff at his house that would tie him in to it. Our man would know that he was a weak link and couldn't risk him being nicked. By the same token, after he'd killed him he didn't bother to go round to Meadows Road and remove the evidence.'

'He wanted us to know Rees was involved.' Bert Conway stubbed his cigarette out in an overflowing ashtray next to his chair. 'He wants us to think that Carstairs is – or was – the main man, and that Rees and Lottie were probably the only others involved. We accept that – and no more fraud enquiry.'

'No. I think you're wrong.' Elbows on the desk, Harry leaned forward and rested his chin on his hands before looking at the others. 'When the accounting's done and the paperwork's in – which should be within the next few days – I think we're going to be looking at a lot more money in this deal than we realise. Carstairs and Rees I can see places for. Lottie's an unknown quantity. The killer, whoever he may be, is also in there somewhere – and crucially for whatever reason cannot simply disappear. That makes three people that we know of. I think there's probably one more, someone who could sink our man, and the murderer's sending him a message.'

'Also, we're talking about two murders when we all know that there are three.' Bert Conway looked round the room for confirmation.

Will nodded in agreement. 'Yes. Leonard Belcher was sent to Izzy Feinemann's to redeem the ornaments that Lottie Groves pawned. The question is, did the killer actually know what she'd hocked? The fact that they weren't there any longer didn't save the lad's life. He could identify the person who sent him, and that was sufficient to sign his death warrant.'

As an afterthought he added quietly, 'It also means, of course, that we're not the only ones after those nick-nacks, and that's very, very important.'

A footfall in the passage outside the office, accompanied by the clicking on the stone floor of the steel segs that he wore on the heels of his boots, announced the presence of Eric Broughton. Finding himself locked out, the boy tapped respectfully and waited. Harry got up from his chair and opened the door. 'Telephone call, sir.' The lad's curious gaze flicked around the room. When the detective office was locked and people were in there, it usually signified that something was going on. Spotting the bottle of Ballantine's and the half empty glasses his question was answered. Secret conference. He shot Superintendent Mardlin a glance. Mr Chote would never have allowed whisky, not even at a secret conference.

Harry moved in front of the boy to cut off his view. 'All right. I'll come downstairs,' he said, pushing Eric back into the corridor.

Five minutes later he was back, a grim expression on his face. 'Kempin's legged it.'

'What do you mean Kempin's legged it?' demanded Will.

'Nate and Bernard arrived at Sevastopol Barracks, and were told by the duty officer that if they could find Kempin they were welcome to him. Apparently he went out on a four hour pass last night and failed to return at ten o'clock. He's been posted absent without official leave – AWOL.'

Will swore under his breath. That was all he needed. The press would have a field day with this latest development.

'It gets worse.' Harry passed across an early afternoon edition of the *Kelsford Gazette* that he had picked up. Will looked at the front page.

Police Hunt For 'The Soldier'

Earlier today the mutilated body of local businessman Mr Ivor Rees was found brutally slain at his factory premises in Clipstone Row. In a statement to our correspondent this morning the Chief Constable of the Kelsford Borough Police, Mr Sydney Hall-Johnson, said that it is thought that Mr Rees probably disturbed the man while he was engaged upon some nefarious activity. Because of the use of a trench knife as the weapon with which to perpetrate his dreadful crimes, this man has become known as 'The Soldier'. In order to effect his safe escape the killer inflicted injuries upon Mr Rees too horrible to describe.

The case bears distinct similarity to the recent murder at her home in Devonshire Gardens of Miss Charlotte Groves, a nurse at the Kelsford War Hospital. On that occasion also, it would seem that Miss Groves disturbed a man in an upstairs room and was killed in an horrific manner.

The Chief Constable, who is of the opinion that the killer has received military training, is advising all citizens of Kelsford to be on their guard until this man has been detained.

Will threw the paper onto the table for the others to read, and with a deep sigh emptied the remnants of the Ballantine's bottle into the four glasses.

'What is this bollocks?' demanded Conway. 'Disturbed someone in the premises . . . nurse . . . the fucking Soldier!'

Will gave another sigh, this time of resignation. 'Why', he asked sourly, 'does Gilmour Bathurst walk with a limp?'

'Because', answered Harry, echoing Will's tone, 'he's got Sydney Hall-Johnson in his pocket.'

The following day was Sunday. Irene Deladier sipped at her breakfast coffee as she turned the pages of the *Gazette*. The majority of the front page was given over to the murder in Clipstone Row.

A short paragraph at the bottom of the second page berated thieves who, the previous evening, had broken into the offices of the *Gazette* and removed several pieces of photographic equipment. Amongst the items stolen were pictures taken at the scene of the recent fatal accident in the High Street. Curiously, not only had the burglars removed the photographs but they had also taken the glass plates from which they were produced.

Setting the paper aside, she buttered a piece of toast. Unlike Will, Irene had slept soundly the previous night, and awoken refreshed and clear minded. For some time now she had been taking stock of her life, trying to decide exactly what it was that she wanted to do. Several things had become clear to her, not the least of which being that for the foreseeable future she was going to be in Kelsford. With this in mind she had thrown herself into helping out with voluntary work in the town. In addition to acting as an interpreter for the Belgian and French refugees who were still arriving, and working as an ambulance driver, she was also active in fund raising for the War Hospital Supplies Committee, which was dedicated to providing little extras for the men who were recuperating before returning to their units at the Front.

Personally, Irene was finding that as time passed she was adjusting to being a widow. Gradually she was coming to terms with the fact that Jean-Claude was now beyond her reach and that in order to survive she needed to move on. Her isolation was emphasised by the fact that apart from her father's immediate relatives, Ann and Reuben Simmonds, she was, despite being born of English parents as much a foreigner here as Matthias and Béatrice Palmaerts. Apart from the occasional holiday visit to Kelsford to see her aunt and uncle, Irene's life had been spent in France.

It was the intense loneliness of her situation that Irene found hardest to deal with. From the first time that she had met Will at the coffee house, despite their age difference, Irene had felt herself drawn to the policeman. Apart from the physical attraction, he was someone with whom she felt instinctively safe.

Sipping her coffee, Irene skimmed an article concerning the health of the troops in Gallipoli, her mind elsewhere. She had not consciously planned to have an affair with Will. One minute she had been making her way through the railway carriage, the next she was lying on the floor beneath him while the world erupted in a terrifying explosion. When she opened her eyes she was conscious only of the excitement pumping through her system and being aware of an uncontrollable desire.

Although brought up in the remote French countryside, by the time she was a teenager Irene was by no means uninformed about the facts of life. When she was fifteen one of the chambermaids working at her parent's château, Claudine Morel, who was a year older than her, had become pregnant by one of the village youths, and had had to leave her mother's service.

Irene's two closest companions were her brother Sam and Stefan. Often when Sam was otherwise occupied Stefan and Irene spent their days out riding together in the surrounding hills. Inevitably, hidden away in some secluded hayrick or mountaineer's hut, the two teenagers had on more than one occasion indulged in mild sexual experimentation. Eminently aware of the fate that had overtaken Claudine they always restricted their activities, by mutual agreement neither of them ever seeking to progress to full intercourse. The interlude came to an end when Stefan left the château to undertake military service in the French Army. When his conscription was completed, and possibly suspecting that an affair could be brewing, Irene's parents suggested to Mirka and Daniel that their son would benefit from a university education, and Stefan was spirited away to Vienna.

When Irene was, sent off to complete her education at the expensive École de Paris pour Demoiselles in Paris, she encountered another of life's previously unsuspected mysteries. To her surprise, several of the older girls, cloistered together in the rarefied atmosphere of a young ladies' finishing school, formed intimate relationships. Things were brought into focus during her middle term when a highly secret and well-thumbed novel entitled *Love in the Harem* was passed surreptitiously around the students, to be read in the dormitory after lights out. The author claimed to have shared the pleasures of harem life, explaining in graphic and erotic detail the pleasures to be derived from the love of one woman for another. While finding the subject mildly interesting, the prospect of an affair with a member of her own sex held little attraction for Irene, and as such she chose not to include herself in the select group of girls who, either from curiosity or natural inclination, became involved in lesbian affairs.

Therefore, when she began her relationship with Jean-Claude, Irene although still a virgin was not as unworldly as many other young women of her age, and by the time the couple had been together for a few months they were fully engaged in an affair. Now, a year after receiving the telegram informing her that her husband had been killed in action, Irene Deladier was keenly feeling the need for physical involvement.

Irene had not seen her cousin since the night of the raid, and wondered if James Simmonds had picked up from the newspaper the piece concerning the death of Byron Carstairs. At the railway station she had noticed that he was not wearing his artificial hand, choosing instead to pin the cuff of his shirt sleeve over the stump. James had mentioned earlier in the day that his wound was causing him some pain, and that he would be working from home for a while. She wondered if the discomfort was a contributory factor to his rudeness towards Sam during the reception at the hospital.

Thinking of her brother reminded her that she needed to discuss with Béatrice the menu for dinner. Sam seemed to be preoccupied about something that he refused to discuss. That this was to do with the recent fatal accident in the High Street Irene was fairly certain. She was also aware that he had been to a meeting at the police station with Will, which, although he would not elaborate, she had the impression had gone badly.

In an attempt to raise her brother's spirits, Irene had invited him to come for dinner, together with the two scientists with whom he was working. She had promised to ask Béatrice to cook something Flemish for Monsieur Kändler, and if the meal progressed late into the evening the guests could stay overnight, returning to the mill the next morning. Perhaps after a good dinner and some of the fine Côtes du Rhone wine that Mme Palmaerts had unearthed, Sam might be a little more forthcoming. It intrigued her that his worries appeared to emanate from the nature of the work being undertaken by Kändler and Duggan.

The ringing of the telephone in the hall came to her ears, followed moments later by a discreet tap on the breakfast room door.

'Telephone call for you, madam,' announced the housemaid. 'A Mr Mardlin.'

Irene placed the coffee cup on top of the newspaper, and with a quiet smile made her way out into the hallway.

Chapter Thirteen

Off the east coast of Scotland, taking advantage of an unusually calm sea and a beautiful summer's morning, the U39 lay hove to on the surface of the North Sea charging its batteries, while the crew took the opportunity to open the hatches and 'clean ship'.

On the bridge Klaus Diessbacher and his second in command Oberleutnant Franz-Georg Heinig leaned companionably against the rail of the bridge on the conning tower. Despite the sunshine it was cool enough on the open sea for them both to be wearing reefer jackets. Fishing about in an inside pocket, Heinig withdrew a leather tobacco pouch and short-stemmed meerschaum pipe. He turned out of the breeze and worked the flame from a brass petrol lighter back and forth across the coarse dark mixture until it was burning to his satisfaction. Since the outbreak of war every engineer in Germany with a lathe and an hour to spare had been making cigarette and pipe lighters from empty cartridge cases or any other scrap brass they could lay their hands on, to give as gifts to men leaving for the war. He ran his thumb absently over the engraved emblem of the U-Boat service, 'für Kaiser und Reich'. It would have been impossible to keep a match alight even in today's light breeze, but the ingenious metal shroud around the petrol-soaked wick allowed the flame to burn unimpeded.

The meerschaum clamped firmly between his teeth, Heinig turned his attention back to the horizon. Diessbacher, after a perfunctory glance at the empty sky, sucked in his breath and scowled down at the lookout in the stern, who was standing straddle-legged against the gentle movement of the boat in the light swell, a pair of heavy Zeiss binoculars in his hands. 'Anything, Peterson?' Even in these conditions he had to shout for the man to hear him.

'Nothing, sir. Empty as a nun's bed.'

'We shouldn't stay here much longer, Franzie.' As always when the U-boat was on the surface in hostile waters, the captain was uneasy.

Most of the crew were on deck, enjoying their first fresh air for several days. Some washing had been hung like a string of signal flags between two temporary poles on the starboard side, while for'ard of the bridge Erwin Fahr, the boat's gunnery officer, had ordered the removal of the waterproof cover from the heavy one hundred and five millimetre deck gun in order to check it over. Looking at the men working, Diessbacher was not concerned with the gun's potential to sink a small surface vessel within minutes, but how long it would take Fahr and the boat's gunner, Seaman Lothar Krüger bent over the elevation wheel of the weapon, to get the cover back on and secured down. Similarly aft, Guntër Schmidt and Steuermann Jacob Kramski were engaged in oiling the swivel on the boat's heavy calibre machine gun.

'Jacob,' he bellowed, 'Get the covers back on her and fasten down – machen Sie es schnell!'

'Ja, Herr Kapitän. Sofort!'

Captain Diessbacher was proud of his vessel and the men under his command. The Thirties class submarine commissioned out of the Kiel shipyards earlier that year was one of the most modern U-boats in the German High Seas Fleet. Sixty seven metres long, its two huge diesel and electric engines gave the U39 a surface speed of sixteen and a half knots, while submerged it was capable of almost ten knots. With its engines throttled back to conserve fuel, the boat had a range of over four thousand miles – which was becoming a problem. For the last seven and a half weeks U39 had been ranging back and forth across a four hundred square mile sector of the North Sea, avoiding contact with any Allied shipping and restricting radio communications to a minimum. Apart from a brief spell in the maintenance yards at Bruges, when the men were allowed an evening's run ashore under the close eye of Bosun Grönemeyer, the crew had in Diessbacher's opinion been cooped up in the sub's hull insert: quite long enough.

Although the crew was aware that this was not the normal 'seek and find' patrol, only the captain and his second in command were aware of the reason for the cloak of secrecy under which they were sailing: to remain off the English coast as a communications link between the man who they had recently transferred to the *Viking Tun* and the High Command in Berlin. Boredom, an ever-present fact of U-boat life, was starting to eat into the crew's morale. It did not help that the vessel had previously spent two months cruising in Mediterranean sunshine – the nearest thing to perfection that a wartime posting could offer. The news that they had to exchange their idyllic lifestyle for a North Sea station had not been well received. The change of climate and enforced inactivity were making the men restive.

Klaus Diessbacher and Gustav Grönemeyer were the only professional seamen aboard, which bothered the captain. Although he had seen active service, none of the rest of the crew had ever been under fire; even Grönemeyer, with thirty years' sea time behind him, had been involved in little more than police actions off the coast of East Africa. However well trained they might be, it was one thing to sink a couple of unarmed merchantmen running supplies to Allied bases in Egypt, and quite another to play hide and seek in the North Sea with the British Home Fleet.

'We need to get moving, Franzie,' Diessbacher growled to his companion. 'Go down on deck and tell Erwin to get that gun secured. I want to be out of here in no more than five minutes.' Heinig nodded his agreement, and was turning to throw his leg over the deck ladder when a bellow from the stern lookout stopped him in his tracks.

'Aircraft three o'clock!'

Grabbing his binoculars from the rack in front of him, Diessbacher threw them up to his eyes and searched the sky on the starboard side of the boat. Clearly visible, skimming in at wave-top level, was the silhouette of a large biplane. Heinig slammed his fist against the attack alarm button and began hurling orders to the men on the deck to secure the open hatches. His words were lost in the ear-splitting blast emitted by the klaxon and were unnecessary: with a precision that was the result of the interminable drills to which they had been subjected, the crewmen had the job completed in seconds.

Taking one last look round, Diessbacher threw himself onto the bridge ladder and slid down into the control centre beneath him. Already the green emergency lighting was coming up to strength as the engine room crew threw the switches on the generators, and the eighteen hundred horsepower diesel engine went to half-speed in anticipation of the Captain's order to crash dive.

The aircraft, flying with the sun behind it to make detection harder, had been about five miles away when Peterson picked it up. If it were carrying a full bomb load its approach speed would be not much more than about eighty miles an hour, but that was still less than four minutes: it was going to be a very close-run thing.

Men were plummeting down the ladder from the deck. Counting them in, after two and a half minutes Diessbacher knew that there were only the gunnery officer and Franzie Heinig to come. Deciding that he could wait no longer, he opened the voice pipe and yelled into it the order to make an emergency dive. As the engines kicked from half to full power, thrusting the vessel forward and down, the two remaining officers, seawater streaming from their soaking uniforms, came crashing down the ladder. With a sickening lurch the bows plunged under the surface of the ocean.

The whoop of excitement emitted by the young pilot of the Short 184 reconnaissance bomber on sighting the U39 was lost in the aircraft's slipstream, but his frantic gestures were immediately picked up by his observer in the cockpit behind him. Slewing the aircraft round to put the sun behind them, Lieutenant Gerard Horton began a steep descent to bring them onto an attack course.

Returning to their base at Rosyth, Horton and his observer, Lieutenant Walter Callister, had just completed a routine submarine patrol over the North Sea. After three months of these sorties, endlessly quartering hundreds of miles of empty ocean, their expectations of actually spotting an enemy vessel were low, so to catch a U-boat exposed and stationary was almost unbelievable.

At two hundred feet Horton eased back the stick and opened the throttle wide to make the final five mile dash to his target. Dropping down further until the seaplane's floats were almost skimming the waves, the two men could clearly see men running for the safety of the conning tower. It was going to be relatively easy, thought Horton, as he saw with huge relief that the German sailors were not attempting to man the heavy machine gun on the aft deck. Unable at this angle to deploy the aircraft's single Lewis gun, Callister could not spray the deck with covering fire, and as the aircraft was only feet above the surface and flying a straight course it presented a very tempting target: a steady machine gunner could have brought it down before the bomb could be released. Still with some distance to go, Horton and Callister saw the boat sinking out of sight. When just the superstructure was visible the pilot released his torpedo, watching it drop gracefully into the water directly over the submarine's hull. He took his aircraft back up to a safe height and began to circle over the dive site. The torpedo was set to detonate on impact, but the full throttle roar of the plane's engine prevented him from hearing an underwater explosion. Even so, Horton was certain that they had hit the sub at point blank range, and remained over the target area to look for debris.

Franz-Georg Heinig hung on to the handles of the periscope columns as the submarine, tilted at an angle of almost forty five degrees, plunged beneath the surface, and the engine room switched smoothly from diesel power to electric. According to his calculations the stern should just have cleared the surface. As he quickly calculated their chances of evading the attacking aircraft, a soft, almost melodic, scraping noise resounded through the hull, and a slight tremor interrupted the submarine's motion.

'Gott in Himmel, that was a fucking torpedo!' Hands tightly gripping the controls of the steering mechanism, Helmsman Kramski put into words what everyone on board had realised the moment they heard the missile glance against the stern rail.

'Silence,' Diessbacher hissed menacingly. He was praying that the aeroplane had only one torpedo on board.

At fifty metres – the sub's maximum submersion depth – the boat's engineer brought the dive to a halt and levelled out. Diessbacher's main worry was that the attacking bomber might have sufficient fuel to remain in the area and could attract the attention of a British warship. On his instructions a fifty litre drum of engine oil, its lid opened, and several articles of the men's clothing and bedding stripped from the nearest bunks were jettisoned through the port stern torpedo tube.

From a height of three hundred feet the shiny blue-black stain spreading slowly over the surface of the waves and glinting brightly in the sunshine was unmistakable. A few moments later the airmen were able to make out other items of flotsam in the waves. Turning in his seat, Lieutenant Horton grinned at his companion and, making a thumbs up sign, banked the aeroplane over and set a course for Rosyth. He took a pencil that was wedged into the fastening strap of his revolver holster, and scribbled quickly in the margin of his flight map the designation that he had read so clearly on the bridge of the submarine during the last seconds of his bombing run: U39.

Ralph Gresham touched a hand to his elegantly striped Guards tie and glanced quickly at his wristwatch. One minute to spare. Tapping softly on the panelled door, without waiting for a reply he entered the first-floor suite of the Grosvenor Hotel and closed it behind him. 'Sorry I'm late, Sir Rowland. The traffic in Oxford Street's horrendous.'

Leigh-Hunt waved a hand dismissively 'Take a seat, Ralph.' He indicated a trolley set out with canapés and sandwiches, along with a silver coffee pot and china cups. 'Help yourself to refreshments.'

Pouring himself coffee, Gresham dropped onto the oversized leather settee opposite the diplomat's armchair.

Sir Rowland stretched his legs and adjusted his pince-nez. 'Bayliss contacted me yesterday. Says there's been a development at their end, which presumably means that Room 40's come across something. I've asked him to join us at half past eleven. Meantime, what progress is being made in Kelsford?'

'Kändler and Duggan appear to be nearing a breakthrough. They're working on something called an organo-phosphate, from which it should be possible to produce a gas in large quantities. It's not dissimilar to the stuff that we and the Germans are both using, except it's a hundred times more potent, and it's heavier than air. For the time being they've codenamed it MD19. At the moment they're trying to achieve the optimum method of delivery, and if they can crack that it'll be feasible to run some field trials, possibly around Christmas. I have to say that the result of the Kelsford fireman accidentally inhaling a small amount was most encouraging.'

'Did you have much trouble with the local police over that?'

'No. The detective superintendent's a sensible man, name of Mardlin. As expected he'd arranged for photographs to be taken of the canisters, but they're now in our possession. There were some newspaper pictures of the scene of the accident – and again we've recovered those, along with the plates from the newspaper offices. None of them showed anything compromising. I had a chat with the superintendent, and I'm quite sure that he'll co-operate if anything else happens.'

Something in Gresham's tone caught Leigh-Hunt's attention. He raised a quizzical eyebrow.

Gresham flashed the silver-haired man a quick smile. 'He's having an affair with Major Norton's sister. Came to us by accident really. We have the usual set-up in place in the town. Rented shop converted into a social club for the Belgian refugees, where they can gather to drink coffee and play cards, buy the odd bottle of wine. The steward, who's also Belgian, was recruited soon after he was admitted to this country. For a small consideration he finds himself in regular employment in good living accommodation, and generally does better than the rest of his contemporaries. In return he tells us what's going on. He was delivering a bottle of wine to Madame Palmaerts's employer's house a couple of weeks ago and spotted Irene Deladier, all comfy-cosy, letting Mardlin in through the back door.'

Rowland Leigh-Hunt nodded sagely. 'Excellent. A word of warning, though. You'll need to be careful that Norton isn't telling his sister things that don't concern her.'

A tap on the door announced the arrival of Commander Bayliss. Leigh-Hunt paused to stare out of the picture window at the busy street below. A taxicab halted in the middle of the road outside the hotel to allow a well-dressed young woman to descend. While she was paying the cab driver a small uniformed bell-boy in a low-crowned pillbox hat, secured firmly under his chin by a thin strap, ran down the hotel steps to gather the bags of shopping that she had deposited. When this war is over, thought Leigh-Hunt, the world will be a different place. The streets of London will be crowded with taxi cabs like this one. No more hansom cabs or horse-drawn carts clopping sedately along; progress would see to that.

He realised that Bayliss was speaking to him. 'We have a problem, Sir Rowland. It seems the Germans might be on to us.'

Leigh-Hunt stiffened slightly and continued to contemplate the street scene before turning to face the other two men, his face an impassive mask. 'You'd better tell us about it.'

'The signals section at Room 40 have picked up an intercept through the Swedish Roundabout from Berlin, routed via New York to Madrid, which specifically refers to Project 19,' Bayliss said flatly.

Located in the heart of London in the Old Admiralty Building, Room 40 had been set up by the Royal Navy shortly after war was declared, to intercept and decode enemy wireless telegraph signals. Fortuitously, two important factors that aided the work of the cryptographers immensely entered the equation at an early stage in the proceedings. The first was that at the outbreak of war, in order to restrict Germany's communications network, the underwater telegraphic cables that linked Germany with France, Spain and America were cut and dredged by the British Navy. The second was the capture, by the Russians from a German cruiser in the Baltic, of a set of code books relating to the three principal German Embassy and military ciphers.

As a result of the cutting of the cables, German High Command in Berlin was forced to send embassy telegrams via the Swedish Diplomatic Service to America, for retransmission to their diplomatic embassies worldwide. Although the Swedes were officially neutral, it was well known in intelligence circles that they were using their status as a cloak to assist the Germans whenever possible. However, signals transmitted by the Swedes to the United States had to pass along the Atlantic cable, which had been deliberately left in place. The reason for it remaining untouched was that the British Post Office had access to the cable and could monitor all transmissions. It was therefore a simple matter for every telegraphic signal sent from Stockholm to the German Embassy in America to be intercepted and passed to Room 40, who set to work decoding the material. Similarly, the replies from the embassies to Berlin were also monitored and read. The system soon became known in the British Secret Service as the Swedish Roundabout.

'Two days ago a signal from Berlin to the German Embassy in the States was intercepted,' continued Bayliss. 'It made specific reference to research work being carried out by the Allies into the production of nerve gas. The disturbing thing is that it referred directly to the research by name as Project 19.'

'What's the origin of the signal?' asked Gresham.

'Now that's interesting.' The commander gave a satisfied smile. 'Yesterday an RNAS reconnaissance plane on coastal patrol a couple of hundred miles off the Firth of Forth caught a sub on the surface. The crew attacked it and they're claiming a kill. The pilot's adamant that the number on the conning tower was U39. According to our latest intelligence U39 should be in the Mediterranean, which means that it's only recently been brought up into northern waters. Its presence seems to have been kept a total secret. According to our source in Potsdam, it's not been added into either the North Sea or Flanders flotillas, and the transfer's not been notified to his office. This is highly unusual, and can only mean that its presence is clandestine.'

'How certain are we that it's been sunk?' demanded Gresham.

'Good question.' Bayliss shook his head slowly. 'These pilots all want a kill. Lieutenant Commander Horton claims he scored a single torpedo hit on the boat beneath the water as it was diving. There was no sound of explosion, and neither he nor his observer saw the hull break up. He's basing his claim on oil and debris coming to the surface a few minutes after the event. They could have scored a hit, in which case the boat is at the bottom of the sea, or the U-boat captain might have jettisoned some items to make it look as if the sub had broken up under water.'

Leigh-Hunt's usually urbane expression was replaced by one of grim concern. 'This means two things. First, if the Germans know about Project 19, then we must assume they know where it's located, which in turn indicates they've got an agent in place. Second, a single agent somewhere in the Midlands wouldn't warrant a submarine being secretly detached to the North Sea. No, that indicates the presence of another agent or more likely a controller near the east coast who needs a direct line to Berlin. Without doubt this is the biggest intelligence undertaking of the war,' he continued carefully. 'We must presume there's an agent in place in Kelsford, and whoever it is will be deep – not some newcomer they've sent in to try out. The Germans can't afford to have him exposed. The second man, who was probably picked up and brought here from Wilhelmshaven by U-boat, will in my opinion definitely be the agent's controller – someone authorised to make decisions.'

Bayliss raised his hand an inch or two, and the older man nodded at him. 'The sinking or otherwise of the sub is a mixed blessing. If it has we've bought ourselves a certain amount of time while another one's recalled to Wilhelmshaven for briefing and sent out again – at least a week, probably two. But it would be better for us if the U39 hasn't been sunk, because knowing its identity we can monitor any signals and track its position, which gives us a huge advantage.'

Gresham nodded in agreement and took up Bayliss's train of thought. 'The standard way of liaising with a submarine is by boat. For obvious reasons a sub can't come in too close to shore, so the rendezvous point is usually a mile or two out to sea with a trawler.'

Leigh-Hunt removed his pince-nez and withdrew a small white handkerchief from his jacket pocket, before polishing the lenses absently. Gresham and Bayliss sat in silence. Leigh-Hunt was thinking not just about this new information but also about a rather more personal matter. While the newly established military intelligence organisation was beginning to function well, the navy's code-breaking section in Room 40 under Captain 'Blinker' Hall had been allowed to remain independent, at the same time becoming of absolutely critical importance. He had to bring the code breakers into his own sphere of control, Leigh-Hunt decided. Had Winston not been in such bad odour over the Dardanelles fiasco it would have been a simple matter, but now he had to be a little more subtle: a quiet chat and the promise of an early promotion to rear admiral for Reginald Hall should be a starting point. 'Fishing port then,' he declared, pince-nez back in place. 'The submarine was sighted off the Firth of Forth and Kelsford is about two hours by train from the east coast, so that's where you start looking.'

'Hull, Grimsby, Scarborough, places like that are too big, with too much coastal traffic,' speculated Bayliss. 'I suggest we need to be thinking about somewhere quieter: Yorkshire coast, Northumbria, possibly even one of the Scottish ports.'

'Then I suggest you get on with it, gentlemen,' Leigh-Hunt replied bleakly.

Part Two

Chapter Fourteen

W hat time are you on duty tonight, Tom?' Emma Weldon stood back from the kitchen sink and stretched to ease her aching back. Washing clothes in the stone sink was becoming increasingly difficult the bigger she got, and to use the galvanised dolly-tub was now more than she could manage.

Tom Weldon glanced over the top of his *Daily Sketch*. 'Same as last night. Ten o'clock.'

'Now that you're up, do you think you could give me a hand to move the dresser out of the baby's room?' Emma put her wet hands flat on her swollen stomach, and looked enquiringly at her husband.

Without looking up from the newspaper, Weldon said, 'No, not today. I'm going out.'

The young woman turned to face him, leaning her back against the edge of the sink. 'It would help if you gave the pub a miss today. There's a lot to do getting things ready, and the bigger I get the more difficult it is for me to manage.'

Behind the paper Tom Weldon's expression froze into one of deep annoyance. Christ almighty, how much longer is this going on for? he thought. If this is wedded bliss then thank God I'm going to be out of it soon. Straightening his face, he put aside the paper and reached for the large brown teapot in the middle of the kitchen table. 'I've got some business to deal with,' he said sourly. 'If I'm out working to earn a living then I'm entitled to have an hour for a pint and to get one or two things sorted.'

Emma Weldon stared coldly at her husband. She could not believe how he had changed in the short time they had been married. Eight months ago everything had been different. She was in service as cook with the Frasers in Craddock Street, earning a comfortable sixty pounds a year, and Tom was the charming beat policeman who used to call in for a cup of tea or, early in the morning, a thick bacon sandwich. Emma was still not sure how it was that things had moved on. There had never been any question of walking out or anything like that. It was one evening in late May when she was on her own in the kitchen. Tom had come in from his beat for a chat and for some supper. Having cleared up the remains of a shoulder of lamb that was left over from the meal upstairs, she was bending over him clearing away the dishes when he kissed her. She had responded, and before she knew what was happening his hand was up her skirt – and she was not protesting. Looking back, Emma could not believe her own stupidity. Matters quickly progressed: they met when they were not working, and then spent afternoons and evenings in his lodgings making love.

It was only two months before she found herself to be pregnant. Because of his position as a policeman, Tom had to marry her or lose his job. With Emma's only family being her widowed mother in Derby, the couple paid for their quiet wedding at Killick Street Chapel, and moved into the rented two-up two-down house in Cowper Terrace, at the back of Wordsworth Lane. While Emma was prepared to settle down and make the best of things, Tom Weldon had never adjusted to marriage, and still insisted on going out with his old cronies.

Emma glanced at the clock on the mantle shelf. It was her only wedding present, from Hettie and Jane, the two maids at Mrs Fraser's. Ten minutes to one. Having come off night duty at six o'clock that morning and gone straight to bed, Tom had got up half an hour ago – and now he was going out again. 'It's just that you're never home. If you're on a day shift you're out all evening. If you're on nights or earlies it's all afternoon.'

Weldon took a sip of his tea. Calm down, he thought to himself. It would not be for much longer. In another five days Christmas would be out of the way and he would be off. If things went according to plan he should collect the last of his money tonight. After Boxing Day he would simply go out to the shops for a paper, and never come back. His passage to Australia was already booked. None of your two quid 'farm labourer's assisted passage': he had paid twenty-five guineas for a second-class cabin with full board. He allowed himself a sly grin: the tickets and everything else were hidden away safe and sound. When he disappeared, Nathan Cleaver would appear to be as mystified as everyone else. Then Nate would follow him out to Australia in a few months' time. Get a bit of sunshine on their backs, and be rid of this whining bitch and the brat that she was carrying.

Until he was ready, though, it was best not to arouse her suspicions. The hint of a smile came to his lips. After all, it was not as if he were going without the little comforts of life. There were more fish in the sea than Emma.

Mistaking the smile, his wife gave a small shrug and smiled back at him. At least, she thought, he did not keep her short of money. Even if his 'business' involved playing cards with Nathan Cleaver in the Trafalgar Arms, he always seemed to eke out his thirty-two and six wages without stinting on her housekeeping. 'I suppose you'll be off down to the Trafalgar, will you?' she asked.

'Possibly,' Tom replied, setting down his empty cup and pulling on his jacket. Possibly, but not just yet: other things first, he thought.

It was cold in the bedroom, and Irene Deladier shivered slightly as, slipping from between the warm bedclothes, she reached out to the nearby chair and pulled on a loose-fitting peignoir.

Will lay back on the pillows and watched appreciatively, as she tied the narrow sash around her middle and stood looking at the afternoon snow falling in a thick white curtain outside. Even after nearly four months he could not get over the excitement of watching her. 'What are you looking for?'

'Elsie and Beatrice have gone out shopping to get the food for tonight's dinner party. They should be back any time, and I don't want them to see you here. The half past two tram's just gone by. They'll definitely be on the next one.' Returning from the window, she slipped back into the warmth of the bed and snuggled up to Will. She ran her hand down his cheek. 'You really should be going, my love.' Almost as an afterthought she added, 'Does Susan know about us?'

His pale brown eyes held hers enquiringly. 'I don't know whether she suspects anything or not. Does it matter?'

Irene bit her lip thoughtfully. It was something that she did, Will had noticed, when she was thinking. 'She could make things awkward if she chose, you being a figure of authority in the town and me being . . .' Irene broke off, not quite sure how to finish.

'You being a woman of considerable means, and the sister of the commanding officer of the secret Watermill project.' Will finished the sentence for her.

'I just want to avoid a mess,' she said resignedly.

'There won't be a mess. Susan's off at the moment on one of her affairs. God knows who with – and I don't particularly care. If she ever works it out she won't say anything, so stop worrying.'

Irene wanted to ask if he and Susan still slept together. Their relationship puzzled her. Despite Susan's philandering, Irene knew that Will and his wife were still good friends. It was a part of him that she did not understand yet. 'When are you coming to talk to Matthias again?' The ongoing enquiry into the theft of the War Hospital funds had on more than one occasion provided the couple with a plausible excuse for Will to be at her house on official business.

'I have to tread carefully. There's not much more Monsieur Palmaerts can tell us at the moment. And I don't want to alert your cousin James by being here too often.'

Will placed his arms behind his head and stretched out. 'The problem with this enquiry is that every lead is a dead end – quite literally. Without a doubt the architect Carstairs was the lynchpin, authorising payments for excessive quantities of materials that never existed. Palmaerts went through the contractors' worksheets since work began in February, and from March until his death Carstairs had also been authorising payment of wages to twenty casual labourers who didn't exist. The scheme was in place from the beginning. Rees was the middle man: he simply substituted the forged invoices for payment.'

'But surely, as treasurer, Jamie would have paid the contractors,' interrupted Irene.

'No, that's where Carstairs was clever. Architects work on a percentage of the overall job. For instance, if the project costs a hundred thousand pounds the architect receives ten per cent for his fee, namely ten thousand pounds. Carstairs, in order to make administration of the building work more manageable, set things up so that each month he told James how much had been spent. James gave him a cheque for that amount, and Carstairs ostensibly paid the individual contractors and suppliers. What we need to find out is what he did with the money that he creamed off, and who else was involved.'

'You think there were others?'

'Yes – it was too unwieldy for there just to be Carstairs and Rees. Too many things that could go wrong. I think there's definitely someone else fairly senior in the hospital's management who's sweating. The interesting thing is that those involved seem to be dying at an alarming rate. I can't prove it, but I've a gut feeling that the Groves woman was part of it, or possibly knew something about what was going on that made her dangerous. And that little soldier Kempin is another link. At first I thought he was simply being framed, but now, since he's disappeared, I'm not so sure. Why did Lottie Groves's murderer try to frame Kempin – and how did he know of Kempin's relationship with Groves?'

'Where do you think Kempin is?'

'If I knew that I'd be a lot further forward,' Will retorted testily. Immediately regretting his ill humour, he turned on his side to face her. 'Sorry, I shouldn't take it out on you.' He decided to change the subject. 'Who's coming to your dinner party tonight?'

Irene paused to think. 'James is bringing Kathleen Doyle, my brother Sam and his two boffins from the Watermill, and an officer I've not met before, a Major Gresham. I could invite you and Susan, of course,' she added mischievously. 'That way, woman to woman, I'd soon know if she was on to us.'

'I don't think so,' Will grinned, not mentioning that he and Gresham were acquainted 'With all those men about she wouldn't make it to the pudding. Are James and Kathy Doyle an item?' Will watched the snow gently drifting past the window.

Irene paused to think; the question had never occurred to her. 'Wouldn't have thought so. It's just convenient for them to partner each other to functions. She's tied up running the hospital, and when Jamie's not working he's trundling round in his captain's uniform drumming up enthusiasm for the war effort. At present he's trying to convince men to enlist in some new howitzer battalion he's raising.'

Will continued to look past her shoulder at the window. 'Pity,' he said quietly. 'It might take his attention away from you.'

Irene pursed her lips. 'You've noticed. There's nothing I can do about it. He started off by being very helpful and protective when I first came here, and I must admit I was quite vulnerable. He's never made approaches, though, and after all he's my cousin.'

'Half the royal families in Europe are sleeping with or married to their cousins,' Will replied pointedly.

As they were talking about families, Irene decided to raise a vexed question. 'You don't get on with my brother, do you?'

'We got off on a bad footing,' Will replied carefully. He knew that Irene and her brother were close, and did not want to upset her. 'What's going on at the mill bothers me.' He thought back to his conversation with Gresham. 'My feeling is that there's something dangerous going on there. Unfortunately, if things go wrong people are likely to get hurt, and that'll involve me having to sort it out.' Slipping a hand beneath the covers, he gave a tug at the silk fastening of her gown. 'But I do like his sister very much,' he murmured.

The afternoon light was beginning to fade, casting long shadows over the laboratory bench, as Paul Kändler stepped back from the cage with a grunt of satisfaction. 'Fifty-eight seconds,' he exclaimed excitedly.

The other man looked past him at the dead rat. 'I think we're probably there, Paul,' he replied slowly.

'Inhalation is definitely much quicker than absorption through the skin,' Kändler declared, his watery blue eyes shining brightly behind thick lenses.

Herbert Duggan peered through the bars at the dead rodent. 'We'll have to do an autopsy, but if the flooding of the bronchial passages in an animal this size can be achieved in less than a minute, then in an human being we're probably looking at three to four minutes, do you think?'

Kändler nodded his head quickly. 'Yes, I'd think so.'

Duggan picked up the trumpet-shaped telephone earpiece and jiggled the metal cradle up and down with his other hand. The operator sitting at the switchboard in the house answered immediately. 'Ask Mr Gresham to step over here please,' the scientist said.

Five minutes later, clad in white overalls, Gresham joined the scientists in the tiled laboratory.

'We're having difficulty stabilising the reaction,' Duggan explained. 'Basically the compound is an organo-phosphate. You need to take a phosphate and replace some of the particles with others made up of carbon, hydrogen and nitrogen. It creates a highly toxic cocktail. The difficulty is working out the correct order to do things in, and of course the quantities.'

Gresham stared down at the amber liquid in the sealed glass phial. One part of his mind was occupied with how to take forward the results of the biochemists' work, while another examined the implications of their achievement: he found it difficult to comprehend that in front of him was the most destructive weapon ever conceived by man. He raised his eyes from the workbench to take in the architects of this instrument of death, as if seeing them for the first time.

Dr Herbert Duggan was a bluff-looking man of fifty-eight, although his neatly trimmed grey hair with its untidy parting made him look ten years older. Twinkling blue eyes and heavy moustache, stained with nicotine by the cigarette that always hung out of his mouth when he was not in the laboratory, gave him a distinctly avuncular aspect. The old brown jacket and loosely knotted plain tie completed the impression of an elderly schoolmaster patiently awaiting retirement.

Paul Kändler was different. Apart from anything else, Gresham thought, he 'looked foreign'. Unlike Duggan, he was a relatively young man, just thirty-one. In appearance they were very different. Kändler was of medium height, with thick and bushy brown wavy hair that stood up from his head like a dark mane before sweeping away from his broad features. The thick lenses of his steel-rimmed spectacles spoke clearly of his short-sightedness. Definitely 'foreign looking', Ralph Gresham decided.

'How stable is it?'

Kändler took off his glasses. 'If you remove the stopper or break the phial we'll all be dead in less than three minutes.'

With extreme care Gresham replaced the container on the laboratory bench.

'Delivery', continued Kändler animatedly, 'is going to be the next question to be resolved. Once we've come to a decision on that we'll be able to proceed to trials under controlled conditions.'

Herbert Duggan began to unbutton his overall. 'Let's go into the conference room,' he said. 'I need a smoke.'

Having secured the double mortise lock on the steel-lined laboratory door, the three men made their way to the room at the far end of the converted barn where daily progress meetings between scientists and their military associates were held. As they walked along the corridor Gresham checked over his shoulder to ensure that an armed guard was positioned by the door behind them. His counterpart was on duty outside the entrance. Before coming into the research complex, the major had checked that the two patrols covering the perimeter of the building were not skulking somewhere out of the weather.

'I think there are two options for exposure to the effects of MD19 which can be achieved by a single delivery method. One creates a quick, direct battlefield assault weapon. The second is equally deadly, and is designed to seal off an area after it's been abandoned to prevent enemy reoccupation.' Duggan's voice was hoarse from years of smoking. The cigarette hung limply in the corner of his mouth, smoke curling up through his moustache into the warm atmosphere. Gresham waited in silence for him to continue, his mind busy. 'MD19 in liquid form has an extremely high boiling point, two hundred and forty-six degrees centigrade, which is two and a half times higher than water.' Duggan took the cigarette from his mouth, appearing more than ever like a schoolmaster delivering a lesson. 'Critically, it has a low vapour pressure making it six times heavier than air, and consequently when released it'll stay close to the ground. The optimum delivery would be as a vapour, which of course means by artillery or mortar shell. The explosion would create a colourless cloud to be inhaled by anyone in the vicinity. Death would be almost instantaneous. It would settle onto everything at ground level, remaining lethal to the touch.'

Kändler took over. 'The absorption route, while being slower, is by far the most insidious.' His little eyes gleamed behind his spectacles. 'In order to create a vapour in the first place, the chemical's dissolved in a non-flammable solvent. When the vapour settles to the ground the solvent evaporates, leaving a minute coating of MD19 on everything it touches. Think about it: even the uniforms of the dead will be infectious. Handling anything in their pockets, such as identity papers, cigarettes, even matches, will be fatal.'

Gresham felt around in his tunic pocket and brought out a gunmetal cigarette case. Tapping it on his hand before opening it, he looked at the scientists. 'How long would it be before an infected area could be occupied?'

Duggan gave a dry laugh. 'That we don't know yet. Could be days, weeks, possibly months. Until we've used it we'll not be able to say.'

'In which case what we need to do now is arrange some field tests.' Gresham stared out of the window at the meadow behind the Watermill. Thirty feet away was a newly erected high steel fence, which ran around the perimeter of the buildings. On each side of it a belt of rolled barbed wire, ten feet deep and six feet high, prevented unauthorised access. His mind elsewhere, Ralph watched the two soldiers, Lee Enfields slung over their shoulders, muffled up in their greatcoats, trudging along the outside of the wire.

'That'll not be easy, Monsieur.' Paul Kändler was watching him carefully.

'Not easy, but not impossible.' Gresham already had the germ of an idea forming in his mind. He would require Leigh-Hunt's approval, but Sir Rowland was a practical man. 'In the meantime, gentlemen, I think we should go and get ready for Madame Deladier's little *soirée*.' As they prepared to leave the conference room he said, 'For the time being please do not mention to Major Norton the stage we've reached. There are certain arrangements I need to make.'

It was half past six when Tom Weldon arrived home for dinner. Emma had recently become reconciled to spending most of her time alone, whether her husband was on or off duty. That he resented the situation in which their earlier relationship had placed him, she was in no doubt. The marriage was not a happy one, and she wondered if he would remain with her after the baby was born. Should Tom leave them, she was well aware that it would spell disaster for her and the child. A woman on her own with a family inevitably finished up first on outdoor relief and then in the workhouse, a prospect that did not bear thinking about. For this reason she continued to patiently accept his drinking and his lack of interest in her. One thing was for certain: any pretence of love, or even affection, between them had ceased long ago.

Hearing the sound of her husband's key in the front door, Emma heaved herself onto her feet. At six months' pregnant even such a simple matter as getting up from a chair was difficult now that she could not bend in the middle. It was at least two months since any form of sexual contact had been possible, and she wondered if Tom was finding solace elsewhere.

Having spent the last two hours in the Trafalgar Arms drinking with Nathan Cleaver and a couple of other off-duty policemen, Tom Weldon was in a particularly good mood. The entire afternoon had gone extremely well. His wife was quite correct in her assumption that while she was indisposed he was involved in a casual dalliance with another woman – more than one, in fact. After spending an hour with his latest amour, he had gone on to meet Cleaver, and had succeeded in completing the all important business that was about to secure his freedom.

Putting an amiable smile on his face, Weldon hung his overcoat up behind the front door. 'What's for dinner?'

'I got a nice rabbit from Smethurst's, so I've done it in a pie. There's a bottle of beer for you in the pantry if you want it.' She was relieved that he was in a good mood. Recently he had often been morose and argumentative after coming home from the pub. He had probably done well at cards, she thought.

'That's good,' he replied, still smiling, although Emma noticed that it did not quite reach his eyes. 'Listen,' he continued, producing from his trouser pocket two half sovereigns, 'I'm going to have my dinner and go up to bed for a couple of hours before I go to work. I forgot to tell you, Sergeant King says that I'm to work over Christmas, and you don't want to be on your own. I've had a good afternoon, so why don't you take these and catch the train over to Derby tomorrow. Stay with your mother, and come back after Boxing Day.'

Chapter Fifteen

Walking back along the river path from Eastgates Bridge to the weir Harry North was lost in deep thought, his coat collar turned up against the cold, penetrating drizzle. He was fairly certain that the post-mortem would show that Tom Weldon had been hit over the head and dumped in the Kell. The question was why, and what was he doing on the bridge in the first place?

Weldon could have been following someone. A fight could have ensued in which the constable had gone over the bridge top. Harry turned the possibility over carefully before deciding that it was not likely. Weldon's lamp was still secured to his belt, which if he was talking to a suspect would have been in his hand; if a struggle had taken place it would probably have been dropped and broken. And Weldon was a big man with a reputation for being able to look after himself in a fight, so putting him in the river would not have been an easy task – hence the blow to the back of the head, presumably delivered by someone coming up behind him, or when his attention was diverted. Tom Weldon had gone to Eastgate Bridge for a reason. Find that, and the rest would be easy.

The real question in Harry's mind was whether the incident tied in with the murders of Charlotte Groves and Ivor Rees. Harry had a disquieting feeling that it did.

Weldon was a popular man among his colleagues, Harry reflected, outgoing and good at his job. During a night shift he was usually guaranteed to bring in some miscreant whom he had discovered up to no good. On the other hand there were rumours that his private life left a lot to be desired. It was common knowledge that he was a ladies' man. Earlier in the year he had been obliged to marry a cook at one of the big houses after getting her into trouble. He also liked a drink and a game of cards. The word was that despite his marriage he was still chasing the local barmaids.

Harry gave a sigh of resignation and glared up at the overcast sky. The dead man's closest friend was Nathan Cleaver; he would have a word with him later in the day. At least it had stopped snowing. Harry hated snow, and as he trudged the final hundred yards to where the body had been found he felt the slush under his feet soaking through the soles of his shoes.

By now, the corpse having been removed to the undertakers, the crowd of onlookers had dispersed, leaving two dispirited constables to the dreary task of checking along the river bank for any items that might have been missed. It was, the inspector knew, a waste of time: the body had gone into the river almost half a mile upstream.

Following the tarmac path towards the park gates, Harry spotted a two-wheeled knife grinder's cart next to a billboard exhorting readers of the *Kelsford Gazette* to make a donation to the Shilling Christmas Fund, 'in order to send a festive present to every man from Kelsford who is serving in the Army and Navy or is held in a German Prisoner of War Camp'. The faded wooden board on the front of the cart proclaimed its owner to be a grinder and cutler. Jeremiah Boam, its owner, was at the front door of the park keeper's lodge in conversation with a stout grey-haired woman, the wife of Reuben Lennox, the assistant park keeper. Harry hoped that Lennox was out: he was in no mood for a detailed discussion about what had happened that morning.

Touching a hand to his cap, the knife grinder pocketed some coins that the woman handed to him and made his way over to Harry. 'Morning, Mr North, sir. This wind's sharp as knives.' A quick grin appeared on his narrow unshaven jaw. The quip was obviously a stock in trade.

'How's business, Jerry?' From the thin rain soaked jacket that the man was wearing, Harry presumed it was not that good.

'Oh you know, sir, comes and goes. Regulars like Mrs Lennox are always good for a tanner here and there.'

Harry nodded in agreement, and was about to carry on when Boam said conversationally, 'Bad job about that young man down there. Changed his beat, had he?'

A sixth sense halted Harry in his tracks. 'Yes. Up to a month ago he used to work the area around Devonshire Gardens, where the nurse was killed. Did you know him?'

'Just to say good morning to. That side of town's quite a good area for me. There's a couple of fishmongers and Felix Friedmann the pork butcher, although his business has gone downhill since the war broke out. It's not very fair really, because the old boy's been here for nearly forty years.'

Harry pulled a packet of Players from his pocket and offered one to the knife grinder.

'Did you see PC Weldon the afternoon that Charlotte Groves was killed?' he asked casually.

'Oh yes.' Boam struck a match, and cupping his hands around it against the weather, held it for both of them to light their cigarettes. 'As I told Mr Cleaver, I was packing up my stuff when I saw Lottie going into the house, then I went off down towards the Prince of Wales. PC Weldon was coming up Devonshire Gardens. He said "Good afternoon" as we passed. It's sod's law: a couple of minutes later and he'd have seen the bloke what killed 'er coming out of the house.'

'Did you tell Mr Cleaver that you'd seen PC Weldon?' Harry asked quietly.

'Yes, sir. He said he'd tie in my statement with PC Weldon's report.' The knife grinder shivered, his damp jacket providing little protection against the December weather.

'Thanks, Jerry. Look after yourself and have a nice Christmas.' Harry's mind was elsewhere.

Back at Long Street an air of shocked disbelief pervaded the station. Tom Weldon's death was the main subject of conversation, along with speculation about how it might have occurred.

Following a quick visit to the front enquiry desk to collect a short steel case opener, kept to open boxes and other items that were handed in, Harry made his way down the corridor to the muster room, where the men paraded for duty.

Along the back wall of the deserted room was a bank of small metal lockers, stacked four high, in which officers kept their personal effects. Searching along the third row, he quickly came to the one that he was looking for. A simple cardboard label slotted between two grooves on the door read 'PC 82 Weldon'. Slipping the jaws of the jemmy behind the lock, Harry levered it outwards. With a sharp crack the soft metal of the door buckled, releasing the flimsy lock.

Inside was a pile of completed notebooks, which Harry placed on top of the lockers; he would go through them later. Next to the pocket books was one of the new-style wristwatches with a brown leather strap, a short curved pipe, some matches and a pouch containing an ounce of dark shag tobacco. From the back of the locker Harry removed a shipping line prospectus by the Commonwealth and Dominion Line, giving details of the various passages available to Australia. The only remaining item was a woman's red elasticated garter with the words 'love you' etched inside with indelible pencil.

Tucked inside the prospectus was a receipt made out to Mr Thomas Weldon, for twenty-five pounds in respect of a single one-way ticket on the SS *Star of Australia,* departing Tuesday 28 December from Southampton for Townsville in Queensland, along with a pocket-size cardboard-covered folder. Opening the folder, Harry saw that it was a passport also in the name of Thomas Weldon. He examined it with a degree of curiosity, as he had never seen one before: it was only recently that legislation had required anyone travelling abroad to acquire one. Comprising a large single sheet of paper folded into eight, the travel document contained a description of the holder along with his personal details. North was interested to see that Weldon described himself as a 'journeyman printer', and the section marked marital status indicated he was a single man. Across the bottom, near to a small square portrait photograph, was scrawled the applicant's signature. Obviously, Harry mused, Thomas Weldon intended to leave his options open once he settled in Australia.

Harry slipped the papers back into the prospectus and gathered up the remainder of the contents before making his way upstairs to the first floor.

The atmosphere in the detective office was very much the same as elsewhere in the building. Clarence Greasley, Bert Conway and Nathan Cleaver were engaged in a muted discussion, while Bernard Ashe busied himself making some tea on a gas ring at the back of the room.

Conversation ceased as soon as Harry appeared in the doorway, and heads turned expectantly towards him. Without speaking, he crooked a finger towards Nathan Cleaver, indicating for the detective to follow him.

In his office, Harry sat down behind his desk and instructed the younger man to close the door, fixing him with a cold and appraising stare. Distinctly ill at ease, Cleaver attempted to return the gaze before dropping his eyes.

'You were Tom Weldon's closest mate, weren't you.' It was a statement, not a question. The unfriendly tone caused the young man to look up at the inspector.

He nodded. 'Yes, sir.'

Placing the passport and travel documents on the desk, Harry said coldly, 'You and I are going to have a long chat about one or two things, Mr Cleaver, and depending on how that chat goes, at the end of it you may or may not still be a policeman.'

Harry North paused on the steps of the King George Hotel to light a cigarette, the woman in room 104 still filling his mind. Elfin face and dark hair almost down to her waist, heavy breasts spilling out of the loose bathrobe as she held it together with one hand and checked the corridor to ensure that it was clear for him to leave. Glancing over her shoulder at the rumpled double bed with an ice-filled champagne bucket beside it, Harry had to concede that for her age Susan Mardlin was still an extremely desirable woman.

Taking a deep draw on his cigarette, he checked his watch: he needed to get back to Long Street before he was missed. From the rooftop of Goodman's cigar factory a hundred yards away the insistent sound of air raid hooters shrieked in the chill afternoon air. They had, Harry realised, been sounding for some time. He had first heard them while he was in room 104, but at the time they had not been important.

A dull droning noise overhead caught his attention, and looking up he saw the menacing cigar shape of a huge dirigible, the two black crosses on its belly clearly visible, looming above him as it floated into view over the hotel.

Throwing his cigarette away, Harry began to run across the road towards a sign with an arrow and the words 'AIR RAID SHELTER' painted in large red letters. For the first time he noticed that apart from a young woman with a child in a perambulator, who was running in the same direction as himself, the street was deserted.

The force of the explosion blew him completely off his feet, hurling him across the pavement into the side of a delivery van that had been abandoned by the side of the road. Stunned, Harry lay motionless for several seconds before regaining his senses. His only hope of safety was underneath the van. Rolling between its wheels and covering his head with his hands, he lay perfectly still. Two more deafening explosions, apparently only feet away, caused the ground beneath him to shake as if in the throes of an earthquake. The sound of falling masonry from a collapsing building nearby replaced the ear-splitting crashes of the falling bombs.

As the smoke and debris began to clear, Harry crawled from his hiding place and pulled himself unsteadily to his feet, staring dazedly around him. He was surrounded by dust and rubble. In the eerie silence of the aftershock he distinctly heard the drone of the Zeppelin's motors as it continued its sinister passage over the town. At that moment the rest of the world seemed to regain its senses, and pandemonium erupted around him.

From the far side of the town the dull thud of the anti-aircraft gun recently installed on the parade square at Sevastopol Barracks began to rhythmically pump shells skywards as fast as the gunners could reload. The intervals between the shellfire were filled with the harsh chatter of a Vickers machine gun from somewhere else in the depot. Subconsciously it registered with Harry that both were wasting their ammunition: the raiders were out of range.

It was difficult to breath in the dust-laden atmosphere. Putting a hand to his face, Harry saw that it was covered in blood. Still dazed, he realised that he must have been cut by one of the shards of glass that were littering the street, along with masonry and plaster.

The front of the King George was gone. Elegant upstairs apartments gaped open into the street. Beds and furniture leaned at impossible angles out of the shattered rooms. As he watched, a grand piano slid gracefully along the polished surface of the first-floor dining room: after hanging out over the side of the building it gradually gained momentum until it embraced an upturned settee that crossed its course. Both were launched into the air, taking a large section of the damaged building with them.

As the dust began to clear Harry saw that where, seconds before, the young woman with the upturned baby carriage beside her had been trapped under some fallen timber, there was now a ten foot high pile of rubble, the piano, reduced to matchwood and wires, perched on the top. Of the woman and the perambulator there was no trace.

'That needs stitching, mate.' A small man in a long warehouseman's brown overall wearing the white armlet and red cross of a VAD worker was examining Harry's face.

'I'll call in at the Infirmary,' Harry replied vaguely. The words sounded distant, as if someone else was speaking them.

'No, it wants doin' now,' said the man gently, as if speaking to a child. 'There's nothin' you can do here. You go across and get on Sammy Carter's wagon with the rest of 'um. The coppers will be here in a minute. They'll sort it all out.' From one of the pockets of his overall he produced a First Aid dressing which, having ripped away the thick paper packaging, he pressed cautiously against the deepest of the gashes in Harry's cheek.

Harry allowed the warehouseman to lead him a few yards down the road to where the walking injured were being helped over the tailboard of an empty coal wagon. Where it had appeared from Harry neither knew nor cared. The driver slapped his reins across the lead horse's back, and set off for Kelsford Infirmary.

The sound of police whistles and running feet still echoing in his ears, Harry could not believe that only seconds before the Zeppelin's bombs had hit he had been walking out through the doors of the hotel.

Who was going to tell Will Mardlin? he wondered.

'Would you stay for a while if you've nothing else on?' Will looked worn out, Harry thought.

'Yes of course.'

The rest of the funeral party was in the process of departing. Susan's father had left five minutes before with Will's parents. James Simmonds, attired in a black bowler hat and dark overcoat with an astrakhan collar, was fussing around his cousin. Madame Deladier, Harry thought, looked unwell: her face under the delicately applied makeup was pasty, and she looked as if she had not slept. He was puzzled that when she had attempted to offer Will her condolences he had deliberately avoided her.

After shaking hands with Will in the hallway, James bustled Irene solicitously out of the front door and into a waiting taxicab. Watching as the driver closed the door behind them, Harry saw her pale face peering anxiously out of the window at Will standing alone on the steps of the house.

Back in the dining room of 23 Lyndon Terrace, Will indicated a comfortable armchair and, going to the tall polished oak dresser standing along the back wall, produced a decanter of single malt whisky.

Pouring them both a generous measure, he set the decanter down on a side table and dropped wearily into the armchair opposite Harry. 'So what do I do now?'

The question was, Harry realised, a rhetorical one. It was little more than forty-eight hours since the body of Susan Mardlin had been recovered from the ruins of the King George, along with the twenty-eight other guests and staff who had been killed when the hotel sustained a direct hit.

Harry had told the nurses at the Infirmary that his injuries had been sustained when the windows were blown out of the Prince Albert as he was walking past. On his release later that evening he had gone straight to the Mardlins' house. There he found Will, stunned by the news of his wife's death, going mechanically through a stack of personal papers. It was, Harry quickly discovered, a meaningless task that he had set himself while he tried to assimilate what had happened. Other buildings in the town centre had been seriously damaged, and it did not occur to Will in his numbed condition to ask the inspector where he had been when he had received the cuts to his face.

His stay on that occasion had not been a long one. It was obvious that Will wanted to be alone, and having paid his respects Harry took his leave.

This afternoon was the first time he had seen Will since then, and he could see that beneath the formal black suit and outwardly controlled appearance the man was suffering.

'So, tell me what's happening.' Will took a deep swallow of his whisky, and stared absently over the rim of the glass at his companion.

Harry shook his head non-committally. 'Nothing that won't keep.' Later he would give the superintendent an edited version of his conversation with Nathan Cleaver – but only as much as he needed to know in relation to the Groves murder. It had only been two days, but it seemed like an age ago.

Cleaver, already extremely worried by the death of his friend and his own involvement, both in concealing his knowledge of Weldon's whereabouts at the time of Groves's murder and also that he was about to leave his wife and depart for Australia, was completely thrown by the fact that the detective inspector appeared to know all about both.

It was when Harry started to talk about his career being finished, with the added prospect of a long term in prison for concealing evidence in a murder enquiry, that a badly frightened Cleaver readily volunteered the story of what happened on the afternoon of Charlotte Groves's death.

Tom Weldon was having an affair with a parlour maid around the corner from Devonshire Gardens in Collington Street. It was his bad luck that at the very time that he should have been out on his patrol he was dallying in the back kitchen of 27 Collington Street with a buxom young servant girl. When he was asked as a matter of routine what area of his beat he was working when Groves was killed, Weldon had deemed it best to say that he was at the furthest point from the scene of the crime. Everything would have been all right had the knife grinder not seen him in Devonshire Gardens. As no one other than Cleaver knew of this, it was an easy matter to protect his friend and not to include the fact in Jeremiah Boam's statement. Cleaver explained that with his friend's domestic life becoming more and more complicated, he had assisted Tom Weldon in his plans to desert his wife after the Christmas holiday.

Thoroughly rattled, and desperate to deflect the man who now held his future in the balance, Cleaver also said something else that instilled in Harry a cold fury.

Satisfied eventually that Cleaver had told him all he knew, Harry dismissed him, with instructions to go back to work and not to say one word to anyone about what had taken place, or he would personally arrest him for conspiracy.

Alone in his office, the detective inspector roundly cursed Cleaver for his treachery and dishonesty. It was not difficult for him now to put together what had happened. Weldon had walked out of Collington Street into Devonshire Gardens after speaking to Boam, and seen the killer – someone whom he knew – either entering or leaving number forty-two. Since then Weldon had been blackmailing that person, which it was obvious was how he had stashed away sufficient money to fund his emigration plans. An interview with the parlour maid at 27 Collington Street would confirm whether that part of the story was true or not. He knew that, friends or not, Weldon would not have told Cleaver what he had seen, as this would have meant sharing the blackmail money.

Harry decided that although it would be Mardlin's place to decide what happened to Nathan Cleaver, he would persuade him to keep the man where he was for the time being, until he was ready to deal with him personally. Neither the Superintendent nor the Chief Constable would want it to get out that two serving police officers, one of whom had just died in suspicious circumstances, had concealed evidence in a murder case.

Will splashed some more whisky into Harry's glass before refilling his own. 'I know Susan had her faults, but I loved her. Perhaps if we'd had children things might have been different.' He lapsed into silence, staring into the whisky glass. If I had prevented her from having that abortion when we were just a pair of kids she would have been able to have children, he thought bitterly.

Listening to the increasing slur in Will's speech, Harry realised he was already drunk. He had probably been drinking steadily all day.

Will gave a wry smile, almost talking to himself. 'She did a lot of silly things over the years, Harry, but she always came back. Now it's me who feels guilty. If she hadn't died it wouldn't have mattered.'

Harry made no reply, simply leaning across the table to fill Will's glass from the decanter.

Will looked at him owlishly, then shook his head sadly. Now that he had relaxed his guard, the drink was taking over quickly. 'Do you know, she didn't even get her motor car.' He had difficulty with the words.

'You can still get it. If that's what you feel guilty about . . .' In his mind's eye Harry could see Irene Deladier's face looking anxiously out of the taxicab.

'No – cancelled it yesterday.' Will drained his glass and unsteadily picked up the almost empty decanter, dropping the glass stopper onto the carpet in the process. Replenishing his glass, he slopped a liberal measure into Harry's half-full tumbler. 'There's someone else,' he mumbled, staring down into the amber liquid in his hand. 'I love her, and I loved Susan. If I could have told Susan she would have said it was all right, but I can't now, can I, 'cos she's fuckin' dead.'

'You can tell me anything you want to and it's safe,' Harry said carefully, 'but the only person who can help you is Irene.'

Even in his befuddled state the import of the words registered with Will. A wry smile came onto his face. 'You're a cunning, foxy old bastard. How did you work it out?' Holding a finger up, he peered at it for a second or two as if attempting unsuccessfully to focus, then mumbled, 'Our secret. No one's got to know.'

Harry leaned forward and gently took the whisky glass from the other man's loose grip. Without another word, finally overcome by emotion and whisky, Will's head dropped forward onto his chest, and he passed out.

Harry sadly regarded the dishevelled figure slumped in the chair opposite as he sipped at the contents of his own glass. God almighty, he thought, what a way to spend Christmas Eve. Closing his eyes, he allowed his mind to drift back to the King George Hotel.

As he knew it would be, the door to room 104 was unlocked; it swung open at his touch. Susan Mardlin was sitting up in the spacious double bed, the covers pulled loosely around her, sipping a glass of chilled champagne from the ice bucket at her side. Her long auburn hair, released from the customary pins that held it high on the back of her head, cascaded around her bare shoulders, and provided a perfect frame for the small oval face. She had never, he thought, looked more lovely.

Her green eyes widened in surprise as the unexpected visitor walked across the room to look out of the fourth-floor window at the busy street. The rain that had supplanted yesterday's snow had in its turn been replaced by a thin watery sunshine reflecting from the wet pavements. A passing army truck threw a spray of dirty wet slush from the gutter over the shoes of a hapless pedestrian, who turned angrily to shake a fist after the departing lorry.

'Hello, Harry.' The soft voice had a mesmeric quality. Harry deeply regretted that she was the wife of a man whom he regarded as one of his few friends.

'He's not coming, Susan.'

'No, that's fairly obvious.' There was a rustling of covers behind him as she got out of bed and pulled on her robe.

'Presuming that you've not come to apply for the position of stand-in, perhaps you'll tell me what's happening.'

Turning from the window, Harry explained slowly that Tom Weldon was dead, and that his death was going to initiate a long enquiry headed by her husband and himself, which he had every intention of keeping her out of.

'How did you find out about us?' she asked.

'Nathan Cleaver – his best mate – has been covering for him. When he was seeing you, his wife thought he was off drinking with Cleaver.'

'So he couldn't keep his mouth shut. Had to brag about it to one of his mates.' Standing in the middle of the room, shoulders drooping, Susan Mardlin looked sad and defeated. Putting her head back, she allowed the tears to trickle slowly down her cheeks.

Harry moved towards her and gently pulled her to him. Putting her head into his chest, Susan put her arms around him, sobbing quietly. After a while she disentangled herself and, moving away, pulled together her gaping robe before sitting down on the bed. Wiping her face with the back of her hand she smiled wanly at him. 'Are you going to tell Will?'

Harry shook his head in silence.

'Thank you.' The words were thick with emotion. 'I'm not a bad woman, you know. I simply have a problem. Will understands – he always has. You'd think that as I get older it would go away, but it doesn't. I'm forty years old, Harry. I used to be good looking. Now I'm just a reasonably preserved middle-aged woman. At one time I wouldn't have looked twice at a man like Tom Weldon. Now I don't have much choice. Will and I still love each other: he never asks questions and he never blames me. He's probably the best man I've ever met, and don't tell me that I don't deserve him. I already know that.'

Harry gazed appraisingly at her for a moment. In different circumstances he would not have hesitated to make a play for her himself. The difference between him and the Tom Weldons of this world was that he did not take things that did not belong to him, especially other men's wives.

Somewhere in the street outside the harsh screech of a factory hooter announced an impending air raid.

'Where did you meet him?' It was not an idle question. If Harry were to preserve her secret he needed some details.

'I went into Long Street one evening months ago, to see if Will was ready to go home. Tom was on duty at the enquiry desk. Someone was sick and he'd been brought in for a few days. Will was out and Tom was just finishing duty, so he insisted on walking me to the tram stop. Said that a lady shouldn't be out unaccompanied on the streets. I'm not stupid. I knew straight away what his game was. After that it just happened. I dropped in at the station a couple more evenings and got chatting. He was plausible, Crude but plausible. The stupid thing is that I never particularly liked him. Any port in a storm really. I suppose you think I'm disgusting, don't you?'

'I've got no intention of saying anything to Will, and no, you don't disgust me. I've been on this earth too long to pass judgements on what other people do with their lives. My objective's to protect Will and see that this doesn't become public knowledge. You need to get dressed and get out of this place.'

'What about Nathan Cleaver?'

A hard expression crossed Harry's face. 'He won't say anything, that I can promise you.' Harry had already decided that his business with Cleaver was personal, and nowhere near finished.

Accompanying him to the door of the hotel room, Susan checked up and down the empty corridor. Before letting him out, she kissed him gently on the mouth. 'Thank you, Harry. You're a good friend.'

Chapter Sixteen

I
t was, Harry had to admit, a good New Year's Eve party: a buffet, free drinks for the guests from the bar downstairs and good company. Two of Reuben's barmen were clearing some space for those so inclined to take to the floor when the pianist decided it was time to strike up. That, Harry decided, would be his cue to slip away: he was not a party person and dancing was definitely not his thing. It had also been a long day and he was tired. By the time the new year rang in he would be sound asleep in bed.

Over the years it had become something of a tradition for Reuben and Ann Simmonds to hold a celebration in the upstairs room of the Rifleman. Just before the war broke out they had stopped working in the pub and left the day-to-day running of the business to Walter and Julia Mardlin, Will's parents, who had worked for the Simmondses since Walter left the army, before the South African War.

Pushing his now empty plate to one side Harry drained the glass in front of him and touched a match to the Goodman's cigar, two or three of which he had slipped into his top pocket before setting out. At a function such as this he was content to do exactly what he was doing now: sit back quietly in a corner with a drink and chat. His companion for the evening, Bert Conway, had gone downstairs to the bar for some drinks. He would be some time, thought Harry: the pub was crowded with the regular Friday night customers in addition to those at the party.

Twenty-seven years before, he reflected, he had sat at this same table at Ann and Reuben's wedding. His mind drifted back to some of the others who had been with him that afternoon.

Jesse Squires and Sam Braithwaite. Since his retirement Jesse and his wife Susan had moved to live down in Cornwall, Susan tending the roses and Jesse spending his days fishing for mackerel in the small boat that he had bought. Sam, always a boozer, died of a heart attack when he was only forty. Tom Norton and Ruth Samuels, she as dark as he was fair, sitting together at the top table and making it obvious to the world that they were a couple. Thinking of Ruth, Harry's eyes searched the room for her daughter. Irene was at the buffet handing a plate of *hors d'oeuvres* to Will. Harry smiled, wondering if she was as much a woman as her mother was reputed to have been. Arthur Mallard, dapper as ever, was talking to Julia and Walter by the piano. Apart from his steel-rimmed spectacles, Will's father, his thick dark hair now iron grey, was little changed from the ramrod-straight army sergeant who with Tom Norton had ended the Collett Lane Siege all those years ago.

'If you fall off the end of that thing you'll break your neck, Harry.' Twenty years of working together meant that off duty Harry and Bert Conway could be comfortable on first name terms. Conway, a widower with no children, was an intensely private man – and despite his bluff exterior had never got over the loss of his wife.

Reaching into his inside pocket, Harry pulled out another cigar and passed it to Conway. 'I don't really like them anyway,' he said, picking up the fresh pint of Starbright that had been placed before him and taking a long swallow.

A flurry of activity on the other side of the room caught both men's attention. Walter and Arthur Mallard were moving their drinks from the lid of the piano where Solomon Weston, the pianist from the Picture House Cinema in High Street, was busying himself arranging his music. Harry consulted his pocket watch. It was half past nine: the last performance at the cinema must have finished at nine o'clock.

'Think I'll slip off, Bert. Got a busy day ahead,' he said, draining his glass.

Conway nodded. 'Same here.' He wondered if his companion was really going home. Harry had lodged with Laura Percival in Tennyson Street for the last fifteen years since her railwayman husband had been killed in an accident at the goods yard, and it was generally acknowledged that they had an understanding. That was the thing about Harry, he thought: you never really knew whether he was telling you the truth or not. It was not for nothing that he had become known as 'Foxy' North over the years that they had worked together. A confirmed bachelor and always discreet, Harry had drifted from one relationship to another – so perhaps he was going home, perhaps not. Perhaps he and Mrs Percival were going to see the new year in together in their own way.

'I might be late coming in tomorrow morning,' Harry said. 'If anybody asks tell them I've got a dental appointment.'

Conway dropped his head slightly and raised his shaggy eyebrows, peering questioningly through the haze of cigar smoke.

'Tell them I'm having a wisdom tooth fitted.'

The first day of January dawned bright and clear. Strolling at a leisurely pace around the town centre, it took Harry just under an hour to find what he was looking for. In an enclosed yard at the back of the Flag and Unicorn, seated on his cardboard box, sat Tuppenny Rice.

Despite the warm sunshine streaming between the buildings into the sheltered space, the diminutive figure complete with woollen balaclava, was wrapped securely in his army greatcoat, buttoned tightly to the neck.

Harry eased his haunches onto a beer barrel and sat in silence regarding the ragged bundle. After almost a minute he took a half sovereign from his waistcoat pocket and, reaching over, laid it carefully on the cardboard box. It lay there for several seconds, glinting softly in the sun's rays, before with slow deliberation a grubby hand extended and the coin disappeared into the folds of the voluminous coat.

'It took you long enough, Mr North.' The whining cant was gone. Thin and cracked with age, the voice was strong and clear.

'Yes, Weasel, I was very slow. I should have pinned you long ago. We're all getting older.'

'You were one of Tom Norton's best kept secrets, but you were very, very good. It was you who followed the Leschenko gang to Collett Lane the night of the shootings in Century Courtyard.'

An eerie cackle emerged from the depths of the balaclava. 'You should know, Mr North. You were there . . . and after Mr Norton was shot it was you and Mr Squires who settled up with me afterwards.'

Harry nodded. He had remembered the previous night. While Tom was in hospital with his shattered hip he had given Jesse Squires ten pounds and asked him to pay off his informant Saul Meakin, known as 'the Weasel'. Up to that point no one had known of the little man's existence, which was one of his principal values as an informant. It had been Meakin who had led Norton to the gang's hiding place in the blacking factory.

Ten pounds was a monumental amount of money to pay to an informant and Jesse decided that young Harry North should accompany him to the dismal house in Dakin Street that Meakin shared with a worn-out prostitute. He and Jesse had kept the secret of the informant's identity, and Harry had always presumed that when Tom didn't return to work, Jesse took the man on for himself. Why the Weasel subsequently left Kelsford or, for that matter, had returned years later, the detective did not know.

It was the rhyme that he should have identified: 'Half a pound of tuppenny rice, half a pound of treacle, mix it up and make it nice . . . pop goes the Weasel.'

'So,' he said carefully, 'for a man who never misses a trick, what is there going on that I should know about, Saul?'

'I'd have to think about that, Mr North.'

'Don't piss me about, Weasel. That wouldn't be a clever thing to do.' Harry's voice was hard and threatening.

Unperturbed, the little man began to hum to himself. 'Half a pound of tuppenny rice . . .'

'Do you ever go by the new hospital?' With all the equipment and unlocked huts on the building site, it was a safe bet that the little vagrant knew his way round it.

'Sometimes.'

'Is there anything that might interest me?'

'There's a nurse who's not all she seems, I've seen her with her soldier friend. She steals morphine.'

'She's already dead,' muttered Harry irritably. Changing tack, he said, 'Tell me, where were you on the day that the woman was murdered in Devonshire Gardens?'

Just for a second he caught the glimpse of something in the thin face peering out at him from under the outlandish headgear. 'Have to think about that one, Mr North, have to think about that . . .'

Harry held his breath. In the enclosed yard the warmth of the sun was accentuating the already overpowering odours emanating from the bundle of clothing.

Weasel began to hum to himself again, 'If you want to know the time ask a policeman . . .'

Harry was beginning to think that he was wasting his money. The man had at one time been a good informant, but with advancing age and his erratic life he appeared to have become at best unstable. On the other hand, the question about Devonshire Gardens had produced a result – of that he was certain. 'Don't waste my time,' he said quietly. 'People who waste my time soon regret it. Bring me something about the Devonshire Gardens murder and I'll make it worth your while.'

As he walked out of the yard, he heard the thin reedy words echoing behind him: 'every member of the Force has a watch and chain of course . . .'

Chapter Seventeen

On a bleak snowy January night, with New Year over and the war grinding its way into 1916, an apparently unrelated occurrence near the village of Castle Donington just south of Derby added another dimension to the events taking place in Kelsford. Overhead, the beam of the powerful searchlight swept the dead ground between the sentry post and the twenty foot high perimeter wire in a slow right to left traverse. Lying perfectly still on the frozen ground, Erhard Siegler and his companions waited until the beam moved to the next section of the wire before moving. With darkness restored, the four men climbed stiffly to their feet and, forcing movement back into their frozen limbs, ran to where the heavy steel mesh had been cut through in readiness.

Crouching by the stout wooden pole to which the perimeter wire was attached, Siegler set to work. The dark rain clouds harbouring the downpour that was about to begin served to block out the moon, but while concealing them from the guards it made the task of finding the hole much more difficult. Almost five precious minutes elapsed before he was able to locate the aperture. Signalling to the others, he crawled through the gap and dropped into the dry ditch on the other side.

In less than a minute all four were through the wire. Tauber and Wiesmann picked up the square of mesh that had been laid on the ground next to the hole and propped it up again to conceal the gap. It would quickly be found in the morning when their absence was discovered at roll call, but for now it would not be detected by the questing searchlight.

They grinned at one another in delight. Life in the prisoner of war camp at Donington Hall was by no means arduous, but as German officers it was their sworn duty to escape and return to the Fatherland in order to continue the war against the British.

With a quick, spontaneous movement they shook hands with each other before, crouching low, they climbed out of the drainage ditch and trotted off along the narrow country lane towards the crossroads half a mile away.

By the time they reached the rendezvous point the exercise had restored the circulation to their limbs, despite the cold winter's night. Siegler, in the lead, almost ran into the side of a waiting baker's van as he rounded the bend near the crossroads. A tall man in a dark mackintosh and with a soft hat pulled down over his face opened the back doors of the van. Tumbling in, the escapees sprawled onto the floor. The man climbed in behind them, while the driver appeared out of the shadows and quietly closed the doors before getting into the cab.

'I take it there were no problems.' The man spoke German with a slight accent, betraying the fact that it was not his native tongue.

'No, it went perfectly.' Now that he was in the van the cold had taken over again, and Siegler found himself shivering. Looking around in the gloom, he saw that the others were also hugging themselves against the cold.

'Have a swallow of this, mein herren, and then please change into the clothes over there. We don't have much time.' Siegler saw that there were four neat piles of clothes, including coats and hats, at the far end of the van behind the driver's cab. The silver flask that the man proffered contained a potent dark rum, which hit his stomach with a jolt before taking off around his system like liquid fire.

'Sorry. Schnapps is a little difficult to come by in these parts,' the man said easily.

'Rum's very welcome, I can assure you.' The voice came from the other side of the van. 'Arno Tauber, Hauptman, Sixty-Sixth Field Artillery.' The stocky Bavarian held out a hairy fist.

'Pleased to meet you,' their host replied. 'Now get changed. We can talk later.'

Wearing warm dry clothes, Erhard Siegler took a second swallow from the flask and leaned back against the side of the jolting van, a feeling of well being creeping over him. He surveyed his companions. Tauber, the short, powerful, artilleryman, now clad in a long overcoat that had seen better days, and a cloth cap with ear muffs tied up on the top, looked remarkably like a small bear. The others were similarly dressed. Young von Otting, the aristocrat of the group, wore a reefer jacket two sizes too large for him, while Josef Wiesmann, like Tauber, wore an old overcoat and had a voluminous woollen scarf wound around his neck.

Relaxing, Siegler enjoyed his first taste of freedom for nearly a year. Like Wiesmann he was an airman, although as a Kapitänleutnant of the Navy Airship Division, and senior officer of the group, he was in a different unit from the young fighter pilot. Siegler's Zeppelin had been brought down during a bombing run over the eastern counties the previous year, while Josef's capture came about after he lost a dogfight over France.

The young Leutnant gave a broad grin. 'Geht's ja gut, Herr Kapitän, nicht war?' he said brightly. Somewhere in the background of his accent was the twang of a Rhinelander.

Helmut von Otting stared coldly across the van at him. 'Don't start congratulating yourself too soon. We're only just outside the wire.'

Siegler had decided to include the Uhlan officer in the escape group mainly because of his ability to speak near-fluent English. In the camp the young Prussian had not made himself popular, with his overbearing attitude and deprecating manner. That he did not like Wiesmann because of his Jewish background was something that the Leutnant made little attempt to conceal. Interesting, thought the airship captain, that Wiesmann was credited with shooting down eight enemy aircraft in single engagements, while the cavalry officer, having been taken prisoner during the retreat from the Marne, had seen relatively little fighting.

The third and oldest man in the group, 'Onkel Arno', was, like Siegler, a professional. A captain of artillery, Tauber had served under the Kaiser for almost a quarter of a century before Dame Fortune put him in the wrong place at the wrong time, and he was captured along with his guns as the German army began its unsuccessful manoeuvre to encircle Paris. Siegler hoped that if they were stopped and checked no one would notice the faded tattoo on the Bavarian's right forearm: the imperial eagle carrying in its claws a banner declaring 'Mit Gott für König und Vaterland'.

It was earlier in the week that the escape had been set up. Each Monday morning a supply wagon from the nearby town of Loughborough came into the camp to allow the German and Austrian officers to purchase extra foodstuffs, such as fresh cheeses and sausage, to supplement the food served by the kitchens. The owner of the wagon was Hanie Wermuth, a Dutchman who had lived in the district for years. Wermuth was a pro-German collaborator, who regularly smuggled in items of contraband such as bottles of whisky or extra tobacco. While wrapping a piece of black bread and wurst for Siegler, a slip of paper was inconspicuously slipped in with the food. With an imperceptible nod, Siegler took the parcel and returned to his hut. Back in their quarters, gathered round the table, the note was examined by the ten occupants of Hut 15.

The instructions were simple and explicit. 'Wednesday night, after lights out, between guard towers five and six, perimeter wire will be cut. Four men only. Rendezvous crossroads, one kilometre due east. Contact will wait until 2200 hrs.'

After some discussion it was decided that the escape attempt should be made. Helmut von Otting was an obvious candidate, as he was the only man in the hut who spoke English. Lots were drawn for the remaining three places, resulting in Siegler, Wiesmann and Tauber being chosen. The rest was easy. After lights out on the appointed night the four men slipped away, and under cover of darkness stole across to where the twenty foot high guard towers, each manned by two sentries and equipped with a searchlight and heavy machine gun, maintained a watch along the perimeter of the camp. Since the flyer Oberleutnant Günther Plüschow's successful escape the previous summer, perimeter security had been tightened up considerably.

Lying out of sight on the cold ground between towers five and six, they counted how long the part of the wire that they needed to get to was left in darkness. It was just under seven minutes, ample for their needs, provided they could locate the gap quickly. If they failed, the four of them would be caught out in the open by the next sweep of the searchlight's beam. The fact that it had taken almost five minutes in the pitch dark, working with frozen hands, to locate the hole had proved almost fatal, mused Siegler. They had only just made it through.

His felt hat removed, the Englishman – for from his accent that was what Siegler judged him to be – handed each of them a brown envelope. He was, the Zeppelin captain supposed, in his middle thirties, just over medium height, clean shaven, with thick dark brown hair parted just off centre over his left eye. Siegler wondered what it was that had kept him out of the army.

Opening the envelope, he found some money and a small buff coloured identity card, issued under the Aliens Restrictions Act 1914 in the name of Marc Van de Walle, lodging at 23 Minden Street, Derby. His occupation was a surveyor employed by the Ministry of Works.

'The papers are extremely good, and will, I can assure you, stand up to the closest scrutiny.' The man smiled encouragingly. The papers were genuine, part of a batch that had mysteriously disappeared from a government department a month earlier during an office move. The harassed civil servant responsible for their safe-keeping had endorsed the gap in the serial numbers as 'stock destroyed owing to damage', as a matter of self-preservation.

'Which of you speaks any English?'

The Uhlan raised a hand. 'I spent a time here before the war studying at Cambridge University.'

The Englishman raised a quizzical eyebrow. 'Excellent,' he murmured. 'In which case perhaps you and Herr Tauber will stay together when we arrive at Loughborough, while the others come with me.' Pausing, he looked around at the foursome, checking the individual appearance of each in their borrowed clothes. Apparently satisfied, he continued. 'I'm sorry, I haven't introduced myself. Please refer to me as Hendry. I'm a British citizen, so I don't require any movement permit. You'll see from your identity papers that you're all shown as living at an address in Derby. The address exists, and other than your papers being physically checked with the Derby Borough Police they'll stand routine inspection. The travel documents are made out for a journey from Derby to Newcastle-upon-Tyne. Herr Tauber and . . . ?' Again the eyebrow was raised enquiringly.

'Otting. Leutnant Helmut von Otting.' The pale blond features regarded the Englishman with slight disdain. The young cavalry officer was less than happy at travelling in the company of traitors and Jews.

Picking up the Prussian's train of thought, Hendry's smile was distinctly chilly. 'You'll take a train to Sheffield. Buy your tickets on arrival at Loughborough railway station. At Sheffield change trains and carry on to Newcastle. When you get off the train at the other end go into the buffet. There you'll be met by a contact who'll take you to a safe house.'

'Your English may be quite good,' he added dryly, 'but you have a distinctly Prussian accent, so don't speak unnecessarily. You're supposed to be Belgian.'

'And the others?' Tauber waved a hand towards Wiesmann and Siegler.

'They'll remain with me. The route we take is not your concern. Sufficient to say that we'll all meet again in Newcastle. If you're captured it's best that you know as little as possible.'

Tauber nodded. It seemed a sensible arrangement.

Hendry resumed his briefing. 'Each of you is carrying papers which show that you're involved in the construction industry. Your cover is that you've been granted permission to travel in order to attend a meeting with British officials from the War Office, to make arrangements for Belgian labour to work on the construction of a new prisoner of war camp being built in the north-east.' The van lurched to a halt, and Hendry pulled open a small hatch. In a low voice he had a short conversation with the driver. Turning back to face the four men, he said, 'This is where we split up. Hauptman Tauber, you and Leutnant von Otting go through to the northbound platform. It's now . . .' he quickly consulted his wristwatch '. . . ten twenty-five. The London to Sheffield train's due in at ten thirty-six. That gives you eleven minutes to purchase your tickets and get on the train, so you'll have to move quickly. Remember, from now on do not under any circumstances speak to each other in German.'

A moment later the back doors were undone. Climbing down stiffly, Tauber and von Otting stretched their cramped limbs, then shook hands with the others and departed towards the patch of light that spilt out from the entrance to the railway station.

'We'll stay here for a short while,' said Hendry, once more consulting his watch. 'Our train's the southbound for Northampton, which isn't due until ten to eleven.'

Siegler eased his back against the side of the van and held out a hand. 'Erhard Siegler, Navy Airship Detachment. This is Josef Wiesmann, Fliegerabteilung Twenty-Four. We're grateful for your assistance, Herr Hendry. You've gone to a great deal of trouble on our behalf.'

Hendry shrugged and passed him the flask of rum. 'It's not a trouble to help out in the war effort.'

'You're British?' Wiesmann was curious.

Hendry gave him a slow smile. 'My family's Austrian. My grandfather came here seventy years ago, in 1845. My father and mother were born here, as was I. Because of our family's business interests, until recently my father, my brother and I travelled regularly to Vienna and Berlin. In August 1914 my father was in Hamburg, and was unable to leave Germany once war had been declared. Since then he's been living with a cousin in Lübeck. He's seventy-three years old and not in good health, Herr Wiesmann. I don't know if I'll ever see him again. Because of our family history, my brother and I were arrested and interned at the military headquarters in York. After three months it was decided that as neither of us were liable for service in the armies of the Central Powers it was safe to allow us to return to our families. But our business is in ruins.' Hendry's face was an inscrutable mask. 'So much for three-quarters of a century of service to the British economy.'

Siegler wondered how many disillusioned men such as Hendry were working to help British prisoners and sabotage the economy in Germany. 'So where are we going from here?' he asked.

'We catch the train for Northampton, and from there east to Peterborough, where we change for Newcastle. Leave all your belongings in the van: Hanie will get rid of them. If you need cigarettes I'll get them from the station kiosk.'

The mention of cigarettes made Erhard Siegler aware of the fact that he had not had a smoke since leaving Hut 15.

Hendry raised the blind at the carriage window, and wiped away the condensation. He stared intently into the night as the locomotive pulled into Peterborough. In the glowing gaslight of the station lamps the platform was a hive of activity, Soldiers of all ranks and units were milling about, and with a feeling of unease he spotted two uniformed constables near the news stand, carefully scrutinising the passengers descending from the train.

That the prison escape had been discovered and an alert telegraphed across the region was, he thought, unlikely. He decided that they had simply arrived at the same time as a troop train, which, while inconvenient, might work for them. More people passing through at this time of night would mean that the police were less likely to check papers.

With a squeal of wheels gripping the steel rails and a great whooshing of steam, the train slid to a halt. One of the two constables, an elderly man with grey hair and a large handlebar moustache, had positioned himself immediately outside their carriage. Deciding that attack was the best form of defence, Hendry signalled to the Germans to follow him, climbed down from the train and approached the policeman. 'Excuse me, officer,' he said pleasantly. 'Do you have any idea if the Newcastle train is running to time?'

Without bothering to consult the station clock, the officer replied, 'It's nine minutes late, sir. Due in at twelve thirty-five.'

'Thank you, officer.' Turning to Siegler, he said, 'That's excellent. It'll give us time for a cup of tea.' Aware that the German had not understood a word of the exchange, he made a small gesture with his hand towards the lighted doorway at the end of the platform. Bidding the officer a cheery goodnight, he set off towards the buffet followed closely by his companions.

Inside the tiny café it was standing room only. Soldiers were monopolising the floor space between the half dozen tables that appeared to have been declared the province of their officers.

Finding a space near to the back wall, and speaking quietly in French, Hendry told the other two to remain there while he fetched some hot drinks. He returned quickly with three steaming cups of thick brown tea. Despite the number of people crammed into the refreshment room, most of the soldiers were only keeping out of the cold, and the serving area was relatively free. Still speaking in French, he said in a low tone, 'We've hit a transit stop of some sort. With any luck most of them will be going south to Dover, or catching the next train for the Midlands. There's a large military depot at Glen Parva on the outskirts of Leicester, and it's a fair bet that's where some of them are bound. Unfortunately a lot of them could be on their way up north to York or Catterick. We'll soon find out.

They did not have to wait long. Hendry and his charges, once safely aboard the Newcastle train, found for themselves an unoccupied compartment, while large numbers of troops milled about on the platform, responding to NCOs' shouted commands, before collecting their mountains of kit and climbing up onto the waiting train.

Accompanied by a great slamming of doors and the noise and chatter of men finding their places, the train pulled out of the station. Hendry became aware that four soldiers were peering into their compartment through the glass partition. Sliding the door back, a young private, his face pitted with acne scars, stepped in.

'Got your papers, then?' the private demanded, holding out his hand towards Josef Wiesmann. Although he did not understand the words, the meaning was obvious. Wiesmann reached into the inside pocket of his jacket and produced his newly acquired identity papers.

'Monsieur,' he murmured politely.

Taking the documents, the soldier scanned them in a perfunctory manner. 'Frogs,' he said over his shoulder to the others. 'Right, get your kit and fuck off. These seats have been taken over by the military.'

A look of confusion crossed Wiesmann's face, and he shot an enquiring glance at Hendry.

'Never mind no-parlez-Anglais. I've told you, get your kit and fuck off. Preferably,' he added, with a smirk for the benefit of his companions, 'towards France.'

Hendry held his breath for a second. The youth could not be more than eighteen, he thought. All their uniforms were brand new, the buttons bright and shiny. The clothing and equipment of men returning to France were usually much more worn and soiled – the brass deliberately dulled so as not to glint in the sunlight for the benefit of a sniper. It was obvious that these troops were either on a training exercise or going to a transit camp before being sent to the front for the first time. Whichever, they had the cockiness of youth, and he could not afford to allow a confrontation to develop.

A commotion outside pulled the soldiers' attention back to the corridor, and they all leapt to attention as a tall figure with a sharply waxed moustache pushed into the doorway. 'You got a problem 'ere, Private Musson?' The harsh and grating parade ground growl originated somewhere in the East End of London.

Hendry saw that the newcomer was a warrant officer in his late fifties, wearing on his sleeve the coat of arms of a regimental sergeant major. The gleaming Sam Browne belt, normally reserved for officers, proclaimed him to be a guardsman. Without having to think about it, Hendry immediately realised he was a pre-war soldier who had been recalled from retirement specifically to train recruits. The Queen and King's South Africa medal ribbons told of service in the Boer War.

'No problem, Sarn't Major. Just clearing these froggies out, sir. Make a bit of space for the fighting men, sir.'

The warrant officer glared round the compartment. 'Come on then, you 'eard the man. Move it!'

Hendry made a slight hand movement to Wiesmann and Siegler. Wordlessly they gathered up their coats and hats and left. The sergeant major stared pointedly at Hendry, not quite certain if he were with the men or not. In the perfectly modulated drawl of an upper-class English gentleman, Hendry said, 'If you will excuse me, Sergeant Major, I think a breath of fresh air is called for.' Pushing past the soldiers, he followed the others out of the compartment.

The remainder of the night was spent standing in the corridor of the swaying train as it clattered its way north.

It was soon after six o'clock in the morning when the three men, tired and ill-tempered, emerged from Newcastle station into the deserted, rain-sodden street. Climbing into the front seat of a waiting taxicab, Hendry gave the driver an address in North Shields and settled back wearily into the seat. It was the first time they had sat down for over five hours.

While the Englishman slumped in the front seat, Wiesmann and Siegler watched silently out of the window as the dismal grey houses slid by. Passing the murky waters of the Tyne, swollen by days of incessant rain, they registered the amount of merchant shipping that even at this early hour was picking its way along the river. Early in the war, ships of the Imperial Fleet had successfully shelled this part of the coast, as far as Hartlepool, in what had come to be known as the tip and run bombardment. Siegler realised that on his return to Germany he must bring this prime bombing target to the attention of Naval Intelligence.

Daylight was beginning to filter through the dark rain clouds as the taxi pulled up in a narrow back street on the east side of the city. Hendry paid the driver five shillings and told him to keep the change. They paused to make a show of lighting cigarettes until the cab had disappeared round a corner at the end of the street. Pulling his collar up against the persistent drizzle, Hendry set off down the road followed by his charges. For the next ten minutes they made their way through a maze of grim and dismal side streets, each a carbon copy of the last: row upon row of narrow terraced houses, punctuated every few hundred yards by the front door of a tiny shop or public house. The rain-streaked brickwork was, Wiesmann reflected, not dissimilar to that of the grim mining districts of his native Rhineland.

Turning left at a dilapidated corner shop, already busy selling penny plugs of tobacco and newspapers to rheumy eyed, unshaven men, cloth caps pulled tightly down over their faces and mufflers wrapped around their necks, Hendry stopped outside a house with a peeling green front door. After tapping lightly on the front window, he pushed open the tall gate to the entry. Inside the dark passageway, he paused to check that they had not been followed before closing the gate and drawing the bolt across. The entry between the house and its neighbour was barely wide enough for a man to walk down. Two lines of washing, one on each side and hanging on slack clothes lines against the brickwork, made it almost impossible to negotiate the narrow passage without turning sideways. At the bottom, in a V from each side to the garden wall between the houses, were two more flimsy board gates. Pressing the latch on the one to the left, Hendry led them into a tiny back yard.

Before they had secured the gate, the kitchen door opened to reveal a beaming Arno Tauber. 'Also, wie geht's?' he demanded, shaking hands with each of the new arrivals in turn. 'It's good to see you.'

Inside the living room the heat from a black iron range was welcome to the tired men. Siegler dropped into an armchair on one side of the fireplace and, holding his hands out, began to massage some warmth back into them. 'What time did you get here?' he asked.

'Just after four,' replied Tauber. 'There was absolutely no problem. We were met by Emile here at the station, and then got a taxi. It dropped us about ten minutes away and we walked the rest.

Siegler noticed for the first time the man standing in the doorway. Thin and in need of a shave, he was dressed in a pair of workman's trousers and an old and faded collarless blue workshirt.

'Any problems?' Hendry asked him in German.

'No. Everything went well at Sheffield, and there were no document checks at this end. You?' From the man's accent Siegler judged him to be Austrian.

'None at all if you don't count a bunch of wet-behind-the-ears Tommies fresh from recruit camp who commandeered our carriage and made us stand up all the way.'

Now that the journey was over Hendry sounded worn out, and it occurred to Siegler for the first time how much strain the man must have been under for the last few hours. If caught, they would be returned to the prison camp, but the Englishman would be shot.

'Please make yourselves at home.' Hendry noted that Helmut von Otting had not offered to vacate his place near to the range for Josef Wiesmann to warm himself. 'Emile and I have work to do. We'll be back early this evening. There's some food and coffee in the kitchen cupboard. Until then I suggest that you get as much rest as you can: we have another long night ahead of us. We'll leave here around nine o'clock.'

'Where are we going?' Von Otting's clipped tones gave the question the air of an inspecting officer asking a new recruit where a speck of dust on his tunic had come from.

Hendry eyed the Uhlan with undisguised distaste. If any of the group were going to present a problem it would be this arrogant young Prussian. 'In the words of your fellow countryman, Count von Bismarck – wait and see.' The look of confusion on the German's sallow features as he tried to recollect when the Iron Chancellor might have said such a thing brought a brief smile of satisfaction to Hendry's tired face. Without further conversation, he and Emile stepped out into the passage, and quietly left through the front door.

At precisely five minutes past seven that evening Hendry and Emile re-appeared at the back gate. Emile had his arm hooked through the handle of a heavy wicker delivery basket of the sort usually carried by grocers' and butchers' boys, while Hendry had a large canvas bag slung over his shoulder. Emile's basket, the Germans were delighted to find, contained a selection of cooked meats and sausages, and two cold roasted fowls. The greatest prize, though, was a litre bottle of peach Schnapps.

'Where on earth did you get this from?' enquired a delighted Tauber. 'I haven't seen any of this stuff since I left home.'

'It's a sad fact of war,' explained Hendry, 'that on both sides the businessmen are pursuing a policy of business as usual. This will have come from the Fatherland through Scandinavia on a neutral ship. Travelling in the opposite direction there'll be fine Scotch whisky and cigars, which will find their way into many good German and Austrian homes.'

Von Otting and Siegler abandoned their game of chess at the table in the middle of the room so the food could be set out. While the Germans devoured the meal hungrily, Emile began to rake the coals in the fire-grate in preparation for leaving the house.

'Wrap up well,' Hendry said, opening his canvas bag. Inside were scarves and woollen gloves, which he piled up on one of the armchairs. 'When we leave here we're going to a safe house on the moors. You can lie low there while I arrange passage on a boat home. It may take a day or two and the moors are not the most hospitable of places, but because they're so isolated you'll be safe from prying eyes.'

Siegler's brow creased in a slight frown. 'We're going inland again, away from the coast?'

'Yes. Think about it. All the ports will be swarming with police. We're taking you to a nice quiet place where the only signs of life for thirty miles in any direction are sheep, and it's relatively simple for one of us to keep a watch on the approach roads. If there are any unforeseen problems it may be necessary to take you further, over the Scottish border. Trust us: we know what we're doing.'

Siegler shrugged in resignation. 'Better bring the chessboard, Helmut.'

Their conversation was interrupted by the sound of a light tap on the front door. All of them froze. From under the heavy pea jacket that he was wearing, Emile produced a long-barrelled Smith and Wesson revolver. Hendry put up a hand for silence and went into the passage.

A moment later he returned, followed by a tall spare figure wearing a long dun-coloured duster coat and deliveryman's flat cap. Emile grunted as he pushed the revolver back into his belt.

'You need to be careful there wi' that, Emile, man, you'll be blowin' yuh bollocks off wi' yon cannon if you're nat careful.' The thick Geordie accent was difficult for Hendry to follow, and he knew that none of the others would remotely comprehend what the man had said.

Not needing to understand the words, the Austrian gave a dry grin. 'You're early, Colly,' he retorted.

'Better be early than late, provided it's nat for your ain funeral.' The man called Colly looked across to Hendry for confirmation. Only he and the Englishman knew that Hendry had brought the time forward for last minute security.

'Last leg, gentlemen.' Hendry ushered them towards the front door. 'Time to be going.'

With a final check around the room to ensure that no trace of their occupancy remained, the men began to file out into the hallway. Siegler picked up the chessboard and pushed the box of wooden pieces into his overcoat pocket.

The back of the Milne-Daimler lorry was only marginally more comfortable than the van in which they had made their escape from Donington Hall. Coleman Farr, or 'Colly' as he was known to his friends, had thrown some blankets and a straw mattress in the back of the covered wagon, and the wooden floorboards were swept clean of traces of the pig meal that he delivered daily to farms near Morpeth and Ashington.

Backs braced against the closed sides of the five ton lorry, their nostrils becoming accustomed to the thick odour of pig food that lingered in the confined space, the men passed the time smoking endless cigarettes and chatting quietly as the driver negotiated the tortuous country lanes. Hendry explained that in order to avoid the busy main road leading north up to the army camp at Catterick, it was necessary for them to take the less used roads along the coast, before cutting back at a right angle and heading west towards the moors.

They had been travelling over three hours before, every bone in their bodies aching from the cramped conditions, they crossed the Great North Road and passed through the sleeping cluster of cottages that was the tiny village of Whittingham.

'How much longer is this going to take?' demanded von Otting, glaring balefully at Hendry.

The Englishman pushed back his felt hat and grinned maliciously at the young cavalry officer. The sooner they parted company the better he would like it. 'About two cigarettes,' he replied, pulling a corner of the straw palliasse under his aching buttocks.

A shadow passed momentarily across Arno Tauber's dark features. The expression was one that had recently become common in the army, but he had never before heard a civilian use it.

The road deteriorated into little more than a cart track, which after about five miles took them into another tiny cluster of cottages. After passing the only building of any size, a large grey stone house standing at a crossroads, the driver forked left and, dropping into first gear, followed the track up a steep winding climb that took them away from the last signs of civilisation.

The sky was beginning to lighten when after a further gruelling half hour the lorry finally came to a halt. Descending stiffly, the men saw that they were in the middle of a vast stretch of open moorland. The rain had finally relented and an icy wind was blowing away the clouds.

'Welcome to Otterburn, gentlemen,' Hendry's voice was as bleak as the moor. 'It's probably the most deserted place in England at this time of the year, and the safest for you to hide. Other than the odd poacher, no one will set foot here until at least April, when the shepherds turn the sheep back out from their winter quarters.'

Having said goodbye to Emile and Colly, Hendry took a compass bearing to confirm their position on the map that he produced from his shoulder bag. He led the party away from the road along an almost indiscernible path. Going was difficult on the soft ground, which after days of heavy rain was a quagmire, and for the next hour, cold and fatigued, the group plodded on in dismal silence.

Losing his footing on a slippery piece of turf, Josef Wiesmann fell heavily, and slid sideways into the waters of a stagnant drainage pool at the side of the path. Cursing fluently, he hauled himself back to his feet covered in thick glutinous mud.

'You flyers aren't used to the realities of life,' jibed Tauber dourly. 'In France it's like this all the time – mud and shit, mixed with shit and mud.'

'And who turns everything into mud and shit?' retorted Wiesmann angrily. 'The bastard gunners!'

'Keep your voices down,' muttered Hendry testily. 'We're nearly at the croft, and there could well be a poacher up here after deer. I'd prefer to see him first, before he hears you lot and thinks the invasion's started.'

Von Otting glowered. They were all worn out. 'We're in the middle of the moon, and you tell us that we're nearly there!'

Ignoring him, the Englishman pointed to the right. 'Over there. Come on.'

They were practically on top of the hut before any of the others saw it. Suddenly the ground dropped steeply away into a gully and they found themselves looking down on a pale patch which, in the gradually growing light, they realised was a thatched roof. Scrambling down the incline brought them to the side wall of what was little more than a large stone hut built into the hillside.

Hendry indicated for them to remain where they were while he checked that it was unoccupied. Watching him move softly forward, the others saw that a pistol had magically appeared in his right hand. A minute later, the revolver held loosely at his side, he reappeared and signalled to them.

The tiny single-storey crofter's cottage, if such it could be called, had been built into the side of the gully to afford its occupants a maximum of shelter. In winter it was protected from the howling gales and lashing rain that regularly swept across the open land, while in summer the gully provided a good deal of shade from the blistering heat of the sun. That it had been empty for some time was apparent. Although the single low-beamed room smelled cold and musty, four dry and clean mattresses had been stacked in one corner, and an old stove in the middle of the floor had a pile of kindling stacked next to it. To complete the furnishings, a wooden table and chairs stood by the wall at the back.

'I suggest you get the fire going and make yourselves comfortable,' suggested Hendry. 'I'm going back up the path. It'll soon be daylight and I want to be sure we've not been followed.'

Nodding their assent, the exhausted men shrugged off their wet outer clothing. Wiesmann opened the hinged door of the stove and began to stack firewood carefully inside. Looking at his watch, Erhard Siegler saw that it was half past six. Looking up, he saw that the Englishman had already left. 'So, how long do you think we can stay here without going completely mad?' he asked. 'We had better billets at Donington.' As he turned with a rueful grin to the others, Siegler caught a worried expression on Arno Tauber's face. 'What's the matter, Arno? No one ever said it would be the Adlerhof.'

The Bavarian was gazing around the cottage thoughtfully. 'I've got a feeling that there's something not right about this.'

'Go on.' Tauber had everyone's attention.

'This escape was set up very quickly – before we really had a chance to think it through – yet every single detail seems to have been meticulously planned. We've travelled hundreds of miles, yet no one has even asked for our papers.'

'That can happen, Arno, and we know the Dutchman's reliable. He got Günther Plüschow out and back home, didn't he?' said Siegler.

'What's the point you're making, Arno?' asked Wiesmann.

'Well, we're not actually out, are we?' Tauber scratched a meaty fist across his unshaven jaw. 'With an escape that's this well planned, you'd expect to be split up and taken to an exit point on the coast, whereas exactly the opposite has happened. We've been kept together and brought inland.'

'This is pure speculation.' There was a hint of asperity in von Otting's voice. 'What we all need is something to eat and a few hours' sleep. In daylight things will look much more sensible.'

'Tell me, then,' asked Tauber, 'how many civilians do you know who could lead a forced march across a wilderness in the middle of a winter's night using only compass bearings?'

Half a mile away, on a rocky outcrop at the top of the gully, lying prone in the camouflaged brushwood hide, the man swept the surrounding moorland with a powerful pair of ten by fifty Zeiss glasses for any signs of life. Satisfied that he was alone, he cupped a flickering match in his almost frozen hands and lit the last Passing Cloud in his packet, before scrutinising the front door of the croft.

Inside the cottage the four men, having got the stove burning, pulled up the chairs and discussed their situation.

'I think Arno might have a point, and if he does we need to decide on a course of action.' Siegler rubbed his eyes: what he really wanted to do was sleep. They were all tired, but if the Englishman was leading them into a trap they needed to be ready.

Wiesmann got up from his chair and walked over to the uncurtained window that looked out along the gully. From somewhere overhead came the noise of an aero engine, followed a few seconds later by the sight of a bright yellow biplane coming in low at about two hundred feet. As a pilot, the fact registered with Wiesmann that the open moors would provide a perfect firing range for aircraft to test their guns. Watching as the RFC machine disappeared from view behind the incline, Josef realised that they would have to be extremely careful not to be spotted from the air. 'First we need to separate him from his gun,' he said over his shoulder, watching to see if the plane reappeared. 'It's daylight now, and he must be as tired as we are. It's very cold out there. When he comes back in we offer him a place by the stove and then jump him. If we're right we'll make him talk, and then decide what to do.'

'If we're right it will be necessary to kill him.' The Prussian looked at the others for confirmation.

'I think that goes without saying,' Siegler agreed. 'At least out here there'll be no problem in disposing of a body. Josef, stay at the window and keep watch.'

'Meantime,' said Tauber, 'I need the toilet.'

Presumably because of the forbidding conditions outside, a corner of the room containing a bucket had been curtained off to afford some degree of privacy. The arrangement was merely a variation on the dry ash privies found at the end of every courtyard in the land. A hinged wooden toilet seat had been fitted onto a large galvanised pail, which could be emptied after use into a pit well away from the cottage.

Closing the curtain behind him, Tauber dropped his trousers. As he settled onto the seat the Bavarian heard a sharp cracking sound as a small glass phial fixed between the wooden seat and the edge of the metal bucket shattered.

Through the binoculars a figure appeared at the window of the shack. A small adjustment brought into focus the slim figure of Josef Wiesmann. As the watcher observed him, his concentration was broken by the sound of an aircraft approaching. Risking a quick glance up, he saw a BE2c reconnaissance plane drift slowly past. Returning to his surveillance of the building, he saw that Wiesmann was no longer visible. He was about to put the binoculars down for a moment in order to rest his eyes when a movement caught his attention.

At first he was not sure, but the front door seemed to have opened slightly. Holding his breath he waited, certain that he was right. Suddenly the door was flung open, and the figures of Erhard Siegler and Helmut von Otting burst out. Both men were clutching at their throats. Almost immediately Siegler dropped to his knees, then slumped forward onto the ground. Von Otting tottered a few paces past him, apparently trying to vomit, before losing his balance. He stumbled sideways, rolled onto his back and, arms outstretched, lay prone.

The binoculars swept back to the doorway. After ten minutes neither of the other occupants had appeared. Rolling over onto his side, the man carefully packed his glasses back into the canvas bag, along with the now cold cigarette end and the spent match. Standing up, he kicked the flimsy hide to pieces and scattered the brushwood untidily. The wind and rain would disperse them within an hour. Having made sure that he had left no traces of his presence, he slung the bag over his shoulder and, keeping to the high ground, strode off in the direction in which the BE2c had been heading.

It took half an hour of brisk walking before he came over the crest of a small rise and spotted, in the soft heather two hundred yards away, a bright yellow fuselage with red and blue roundels. Standing beside the machine were two figures, muffled up against the cold in leather coats and flying helmets. One of them gave a brief wave of recognition.

As he joined them the taller of the two men threw away his cigarette. 'You look absolutely worn out. Everything go all right?'

'Fine,' he replied tersely. 'They're down already. Siegler and von Otting are on the ground outside, so it must have been either Wiesmann or Tauber who used the bucket.'

Gresham's mouth twitched. 'I do hope you haven't been anywhere near, Ted.'

Bayliss shook his head, 'You jest. I stuck on the high ground until I was well clear. You wouldn't have any ciggies, would you? I smoked my last back at the hide.'

'We don't need to be here too long.' Handing Bayliss his gunmetal case, Gresham nodded to the pilot, who was studiously examining one of the aircraft's wing struts. Raising his hand in acknowledgement, the figure in helmet and goggles climbed into the rear cockpit seat and began to prepare for take-off.

'What about him?' Bayliss asked casually.

'Percy? Good man. He's been with us for some time; recruited him before the war. Grammar school lad, no pretensions and very bright. While this present caper was being set up we sent him off to Farnborough to learn to fly. Most worthwhile, I have to say. During the wee small hours, while you were slogging round the countryside, we were doing a spot of charpoy-bashing, a good night's kip followed by eggs and bacon in York, and then simply cabbed on up here from a local airfield.'

Bayliss gave him a sour look, which said his turn would come. He cupped his cigarette against the wind. 'Going to be a bit cramped on the way back, isn't it?'

His companion nodded. 'Yes, I'm afraid so. Got you some flying kit, but you and I are going to have to squeeze into the observer's seat together. It'll make the plane heavy to handle and play havoc with the fuel consumption, but they do it all the time in France. Before we leave the area I've asked Percy to do a recce; make sure the other arrangements are in place.'

Edward Bayliss took in the barren landscape around them. He would not be sorry to be on his way back home to a hot meal and a warm bed, but the flight back to Kelsford would be a long cold one. 'What about the bodies?' he asked.

Gresham pushed the cigarette case back in his pocket. 'The dosage in the phial was tiny: they put in what they considered to be sufficient to kill up to ten men. Later today, when Kändler and Duggan arrive, the bodies will be removed by orderlies in protective suits. They'll be taken up to Catterick. We've arranged a secure facility there for Duggan to perform post-mortems – and after that cremation, to remove all traces. In a couple of days we'll put some sheep in the gully. No doubt they'll keel over and die quite quickly. We'll have to do the same thing every day until the ground's clean. Once that's done we'll fire the croft and have a squad of Sappers fill in the gully. When they're finished no one will ever know that there used to be a cottage there.'

A signal from the BE2c indicated that Percy Longman was ready to take off. Bayliss, clad in warm flying leathers, scrambled up into the forward cockpit while Gresham swung the propeller. Five minutes later the biplane, wallowing heavily under the weight of its extra passenger, was airborne.

Gaining about three hundred feet, the pilot dipped the wings gently to starboard and began a wide sweep of the area. Staring down from his precarious position, Bayliss could see the country lane in which Colly Farr had deposited them several miles away to the east. Cautiously driving along the almost hidden path was a convoy of ten army lorries. One more had left the track and was stuck; it had already sunk down as far as its axles. As they watched, two of the wagons peeled off to the left and halted. A group of soldiers got out of one, while men on the tailboard of the second began to drop off rolls of barbed wire and what looked like painted signboards.

Half-turning in his seat, Bayliss gesticulated to Longman to take the plane down for a closer view. The pilot throttled back the engine and, making a series of broad circles, brought the aircraft down to fifty feet.

As they skimmed the moor, Bayliss could see that the soldiers were stretching out the coils of wire to make a perimeter fence. Every hundred yards or so a large square sign bearing a red skull and crossbones was being hammered into the ground. They were designating the area as a minefield in order to keep out any curious locals. It was, he could see, a thankless job. The ground was either rocky and unworkable or a bog.

As he watched, one of the soldiers, armed with a large sledgehammer, stepped back from the track and, missing his footing, disappeared up to his knees in the freezing mire. Bayliss glimpsed a tall figure with a waxed moustache waving his arms at the nearest soldiers to fetch a rope. Swinging in his seat, he signalled frantically to Longman to go round again, and made a downwards gesture. Obviously unhappy at taking the overloaded plane any nearer to the ground, the pilot glared at him and shrugged.

As the BE2c came round for the second time they saw that the soldiers had a line round their terrified comrade, now chest deep in the icy mud, and were attempting to pull him to safety. Bayliss gave a raucous bellow of laughter as he recognised the figure in the bog as the soldier who had commandeered his railway carriage on the train up to Newcastle. He was still chuckling as Percy Longman began to climb to a safe height before setting a course south for Kelsford.

Chapter Eighteen

Sam Norton put down his soup spoon and, breaking a bread roll on his side plate, gazed speculatively at the other guests. The lobster bisque was very good, but he did not have much appetite. It had recently become something of a ritual for him, together with Herbert Duggan and Paul Kändler, to eat with his sister on a Sunday evening at the house in Kingsbury Lane. Tonight was different, however: rather than the usual quiet soirée, Irene had arranged a more formal affair.

Seated on his right, next to Herbert Duggan, were his cousin James and Kathleen Doyle, Paul Kändler sat opposite with Ralph Gresham, and at the far end was Will Mardlin. Sam noticed that either by accident or design the superintendent had been placed next to his sister. He wondered what Irene's motive was for bringing them all together.

James continued to remain decidedly cool towards him, Sam considered. It was sad, he reflected, that his cousin genuinely resented the fact that having been gassed he had neither died nor been posted back to France.

Sam and Will had exchanged polite conversation over pre-dinner drinks, but it had been a strained half hour. It was the first time that they had met since the incident in which the fireman had been killed, and it was clear that the matter stood between them. Sam would have liked to confide in the bluff-looking policeman that he was himself desperately worried about what was going on at the Old Watermill, but he knew this was impossible. He had noticed a subtle change in the demeanour of the two scientists over the last few days, an undercurrent of excitement, and he wondered if they had made a startling discovery that he was not privy to.

Two days before, late on the Friday morning, Ralph Gresham had landed unannounced in an RFC reconnaissance plane on the meadow at the back of the mill. Bundled into the observer's seat with him was a man in civilian clothes whom Sam had never seen before. Ralph introduced him as a Ministry boffin who had come to look the place over. That he was lying Sam was certain.

Far from making a tour of the mill and its laboratories, the man went directly to the room set aside for Gresham's use on his increasingly frequent visits. He remained there until mid-afternoon before being spirited away again in the aircraft.

If Sam needed further confirmation that things were moving, late on Friday evening a telegram from the War Office addressed to Gresham was delivered to Sam's office, stating that Major Gresham was, with immediate effect, promoted to lieutenant colonel.

Picking up his soup spoon again, Sam addressed himself with little interest to his meal. As his eyes came up from his bowl, for a fleeting second he saw a glance pass between his sister and Will Mardlin. With a sharp pang of misgiving, he wondered if Irene could be stupid enough to involve herself with the policeman. The quick glance of defiance that she shot him convinced him he was right. He would need to talk to her: Irene was an extremely wealthy woman, and Sam had no intention of his sister being taken advantage of. If Will caught the exchange he chose to ignore it.

'We need another two hundred men and the lists can be closed.' James Simmonds was expounding on his favourite subject, the newly raised Kelsford Howitzer Battalion.

'Presumably,' commented Gresham politely, 'men are getting into local units of their choice before this new conscription policy puts them where they don't want to be.'

Simmonds nodded enthusiastically. 'Precisely, Colonel. I think that in forming men into pals battalions Lord Kitchener has hit on a sound plan. This battalion of ours will be accepted as the Kelsford Pals, I hope.'

From the opposite side of the table Paul Kändler peered myopically through his steel-rimmed spectacles. 'In truth I think that the mistake the Allies are making is in thinking they can win the war without the Americans.' His pale blue eyes blinked rapidly behind his thick lenses. 'It's an unfortunate fact that over recent years British industry has lost its pre-eminence.' An apologetic smile lit up his chubby features. What he was saying was not at all palatable to the British, and especially not to those like James Simmonds. 'It's a matter of economics. Over recent decades your overseas empire has been draining the nation's resources rather than augmenting them. At home the production of commodities such as steel and grain have been overtaken by both Germany and America. Britain can no longer support her own needs without imported materials from the United States.' James Simmonds was ready to explode, but the Belgian continued. 'In order to prevent those supplies reaching England, sooner or later Germany will have to begin destroying American ships that are bringing supplies across the Atlantic. When that happens, when the U-boats begin an indiscriminate torpedoing of merchantmen, then President Wilson will bring the Americans into the war.'

'That's a preposterous suggestion!' Simmonds could no longer control his anger. 'Once the available manpower in this country has been fully mobilised

– and conscription will address that – we'll roll back the Germans in one huge push.'

Gresham cut in smoothly. 'The problem with the conduct of the war, especially in France, is not a simple one. Everybody has their own ideas of what is best. Time alone will tell who is right and who is wrong.' Before Simmonds could take up his argument again, Gresham switched his attention to his hostess. 'The soup, Irene, is superb. Pass my compliments to Madame Palmaerts, please.'

Irene smiled gratefully at the dark-haired officer. Jamie could become quite a boor when he was allowed to expound upon his favourite topic. He would take umbrage at being challenged by someone who was not only a civilian but a foreigner to boot.

'Thank you, Ralph. Will you be staying long at the mill?' From the glare that Sam shot her, Irene knew that this was an uncomfortable question for him.

'No, I'm going back to London tomorrow morning,' he replied, smiling politely as he tried to ignore the persistent foot that, stretched under the table, was gently massaging his left ankle. Kathleen Doyle was definitely not, Gresham decided, his type. He much preferred the dark and sultry good looks of his hostess to the red hair and bold features of the woman opposite him. 'Could you pass the butter please, Will?' he asked, giving the policeman an enigmatic smile.

For the remainder of the meal the conversation concerned mundane happenings around the town and the vagaries of the war. After Simmonds's outburst the two scientists remained very quiet, taking little part in discussions about the newly imposed rules on conscription, or the collapse of the campaign against the Turks and Mr Churchill's consequent fall from grace.

Soon after ten o'clock, as the coffee cups were being cleared away and the gentlemen were finishing their cigars, Matthias Palmaerts slipped unobtrusively into the dining room and, with a quick acknowledgement to his fellow countryman, informed Gresham that the car had arrived to take him and his party back to the mill. It was the signal for the evening to draw to a close, and a few minutes later, as the car with Gresham, Sam and the two scientists eased away from the kerb, a taxi pulled up to collect Simmonds and Kathy Doyle.

'Can we give you a lift, Will?' asked Simmonds.

'Thanks, James, but I think I'm going to walk. The air will do me good.'

Five minutes later Will was at the back door, and Irene Deladier, the kitchen in darkness so as not to silhouette her in the doorway, let him in. Closing the door softly, they embraced quickly before making their way out into the hallway. About to mount the stairs, Will was momentarily taken aback by the sight of Béatrice Palmaerts standing in the entrance to the dining room, a tray of empty glasses in her hands. Inclining her head a fraction, she murmured a quiet 'Monsieur'.

Up in the bedroom, Irene leaned forward and kissed him on the lips, then, pulling at the knot of his bow tie, slipped it from around his neck and started to release his stiff wing collar from its studs. Running the back of his hand softly across her cheek he asked, 'Is she going to say anything?'

'Béatrice? No. She worked it out some time ago, and she's totally discreet. I doubt she's even told Matthias. Anyway, without her to let you out through the kitchen in the morning, how are you going to stay the night?'

Will was surprised: he had never stayed all night. Until now they had only been together when the staff were out, and the Palmaertses were in their own quarters.

Slipping his dinner jacket off, he moved behind her and began undoing the buttons at the back of her high-necked dress. As it slipped to the floor he reached around in front and, undoing the lacing of her high corset, eased it open, caressing her taut nipples. 'Did the evening work out as you hoped?' he asked, absently kissing the back of her neck. The corset fell away to join the dress on the floor, leaving her wearing only a pair of long pantaloon drawers.

Irene considered the question. In the time since his wife's death she and Will had become very close. At first she had wondered if they were going to split up, as Will seemed to be carrying an enormous burden of guilt about their relationship. Considering Susan's lifestyle, as she had tried to explain to him in the days after the funeral, this was completely irrational. The thing that bothered her more than anything was the rift between the two men in her life. 'I think so. The main object was to get you and my brother on speaking terms. Jamie and Kate are easy. Ralph Gresham . . . there's something about him. You never really know what he's thinking.'

'I think he fancies you.'

'He's not my type and I'm spoken for. He'd do better with Kathy Doyle. She nearly slipped off her chair trying to get her toes up his trouser leg. It must be something to do with being a nurse, seeing all those naked men every day. I'm really surprised Jamie hasn't taken her on.'

'Perhaps he has.' Will's hands had moved down and were undoing the drawstring of her pants. Irene's breathing was becoming ragged. Pulling away, she stepped out of them and turned to face him 'Do you think we could talk about this later?' Her voice had taken on the throaty timbre that he had come to recognise so well.

The north coast of England in midwinter, and Whitby in particular, was, Siegfried Keppler decided, just about the most inhospitable place on the planet. Walking along Pier Road and past Coffee End, he made his way up towards the battery at the river mouth. He glanced over the twenty foot drop to the exposed strip of sand where about thirty of the narrow fishing boats that the locals called cobles were beached, waiting for the next tide to float them off again. He did not envy the men who were preparing the fishing lines for the next trip out. The icy wind funnelling down the estuary was enough to freeze a man to the bone. As he watched, another coble, its sail down, was being rowed across from the far side of the river by four figures wrapped in heavy oilskins.

In front of him, spread out on the broad quay, was what was left of the morning's catch. While some of the herring spread out on trestle tables were being gutted and cleaned by the small army of fishwives, clad in their uniform of greasy aprons and headscarves, hands blue and numb with cold, the majority were being posted into wooden barrels for salting down. The whole quay reeked of fish guts. In these temperatures, Keppler reflected, if one of the women cut herself the first she would know of it was when she saw the blood.

Out on the battery, with nothing to stop the fierce wind blowing off the North Sea, the chill factor dropped by several more degrees, and he knew that he could not remain there for long. Shielding his eyes he scanned the horizon. This stretch of water used to be referred to as the German Sea, and after the war would revert to its old name, he mused idly, his mind on other matters.

A movement far out to the left caught Keppler's attention and, wiping his streaming eyes, he peered intently at the small fishing boat that was yawing about in the heavy seas. Once he was satisfied that it was the *Viking Tun*, he turned and made his way back along the harbour.

A pair of herrings wrapped in newspaper and tucked under his arm for lunch, Keppler crossed the swing-bridge at the drinking fountain and made his way up Church Street, where he slipped in through the open doorway of the old-fashioned pub near to Arguments Yard. It was almost lunchtime, and the bar was packed with fishermen who, having tipped their catches on the fish dock, were now taking a well-earned pint while their women prepared the fish for sale.

He settled into a corner seat with a pint of bitter, dropping the parcel of fish on the table in front of him. During his stay in the port he had become a regular visitor to the local pubs, and had developed a taste for the warm English beer that the British working class consumed by the gallon. More importantly, though, posing as a Swedish sailor who was between ships, he was able to mingle with the men of the town and could now pass unnoticed, sitting quietly over a pint, listening to the daily gossip. The fact that he made regular trips on the *Viking Tun*, which came into Whitby every fortnight, lent credence to his cover as a casual hand. It was a good plan, Keppler deliberated. Even the harbourmaster knew his face now, and the possibility of anyone asking to see his papers was remote.

The Scottish fishing boat's visits to Whitby were carefully timed to coincide with the presence of U39 off the coast. When Keppler had information to pass back to Berlin, a radio message sent by Ludwig Heitmann from the transmitter hidden in his workshop to the submarine fixed a rendezvous out at sea, at which the sealed oilskin packet containing his reports were passed over in the cold grey dawn. Captain Diessbacher had strict instructions that should his vessel come under attack during his return passage to the U-boat pens at Brugge he was to drop the package over the side, weighted down with a plumb lead.

A grizzled old seaman wearing a battered hat paused by his table. 'Bastard of a day, Sven,' he ventured. 'I see Tam's comin' in. Are you planning to take a couple of days' work?'

Keppler nodded. 'Need the money, Arnie – if he's going out on the evening tide, that is.'

The old man grunted an acknowledgement, and pushed his way through the throng at the plank-topped bar.

Most definitely going out today, thought Keppler. It was crucial that the latest information from Nemesis be sent to Berlin as a matter of extreme urgency. The fact that during the last week the British had deliberately murdered four German officers in a field trial of MD19 did not particularly perturb him. In warfare such measures were often necessary, and the loss of four men in the context of what was happening at the Front was negligible.

Until recently Nemesis had maintained a deep cover, hardly ever communicating with Keppler. Now, however, the situation had changed. The information coming in from the agent during the last five weeks was dramatic. Not only had the Kelsford laboratories finally produced MD19 that was almost ready for use as a weapon, but it had been tested on human beings. According to Nemesis the scientists still needed to refine their formula in the light of the autopsies, but it was anticipated that by midsummer a full-scale release of the gas under battlefield conditions would be feasible. It would, Keppler decided, be worth an uncomfortable two days on the tiny fishing smack to relay his findings to his masters in Potsdam.

'I've spoken to General Thompson, and he's aware that within the next month or so we'll be in a position to proceed with the use of MD19 on the battlefield. After that the Ordnance Depot – Thompson – will be required to undertake its overall production.' From the tone of his voice it was apparent that General Sir Hedley Thompson had not risen in Leigh-Hunt's estimation.

'What was his reaction, sir?' enquired Ted Bayliss.

'Mixed, as one would expect. He's appalled at the prospect of eliminating large numbers of the enemy's troops without giving them a sporting chance to wipe out a similar number of our own. The outlook of men such as Thompson and Haig is a mystery. Their perception of modern warfare is still based on the premise that if we each have a million men at the start of a battle, and at the end of it I have one man and you have none, I've won. Though he deplores what we're doing, he also voiced concern that he's not being told on a day-to-day basis what's going on.'

'Not really possible.' Gresham eased his position in the armchair. Bayliss could clearly see the pale mark on his tunic cuff where the major's crown had been moved over to allow the star of a lieutenant colonel to be added. Gresham allowed himself a hint of a smile. 'Memos flying round between Whitehall and Greenwich: hardly on.'

Leigh-Hunt stood up and walked across to the buffet table that had been set up in the hotel suite. He had a weakness for vol-au-vents, and selecting one from the tray he moved over to the elegant Adam fireplace. Despite the niggling worries he felt about the latest developments, it was the nearest he could allow himself to prowling. 'The autopsy reports on the Northumbrian trials – have they been completed?'

Gresham handed him a slim buff folder and another to Bayliss. Opening his own copy, he glanced at the single sheet of paper, which was dated Saturday 29 January 1916. Ignoring the service details of the German officers, he went to the main body of the report. '"Bodies examined by Dr Herbert Duggan at 1500 hours on the day of death, Friday 28 January. Considerable swelling and bloating of the cadavers commensurate with exposure to an insecticide based compound. Bronchial passages flooded with mucus, retinal damage indicating loss of vision prior to death. Evidence of uncontrollable vomiting and defecation in the final paroxysm. Cause of death, asphyxia. Estimated that death would have occurred within three minutes of exposure to the compound MD19." That would fit in with what Ted witnessed in relation to Siegler and the Uhlan.'

Edward Bayliss nodded in agreement. 'Von Otting and Siegler made it out through the door into the fresh air, probably within the first minute and a half. Once outside they went down like roped steers, dead before they hit the ground. According to the clearance team, Josef Wiesmann was inside, sprawled on the floor, while Tauber was in the toilet cubicle. It was he who broke the capsule.'

'And that leaves us where in relation to time scales?' Leigh-Hunt popped the last of the smoked salmon pastry delicately into his mouth.

'Burke and Hare need a little more time to make adjustments to their formula before they're entirely satisfied, Sir Rowland, but they estimate that the gas will be ready for the main summer campaign in France.' Noticing the sharp disapproval of his levity, Ralph Gresham gave a cough of apology. 'Sorry, Kändler and Duggan.' He had forgotten that Sir Rowland Leigh-Hunt was totally devoid of any sense of humour. 'Let's move on to the second, and more worrying, item on the agenda.'

Leigh-Hunt settled into the third armchair and extended his hand towards Commander Bayliss, who produced from his briefcase three pale green folders, handing one each to Leigh-Hunt and Gresham before opening his own. Sir Rowland adjusted his pince-nez and began to read the Naval Intelligence sheets. 'Carry on,' he murmured, without looking up from the typed sheets.

'It would appear that our friend Nemesis is better placed than we realised.' Bayliss did not need to consult the green folder: he had read and re-read the intercepted signal transcript that it contained a dozen times, before settling down to prepare the intelligence appraisal that the other two were studying. 'On the 8th of February, eleven days after our field trials in Northumbria, a message was telegraphed from Berlin to the German Embassy in New York. A copy of it is in the file, and I have appended a translation for you. The message is short and to the point. It states that German intelligence has received a report from a highly reliable agent to the effect that Britain has developed and tested a new form of deadly nerve gas, designated MD19. It adds that the tests referred to were conducted on German prisoners of war. At the present time the ambassador is not to divulge this knowledge to the American administration, and is to regard it as top secret. The closing sentence is most interesting: 'Any further developments reported by agent Nemesis will be signalled for your information.'

Sir Rowland gave Ralph Gresham a hard stare. 'What's your evaluation?'

Gresham pursed his lips while he deliberated. 'Let's work backwards. The signal was intercepted eleven days after the trials. Say it rattled around Berlin for a day before they decided that the information was too good to keep to themselves, and sent it off to America. We've already decided that there's someone on the east coast acting as Nemesis's controller: he would have needed to receive the information from Nemesis and arrange for it to be delivered to Berlin. I doubt he'd have trusted an open radio link. The information would have been sent by direct courier or even by Nemesis himself. After that a rendezvous with the submarine – which I think we can now safely assume is still the U39.' He paused long enough for Ted Bayliss to give a nod of agreement. 'Then about five days for the sub to get the information back to a Channel port, or even steam direct to Wilhelmshaven, and that brings us back to . . .' He hesitated, reckoning out the days.

Ahead of him, Bayliss said quickly, 'Four –at the most five – days from the time of the trials for Nemesis to acquire the information and pass it to his controller.'

'Does the intercept say anything about the autopsy results?' asked Leigh-Hunt.

Bayliss shook his head. 'No, Sir Rowland.'

'So Nemesis didn't have the results of the autopsies when he contacted his controller?'

'It's possible, but not necessarily significant.' Gresham looked thoughtful. 'If he has the access that he appears to have, that sort of information could be passed up the line later.'

'The security on this project is as tight as anything that we've ever undertaken. How long is it going to take to trace the leak?'

The twitch pulled briefly at Gresham's mouth as he studied a point somewhere over Leigh-Hunt's shoulder. 'At the moment it's extremely difficult to say. While the project's top security it's also big. Big means people, and people present problems. In the setting up of the trials alone there were the Dutchman Wermuth, Coleman Farr, that Polish actor, Gajewski from the Yorkshire unit who poses as an Austrian, the two operatives to shadow von Otting and Tauber on the train to Sheffield and Newcastle, to make sure they didn't get themselves into trouble.' He paused. 'Then there was the house in

North Shields, and setting up the croft on the moors.' How many other things might we have missed, he wondered.

'Is the Dutchman reliable?' Sir Rowland seemed to distrust the Dutch as a nation. There was a story that many years ago while he was sabreing his way through the serried ranks of Whitehall, his wife had been suspected of a dalliance with a Dutch diplomat.

'Yes. We used him last year to get Plüschow and the other fellow, Oscar Treppitz, out of Donington. We arrested Treppitz at the docks and let Plüschow get back to Germany. Plüschow took back a load of duff information that Hanie Wermuth had been feeding to him for months. It caused havoc in Berlin and confirmed Wermuth's reputation inside the camp, which paid dividends with this last operation.'

The three lapsed into silence, turning over the implications of their discussion.

'There's something else that, while it may not come to anything, you both should be aware of.' Leigh-Hunt and Bayliss looked at Gresham expectantly. 'In recent months there have been two unsolved murders in Kelsford: one in June last year of a prostitute, and the second of a haulier and contractor in August.' Ralph paused. He was far from certain that the murders were of any relevance, and had pondered whether or not to bring the subject up. He had decided that he had nothing to lose by mentioning it: if he did not, and it became relevant later, Sir Rowland was not a forgiving man. 'They appear to be connected to each other, but at present there's nothing to indicate that they have anything to do with our interests.' He paused again, and decided that now he had brought the matter up he was right to continue. 'However, the two detectives investigating the murders are very experienced. Although little progress has been made, Superintendent Mardlin is highly capable and most persistent.' A quick glance at Leigh-Hunt confirmed that the older man recollected their previous conversation concerning Mardlin's association with Sam Norton's sister. 'His deputy, an inspector by the name of North, is equally diligent, and between them they'll find out who's responsible eventually, but in the process they'll leave no stone unturned - unfortunately. Because of the brutal nature of the killings, the local press mounted a campaign to have half the soldiers in the town arrested. One soldier, who was a leading suspect, went AWOL, adding fuel to the fires. While tracing him is of paramount importance, the indications are that Mardlin's not convinced that he's the killer. He's looking elsewhere for a solution. My point is that in the course of their investigations there's a distinct possibility that Mardlin and North may become a danger to us.'

For once, Sir Rowland's urbane mask of imperturbability was replaced by one of grim displeasure. 'And, of course, although you resolved the matter with him at the time, Mardlin was also involved in the security leak when the fireman died. Presumably he's still in conflict with Major Norton over that?'

Gresham nodded. 'Yes, despite his relationship with the sister.' He shot Ted Bayliss a look that said 'I'll explain later.'

'It goes without saying, Ralph, that he mustn't be allowed to compromise this project. If it becomes a problem take whatever steps are necessary.'

Gresham nodded once more in acknowledgement. The instruction might not be so easy to carry out. He was all too aware that Will Mardlin would be digging, and the problem with people who dug deep enough was that they usually found something.

'Is there any good news?' Leigh-Hunt asked morosely.

'Well actually, yes,' volunteered Bayliss. 'We might have a lead on the controller.'

Gresham badly needed a cigarette, but he knew that Sir Rowland would not countenance smoking during the meeting. He waited patiently for the Navy man to continue.

'For some time now there's been absolutely no submarine activity in the sector off the east coast between Scarborough and Berwick-on-Tweed, which makes us suspect that there's something going on the Germans don't want to draw attention to.'

'Such as a submarine lying low off shore,' ventured Leigh-Hunt.

'Exactly. Looking closely at that sector, we've been checking on the movement of vessels in and out of the ports along that stretch of the coast. For some months now, as a counter-espionage measure, harbourmasters have been instructed to keep confidential logs of all fishing vessels entering and leaving their quay that aren't registered to that port. One particular boat stands out: a Scottish motor trawler named the *Viking Tun* which originates from Skye. It's registered to a skipper by the name of Thomas MacLeod, and it visits Whitby regularly ever two weeks, drops a catch and sails on the next tide, returning with another catch a couple of days later.'

'Ideal cover for picking up a passenger, making a rendezvous at sea with a sub, then dropping the passenger off again.' Gresham was pleased: now they could set to work.

'When was the last time that *Viking Tun* berthed in Whitby?' demanded Sir Rowland.

'The 2nd of February.' The tension in the room was oppressive. 'We're waiting for the next visit to see who, if anyone, goes aboard.'

Leigh-Hunt removed the pince-nez and polished it carefully on his silk handkerchief. 'Don't rush things. I don't want any mistakes,' he said carefully, 'Ralph, arrange for extra men to be drafted to the Old Watermill, and include among them a couple of our own operatives. I want extra security in case the Germans attempt to sabotage the site. When this is wrapped up I want Nemesis and his controller removing permanently.' The other two gave brief nods of agreement, collecting their papers ready to depart. Sir Rowland looked across at Gresham. 'I think you're right to be cautious about Superintendent Mardlin. Please keep a close eye on his enquiries and let me know if we need to intervene.'

Chapter Nineteen

U naware that interest in his whereabouts was not limited to the Kelsford Police, but also included a select group of men in Whitehall, Frank Kempin could not believe how well life had turned out. He had secured his release from the army by the simple expedient of deserting, he had a woman to share his bed, and a benefactor who was sending him a postal order every Friday. Things really could not be better.

It was almost eight months to the day since he and the girl had moved into the house in Mansfield Street, and to date no one from Kelsford had come knocking on the door – nor had any details of the job that he was supposed to be waiting for been passed to him. That was the one thing that puzzled him about his new situation. After five months his payments kept arriving each week, but so far he had not been required to fulfil his part of the bargain.

Pushing aside his plate, with the remains of the late breakfast he had just consumed adhering round the edge, he picked up the steaming mug of tea that Lisa had placed in front of him, and with a practised action blew across the top of the cup before pouring a substantial amount of the hot liquid into the saucer, which was in his other hand. Slurping loudly, the little man drank down the contents of the saucer in one long swallow, then pushed back his chair and sat looking contentedly out of the window into the narrow street.

In August the previous year, having been released three weeks earlier by the police on bail, Kempin had decided that it was time to disappear. After what he considered an arduous day in the cookhouse, Kempin had gone to see the duty corporal, a thin-faced Liverpudlian, with whom he had formed an association based upon Kempin's ability to procure certain 'amenities', and obtained a four hour pass for the evening. In fact, it was Frank Kempin's access to 'amenities' that was giving him as much cause for concern as the police enquiries. Superintendent Mardlin's prediction that he would become *persona non grata* as Charlotte Groves was infected with venereal disease was coming true. Two of the men who had enjoyed Lottie's favours were in the barracks hospital and would eventually be brought before the commanding officer to face charges, as contraction of a sexually transmitted infection was a disciplinary offence. If anyone else went down with the clap Kempin knew that he was in grave danger of having his head pushed into a pot of boiling soup. At least the Scouse corporal was not yet pissing through a button, so his evening pass was stamped without question.

On walking into the saloon bar of the Generous Briton, in Kirkstall Street, Kempin had been surprised to find a sealed envelope waiting for him behind the bar. Lisa the barmaid simply said that a young boy had left it with her ten minutes earlier. This in itself alerted the streetwise Kempin. It was common knowledge in the pub that he and the barmaid were on more than friendly terms: not only did someone know where to find him, but also exactly whom to leave a message with.

Taking himself off to an empty table, Kempin pushed a thumb under the flap of the envelope and opened it. Inside was a single sheet of cheap notepaper, along with a postal order for five pounds.

The note was written in boldly printed capital letters:

> *YOU ARE BEING SET UP TO TAKE A FALL. THERE ARE THOSE WHO DO NOT LIKE THE POLICE AND WHO WOULD SEE YOU SAFELY AWAY. TOMORROW MORNING CATCH THE TRAIN TO LEICESTER. GO TO MRS RILEY'S LODGING HOUSE IN ABBEY STREET WHERE YOU ARE EXPECTED. YOU WILL BE GIVEN THE KEY TO A HOUSE. STAY THERE UNTIL YOU ARE CONTACTED. IN EXCHANGE YOU MAY BE NEEDED TO DO A JOB LATER ON.*

The arrival of the note, just when he had decided to disappear, was to the wily little soldier a godsend, and the five pound postal order was as good a guarantee as he was going to get. The job that his unknown benefactor had in mind was something he would worry about later. That a postal order had been enclosed, not a banknote, showed that the sender knew what he was doing. Any main post office would cash the order without question, whereas trying to change a five pound note would without question result in a constable being called.

Kempin did not have to consider his decision for longer than it took him to sink his pint of bitter and order a second. The army had been his passport out of Manchester, where the local police were still looking for him in relation to a serious assault on a prostitute whose performance had not come up to his expectations. Now, with this latest enquiry hanging over him, it was time to move on again.

He glanced across the bar, catching Lisa's eye and signalling that he wanted to speak to her when she had finished serving the men who had just walked in. The girl could come with him, he decided. That Lisa was not her name he was well aware. He didn't really care what her true identity was, or where she had come from before starting work at the Generous Briton. What he did know was that she was wanted by the police for skipping bail over some money she was alleged to have stolen from her employer while in service, and a woman who was wanted by the police was very vulnerable. Frank Kempin liked women who were vulnerable: he had known several in Manchester. With the offer of a secure hideout an hour's train journey away in Leicester, it took no time at all for Lisa Abbott to decide to leave Kelsford the next morning.

Kemplin finished his beer and slipped off down to the address in Grey Street where Lisa rented a room. It was a flea pit, and no one questioned the fact that the soldier went up to the single room at the back of the house that was shared by the girl with a middle-aged prostitute, whose offer of a quickie for a tanner while he waited even Kempin refused.

At half past eleven, when Lisa returned from her work at the Generous Briton, she brought with her the second-hand suit Kempin had instructed her to slip out and buy from Mrs Crowdell's used clothes shop. Thrusting his now redundant army uniform beneath the single bed, Kempin pushed his way under the thin blanket next to the barmaid, and without further preamble pulled down her drawers.

Kempin was quite aware that Lisa was not unversed in the matter of sex, as on more than one occasion during their acquaintance he had waited for her after work, and had intercourse with her against the wall in the yard at the back of the pub, in return for a couple of bob. As on this occasion, his only complaint was that her participation showed a decided lack of enthusiasm. The difference tonight was that she recognised this would be part of the bargain they had struck. Far from being insulted by the woman's lack of ardour, Kempin was satisfied with the outcome. He had very definite plans for Lisa when they reached their new abode, and if she were not over eager at least she was compliant.

Neither of them had visited Leicester before, and it took them nearly twenty minutes after leaving the railway station to find their first landmark, the tall grey clock tower surrounded by criss-crossing tramcar lines that marked the town centre. From there, enquiring at a newsagent's shop about the location of Abbey Street, they were directed to follow the Haymarket past the Palace Theatre to the first turning on the left. Abbey Street was not particularly inviting. The narrow road was flanked on either side by a long line of dilapidated red-brick houses, broken up by a series of dark and evil-smelling courtyards that concealed more slum properties at the rear. Walking down the mean little street, Lisa hitched her skirts well above her ankles to keep the hem of her cheap dress from trailing in the accumulation of rubbish and filth that littered the footway. A sharp stench of human excrement and pigswill drifted on the breeze from the communal privies and stinking sties nestling in the courtyards.

Kempin stopped a shabbily dressed old man with one leg who was making his way painfully in the opposite direction. 'I'm looking for a lodging house run by a woman named Mrs Riley.'

Eyeing him sourly, the man, who on closer inspection Kempin realised was probably only in his fifties, gave a sideways flick of his head towards the run-down houses behind him. 'Take your pick,' he grunted, and with a practised swing of his crutch moved on, contriving to catch Kempin's ankle a painful crack as he did so.

'Bloody old bastard!' muttered Kempin, nursing his injured ankle.

'Over there.' Lisa pointed across the road.

Kempin found himself staring at the dingy brick frontage of a pub with a faded sign over the door proclaiming it to be the George III. Over the doorway was the customary four-sided tapering gas lamp common to police stations and public houses, with the name of the premises on two faces, while the other two identified the licensee as Edgar Armstrong. The door of the house next to the pub was standing open, and sitting just inside on a kitchen chair taking in the morning sunshine was a wizened old crone wearing an ancient black crêpe bonnet tied under her chin and a matching black shawl wrapped tightly around her skinny shoulders. Like their owner both had seen better days. Sticking out of her toothless mouth, a thin column of blue smoke curling upwards, was a short stubby clay pipe. In the window next to the chair, barely discernible through the grimy glass, was a sign that read 'Sarah Riley, Registered Lodging House Keeper – Beds 3d, Rope 1d a night'.

With a satisfied nod, skirting a pile of horse manure, Kempin made his way over the road, leaving the girl to follow. 'Mrs Riley?' he demanded.

The crone took the pipe from her mouth and, hawking, aimed a globule of phlegm an inch from the man's foot. Close up, the stale odour from her unwashed clothing was nauseating.

'Sadie's not here. Who wants her anyway?' she asked without looking up.

'Don't piss about, ma. I'm not a scuffer.' Kempin was tired and edgy, time was getting on and he needed some proof of the existence of the accommodation that the writer of the note had promised.

A large, equally unkempt man with several days' growth of heavy black beard materialised from inside the room. 'No, you ain't a scuffer, and you ain't from round 'ere neither.' The man's voice, cracked and hoarse with years of smoking and strong drink, was broad Leicester. He was in his early forties and was, decided Kempin, some sort of minder. As if conjured up by sleight of hand, the one-legged man reappeared behind them, accompanied by a heavy set labourer carrying a short stick under his arm that the Irish called a shillelagh.

Lisa eased herself into a position where she could take a kick at one or other of the new arrivals. She judged that the one-legged man would be very fast and deadly accurate with his crutch.

Kempin, born and bred in the back streets of Manchester, sensed rather than saw the men behind him. Ignoring the minder in the doorway, he addressed the old woman once more. 'I've obviously got the right place. I was told to collect a key. We've just got off the train from Kelsford,' he said evenly.

The woman examined the bowl of her pipe, which appeared to have gone out, and tapped out the dottle against the leg of her chair in disgust before turning her gaze to the soldier. 'Got any snuff?'

Kempin shook his head and said, with an ingratiating smile, 'Don't use it, Sadie, but if I get that key I'll find you a penn'orth of twist and a glass of something next door later on.'

Sadie Riley pulled back her lips to reveal a black hole punctuated by the irregular stumps of rotted teeth. Fishing in the pocket of the filthy apron around her waist, she produced a large mortise key.

'Gimpy'll show you where to go.' She nodded to the one-legged man. 'And if she's intending to work, you'll need to clear it with Armstrong.' The conversation over, the crone delved once more into her apron pocket, this time for a clasp knife and the remains of a plug of pipe tobacco which she began to cut into small pieces.

In silence, Gimpy led them a short distance back up the road, and turned right into an equally drab and even narrower alley named Mansfield Street. They halted outside number forty-two.

'Do you want some more tea?' Snapping out of his reverie, Kempin shook his head.

'No, I'm going out. If the postman brings an envelope you don't open it – understand?'

Lisa Abbott shrugged her shoulders and began to clear away breakfast. Each Friday the postman delivered an envelope, which Kempin always pushed into his pocket unopened. Later on he would disappear for an hour or two before returning, stinking of ale, to fall asleep in front of the parlour fire. It did not take a genius to work out that the weekly envelope contained money.

Pulling on his cap and tying a muffler around his neck, Kempin made his way over to the door. 'Don't forget: you open it and you'll get a pasting.'

As the door closed behind him the young woman shrugged again, and continued to stack the pots in the sink. Had she not been dodging the police in Kelsford, Lisa would never have been involved with the miserable little deserter. In exchange for a safe place to stay for the last few months, Lisa had to go out each evening and work the nearby streets. At first, while prepared to sleep with Kempin, she had refused point blank to work as a prostitute – but her new-found protector had other ideas. He was not, she soon discovered, averse to using physical violence, and his recent promise to give her a pasting was not an idle threat. Within a week of moving to Mansfield Street, Lisa was out with the other girls working a beat.

It was obvious to her from an early stage that the envelope must contain some sort of payment, and she soon found out that Kempin hid the contents of the packages behind a loose skirting board at the back of the Welsh dresser. It was an easy matter to prise the skirting away when he was out, and check the hidey-hole's contents. Each envelope, she discovered, contained a postal order for two pounds. What annoyed her was that he also took her earnings, leaving her just enough money to buy the food that she cooked.

He was in for a bit of a shock, she decided. Sadie Riley, or Mother Clipstone as she was known, because of a gaol sentence she had served as a young woman for clipping gold coins then smoothing the edges with an oiled sharpening stone, had told Kempin on the first morning that if he intended Lisa to work the streets he would need the permission of Big Nobby Armstrong. This was emphasised the same evening when they paid their first visit to the George III. The hoarse-voiced minder, whose name was Growler Doughty, accompanied by an equally large Irishman, escorted Frank Kempin from the bar into the back yard and left him under no illusions as to where he stood.

Although many of the rookeries and tumble-down hovels of twenty years before had now disappeared, the Belgrave district and in particular Abbey Street, along with the courts and yards running down to the Great Northern railway station, was a fiercely Irish domain in which any illegal activities were subject to the approval of Nobby Armstrong, the landlord of the George III. Lisa quickly discovered that Big Nobby, also known as the Baron, was a huge Dubliner, who despite being almost sixty years old could take on any two men who cared to put up against him and leave them to regret their temerity.

For Lisa to work as one of the girls in the district, the fee for Armstrong's consent was ten shillings a week, payable by Kempin to one of the Baron's collectors. At Lisa's protests that this was five tricks at two bob a go, Frank merely gave a lopsided grin and told her that she was 'going to have to get her arse moving', because he wanted another two quid on top of that. At just turned twenty, Lisa, fair haired and slim, was quite an attractive girl and still had an advantage over most of the other prostitutes in the Abbey Street area: she was not a heavy drinker and was careful of her appearance. Unlike so many of her sisters in the trade, she was very clean and fastidious in her domestic and personal habits. Number forty-two was clean and tidy, and she never brought clients back to the house.

Armstrong, they soon found out, controlled all the lodging houses between Belgrave and Wharf Street on the east side of the town. Wharf Street was the domain of Michael Shaughnessy, another expatriate Irishman and a cousin of Armstrong. Because of their family connections the two men ran their districts amicably, and provided everyone obeyed the rules there was never any conflict between them.

What Kempin did not know was that when Lisa had gone out to work the previous night, Gimpy had been sent to meet her at the corner of Orchard Street and Belgrave Gate, and to take her to Mother Clipstone's. Knowing better than to ignore the summons, she made her way back up Abbey Street, and five minutes later was let into the lodging house by Growler.

The house the girl decided, was a midden. In the front room downstairs the only piece of furniture was a threadbare sofa, upon which Sadie Riley was sprawled. Pouring a glass of rum from a stone jar standing on the floor beside her, the old woman gave Lisa a glazed stare. 'Upstairs, through the door,' she mumbled.

Lisa could see that the hag was extremely drunk, and without bothering to reply she followed Growler through into the back room, which served as an eating place for the inmates, and climbed the narrow stairs. The young woman had never been up to the first-floor dormitory before, and she looked round with interest. At the top of the stairs the walls of the two tiny bedrooms and the landing passage had been knocked down to make one big sleeping area, illuminated by two guttering gaslights. At the far end an open archway had been knocked through into the terraced house next door. On the other side to the left was a closed door, which gave access to the first floor of the pub. The air in the enclosed room was dank and unpleasant. Along each of the walls was a row of iron cots with a straw mattress and a single blanket, most of which at this time of evening were unoccupied – although Lisa could make out in the bed nearest the window an untidy bundle that, by the trousers and boots dropped by the bedside, she assumed to be a man. Stretched across one end of the room, wrapped around metal cleats fixed to the walls, were two lengths of clothes line for those who could not afford the price of a bed: they could hang their arms over it and attempt to sleep standing up.

The layout had two purposes, she realised. The capacity of the lodging house had been doubled by knocking through into the house next door, and by putting a door into the pub on the other side, anyone could come and go through the back yard of the buildings either side. Any police watching the George were wasting their time, and in the event of a raid an easy escape route existed.

Growler tugged impatiently at Lisa's sleeve and tapped deferentially on the door leading into the pub. He stood back to allow her through, then closed it behind her. This room was only marginally less depressing. It was small and furnished with two beds arranged in an L shape, so that anyone attempting to come into the room had to climb over one of them. On the one furthest from her, a double, sat Nobby Armstrong. Lisa wondered if any of the men of her recent acquaintance ever shaved: a minimum of three days' growth of beard seemed to be regarded as a badge of office. On a small side table by the bed stood a bottle of Bushmill's.

Patting the coverlet next to him, he held out a second glass of whiskey and said in a thick southern Irish accent, 'Sit down, Lisa. It's time you and I had a little talk.'

The girl obediently did as she was bidden, and took the glass from him.

'So, where's your Frank tonight?'

'Out for a drink, Mr Armstrong.' She knew better than to call him Nobby. The grey whiskers and soiled vest spilling out over his trousers would make it difficult for anyone who did not know who he was to pick him out from those who worked for him. It was a deliberate ploy: never attract attention to yourself. The sour odour of sweat assailed her nostrils as he leaned towards her, his eyes taking in the deep cleft between her breasts where the buttons of her dress, deliberately arranged for the benefit of potential clients, were left undone.

'They say that he's wanted for murder up in Kelsford.'

She shrugged. It was an eloquent gesture that she had learned a long while ago: it said so many things – 'Sorry, I can't help you', 'I don't know', 'Screw you, I'm not interested'. This time it said 'Perhaps he is, but it's none of my business.'

'What do you think, Lisa?'

The girl returned his steady stare. 'He had a tug by the coppers middle of last year. Woman he'd been screwing – a working girl – got herself killed by some maniac who chopped her up. Then on the day before we came here he was given a note. It said he was going to be fitted up, and he should move to Leicester, collect a key from Sadie Riley's place and hide up for a while. The afternoon we arrived he picked up a copy of the *Mercury* and saw that a bloke named Rees had been skewered on the end of a bayonet at his factory in Kelsford. Headlines said they were looking for a soldier.' She allowed herself a genuine grin at the recollection. 'He 'bout fucking shit himself. He was so scared it wasn't true. Kept going on about being kippered by the police. Mind you, they're a bunch of bastards up there, so they might be trying to sort him. But I don't think he's got the bottle.'

Armstrong flicked a beetle from the back of his hand onto the bedcover, and, picking it up between his finger and thumb, squashed it with a sharp crack. Wiping his hand on the blanket, he picked up his whiskey glass and drained it. 'So who's sending him postal orders every week?'

Lisa pulled a face, figuring that the postmaster at the Belgrave Gate office must be on his payroll. 'I don't know. He just said that he was being kept hidden away here ready to do a big job for someone when the day came.'

The Irishman grinned. He had yellow nicotine-stained teeth that gave him the appearance of an old grizzly bear. 'Your man's not very bright. I'd say that he's being set up by someone, but not necessarily the police.' He eyed her speculatively. 'You'd be better off without him, you know.'

Lisa took a sip of the Bushmill's, a wary look coming into her eyes as she waited for Armstrong to continue.

'Whoever installed you and your man in that house paid cash up front for the rental. It falls due again next month, and it won't be renewed. I've seen to that. Now if your Frank were to move on and you were to stay here, I think we could make some progress.' Reaching over, he slid his free hand between her knees. 'You're a presentable girl and you keep your place shipshape. How'd you like that little house to yourself? You would work direct for me. There are plenty of high class gents in this town, businessmen and the like, who get piss all at home and would pay ten bob a time for you in a nice comfy bed. Let's say you get three quid a week, and you don't have to go outside your front door.'

For the first time she allowed a slow smile to spread across her face. The proposition beat washing dishes in a scullery in Kelsford, and was certainly better than hitching her skirts for all and sundry down a draughty back alley.

'And I think there'd have to be a private arrangement between ourselves, starting right now.' The hand pulled her skirt above her knees and, as her legs parted, Lisa watched with professional detachment the fires of lust springing up in the big man's eyes.

'When will you sort out Frank?' she asked, easing her hips to give him better access.

'Tomorrow,' he gasped, as she bent her head down over his unbuttoned fly.

It was nearly half past seven. Frank Kempin had been out and about in the town centre pubs for most of the day, and while he was not entirely drunk he was certainly far from sober. He decided to have a last pint in the Prince Leopold in Welford Place before wending his way home for some supper, and to see if his postal order had arrived.

Out at the soakaway that served as a urinal in the back yard, Kempin pushed a hand against the whitewashed wall while he relieved himself unsteadily into the stinking drain between his feet. The first intimation he had of something being wrong was when two burly figures in flat caps and workmen's jackets took up position on either side of him. Glancing to his left he saw Patrick O'Rourke, one of Big Nobby Armstrong's enforcers. On his right stood Growler Doughty.

'Mr Armstrong's sent a message for you.' Growler's harsh tones were accentuated by a cigarette dangling from the corner of his mouth. Removing it, he spat into the soakaway. 'He says to tell you your franchise has been withdrawn, and it's time for you to move on.'

On the other side of him, standing in close, O'Rourke's bovine features looked as if they had been carved out of a piece of wood then repeatedly beaten with a hammer – or, as his employer sometimes joked, 'When he was a lad he caught fire and his dad put him out with a shovel.' His broad nose lay almost flat to his face, and his breath was drawn in a series of laboured snorts, bearing witness, along with the scarred, half-closed eyes, to a lifetime spent in fairground boxing booths, before a combination of alcohol and repeated blows to the head had rendered him punch drunk.

Kempin was confused. The effect of the alcohol drained swiftly away, to be replaced by a rush of adrenalin. That he had inadvertently crossed the gang boss was apparent, but he had no idea how.

'Whatever this is about, Growler, I can square it with Mr Armstrong. Tell him I want to talk to him.'

'You're supposed to be listening to messages, not fuckin' sending them.'

Doughty's rough tones were as difficult to grasp as the old bruiser's. 'I think you need some help to convince you.'

Kempin heard the click of a lock knife engaging. Glancing down, he saw a gleaming five inch blade curving up to a wicked point.

Taking a cue from his partner, O'Rourke grabbed Kempin by the lapels of his jacket, lifted the little man off his feet and spun him round against the wall. It was the mistake that gave Kempin his opportunity. O'Rourke gave a thin scream of agony as the razor blades, carefully sown into the lining of each lapel, cut deeply into his fingers, slicing down to the bone. Releasing his grip, he staggered back, staring at the blood pouring from his ruined hands.

Ducking away, Kempin lashed out with his right boot, catching Doughty a crippling blow in the groin. Without pausing for breath, he dived across the pub yard and threw himself against the back gate , hauled himself up and dropped over into the alleyway at the back.

Reducing his pace to a walk, Kempin made his way into the Market Place. Slipping under the tarpaulin of a deserted stall, he squatted down to recover his breath, listening intently until he was satisfied that there was no sound of pursuit. He began to gather his senses, and attempted to work out what was happening. Whatever he had done to alienate Nobby Armstrong was now of little consequence. Having maimed one of his heavies and ruptured a second, Kempin knew he would be dead by the next morning if he did not leave Leicester as soon as possible. He probably had about half an hour before Armstrong would have put the word out. Going through his pockets, he found that he had nineteen and six in cash, hardly sufficient to begin a new life but enough to get on a train and out of town.

After a lifetime of ducking and diving, Kempin had learned never to take anything for granted, and his one motto was always to be prepared. Prepared, that is, to disappear at a moment's notice. Every Monday morning he made a point of taking a stroll to both of the town's main passenger railway stations and picking up timetables, to carefully study and keep in his back trouser pocket. Feeling in his pocket, he withdrew them. The beer and the recent events had left him with a dull headache, and he now found considerable difficulty in the dim light under the stall in focusing on the bold print of the LMS timetable. Running a finger along the days he found Friday 28 April. There was a train to London at nine forty-seven. It must, he reckoned, be about ten minutes to eight now, so he needed to remain out of sight for about an hour and three-quarters before making a dash to the railway station.

Peering around cautiously from his hiding place, Kempin made certain that he was alone before scrambling out and making his way down through Cheapside towards the Clock Tower. Staying close to the buildings, he made his way around the open space and turned off along the Haymarket into Belgrave Gate, where he paused in one of the deep shop doorways opposite the Floral Hall picture house.

His plan was simple. He would buy a ticket and sit in the darkened cinema until about half past nine, then jump into one of the hansom cabs that always parked at that time of night outside the Palace Theatre, next door. It was less than five minutes by cab to the London Road station, where he would purchase a last minute ticket and board the train for London. He hoped that Armstrong would be anticipating him remaining in the town rather than cutting and running immediately. If he were right, the Baron's men would be searching for him in the local hostelries rather than covering the railway stations.

There was already a queue forming outside the cinema for the evening's second performance, which according to the billboard commenced at eight o'clock. Kempin read on a poster next to the main door that the two films were *Antwerp under Shot and Shell* and *Defenders of the Empire*. They were of no concern to him: he was more interested in spotting any of Big Nobby's men hovering around the cinema entrance. Satisfied that there were none, he waited until those queuing had secured tickets before dashing over, paying ninepence for a seat, and hurrying into the safety offered by the cinema's darkness.

Inside, having presented his ticket to a bored looking woman, he selected a seat on the back row between two couples who, it appeared, were more interested in each other than the captioned images flashing up in front of them. At the front, immediately beneath the screen, seated at an out of tune piano, a grey-haired woman in a dark dress and pearls was banging out a series of unrelated chords, which he presumed were intended to coincide with the film's script.

Settling down in his seat, Kempin took a long careful look round. Everything seemed to be normal. The couples either side of him would, he decided, prevent an unexpected ambush if his entry into the cinema had been detected. On his left he noticed, with mild interest, that a soldier wearing the unbuttoned tunic of a Sherwood Forester was already busy exploring inside the blouse of his companion., a dark-haired young woman.

For a short time he debated the possibility of slipping through the back door of the picture house, which was almost opposite his house in Mansfield Street. If the street was clear he might be able to dive in quickly through the front door and retrieve his nest egg from behind the skirting board. Tempting as it was, he decided to leave it: the risks were too great. Perhaps he would ask Lisa to send it to him later.

The evening's performance finished at exactly the right time. At a minute to half past nine the final reel of *Defenders of the Empire* lurched to an entirely predictable end, and the audience began to collect their hats and coats before venturing out of the warm, smoky atmosphere into the winter evening. Kempin breathed a sigh of relief at his good fortune. It would be safer to leave the cinema as part of a crowd, and slip unobserved into one of the waiting cabs.

As the gaslights in the auditorium were turned up, he realised that something was not right. A line of policemen led by an inspector began to file down each side, stationing themselves at the ends of the rows. Each emergency exit had an officer standing by it. Everyone's attention focused expectantly on the stage as the tall figure of the inspector mounted the short run of wooden steps. Taking up a position in the centre of the stage, he held up his hands to quieten the babble of conversation that had broken out.

'Ladies and gentlemen, I'm sorry to delay your departure. I hope the routine check that my officers are about to conduct will not inconvenience most of you for more than a few minutes. Some of those who did not previously volunteer to serve their country by joining the Colours have also chosen to avoid being legally conscripted into His Majesty's Armed Forces. It is therefore my duty to conduct periodic checks of groups gathered in places such as this, to determine that there is no one among the company who should have reported to the Magazine Barracks. Would all ladies, and those gentlemen over forty years of age, please leave by the exit that has just been opened at the rear of the theatre. Those gentlemen remaining, please form a line in front of the stage and be prepared to supply some proof of your identity.'

Kempin gave an audible groan as he prepared to join the group of truculent young men who were being shepherded by the constables towards the front of the cinema.

Chapter Twenty

With a dull thud the square flap of the cell door dropped open. Frank Kempin looked up from his place on the wooden boards that served as a bed, and glowered at the face peering in at him.

'That's him,' Will said to the gaoler with grim satisfaction as he slammed the trap closed and slid the retaining bolt into place.

'Worth the journey then, Mr Mardlin.'

Will nodded. 'Yes, definitely, Amos. This place hasn't changed much since I left.'

The old-fashioned cell block in the basement of the New Town Hall dated back forty years, to when the building first opened and Leicester Borough Police had established the Central Police Station there. The two cells next to Kempin's were unoccupied, their temporary tenants removed upstairs to the dock of the police court. The whitewashed walls bore the familiar graffiti that had been scratched into them over the years by bored men and women awaiting the next stage of their incarceration.

The gaoler picked up a pen awkwardly in his left hand, dipped it in the inkwell and handed it to Will. 'If you could just sign the book for visiting him, please, sir.'

Will took the pen and carefully inscribed his name and the time of the visit in the heavy ledger. A signature in the book by every officer visiting a prisoner in custody was something that he had been responsible for introducing during his time as inspector in charge of the Detective Department at Leicester. One detective's criminal was another's informant, and occasionally a secret visit by the prisoner's sponsor could ensure counterproductive results. It was not unknown for a prisoner to be told how little the arresting officer really knew, or put in possession of information that could secure his release. It had been an unpopular innovation, but one which put an end to many irregularities.

Will looked at the man's empty right sleeve, pinned up at the elbow. It was always the right hand or arm, he thought.

'When did it happen?' Will remembered Amos Goulding before the war as an active young sportsman who was an avid cricket player. He and his brother lived with their parents in Cambridge Street just around the corner from Susan's mother and father: they had joined the police together in 1910. Amos must have been one of those allowed to volunteer on a temporary release during the early days of August 1914.

The young man flexed the stump of his arm. It made him look like an injured bird, Will thought sadly.

'Loos, last September. We were taking out a trench system. As we went round a corner in the zigzag the Jerries had set up a machine gun in the trench. Took it straight off, close range. I was lucky really. It killed the other five blokes outright.'

'Was that when you got this?' Will's outstretched fingers brushed gently against the red, white and blue ribbon of the Military Medal on Goulding's chest.

'I managed to get a grenade away before I went down.'

Will nodded and closed his eyes, suddenly filled with emotion at the senseless waste. He did not need to see the citation to know what had happened. Amos Goulding was the lead man of the trench-clearing team – rifle trailing in his left hand because there was insufficient space to use it in a trench; a grenade, the pin pulled, lever held down in his right. Rounding the corner, his reactions had been a split second faster than those of the German machine gun crew, lobbing the grenade as the gunner opened fire.

'When were you thinking of talking to him, sir?'

He stared for a long moment at the blank door facing him, forcing his mind to return to the cell. The deserter. 'Soon, Amos,' Will replied softly. 'Very soon.'

As he put his foot on the first tread of the narrow staircase leading up from the cell block into the police station, Will paused. Although he dreaded the answer, he could not leave without asking. 'And George?'

There was a long pause. 'My brother was killed at Ypres, sir, last May.' For the first time the young man's voice betrayed his emotion.

'Well, we've got the right man. First we find where he's living, and turn it over, then take him back to Kelsford and talk to him properly.' Will looked round the small group of men in the detective office at the Central Police Station.

Once the telephone call had been received at Long Street the previous night to inform them that Frank Kempin was in custody at Leicester, Will had set to work swiftly in order to prevent the military sending a provost party to collect the prisoner before he could interview him. Kempin's commanding officer at Sevastopol Barracks was more than happy for the police to deal with the soldier and return him to Kelsford.

At seven o'clock that morning, armed with a warrant for Kempin's arrest on suspicion of the murder of Ivor Rees, Mardlin and his team of detectives had boarded the Leicester train.

'He claims to be of no fixed abode. That's patently a lie, but we haven't questioned him at all, sir.' Palmer Osborne almost called Mardlin Will. It was with a conscious effort that he added the 'sir'. After Will had left Leicester to become superintendent at Kelsford, Osborne as senior detective sergeant was promoted to replace his old mentor as inspector. Knowing how Will worked, and having identified Frank Kempin as wanted for interview in connection with the Kelsford murder, Osborne's immediate instruction to his men was that no one was to talk to the soldier until the Kelsford officers arrived.

Harry North chuckled. 'Really bad luck for him. On the trot all this time, and he gets picked up on a conscription dodgers haul.'

Osborne grinned back. This was not the first time that he and Harry had met. A year earlier he had been up to Kelsford to bring back a Leicester man who had killed a blacksmith at his smithy in a brawl over money, and Harry had been the officer who had arrested him.

'It was one of those things. Kempin's photograph was among twenty-odd on the Wanted board in the muster room. Cornelius Carson, the superintendent in charge of the raid, had the duty inspector take the board with them. Once everyone was lined up the board was put on the stage and compared with the men being checked. Three of them, including your man, were among the pictures, although I must say he was the only one up for murder.'

'Right, this is what we do.' Will folded his hands in front of him on the desk. 'Bert, you and I will go down and talk to Kempin. We need to know where he's living.' Will consulted his pocket watch. Half past nine. If things went well, Kempin's absence from his lodgings would still be attributed to a late night out. He looked meaningfully at Conway. 'I don't want this to take long. We need to get in and search his room before somebody starts shifting things. All right?'

Bert Conway nodded, and lifted his hand in a small gesture of understanding.

'Harry.' Will turned to his detective inspector. 'As soon as we have an address I want you and Palmer to get down there and do a search. I think we're looking at a room in a flop-house, but it might not be. Take Clarrie, Bernard and Nate with you. Once you know what you've got, send one of them back here. Palmer, do you want to add anything before we make a start?'

Palmer Osborne considered a moment before replying. 'Depends where we're going. Odds on it'll either be Wharf Street or Belgrave. Whichever, there are some handy lads down there. A lodging house will be the most difficult. By the time you've got into the building, through all the shit and dossers, whatever you're looking for will be long gone.'

'Are there going to be problems getting out?' asked Harry. He well knew that once the element of surprise generated by a fast run in was spent, these could be dangerous places to linger.

'You mean when Big Nobby's or Shag Shaughnessy's men start popping up out of the drains? It's always a risk, but if we make sure they know we're sorting an outsider and not one of their own I think it should be all right. I've detailed half a dozen men from Woodboy Street station to be in the black maria on hand. We'll call in on the way out and let them know exactly where we are going. And whichever side we're going to, I'll take a couple of the uniform men who work the area, so everybody knows that if there's undue trouble they'll be kicking the shit out of them for a long time to come.'

Frank Kempin looked much as Will remembered. The dreary room at the end of the cell block that was set aside for prisoner interviews doubled as a cell when all the others were full on a Saturday night with weekend drunks and inept criminals. With the table and two chairs in the middle there was very little spare room. Will was already seated when Bert brought Kempin in, before closing the door and standing with his back to it, arms folded.

As before, Kempin adopted a sullen, truculent demeanour.

'You already know who I am. This is Detective Sergeant Conway.' Will leaned his elbows on the table.

Kempin shot Conway a ferrety sidelong glance before studying a cigarette burn on the table.

'The first thing I want to know is where are you living?'

'No fixed. I sleep where I can lay my head.'

Had Kempin been watching the detective instead of looking down at the table, he would have known better than to make such a basic error of judgement. The back of Will's right hand caught him a crashing blow across the side of his face, lifting him from his chair and hurling him into the wall. The sudden startled expression on Kempin's face turned to one of fear as, huddled against the wall, he tasted the blood from his split mouth.

'There's no need for this,' he gasped as Bert Conway moved from the door towards him.

'Let me repeat the question,' said Will dispassionately. 'I want to know where you're living.'

Kempin flashed a look round the room as if seeking escape. Conway picked him up one-handed and, holding him against the wall, drove a fist into his stomach before dropping him, retching, onto the floor.

'All right, all right, I'll tell you.' The voice was hardly more than a whisper.

Will gave the sergeant a nod. Setting the upturned chair back in place with his free hand, Conway picked the soldier up again and dumped him on it, before returning to his place by the door. Kempin, obviously terrified, was dabbing his bleeding mouth with his shirt cuff.

'So, where are you living?'

Kempin gave a sigh. 'Mansfield Street, number forty-two.'

'Who else is there?'

A shifty look came into the soldier's eyes for a fleeting moment, before he decided that lying was going to be extremely dangerous. He dabbed his lip again. 'A girl. Just a girl – name of Lisa.'

'Lisa what?'

'Abbott. Lisa Abbott.'

'She a local girl or did you bring her with you?'

'She came with me from Kelsford.' His voice had returned to a whisper.

'Why would she do that?' Will's voice was more relaxed now: the man was telling him the truth, and was not going to start playing games.

Unsure, Kempin shot a nervous glance at Conway, who was regarding him impassively from the doorway. 'I was seeing her, and when I left she decided to come along.'

Will leaned back in his chair. The move was not lost on Kempin: he was making room for Conway to move in.

'Don't piss me about, Frank. You were starting to do reasonably well.'

Kempin attempted to pull his head back out of the sergeant's reach, but found it touching the wall. 'She's on the trot,' he said quickly, looking earnestly at the detective. 'Something to do with nicking some money. I honestly don't know the details, I never did – I never needed to ask her. When I did a runner she came with me. Wanted to make a new start.'

Conway reached into his pocket, bringing out a hardback notebook and a pencil. He tore out a sheet and scribbled on it before opening the door to the cell corridor and calling to Amos Goulding. After a brief whispered conversation he handed the note to him.

Once the door was closed again Will continued. 'You said "when I did a runner". Why was that?'

'Come on, Mr Mardlin. They'd just found a body and it was all over the papers that they were looking for a soldier. That could only be me, couldn't it?' Kempin gave an uneasy smile, watching Bert Conway nervously.

Will relaxed. They had discovered what they needed to know for the time being. The rest would come later, back at Kelsford. Harry North and Palmer Osborne would be on their way to Mansfield Street within minutes, with luck before the woman became worried that Kempin's failure to return home might be ominous. The fact that Kempin was now addressing him as 'Mr Mardlin' signified that the man was anxious to find some way out of his situation.

He exchanged the briefest of eye contact with Conway. Time to change their approach. Conway pulled a packet of Woodbines and a box of matches from his pocket, and offered one to Kempin. The little man accepted a cigarette cautiously. Lighting one himself, Conway settled back to wait for the superintendent to pick up his thread.

'You did a runner because you killed a man.'

'No.' Kempin shook his head vehemently. 'Ask Lisa. We set up to leave the night before the body was found. We was here in Leicester when they turned him up.'

'That's right, Frank.' Conway's gravelly voice had a silky edge to it. 'You set up with the girl to do a runner the night before Rees was killed. Then, the morning after you spiked him in the factory you both slipped away on the train.'

'No, that's not how it happened.' There was panic in his voice again. He was going to have to tell them about the note; they would find out anyway. 'There was a note. The night before we left a note was left at the pub where Lisa worked. It said I was being set up and should get away as soon as possible. Told me to go to the house in Mansfield Street.'

'You kept the note, of course,' Will said softly.

'No, no, I binned it. Not the sort of thing you'd keep, is it?' The shifty confidential look returned to the man's face.

Conway dropped what was left of his Woodbine on the floor and ground it out with the toe of his shoe. 'You're lining up for another slapping.'

'No, honestly, Mr Conway, I binned it.'

Conway shot a sideways glance at Will, who shook his head imperceptibly. That Kempin would not have thrown the note away they both knew. The soldier would have kept it as insurance against an event as this. The fact that he was denying it meant the note contained details he did not want to pass on. Most likely, Will thought, it said who his contact in Leicester was. Kempin and the girl would certainly not have been given an address and simply told to walk in: they would have needed to collect a key from someone.' 'Don't worry, Frank, we'll find it,' he said easily. 'You've been here for months. What have you been doing for money?'

Kempin took a deep breath, deciding that he had nothing to lose. 'The girl earns a few bob for us. Does a bit of tomming.'

Will sat back in his chair. Kempin said that the story about Rees's murder was all over the papers – not all over the *Gazette* – which meant that he had read about it in Leicester. He knew that Kempin was not the killer of either Charlotte Groves or the Welshman. The little man was a petty criminal and a pimp, but he would not have the brains to plan or the nerve to carry out two murders. If the story about the note was true, then not only was Kempin's hiding place known to the killer but he had actually placed him there in order to send the police off on the wrong track. Which also meant that Kempin was in considerable danger.

'Listen to me, Frank,' he said carefully. 'You're truly a little shit, but I actually believe you when you say that you haven't killed anyone. Now that means two things. First I'm your only friend in the world – because everyone else does think that you killed those people – and we both know how difficult it could be for you if we don't find somebody else to hang.'

Kempin's face was ashen as the full import of his situation began to sink in. He knew his chances of being released from custody were non-existent.

'Second, whoever the killer is he's decided to set you up for it. Did you really think that a fairy godmother would put you in a safe house fifty miles from Kelsford and keep you here for months? No, the murderer wanted you to disappear on the day Rees's body was found, so it looked as if you'd done it. He wanted you within striking distance, where he could get hold of you. I'll wager that you, my friend, had you not been nicked, were due in the very near future to have left a detailed note in a fit of remorse, confessing everything, before you cut your throat with your very own shaving razor.' Will thought for a moment that Kempin was going to pass out. 'I'll tell you what's going to happen,' he continued. 'You're going back with us on the train to Kelsford, where you'll spend a day or two in the cells while we have a few more little chats. Then when I'm satisfied that that you have nothing else to tell us, you're going off under close escort to Colchester military prison to await court martial for desertion. I doubt that at this stage of the game the army will shoot you, but you'll go away for a very long time. Anyway, once you're locked up in the glass house with all of those soldiers to guard you, you'll be safely out of the reach of the killer. Which gives me time to find out who he is, and that should lighten every day during the twenty years that you spend breaking up rocks with a big hammer.'

At the house in Mansfield Street, Harry North and Palmer Osborne had almost completed their search of the premises when Will arrived. Walking into the parlour through the open front door, he paused to take stock. The room was surprisingly clean and tidy, and was devoid of the usual fetid odours that permeated such houses.

The crowd that had gathered outside in the street was, as he expected, not the friendliest. It could be worse, though, he thought. Lying just off Churchgate, Mansfield Street was not strictly in the Belgrave quarter, so those gathered outside were mostly curious rather than those who might have been expected to present real trouble.

Nobby Armstrong had been aware of the police raid within minutes of their arrival. The fact that Kempin was now in custody annoyed him, because he wanted to have him killed by his own men. However, he also wanted the premises and the woman living there to be left alone, and as a consequence he gave instruction that the police were to have their hour of poking around, before business returned to normal. Who knows, he thought: one day there might be another chance at Kempin.

'Where's the woman?' Will asked Harry, who was watching as Greasley and Ashe carefully sifted through the contents of a Welsh dresser.

'In the back with Nate Cleaver.' Harry indicated the kitchen. 'She doesn't like us at all,' he added, as Will pushed the door open.

Standing with her back to the sink was an attractive young woman of medium height, her blonde hair pulled back in a tightly pinned bun. From the apron tied around her waist it was obvious that she had been doing some housework when Harry and his men descended upon the house.

The woman's face as she scowled at Nathan Cleaver was a mixture of anger and fear. The fear Will understood: he was not yet sure about the anger.

'Who have we here then?' he asked.

'Ada Manners, sir, alias Lisa Abbott. Until recently of Lyndon Terrace, Kelsford. Specialises in a bit of larceny servant when the mistress isn't around.' Cleaver's face bore a smug, self-satisfied grin.

The look on the girl's face would have deterred a less sensitive man than Cleaver. 'Fuck off and find some hard-working serving girl to write up, you bastard. That's what you're so good at, isn't it?' Spoken in a low clear voice, every word was loaded with hatred.

'I know who Ada Manners is, Nathan. Go and help Sergeant Greasley in the parlour, please.' Will now knew what this was all about.

When they were alone, speaking in a quiet voice, he said, 'I've been wanting to speak to you for some time, Ada. My name's Mardlin.'

'I know who you are,' she cut in, the anger still bubbling. 'You lived just up the road at number twenty-three with your tarty wife didn't you. Train that lying fucker out there yourself, did you?'

It was too late: Will knew that now. Too late to tell her that he knew she had not stolen half a guinea from her employer's dressing table. That Elspeth Sutton had probably made a false complaint because she was jealous of the attention her husband paid to the pretty young servant girl. Too late to tell her he knew Cleaver was dishonest and had lied in his evidence, and that she was telling the truth when she had said, 'No sir, I've stolen nothing.' Above all, it was too late to tell her that he had long ago marked the file against her as 'no action'; that she had never been in any danger of being prosecuted. With a sigh of resignation, he looked past her out of the kitchen window.

'I have a problem here, Ada,' he said, meeting her cold gaze and holding it. 'Frank's coming back to Kelsford, irrespective of what else happens. You've absconded bail while awaiting trial for theft. Answer my questions now, and I might be able to do something about that for you.'

'Such as?' she asked suspiciously.

'I need to know everything you know about Frank Kempin. Who he sees; what he does; what post comes for him; where he gets his money – the lot. In exchange I'll write a letter and have it brought here today before I leave for Kelsford, saying that all charges against you have been dropped. That way you can either go back to Kelsford – in which case I'll see that you get good references, a decent job and no one will be any the wiser, or you can stay here. But if you do that, you'll know that when someone knocks on your door it won't be to lock you up.'

The young woman watched him closely, looking for the tell-tale signs of a lie. 'And if I don't?'

Will's expression hardened. Regretful as he was about Cleaver's duplicity, he could not afford to lose Kempin. 'Back to square one. I arrest you, charge you with helping Frank in anything he's been up to, and I get the Sutton file out again.'

'I don't seem to have much choice, do I?' A surge of elation churned her stomach. Feed Frank to the vultures, free herself from the Kelsford charges, and leave things open to work for Nobby Armstrong. It had suddenly become a very good day.

'How much longer is he going to be in there?'

Palmer Osborne consulted his watch. 'Your guess is as good as mine. If he's getting anywhere with her then he's doing better than we were.'

Harry offered Osborne a cigarette. Will had been in the kitchen with the woman for over half an hour. Greasley and the two detectives had gone back to the Town Hall police station to get something to eat, in readiness for the train journey back to Kelsford with their prisoner, while he and Osborne waited for the superintendent.

'She was all right until she saw that man of yours, Cleaver. He sent her into a spin. She started coming off the walls at him. Presumably there's history. Did he nick her?'

Harry grunted noncommittally. 'Long time ago. Obviously they had some grief.' He needed to find out as a matter of some urgency what Will intended to do about Cleaver's involvement in concealing evidence over Lottie Groves's murder. His problem was that if Will had him moved back into uniform, he could no longer guarantee that the man would keep his mouth shut about Tom Weldon and Susan Mardlin. Harry needed to deal with this himself, and as it happened he knew exactly what to do.

As if prompted by some sort of telepathy, Osborne glanced at the kitchen door to ensure that it was closed before saying, 'By the way, how's Woppy these days?'

Harry looked at him blankly. 'Who?'

Osborne grinned. 'Woppy-tupper – Susan, the best shag in the Midlands.'

Harry stared glumly at his shoes. He should have known of course that Susan's philandering could not have gone unnoticed during the years that Will had been on the Leicester Force, and that she would inevitably have been given a nickname. After a few seconds he replied, 'Susan was killed just before Christmas in an air raid.'

Osborne was genuinely appalled, both at the news and at his gaff. 'Shit. I'm so sorry, Harry. I didn't mean anything – she was a nice woman – it's just that she was famous.' His embarrassed outburst was cut short by the handle of the kitchen door turning.

'Forget it, Palmer. Anyone can make a mistake,' Harry said quickly as the door opened and Will came out, followed by the girl.

Going to the dresser, she slipped her hand behind it and eased away a piece of skirting board. She put her hand into the gap and brought out a small handful of postal orders. Passing them to Will, she said, 'One comes every Friday for him. Some of them he cashes – if I've had a bad week. Otherwise he stashes them. He thinks I don't know about his little nest egg.

Taking the bundle from the superintendent, Harry saw that each was for two pounds and bore the stamp of a post office in London. There were fourteen in all. With the average working man taking home around thirty shillings a week, there was over four months' wages in the orders. Wrapped around the postal orders was a single tattered sheet of paper. Unfolding it, he saw that it was the note that had been left for Kempin at the Generous Briton. With a satisfied smile, he handed it to Will.

His colleague checked the bundle to ensure that they were all issued by the same post office, then peeled off four of them before placing the remainder in his inside pocket. 'Compensation,' he said enigmatically, handing the four that he had detached to Ada Manners.

A brief look passed between them before, nodding, she slipped them into her apron.

At the corner of the street Harry patted his pockets. 'I need some cigarettes for the train. You carry on; I'll catch you up.'

When he came out of the tobacconist's in Churchgate a minute later the other two were almost out of sight. Turning in the opposite direction, Harry retraced his steps to Mansfield Street. The crowd of onlookers had long since dispersed. Checking that there was no one around, he tapped softly on the front door.

Chapter Twenty-One

C rafty bitch!' The words were uttered so softly that the woman could not have been speaking to anyone but herself. Leaning forward, she extended her arm into the recess between the pipes. Her outstretched fingertips just touched the small brown paper parcel tucked away at the back against the wall. One of the hot pipes began to burn her arm, making her withdraw it. That the only light in the room, from a single gas mantle on the wall behind her, was casting a shadow into the spot where she was looking did not help.

Standing on tiptoes enabled her to stretch an inch or two further. She was now able to hook her index finger into the string around the parcel, and she began to withdraw it from its hiding place. The small three-legged stool that she was standing on tilted, threatening to tip over, and forced her to relinquish her hold in order to regain her balance. She paused to gain her breath, a hand resting on the wall next to the pipes. 'The crafty bitch,' she repeated. 'Fancy putting it there, right under our noses.'

So intent was she on retrieving the package that she did not realise a man had silently moved in close behind her, picking up the end of the length of clothes line that was conveniently hanging from the heating pipe and holding it loosely in his hand.

Straightening her back, the woman moved her head gently from side to side to ease the ache in her neck, eyes fixed on the package. The heat in the boiler room was unbearable, and perspiration was trickling in rivulets down her face and body. Large, unsightly patches of moisture stained her armpits and the back of her dark blue dress.

In a single fluid movement the man flipped the trailing end of the rope around her neck, kicking away the stool at the same time. With an audible crack her neck broke cleanly, leaving her dangling in mid-air, feet thrashing in a reflex action, hands dropping to her sides before she became perfectly still.

Carefully lowering the body to the ground, the man undid the end of the rope from the pipe round which he had wound it earlier in the day, and drawing it back over the pipe he tied it to a small pulley that was attached to a hook on the wall behind him. Satisfied that the rope was secure, he heaved downwards, drawing the body first into a standing position, then off the ground until the feet were dangling about six inches above the concrete floor.

It took several attempts before he managed to successfully adjust the length of the rope: finally, when he placed the stool beneath the corpse its toes, pointing downwards in death, brushed the top. Satisfied with his efforts, he detached the rope from the pulley wheels and wound the slack end several times round the central heating pipe, before tying it off with a double hitch knot.

Placing the now redundant pulley in the Gladstone bag that he had brought with him, he checked that no trace of his presence had been left before kicking over the stool. The corpse swayed about in a grotesque dance before settling back into the quietude of death. Extinguishing the gas mantle, he checked that the corridor was clear. Closing the door behind him, he left as unobtrusively as he had entered.

Having settled down in a window seat, Will ordered a pot of coffee and rolls from the waitress before opening his copy of the *Sunday Herald*. Turning to the second page, he began to read an article by Horatio Bottomley about the progress of the war in East Africa. Phipps, the owner of the coffee house, was busy attending to the needs of those who preferred the relaxed atmosphere of his establishment to the more austere tones of a Sunday morning service delivered in a draughty church. Will and Irene had arranged to meet here as, having been unable to make their Saturday afternoon rendezvous, it was the only public place where they could contrive to bump into each other. Glancing up at the ornate clock on the far wall, Will saw that it was ten minutes to eleven: she was not due until the hour.

Idly scanning the pictures of bearded army officers in slouch hats that accompanied Bottomley's querulous demands about the steps that were being taken to recover enemy-held territory in German South-East Africa, Will looked up as the tiny bell over the front door announced the arrival of a new client. To his annoyance, it was not Irene but James Simmonds. Immediately spotting Will, the solicitor raised a gloved hand in greeting and made his way over. Hiding his irritation, Will had no choice but to invite Simmonds to join him. Placing his homburg hat on the table, Simmonds ordered coffee for himself and gave Will a nervous smile.

The detective sensed that something was wrong. Over recent weeks, since he had been investigating matters at the war hospital, he had seen quite a lot of Simmonds, and he found his gung-ho patriotism more than a little wearing. Today, though, the man seemed ill at ease. 'Have you got a problem, James?' he asked.

'I'm not sure. If I'm honest, I came here looking for you. I'm worried about Kathy. She should have met me yesterday, and she failed to turn up.'

Will gave him an enquiring look. For all his faults, James Simmonds was a very practical man, not the sort to come looking for a policeman over a missed appointment. He paused while the waitress placed a tray of coffee and biscuits in front of Simmonds. 'Would you like to tell me about it?'

'This is slightly embarrassing.' James rearranged his hat on the table, the coffee untouched. 'We had an arrangement to meet yesterday evening at the Marlborough Hotel. Between ourselves, old man, Kath and I have had a bit of a thing going for some time now. We meet over there at the weekend, have a spot of dinner and stay the night.' Will knew the Marlborough quite well. It was a large expensive hotel on the main Derby Road, about five miles outside Kelsford. 'She didn't show up, which is something she's never done before. I waited for over an hour, then cancelled the booking and drove back to Kelsford. I went to her flat but she wasn't there, nor had she been all day. I called round again this morning.' James gave an embarrassed cough. 'I have a key. She still isn't there and her bed hasn't been slept in. I really am rather worried.'

Will took a sip of his coffee. A movement in the doorway caught his attention as Irene came in from the street. She looked across, thrown by Simmonds's presence at the table. Will waved, as if surprised to see her. Interpreting the signal correctly, Irene came across to join them. Simmonds's discomfort deepened visibly at his cousin's arrival.

'Leave this with me, James. If you've not heard anything by tomorrow telephone me at the office and I'll make some enquiries.'

Simmonds nodded. Red faced with confusion, he picked up his homburg and excused himself. 'Sorry to rush, Irene. I have a client to see. Many thanks, Will. I'll speak to you tomorrow.'

Watching through the coffee house window as the tall figure disappeared down the street, Irene said, with mild amusement in her voice, 'A client on a Sunday morning? What on earth was that all about?'

Will explained. 'At least it answers our question about whether he and the good matron are at it.'

'Doesn't it just.' Irene was grinning happily. 'The Marlborough to boot . . . at least they do it in style. What do you think has happened?'

'I think Kathy might have other fish to fry, and has taken herself off for the weekend without telling your cousin.' As an afterthought, he added darkly, 'I wonder where Ralph Gresham is.'

'Not with Kathy Doyle I can assure you,' she replied tartly. 'He arrived by motor car last night at the Old Mill, and he's joining us for dinner this evening along with Sam and the mad scientists.'

'Us?' Will raised an eyebrow.

'You're included, unless you prefer to cook for yourself. Béatrice has tracked down a couple of brace of pheasants which she's going to casserole

'– and it would be nice if you and Sam made an effort to get on better,' she added seriously.

Will gave Irene a less than gracious look. 'And what time am I to report for this little soirée?'

'Half past two. Béatrice will be on her own in the kitchen, and will let you in as usual.'

'Isn't that a touch early for an aperitif?'

Irene raised her cup in polite acknowledgement to an acquaintance at a nearby table. 'Not for what I'm serving,' she murmured.

Will was interrupted in his discussion with Harry by the insistent ringing of the telephone bell in his own office. It was four days since Kathy Doyle had been seen, an absence which was beginning to give Will cause for concern. At first he had been inclined to think that she was simply sending a message to James Simmonds that she wanted to finish their affair, but it was unusual for her not to pay a visit to the wards during a weekend. By Tuesday afternoon it was obvious that something was wrong.

While it had its uses, Will was not convinced that he really approved of the telephone: it made everyone too accessible. It seemed to be contrived to disrupt one's day. It took him some time to calm down the man on the other end of the instrument enough for him to grasp the substance of what he was saying. When eventually he understood, he said calmly, 'Stay there, James, and don't touch anything. I'll be with you in a few minutes.'

Pulling his coat on, Will went back into Harry's office and said tersely, 'Come on. The caretaker at the war hospital has just found Kathy Doyle in the basement.'

In the detective office, Clarrie Greasley was going through a file of evidence with Bernard Ashe. 'What you need to remember, son, is that a jury knows nothing about a trial or trial lawyers. A barrister will take the facts and mix them all up with the specific intention of confusing the jury. By the time he's finished they're not sure what happened: they only know what he wants them to think happened. Your job is to sort that out for them. At the end of an interview with a prisoner you need to bring it all back together – put it all in place. It's easy. You simply say, 'Let me just go over what you're telling me happened. You went into the house through the back window to see if there was anything worth nicking, spotted the cashbox and decided to steal it. You put it in your bag and climbed back out through the window.' Nice and simple, Bernard, but now the jury are back on track . . .'

'I'm sorry to cut across your lesson on the finer points of barrister shafting, but we've got some work to do,' said Will from the doorway. 'Get your coats.'

Despite the abruptness of his interruption, the point of Greasley's tuition was not lost on Will. Ashe had potential. On the other hand he was going to have to do something about Nathan Cleaver. His dislike of the man had been heightened by what had happened to Ada Manners. Thanks to Cleaver's duplicity she had changed from an honest servant girl into a devious young woman who had accepted a criminal lifestyle.

Ten minutes later they were standing in the main entrance hall of Kelsford War Hospital. A shaken James Simmonds and the caretaker, named Biggs, were waiting for them at the top of the stairs that led into the basement. Will signalled for the others to carry on while he spoke to Simmonds.

'Mr Biggs telephoned me after he found her, Will. This is dreadful. Why would she do such a thing?'

'That's something we need to find out,' Will replied thoughtfully. 'Perhaps you and Mr Biggs would like to go home now, and I'll arrange for someone to see you during the evening to take a short statement.'

Simmonds looked desolate, and Will felt a wave of sympathy for him. He was still dealing with Susan's death, and could understand the emotions that the man was experiencing. 'Get a cab and go home, Jamie,' he said kindly. 'Leave us to deal with things now.'

Simmonds rubbed his hand across his eyes, then straightened his shoulders and looked Will in the eye. 'Thank you. I'll do exactly that.'

Leaving the solicitor to arrange transport for himself and the caretaker, Will made his way to the basement.

'Jesus Christ, it must be a hundred degrees down here,' exclaimed Clarrie Greasley, as they removed their coats and dropped them in an untidy heap in the passageway outside the boiler room.

Stepping through the doorway, Will peered into the dimly lit area. The heat generated by the huge pipes in the low ceiling that carried scalding water into the rest of the building was intense. As his eyes adjusted to the gloom he saw, hanging in the far right corner, perfectly motionless, the body of Kathleen Doyle. The dark areas of sweat that had stained her dress were gone. Head tilted to one side by the rope that was twisted round her neck, she looked like a broken doll.

Two men from Poleworth's funeral parlour stood respectfully to one side, awaiting Will's instructions. He turned to Ashe, knowing that this was the first hanging the young detective had seen. 'When she's been cut down I want you to go with the undertakers, strip the body and search the clothing, list everything that you find. Check the body over carefully, then wait for Dr Mallard. Once he arrives you can leave him to deal with anything else.'

'It's a woman,' said Ashe apprehensively.

'She's dead, for fuck's sake,' snapped Harry from behind them.

Will nodded in agreement. 'I want a proper search by a police officer, not some Sarah Gamp from the mortuary who's going to pocket anything portable. Do you understand?' Ashe licked his lips nervously and Will relented slightly. 'Get yourself over there, Bernard. Help the undertakers take the strain while they cut the rope.' He gestured to Poleworth's men. 'Cut the rope well above the neck, please, and leave it in place. Dr Mallard will want it for the post-mortem.'

The senior mortician inclined his head slightly, although he knew perfectly well what to do; he accepted that it was part of the detective superintendent's job to give specific instructions. While his assistant and Ashe positioned themselves either side of the corpse to take its weight, he reached up and began to saw at the rope with a pocket knife.

Harry, Will and Greasley quickly exchanged knowing looks, and by unspoken agreement edged back into the fresh air of the passage.

As the rope parted, the dead weight of the body slumped heavily across the shoulders of the two men who were supporting it. They staggered slightly under their burden, then lowered it as gently as possible onto the canvas sheet laid out on the floor. Ashe jumped back with a startled squeal of fright as, with a loud groan, the gases that over the last three days had accumulated in Kathleen Doyle's body escaped in one final exhalation. An incredible stench of corruption engulfed the enclosed space. Beating a hasty retreat along the corridor, Will and his two companions pushed handkerchiefs into their mouths and noses, and caught the harsh sounds of Ashe and one of the undertakers vomiting.

Will disliked mortuaries. The smell of disinfectant mingled with the unforgettable odours emitted by decaying flesh always made him feel queasy. Consulting his watch he saw that it was a quarter past seven, almost three hours since the body had been removed from the hospital boiler room. He shivered as the door behind him opened to admit Harry North, along with a blast of cold air.

Harry undid his coat, and shook out the wet umbrella that he was carrying, leaning it against the wall. 'I hate summer rain,' he grumbled, taking his bowler hat and tipping an accumulation of rainwater from the brim onto the stone floor.

'Come on. Let's see how young Ashe has got on,' said Will morosely.

Inside the small post-mortem room the smell of chemicals went some way towards alleviating the dankness in the air. A distinctly pale Bernard Ashe, shirt sleeves rolled back over his forearms, was standing to one side of the scrubbed table, studiously trying not to see what Arthur Mallard was doing with his scalpel.

Catching sight of Will and Harry out of the corner of his eye, the doctor paused in his examination and stepped back from his work. 'Evening, gentlemen,' he said conversationally, as if they had just joined him for drinks in a comfortable hostelry. 'Just making a start – although I have to say that I don't expect to find anything untoward. I think the cause of death is going to be quite simply hanging.'

Will glanced quickly at the body. The stomach cavity, which Mallard had been about to explore when their arrival interrupted him, was laid open by an incision from the pubic area to the sternum. Moving his gaze further up the body, Will took in the blackened face, bulging eyes and Titian hair of the woman who had recently been his dinner companion. He had hoped to arrive before Mallard began cutting. Like most people, he found autopsies highly distasteful.

Ashe was staring fixedly at a point on the scrubbed wooden surface a few inches from the rope embedded in the woman's neck.

'What's the story, Arthur?' asked Will.

Harry popped a peppermint into his mouth and offered the bag round. Will gratefully took one before passing them to Ashe, who declined with a quick shake of his head. The sweet started the juices working once more in Will's mouth, while the strong flavour of the peppermint seemed to dull his olfactory senses.

Mallard sniffed loudly as if he were starting a cold. 'Death occurred around seventy-two hours ago, sometime Saturday afternoon. The rope has not been interfered with by the undertakers, and that's what killed her. From the evidence at the scene, as described by young Bernard here, it looks as if she tied the rope around the central heating pipe, got onto the stool and looped it round her neck, then kicked the stool away. She was fortunate to break her neck instead of strangling herself. At least it would have been quick.'

Will moved across to a nearby bench, where the woman's clothes had been neatly piled by Ashe. He picked up each item in turn. At one side, laid out on the table, were a fob watch attached to a short leather strap, of the sort worn by nurses, and a small notebook in a leather folder with a pencil attached through a loop. Opening the notebook, he saw that it contained patients' names and medical details. There was also a door key, which he slipped into his jacket pocket.

Unfolding the long blue dress, after a cursory examination he laid it out on the table to view it more closely. 'Who undressed the body, Bernard?' he asked over his shoulder.

Ashe did not answer immediately, then mumbled something that Will did not catch.

'Come on, man, it's a simple enough question. We none of us want to be here!'

The sharp rebuke seemed to return Ashe's focus to the job in hand. 'I did, sir. There was no female attendant here, and you said you wanted the job doing properly.'

'That's better. As you took the clothes off, what exactly did you do with them?'

The young detective took a deep breath. Dr Mallard had just plunged his hands into Kathleen Doyle's stomach cavity and was in the process of setting aside a coil of wetly glistening viscera in search of her liver. Very soon Bernard knew that for the second time that day he was going to be extremely sick. 'I put them on the table,' he said hoarsely.

'I said exactly. What did you do with the dress exactly?'

Ashe took a deep breath and looked up at the ceiling. 'I went through the pockets of the dress while it was still on the body. The watch was pinned to the front left side. In the right pocket there was the notebook. After I stripped the dress off I folded it and put it straight on the table.'

'Thank you. When Dr Mallard has finished I want you to take the clothes and effects in a bag to Long Street and book them in. Then you can go home and get a good night's sleep. We'll see you in the morning.'

Bidding Arthur Mallard goodnight, the two senior detectives went back out into the passageway and closed the door of the post-mortem room behind them.

'Give me a cigarette, Harry,' Will said.

'You don't smoke,' Harry said pointedly.

''Just give me a cigarette, and I'll tell you a secret . . . I don't like PMs.'

'I don't know anyone other than doctors who do,' grunted Harry, passing a cigarette over to Will and lighting one for himself. 'Do you want a drink?'

Will shook his head. 'Later. There's something I need to look at first.'

The heat in the boiler room was still unbearable, Will turned up the gas mantle on the wall to give some illumination. Although the dreadful stench of corruption that had filled the room a few hours before had almost gone now, the hot dry air made breathing difficult. 'If you were going to top yourself, why would you come down here?' He was standing motionless in the centre of the room, looking carefully at the pipes.

'It's out of the way, and you're not going to be disturbed,' replied his companion.

Will shook his head uncertainly. 'But you're also not going to be found for some time. She went missing on Saturday, which according to Ducky Mallard is when she did it. So she knew she wouldn't be found until Monday at the earliest, possibly later, depending on when the maintenance man came down to check his boilers. Kathy Doyle was a nurse. She would know what happens to a corpse left hanging for several days in these temperatures. I think that if she wanted to commit suicide it would have been at home in the comfort of her own flat. Quick and clean, knowing that James Simmonds would be coming to look for her within hours.'

'Are you saying this isn't a suicide?' asked Harry.

'I'm saying that I'm distinctly unhappy.' Will was checking along the back wall. 'The floor in the PM room is tiled. When we cut her down we laid the body on a sheet, yet her dress had traces of concrete dust on the back – as if she had lain on the floor before she killed herself.'

'Or after she was dead,' Harry mused.

'There's a hook on the back wall that would take a pulley,' Will said, scrutinising the top of the pipe where the rope had been tied. Stepping back, he indicated for Harry to take a look. 'Along the top, directly in line with the pulley, there are marks where the rope's been undone, then repositioned a few inches further along.'

Harry pursed his lips thoughtfully. 'Presumably the rope was tied onto the pipe in readiness and left hanging loose. I doubt that the woman would even have noticed it in this light. There are no signs of a struggle, so we can assume that the killer came up behind her, whipped the rope over her head and broke her neck with it. He'd then pass the rope over the pipe to a pulley on the back wall, haul her up and tie the rope off round the pipe, to make it look like suicide.'

While Harry was talking, Will placed the three-legged stool where the body had been found and stood on it. From his new vantage point he could clearly see the recess in the brickwork. Feeling around inside, he quickly found that it was empty. 'I bet she was standing off-balance against the wall, with her back to the room, looking in there,' he said.

Getting down from the stool, his face was troubled. If their suppositions were correct – and he was sure they were – then was this a further complication. Or was it a link that was going to open doors in the investigation of the other murder enquiries? If this was a murder, then both of them knew that it was not a coincidence. 'What we need to know is who wanted her dead, and how they convinced her to come down here on her own. If I had to make a guess I'd say she was looking for the same thing that we are – whatever it was that Charlotte Groves hocked at Izzy Feinemann's. Let's have a look in her flat; then we'll go and get that drink.'

The two detectives let themselves into Kathleen Doyle's first-floor flat at the rear of the hospital complex. They were surprised to discover that the apartment, which was larger than they had anticipated, was equipped with electric light, but quickly realised that the new complex must be at least partially lit by electricity. Much as they had expected, the four rooms that made up the flat, a kitchen, sitting room, bedroom and bathroom, were neat, tidy and spotlessly clean. Apart from some general books on medicine, and a few nondescript pictures hung on the walls, there was little to give them any insight into the dead woman's life.

Opening a tall wardrobe in the bedroom, Harry began to riffle through the half dozen uniform dresses hanging on a rail. Behind them were a similar number of outfits and suits for social and off-duty occasions. A small grunt of appreciation drew Will's attention. Hanging from the back of the rail, the shoulder straps carefully attached to a wooden hanger, was a gossamer-thin peach-coloured night dress, the neckline of which plunged open to the waist. On a woman of Kathy Doyle's ample proportions it would have left remarkably little to the imagination. Will wondered if she had worn it for Jamie on the night he returned with her from Irene's dinner party.

Pulling a hat box from the shelf above the rail, Harry sat down on the bed. He took off the lid, began to examine the contents and gave a low whistle. 'I think we might just have hit gold,' he called to Will, who had moved into the sitting room to continue the search.

Will looked over his shoulder. The inspector was holding a brown paper parcel about six inches square. From a tear in one corner a thin trickle of white powder was making a pyramid in his open palm.

Licking his forefinger, Will touched a few particles to his lips. 'Morphine.'

They stared speculatively at each other for a moment. Harry tilted the hat box towards Will. Inside were four more identical packets. 'We know now why she was killed,' he said.

'We do,' murmured Will. 'And I was about to bring this in when you called me. It was in the sideboard drawer.' He handed his partner a Kelsford Bank of Commerce pass book.

Opening it, Harry gave another low whistle. A long series of entries over a period of several months showed that Kathleen Doyle had made deposits during the preceding year of over a thousand pounds. 'The first deposit is early last year. She's got to have been either a user or selling the morphine on the black market. If she was selling it, was she doing it independently – or is this part of the War Hospital fraud?'

Will sat on the bed, a thoughtful expression on his face. 'Look at the date of the first deposit: 2nd April 1915. That was when Lottie Groves was sacked. She was an addict, so she'd need someone on the inside to get her stuff. She wouldn't have had the sort of money that's been going into this account, so we need to look somewhere else for that. I think this represents Kathleen Doyle's cut from the hospital fraud. Why would a matron steal morphine for a sacked nurse? Groves has to have been blackmailing her. Did she know something about the fraud, or was Kathy Doyle supplying someone else and she found out? First of all we need to get Ducky to check the body and see if our matron was a user.' Walking over to the wardrobe, he opened the door and pulled out one of the dark blue dresses. 'It wasn't Charlotte Groves that Jerry Boam saw going into 42 Devonshire Gardens. It was Kathy Doyle.'

Chapter Twenty-Two

Béatrice Palmaerts opened the door almost immediately to Ashe's tug on the doorbell and admitted the two men politely. She was dressed as Will remembered her on the first night that they had met at the house in Devonshire Gardens: the skirt of her long grey dress smartly pressed and her pristine white apron crisply starched. He was acutely aware that not only was she a party to his involvement with Irene, but also that in the not so distant past she would probably have been the mistress of a household like this, rather than merely the cook.

'Madame Deladier is expecting you, Mr Mardlin. Please go into the sitting room.' Despite the politeness of the heavily accented words, Will caught a distinct humour in her dark eyes as she ushered them into the large room that overlooked Kingsbury Lane.

It was the first time that Ashe had been to the house, and he was visibly impressed with the tasteful surroundings. From the outset Irene Deladier had ensured that Kingsbury Lane was not cluttered with unnecessary furnishings and nick-nacks. Two comfortable armchairs flanked a large fireplace, the mantelshelf of which was devoid of ornaments. Along the bay window a brocade chaise-longue was arranged, so that anyone sitting on it could converse comfortably with the other occupants of the room. The clutter of antimacassars that habitually adorned such items were missing.

When Irene appeared in the doorway Ashe was studying a sepia photograph of a group of people posing beside a large motor car, which was standing outside what appeared to be a small castle.

'Good morning, gentlemen, Monsieur Palmaerts will be joining us in a moment.' Walking across to the slightly embarrassed policeman, she picked up the photograph from the sideboard and held it out to him for closer inspection. 'My home in the Haute-Loire, the Château des Trois Reines, at St Martin.' Irene stood for a moment, looking at the picture. It showed herself, Sam and Stefan in the foreground, with her father standing to one side, leaning against the car door, his foot on the running board of the Daimler. Ruth Norton was sitting in the back wearing a broad-brimmed straw hat, with an open parasol over her shoulder. It had been Sam's twenty-first birthday, in August 1911: they were about to set off into the mountains for a picnic. This was the only picture she had managed to bring with her from France. Carefully replacing it on the polished surface of the sideboard, she said quietly to Bernard, 'Small things become precious, monsieur.' Without realising, she had lapsed into French.

A polite tap on the door announced the arrival of the accountant carrying a bundle of documents.

'Come in, Matthias,' Irene said. 'Are those the papers that Mr Mardlin asked you to look at?'

'Yes they are, madam.' Palmaerts turned to address Will. Like his wife, the Belgian had not changed at all since their first encounter: his black beard was neatly trimmed and the ends of the moustache were waxed into fierce points. 'I am deeply disturbed, Monsieur Mardlin, that I did not notice this discrepancy earlier. The number of patients that Madame Doyle was showing as being treated at the hospital during the period April 1915 until last month exceeds the number of beds by almost ten per cent. We have a capacity for three hundred and ten patients, while the figures indicated that three hundred and sixty have sometimes been accommodated.'

Will took the sheets from the accountant and glanced through them. 'I don't think this is any reflection on your efficiency, Monsieur Palmaerts. You wouldn't expect the matron to be dishonest.'

The expression on the accountant's face indicated that he did not share the policeman's optimism.

'Detective Constable Ashe will take these papers back to the police station. I think, Madame Deladier, that there were other matters you wanted to discuss with me?' He gave Irene a meaningful look.

'Yes indeed,' she replied. 'I'll arrange for Béatrice to bring in some coffee while Matthias explains the figures to you, Mr Ashe.'

Out in the hallway, she closed the door behind them, pulled a mischievous face, and spoke in rapid French to Béatrice before turning back to Will. 'When your young man's had his coffee, Béatrice will tell him that you've already gone, and then let him out.'

Will gave the housekeeper a self-conscious smile and followed the slim figure up the staircase to her rooms on the first floor. He chuckled at Irene's reference to Bernard Ashe as a young man. They would, he thought, be about the same age.

In the familiar surroundings of her private living room, Irene poured a glass of Scotch, added some water from a carafe and handed it to Will. Despite it only being mid-morning he took it from her, dropped into an easy chair and sipped the whisky gratefully.

'You look worn out,' she said, standing behind him, hands on his shoulders.

'I've got a lot on my mind, and I've not been sleeping too well.' Irene was right: he was tired. Since their return from Leicester it had been a busy time for Will and Harry. Several days spent talking to Kempin with few results had served to confirm that the soldier knew nothing more than he had already told them. Yesterday they had released him into the custody of a military escort, to be taken away to the infamous military detention centre at Colchester.

So far no reply had been received to the note sent by Will to the Metropolitan Police, asking for a visit to be made to the post office at Brushfield Street in Spitalfields, where Kempin's weekly postal orders had been purchased. Will was hoping that the postmaster would be able to identify whoever it was that had obtained them.

Will's comment that he did not like post-mortems was something of an understatement. No matter how tired, when he closed his eyes each night his mind was filled with the sight of Kathleen Doyle's bloated face and disembowelled torso. Whenever he dealt with a murder it was always the same. The images would eventually fade: it was just a matter of time before he pushed the details of the autopsy room into the recesses of his memory.

'I've got to go down to London tomorrow for a couple of days, but I'll be back on Saturday. Why don't you come and stay for a while? You need some company, and someone to talk to.'

Will thought about the proposition. Towards the end of the previous year Irene had become involved with both the War Refugees Commission and the Belgian Legation in London. Her family connection with the Kosminski empire meant that she could arrange financial aid, without which much of the commission's work would not have been possible. It was the sort of task that she was good at, and a trip to London a couple of times a month broke up the monotony of living alone in Kelsford.

The offer was very tempting, and Will knew that instinctively she had identified the source of his problem. For twenty-odd years Susan had been there for him to talk to and discuss his problems with when he was at a low ebb. Now he roamed around the house in Lyndon Terrace when he wasn't at work, completely at a loose end. Edith and Mrs Lynam cooked and cleaned for him, but they were no company.

'What about the neighbours?' he asked. 'I don't think they'd approve.'

'Baisez les voisins,' she replied matter-of-factly. That Will did not understand her use of gutter French brought a smile to her face, and she translated for him. 'Fuck the neighbours.'

Will gave a tired grin. 'It's a nice sentiment, but it won't work for either of us. You've got a reputation to consider, and unfortunately so do I, but thanks for the offer.'

'I suppose you're right.' She gave a Gallic shrug that Ada Manners, had she seen it, would have immediately added to her repertoire. Taking Will's glass, she poured him another drink, and settled down in the chair opposite him. 'Does anyone other than you and Harry know that Kathy Doyle's death might not be a suicide?' she asked seriously. Will had already told her of his suspicions that the matron had been murdered.

He shook his head and took a sip at the whisky. 'No. We don't want to complicate things, and I don't want to alert the killer to the fact that we're on to him.'

'Him?' The question hung in a pregnant silence.

'Him – her – I don't know.' Will stared down into the amber liquid in his glass. 'It's fairly clear that there were two people involved in Charlotte Groves's death. One of them was Kathy Doyle, who's now dead. The other, the person who planted the trench knife for us to find and then spirited Kempin away after Ivor Rees was killed . . . Who that is – your guess is as good as mine.' Putting his head back in the chair, Will stared up at the ceiling. 'We need to go back and start with the Groves murder to make sense of what's happened since.' He closed his eyes, marshalling his thoughts into some sort of orderly progression. This was what he needed to do. Talk to someone outside the investigation; someone who would simply listen while he worked through all the conflicting details. 'Payments were made into Kathleen Doyle's bank account from April 1915. She made the deposits personally, and told the cashier that she was in receipt of a remittance from an uncle in South Africa. That was untrue. From what we've since discovered, it's reasonable to presume that Doyle, who according to the post-mortem was not an addict, was supplying Groves with morphine.'

'Why would she do that?'

Will brought his gaze down from the ceiling. 'I think Doyle's part in the hospital fraud was to falsify the patient figures, to inflate the budget for an increased amount of food, bedding, drugs – everything that makes an hospital tick – which was then diverted. Groves probably stumbled on this, and initially blackmailed her matron. Once Simmonds found out that Groves was being employed at the hospital she had to go – which created a problem for Doyle, who had to supply the woman with drugs at her home. Lottie, now out of work, continued to blackmail Doyle, and in addition went on the game to support herself.'

'How would Jamie know about Groves?'

'From his stay as a patient at the 5th Northern General in Leicester. He was there when she was dismissed, and would undoubtedly know why. So when he saw her working here at Kelsford she was dead in the water.'

Irene nodded as the pieces began to slot into the puzzle. 'You really think there were two people involved in the murder?'

Will rubbed a hand across his jaw. It was a habit when he was thinking. 'I'm not certain about anything, but it seems to fit in with what we know. Groves was killed with a trench knife – that's a man's weapon, not a woman's. When the knife grinder saw Doyle going into the house she wasn't carrying anything. I think Groves was expecting Doyle and let her in, and Doyle distracted her long enough to lift the door catch – so that when it closed it didn't lock. Her accomplice slipped in after her and went up to Groves's room to wait for her.'

Will lapsed into silence for a moment. No one other than Harry North and himself knew about Tom Weldon's part in the affair, and it was this that confirmed Will's theory that Doyle had an accomplice. He was fairly sure that Jeremiah Boam was wrong when he said that if Weldon had been a couple of minutes later he would have seen the killer coming out of the house. Will was convinced that a minute or two after Boam left the street the constable saw the person who slipped into the house through the unlocked door – and knew him. Kathleen Doyle had gone into the house before Weldon arrived: he knew nothing of her involvement. Weldon, Will was certain, used his knowledge to blackmail the killer, and it was this knowledge that resulted in his own death.

'Why would they decide to get rid of her when they did?'

Will swirled the whisky around in the bottom of his glass. 'We know that whoever Doyle was working with was – and still is – prepared to commit murder to preserve his own safety. My guess is that Kathleen Doyle – a hospital matron earning about three quid a week – became involved in an affair with a wealthy solicitor, and was onto a good thing that she couldn't afford to have spoiled. No doubt Groves also realised this, and upped the stakes: she threatened to tell James what was going on if Kathy didn't pay up. Doyle couldn't allow that to happen, so she decided Lottie had to go. I think it would have been reasonably easy for her to convince her accomplice that Groves constituted a serious security risk, and get him to do the job for her.'

Irene bit her bottom lip. 'Where does Kempin fit in?'

'They needed a suspect for the murder. Doyle knew that Groves was involved with the soldier through the hospital records. Kempin was being treated at the war hospital for gonorrhoea. All hospitals with a venereal diseases clinic maintain a contacts register, which is one of the most confidential documents kept by any medical establishment. It contains a list of patients being treated for venereal disease and details of their recent sexual contacts. Any of those contacts could have infected the patient – or vice versa – so discreet enquiries are made among people on the list, and they in turn are asked to supply details of any other contacts they've had. While the intention is to limit the spread of infection, as a document it's dynamite. Apart from the consultant at the clinic, the only other person who'd have access to it would be the matron. The Leicester clinic was in Knighton Street off Aylestone Road, and even as detective inspector I was never allowed to have sight of that register. Doyle must have spotted Kempin's name cross-referenced to Charlotte Groves. After that it wouldn't be difficult to trace Kempin's visits to Devonshire Gardens.'

'What about Ivor Rees? Why was he murdered?'

'Groves died to protect Kathleen's personal safety. Rees, I think, was different. I think both he and Doyle were killed to tidy things up. Rees's killer knew that Kempin was suspected of Groves's murder, because he had engineered it by planting the trench knife on the tram. The murderer arranged for Kempin to leave Kelsford, go to Leicester and stay in Mansfield Street. Palmer Osborne checked with the letting agents in Leicester: nine months' rent was paid on the house by money order wired from a bank in London. The bank merely has the name Vivian Smith on record, and can't tell us anything about the person. What it does mean, though, is that Ivor Rees's murderer set up Kempin beforehand.'

Irene turned over what Will had said. 'So Rees and Doyle were killed over the hospital fraud, and Charlotte Groves's murder was probably a matter between her and Kathleen.'

Will spread his hands in a vague gesture. 'I'm just putting up possibilities. James and Matthias identified the existence of the fraud just before Byron Carstairs died. Bert Conway went to Sheffield and checked that out. There's no question that Carstairs death was anything other than a result of the air raid. But he was the lynch pin of the whole thing, and with his death things began to unravel. The question is, who else is involved in the fraud, because that's where we'll find our killer.'

'Was Rees a drug addict?'

'No. He was simply a crooked small-time businessman who saw an opportunity to make some easy money.'

'And why', Irene continued, 'was it necessary to kill Kath Doyle?'

Will made a face. That was the central question. He only had a theory, but he felt it was a good one. 'For the same reason that Doyle had Groves killed: she had become a danger. Kathleen was involved in everything from the outset, and she knew who killed both Groves and Rees. The war hospital fraud was under investigation. If she were linked to the Groves murder and interviewed, she might well have caved in and revealed everything. Someone's taking out insurance and removing anyone who's a weak link. Rees was a weak link because he was a minor player who knew too much. Doyle was a weak link because if anyone worked out that it was her and not Groves who Jerry Boam saw going into the house we'd soon put the rest together.'

Irene eyed Will appreciatively. She was beginning to realise that he was very good at what he did. 'How do you think Kath Doyle was persuaded to go down to the boiler room?'

Will drained the remaining whisky before answering. Things were beginning to come together in his mind as he talked, but he was painfully aware that without any evidence it was all speculation. 'Before she was killed Charlotte Groves acquired something that proved what Doyle was up to. Whatever it was, the indications are that she concealed it in an ornament and pawned it with Israel Feinemann. After killing Groves, the murderer took the pawn ticket, found a kid on the street – Leonard Belcher – and, no doubt having given him a tanner, sent him off to redeem the pawn. He must have been absolutely furious when the lad came back and said that it had been sold.

A complication now, of course, was that Leonard could identify him, so either he or Kathy must have walked with the boy to the locks and pushed him in. Afterwards they were desperate to recover whatever was in the ornament. I think the only thing that would have got Kathleen into that boiler room on her own would have been if she thought that what she was looking for was down there. Our killer, who she thought she could trust, would have put the idea into her head that Groves had hidden what they were looking for in the pipe work. She worked at the hospital , after all. That would have worked: Groves could have concealed the evidence and used the pawn shop to set a false trail.'

'Where do you go from here?'

'The best lead we have for the time being is the postal orders that we recovered from the house at Leicester. They were all issued by the same post office. That was a mistake, because the London police should be able to find out who was buying them.' Getting up from his chair, Will moved restlessly to the window and stared down at the busy street. At least he was getting one or two things clear in his mind.

Something unrelated had happened earlier in the morning that was puzzling him. Lying awake the previous night, he had decided that it was time for Nathan Cleaver to go. It was his intention to see the man today and tell him that he was going back in uniform. Before leaving the office he had discussed the matter with Harry, who had merely said that he agreed with the decision and had been thinking the same. What surprised Will was Harry's next comment: that he shouldn't worry about it, as there was a rumour going round that Cleaver was on the point of resigning. He would clarify matters during the morning, while Will was out.

Putting this to one side, Will went over to Irene and kissed her lightly on the mouth. 'Perhaps I'll have another whisky before I go.'

The atmosphere in the detective inspector's office at Long Street was electric. Nathan Cleaver's face was suffused with rage. 'I'll take my chance on you having a go at me because I didn't say Tom Weldon was in Devonshire Gardens when the Groves woman was killed. You move me back into uniform and everyone in this town is going to know that Tom was shagging the arse off Mardlin's wife.'

'Not "having a go": criminal charges,' said Harry quietly. He was as calm as the other man was angry. 'Conspiracy to pervert the course of justice is a serious offence. Judges don't like it. They go very heavy when it's a policeman involved – at least three years. By the way, I had a word at 27 Collington Street. They haven't got a maid, and the cook is sixty-three years old with a face like a robber's dog, so your good friend Tom Weldon was setting you up as well.'

Cleaver glared maliciously across the desk. 'I've been thinking about this. You'd have a job to get a jury to convict me. First off it's my word, the word of a respected police officer, against Boam's. All I need to say is that he's lying, that he never told me in the first place. He read the papers and decided to draw attention to himself by telling you a cock and bull story on the day Tom died. You've got no evidence, none at all. My word against his.'

'"The word of a respected police officer"...' Harry held the man's gaze. 'How about "the word of a convicted rapist"?' He spoke slowly, placing emphasis on every syllable.

The expression on Cleaver's face changed to one of puzzlement. 'What do you mean, a convicted rapist?'

A tiny smile played around Harry's mouth as he reached into his desk drawer and pulled out two handwritten sheets of paper. As he pushed them across the desk, Cleaver could see that they were statement forms headed 'Kelsford Constabulary'.

'What's this about?' he asked guardedly.

Harry's lips parted under his thick moustache as the smile broadened, but his eyes remained cold and hostile.

'Read it,' he said softly. 'It's Ada Manners's statement of how, on the day that you interviewed her in this police station, you promised that if she allowed you to have sex with her you'd ensure that she wouldn't be prosecuted for stealing the money from Elspeth Sutton. It goes on to say that when she refused you brought her in here – into this office, which was empty – and raped her.'

Cleaver stared at him in disbelief; then the anger returned.

Harry's eyes never left the detective's face. 'Forget three years for perverting the course of justice. On the rape charge you'll get seven to ten, guaranteed.'

'That's rubbish, and you know it. She's trying to get her own back because she doesn't like me. She'll never make it stick, because it didn't happen.'

'She doesn't like you because you wrote her up, and you forced her to have sex with you against her will – you raped her.' Harry paused, enjoying the moment. 'And she'll make it stick. You see, Nathan, in her statement she not only describes this office in detail, she describes quite clearly a small port wine birthmark on your stomach, just below your navel. The only way that she could know about that is if she's seen you with your trousers around your ankles.'

'I don't understand. This is impossible. Just what the hell is going on here?' Cleaver was shaken, and his bewilderment served only to deepen Harry's satisfaction.

'You do have a birthmark on your belly, don't you, Nathan.' It was a statement, not a question, the tone as soft as silk.

'You know I do. It's in my medical file.'

Comprehension suddenly dawned in Cleaver's eyes. Grabbing the statement, he looked at the date. Friday 11 February 1916: the day that they had raided 42 Mansfield Street.

'You bastard,' he gasped. 'You've fitted me up! This statement is a pack of lies concocted by the pair of you. You described the office and told her about the birthmark.' His brain was working overtime, and the words came tumbling out. 'She's a prostitute. She was on the run from theft charges and was living under a false name. Her word isn't worth jack shit.'

Harry's cold eyes held him unwaveringly. 'Ada Manners was never on the run. No wanted notices were ever circulated and no warrant was ever issued for her arrest. Owing to a conflict of evidence the file against her was marked for no action within days of you submitting it. Any jury could see that she was a simple servant girl who'd been written up by an unscrupulous detective. We'd never have dared to take it to court. As a matter of fact, there's a statement here that I took myself from Mrs Sutton, saying that she later found the half guinea and wishes to withdraw the complaint altogether. She even apologises for the slur on the girl's good name. Ada Manners was in love with a soldier, and wanted to leave Kelsford because of what you'd done to her. They made a new start in Leicester. She had no way of knowing that he was wanted by the police. The girl used a false name because they weren't married, and she was terrified that, having raped her once, you might find her and do it again. Where you get the notion that she's a prostitute from I have no idea. Since Kempin's arrest, Ada Manners lives on her own in that little house in Mansfield Street, and has started to take in clerical work for several businessmen in the town. Some of them are local councillors; there's even an alderman, I'm told. Every one of them is more than satisfied with her undoubted talents, and would give her a gleaming character reference.'

'Kempin! Kempin knows different. He pimped for her!' There was an air of desperation in the younger man's voice.

Harry shook his head. 'Frank Kempin went off yesterday to Colchester Detention Centre to await court martial for desertion. He's looking at a minimum of ten years' hard labour. I spoke to him before he went off to the glass house, because living off the earnings of a prostitute would constitute a further court martial offence – take his sentence up to twelve or fifteen. He didn't want that, and he was very eager to set the record straight that Lisa Abbott – as he knew Ada Manners – kept house for him as his common law wife while they lived in Leicester. She never needed to work, as he received a postal order every week that was sufficient for them both to live on.' His smile broadened. 'I've got his statement here in the drawer.'

Speechless in disbelief, Cleaver stared at the detective inspector.

Harry pushed an envelope across the desk towards him. 'Tom Weldon's ticket to Australia was negotiable. I contacted the steamship company and got the date and name on it changed. Your boat leaves Southampton on Monday. You've got two choices, Nathan. You leave this office, walk out of the station – without speaking to anybody – and catch that boat, or I arrest you right now for the rape of Ada Manners and for attempting to pervert the course of justice. Don't bother to clear your desk.'

Harry was still smiling as the door slammed and the footsteps echoed hollowly along the marble passage. For a man who liked fitting people up, Nathan Cleaver had taken his present situation remarkably badly.

Chapter Twenty-Three

Returning from his early morning rounds of the perimeter guards, Sam Norton paused in the vehicle yard at the back of the Old Watermill to light a cigarette, and to read again the letter that had arrived for him in the previous evening's dispatches. The French postmark gave him a strangely homesick feeling. It had been with a slight thrill of excitement that, recognising the handwriting, Sam tore open the letter from his old friend André Tessier, whom he had last seen riding out from St Jean towards the lines at Ypres, almost a year before.

André's letter explained that on the second day of the battle, like Sam, he had been badly gassed and sent back to a hospital in Lille for treatment. Unfortunately his situation was far worse than his friend's, and after several months he had been invalided out of the army. Having lived since then on a small disability pension, André was seeking permanent civilian employment – and wondered if Sam would be prepared to recommend him to Kosminski's in Paris.

Delighted to find that his old comrade was still alive, Sam immediately wrote back and promised his help. Then he penned a letter to his mother, asking her to arrange a position for Tessier in the company. It would, he thought, be wonderful for them to meet again in France after the war.

Looking around the yard, Sam's eye came to rest on a small Siddeley-Deasy truck, identical to the one that had been involved in the accident in Kelsford. Its canvas covers were thrown back to reveal a row of orange canisters, neatly stacked along one side.

Ever since he had discovered the true purpose of the work being conducted at the Watermill, Sam had felt that he was being marginalised. He was certain that Duggan and Kändler had made a major leap forward in recent weeks, the details of which were being deliberately withheld from him. There was an air of urgency in their attitudes, and while they answered his questions politely, and appeared to explain what they were doing whenever he asked, Sam knew they were keeping a great deal back. He decided that he would speak to Irene and ask her to discontinue the Sunday evening dinner parties, which he felt were a charade. Making polite conversation across the dinner table to Ralph Gresham, whom he detested more each time he saw him, and the two scientists, whom he knew were quietly laughing at him, was becoming more and more difficult. Sam knew that his sister felt she was making his situation easier, but in fact she was exacerbating it. The inclusion of Superintendent Mardlin did not help matters, as Sam was now convinced that he was involved with Irene.

The recent arrival by aeroplane of the mysterious stranger had served to deepen the young officer's suspicions. The man had remained for no more than a few hours before climbing back into the machine and taking off. In answer to Sam's enquiry, Gresham had merely replied that he was 'from the Ministry', and not to worry. Sam was worrying, though, about him and about what was being produced in the tightly secured laboratories. The aircraft that brought Gresham and his companion had flown in from the north. London and the Ministry lay to the south, so where had they really come from? Later that afternoon, carrying overnight bags, an agitated Paul Kändler and Herbert Duggan had been whisked away in the staff car that was a permanent feature at the Old Watermill, and did not return for several days.

The sound of a motorcycle engine approaching along the driveway took Sam's mind back to the previous summer, and the Brummie lance corporal who had set off from the farmhouse at St Jean for Steenstraat. He wondered if the man had made it, and if the two Frenchmen to whom he had given his horse had ever arrived at the casualty clearing station. The pleasure of hearing from André Tessier was replaced by a feeling of profound depression. In their own ways they were both trapped by the circumstances into which fate and the war had thrown them. André was living on a pension and seeking employment, while Sam, having escaped the dangers of life on the front line, was now in a virtual prison under the watchful eye of a man whom he knew virtually nothing about.

Handing over the day's dispatches to the courier, Sam threw away his cigarette end and went into the office. Lifting the telephone receiver, he asked the operator for Irene's number in Kingsbury Lane. When she answered he explained that he would be sending over two letters for her to take to the Kosminski office when she next went to London. At least, he thought, she could escape Kelsford once in a while.

Adjusting the focus of his field glasses, James Simmonds watched as the uniformed motorcyclist accelerated along the lane away from the Watermill towards Kelsford. Easing onto his right side, he scribbled the time on the notepad with his left hand. His writing was now almost as neat as when he had written right-handed, but he still felt extremely awkward. He decided that he would give it another half hour before leaving his hiding place in the trees that overlooked the lane. Pursing his lips, Simmonds checked the entries in his notebook. Under today's date, Wednesday 3 May, there was little listed since he had begun his vigil two hours earlier. Other than the motorcyclist who had just left, the only movement since six o'clock had been a supply lorry arriving. When the driver stopped to report to the sentries at the gate, Simmonds had caught a glimpse through the canvas flap at the rear of several metal canisters and lengths of jointed piping, of the type used in France to deliver chlorine gas from trench emplacements.

A light drizzle fogged up the lenses of his field glasses, and the solicitor decided to call it a day. Packing them into the canvas shooting bag that was lying on the damp ground beside him, he pulled his soft hat over his face and stretched his cramped limbs, before beginning the long trudge across the fields to Kelsford. As he walked, Simmonds turned things over in his mind. Each day he was learning more about the activities at the Old Watermill. Something that interested him greatly was the fact that security had recently been dramatically increased. The patrols around the perimeter wire had been doubled, and there was an increase in the number of vehicles entering and leaving. The logical conclusion, he reasoned, was that the operation was reaching a critical stage.

Several weeks earlier he had seen a BE2c spotter plane landing in the field at the back of the main buildings. This had particularly intrigued him, as there were two men squashed into the observer's seat. One he identified as Ralph Gresham, but the other, dressed in civilian clothing, he had not seen before. A few hours later the BE2c departed with the unknown stranger on board, leaving Gresham at the project site. Why, he asked himself, would it be necessary to fly an overloaded aeroplane into the research centre, and where had it come from?

Simmonds decided that he would wait until he was in possession of more information before discussing the matter with Will Mardlin. The drizzle was becoming heavier now, and he brushed some raindrops from his moustache before checking his wristwatch. A few yards in front of him a startled magpie took off, heading for the safety of the trees.

Looking at the watch, a Christmas present from Kathy Doyle, set Simmonds's mind on a different train of thought. Will had been wrong in his assumption that one of the reasons why Charlotte Groves had been killed was so she would not betray the matron's activities. Doyle had been both James Simmonds's nurse and mistress, and she was stealing drugs from the hospital not only to supply Groves but also him: since losing his hand, he had come to rely on the illicit morphine. Will's reasoning that the woman's greed had become a serious risk to their activities was correct, however – and this was a risk that necessitated her removal.

Kathy was a different matter, entirely. Simmonds deeply regretted her death, and felt a daily sense of loss without her. It also presented him with a practical problem. He had an ample supply of morphine, but that would not last indefinitely and he needed to identify a new source. Thinking about it as he walked, James decided that it might not be too difficult. He knew a man in the East End who would have the necessary contacts.

The drizzle had developed into a steady downpour, and it was beating insistently on the window of Will's office. He drummed his fingers lightly on the desktop as he reread the telegram that Eric Broughton had just brought in:

ENQUIRIES AT BRUSHFIELD STREET POST
OFFICE SPITALFIELDS NEGATIVE STOP UNABLE
TO IDENTIFY PURCHASER OF POSTAL ORDERS
STOP SIGNED ABSOLOM DETECTIVE INSPECTOR
COMMERCIAL STREET POLICE STATION H DIV
METPOLSTOP.

Will looked up as the figure of Harry North appeared in the doorway. 'Come in. I need to talk to you.'

Harry closed the office door behind him and sat down before taking the telegram. Like Will, Harry read, then re-read the text. 'They're playing games. Do you want me to go down there?'

Will gave him a meaningful look. 'More to the point, I think I need to go down there. How do you feel about coming with me?'

Harry considered the situation. The response to the Whitechapel enquiry was obviously a smoke screen: finding out who had sent the postal orders should have been an easy task. The Metropolitan Police was going through what at best could be described as a traumatic time. Over a long period many who were in a position to know had been questioning some of the associations that existed between Metropolitan officers and criminal elements. The response from Detective Inspector Absolom was suspicious, to say the least. Will's implication was that he intended to go down to Whitechapel and conduct his own enquiries, without telling the London police. This in itself was not only a breach of protocol but also, in view of the nature of the area, somewhat hazardous. The correct procedure was that any officer from an outside force should inform the police at Commercial Street of his intentions, and then on arrival in London report to the station – where Inspector Absolom would detail one of his men to assist in the enquiry. The reply from Commercial Street indicated to the superintendent that if he followed procedure all traces of suspects to be interviewed or evidence to be gained would disappear long before he got off the train at St Pancras.

Harry nodded. 'That's not a problem. When do you want to go?'

Will smiled at him gratefully. 'Tomorrow.'

'I'll sort out an early train,' Harry said, standing up to leave.

Will held up a hand. 'Before you go, why did Nate Cleaver put his ticket in so suddenly?'

Harry sat down again. It was the question he had been avoiding. 'I've been meaning to talk to you about that.'

Cleaver's departure was the subject of much speculation around Long Street, and the rumours included his coming into a large sum of money and being diagnosed as terminally ill.

'I talked to Cleaver,' he said carefully. 'I put it to him that there was a conspiracy between him and Weldon to pervert the course of justice, and he accepted that rather than be charged he would put his ticket in and leave quietly – and quickly.'

Will rubbed a hand across his jaw, a deep feeling of annoyance building up inside him. 'It wasn't your decision, Harry. I'd have put Cleaver back in uniform, then prosecuted him. What the bloody hell do you think you're playing at?'

Returning his colleague's steady gaze, Harry replied evenly, 'I knew that you'd be annoyed, but think about it. At present we have two, possibly three if you count the Belcher lad, undetected murders – and one, Kathleen Doyle, which only you and I know about. There's a major financial fraud about to surface, and a public outcry over a maniac killer on the loose. If we admitted that one of our own men deliberately covered up evidence in the Groves murder, that fat barrel of shit at the *Gazette* would hang us out to dry. Yes, according to the system you should have made the decision on Cleaver, and as detective superintendent your hands would have been tied. My way, Cleaver disappears, everything gets buried, I get a bollocking and we carry on with the job of finding out who killed those people.'

Will took a deep breath. Harry was right, of course. If the positions were reversed he would have done the same thing. He had to keep this between the two of them, and accept what Harry had done. At the back of his mind, though, he had an uneasy feeling that everything was not right: there was something the detective inspector was not telling him. 'All right, Harry. Leave it at that.'

'Tell her we want three pints and you're paying – that way she won't charge you.' Clarrie Greasley held out his empty glass expectantly to Bernard Ashe. The young man looked distinctly uncomfortable.

'Go on, you're knocking her off,' put in Bert Conway, giving the blonde girl behind the bar his version of a charming smile.

'I am not "knocking her off",' hissed Ashe, as he took the other two men's glasses. Getting up, he went over to the bar and engaged the barmaid in conversation while she pulled three pints of mild.

'So, what's the story, Clarrie?' asked Conway, pushing a packet of Gold Flake across the table.

'I'm buggered if I know,' replied his companion, 'and if I'm honest I'm not bothered. He was a liability. What he didn't know or couldn't prove he made up – and that's not good for anybody. All I know is that last Tuesday he went in to see Foxy North, spent about twenty minutes in the office, came out with a face like a cracked pisspot and walked off, never to be seen again. After that you know as much as I do.'

Ashe placed the pints on the table and sat down. 'Are we talking about Nathan?'

The others nodded. 'What do you know about it?' growled Conway.

Ashe was used to his sergeant's brusque demeanour. 'Only what's going round the nick, but it seems to me that all this about him putting his ticket in and scooting off to Aussie has come up since we did that job in Leicester.'

'Meaning?' asked Greasley.

'Well, I wonder if it could be something to do with the woman Kempin was living with. When Nate and I left the house, he went back to the Town Hall station and I nipped off to do a bit of shopping.' He paused, glancing across at the bar. 'I wanted to get Connie a present.'

The two older men shot each other despairing looks. 'Go on,' said Conway.

'As I was coming out of a shop in Churchgate I saw you, Clarrie, with Mr Mardlin and Inspector North walking up the road, then Mr North left you and went into a tobacconist's on his own. After a minute he came out, but instead of following you he went back down to Mansfield Street. As it's a bit of a dodgy area I followed to make sure that he was all right, and I saw him knock on the door at forty-two and go back into the house. It could only have been to see the woman.'

'Now we're getting somewhere,' said Conway, picking up his glass.

'Let's think about this,' mused Greasley. 'We all know that Nate Cleaver wrote the Manners woman up over that money missing from her employer. Mardlin latched onto that from the beginning, because he marked the file "No Further Action". At the house in Mansfield Street Mardlin spends a long while with her in the kitchen. Then when they come out she shows us where the postal orders are. He slips her a couple for her trouble and we all leave. Except Foxy makes an excuse that he needs some ciggies and goes back.'

'Bert Conway took a swallow of his beer. 'They're a devious pair of sods. I wonder what they cooked up.'

Greasley looked pensive. 'It seems to me that Mardlin found something out when he and the girl were in the kitchen. He tipped Foxy the wink, and while we all went off to the nick good old Harry went back for another chat. Whatever it was, they came away with something that well and truly shafted Cleaver.'

Ashe glanced from one to the other. 'Do you really think they'd stitch up Nate?'

Greasley gave a hollow laugh. 'Harry's been around for ever, and believe me he came up in a hard school. He was tramping the streets of Kelsford when Jack the Ripper was carving up women. He was a young bobby when old Joe Langley was the detective inspector, and they reckon Joe was so bent he finished up in the asylum. Foxy's the only man I know who could follow you into a revolving door and come out in front of you. I spoke to one or two of the lads at Leicester who worked with Will Mardlin. They all reckoned he was good – but he liked to get his own way. I'd say that he and Foxy make a very dangerous team. Tell you one thing, though. I don't think either of them would do a job on someone who didn't qualify, and I think Nathan Cleaver most certainly did.'

Bert Conway's lugubrious features bore a look of satisfaction; he had never liked Cleaver. 'We might know the truth about this one day. Whatever, they must have been bloody good for Cleaver to pack his bags and jump on a boat for Australia.' He consulted his pocket watch. 'Time to be off, Clarence. You and I have a bookmaker to consult before the two o'clock race.'

Finishing their beers, the two sergeants looked enquiringly at Ashe, who shook his head. He had no intention of becoming involved with them in an afternoon at the local races.

After they had left, he took his glass over to the bar and began to chat with Connie Armitage, with whom, as Conway had correctly speculated, he was going out.

As he watched the slim young woman serving a customer at the far end of the bar, Ashe turned something over that he had been thinking about all day. Nathan Cleaver was Tom Weldon's best friend. He had never liked either of them, and they were in his opinion two of a kind. Weldon's death was shrouded in mystery and he wondered if it was there, rather than with Ada Manners, that his two colleagues should be seeking the truth of Nathan Cleaver's unexpected departure.

His mind returned to the present as Connie, with no customers waiting, came back to his end of the bar, took a clean tea towel and began to polish an already gleaming pint glass. 'I've got a bit of leave due soon, Con,' he said. 'I wondered if you fancy a day or two away at the seaside.'

Chapter Twenty-Four

The following morning, Friday, Will and Harry caught the seven twenty-five train from Kelsford Midland station for London. There was an early morning chill in the air, and the warmth from their breath left a film of condensation on the carriage windows. Wiping the glass with the back of his hand, Will peered out at the flat countryside flashing past. 'Have you got any contacts in London?'

Harry shook his head. 'I've been down there a few times, and I did an enquiry at Leman Street a year or two ago, but as far as contacts are concerned . . . no.'

The motion of the train eased as it began to slow down, with a whistling escape of steam, before halting at Market Harborough station. Will, his mind elsewhere, gazed absently at a knot of people gathering up their belongings in readiness to board the train. A tall woman wearing a wide-brimmed crêpe hat was busily shepherding a small boy in knickerbockers and a tweed cap into the next carriage.

'How long have you been in the department, Harry?' Will realised that he knew very little about his companion's background. At first he had been worried that in his drunken state after Susan's funeral he had let slip the secret of his relationship with Irene Deladier, but in truth Harry had become a good friend since Will's return to Kelsford, and one whom he could trust implicitly.

Harry brushed a finger through his snow white moustache before answering, and smiled – more to himself than to Will. 'Tom Norton got me in. He was a detective sergeant then. I hadn't been on the job very long when there was a payroll robbery just before Christmas 1887. That's when I first came into the department, because they were so short handed. The detective inspector in those days was Joe Langley. He was a real old bastard: I never remember seeing him sober. Tom took over from him. He was probably – present company excepted – the best I ever worked for.'

A cab dropped the two detectives in Whitechapel at the corner of Liverpool Street and Bishopsgate. Paying the driver, Will enquired about the location of Brushfield Street, and once they had been given directions they set off along the busy main road.

About halfway along Brushfield Street, sandwiched between a corn dealer's and a rope and twine manufacturer's, was a small double-fronted shop with the words Brushfield Street Post Office over the door. A large board fixed to the wall just below the bedroom window bore the name J. Aldwinkle.

The two men paused on the opposite side of the road for a minute or two. It was as much a general store as anything else, Will decided. The window to the left of the entrance was laden with all manner of household items ranging from pots of furniture polish to patent medicines and cordials. The right-hand window was stacked with stationery: Bottles of Lyons Blue Black Ink stood alongside half a dozen small stone jars of Stephens Scarlet Writing Fluid, a selection of lined letter pads and several boxes of pens and nibs.

It was Friday lunchtime, and the shop appeared to be busy. As they watched, an old man wearing a cloth cap and muffler came out of the door, counting a handful of change into his pocket before making off towards Commercial Road.

Eventually, judging the premises to be clear of customers, the detectives crossed over and went into the shop. The sound of the bell above the door, tinkling as they entered, summoned from the back room a diminutive little man in a tightly buttoned dog's-tooth jacket which had seen better days. Will wondered if he was about to go out, or if the old-fashioned, curly brimmed bowler on the postmaster's head was a badge of office.

'Good morning, gentlemen. How may I help you?' The man was elderly, probably in his sixties, with a large untidy grey moustache, twice the size of Harry's and almost completely hiding his mouth.

Smiling pleasantly Will produced from his pocket the small blue-covered warrant card that proclaimed him to be an officer of Kelsford Constabulary. 'Detective Superintendent Mardlin. I was hoping that you could be of some assistance in an enquiry that I'm making regarding a series of two pound postal orders that have been bought from your post office.'

The bowler hat bobbed up and down momentarily as the postmaster gave a quick nod. 'This'll be what the detective was here about a day or two ago. I told him that those orders were bought by Mr Hardesty from the Tivoli.'

'Ah yes . . . they cabled me about that.' The smile became even friendlier. 'My colleague and I have just come from Commercial Street Police Station, but unfortunately the detective who spoke to you is out on a job at the moment, so we decided to pop round and speak to you ourselves. It would oblige me if you could tell me exactly who Mr Hardesty is.'

'He manages the Tivoli Palace Theatre round the corner in Needlegate,' came the ready reply. 'Is there some sort of problem? The gentleman who called previously – Mr Absolom – was a little vague about the matter.'

'Not at all. A few of the orders have turned up among some stolen property, and we needed to resolve whom they originally belonged to, especially as they have all been purchased over a period of time from the same office. Do you know Mr Hardesty well?'

'He comes in about once a week for his tobacco, and of course until recently every Thursday for a £2 postal order. Apart from that I don't know him very well. The Tivoli changed hands about eighteen months ago, and he came here to manage it for the new owners.'

'You wouldn't happen to know who the new owners are, would you?' enquired Harry.

'No, I'm sorry, I don't, but I'm sure Mr Hardesty will be able to tell you.'

'I'm sure he will,' Will put in smoothly. 'Have you seen Mr Hardesty recently?'

The bowler hat twitched to left and right as its owner shook his head. Blowing out his moustache, the little man paused to think. 'The last time I saw him was a week or two ago, when he last bought an order.'

'Did he ever say what the postal orders were for?'

'Oh yes.' The postmaster gave a satisfied smile. 'He did. The theatre's got an agent in the Midlands who's commissioned to find new talent for them. They pay the gentleman a retainer each week.'

Waiting for a horse-drawn delivery van to pass before they crossed the busy thoroughfare, Will's face bore a strange expression. 'I think at last we've cracked the whole crock of shit wide open.' He spoke quietly, trying to hide the excitement in his voice.

'What have I missed?' demanded his companion.

Will took a deep breath, ignoring the empty road in front of him. 'Charlotte Groves.' He let the words hang a moment. 'Don't you remember, at the bottom of the box in her wardrobe there was a programme for the Tivoli Palace. We assumed she'd been down on an away-day and pulled in a show before she caught the train home. We want our arses kicking, Harry. Charlotte Groves came down to London all right – specifically to visit the Tivoli Palace.'

Harry cursed under his breath. 'I'm getting too old for this game. If she came down to the theatre to meet someone she wouldn't have needed to pay for the show, and there wouldn't have been a programme – so, just like us, she was on a fishing expedition. The question is, did she find out what she wanted to know?'

Harry stared down at the polished toe-caps of his dark brown leather shoes. 'I think we need to talk to Mr Hardesty.'

'Let's take a walk past the theatre while we make our minds up.'

Will and Harry were strolling along Bishopsgate towards Spital Square.

'Presumably we're not going anywhere near Commercial Street nick,' ventured Harry.

Will shook his head. 'Definitely not. From the looks of it Hardesty, as manager of this place, is giving somebody at Commercial Street – presumably Absolom – a regular drink to ensure that he and his premises are left well alone and that his licence gets renewed every year. Any out of town enquiry that comes up with Hardesty's name on it is going to be returned as "nothing known".'

Harry indicated a turning on their right with the name Needlegate affixed halfway up a warehouse wall. Turning in, they found themselves flanked on either side by the high brick walls and narrow windows of dismal grime-streaked factories. The street, which was less than two hundred yards long, met another that ran across at right angles. Halfway down, on the left-hand side, was one of the myriad of music halls that abounded in working-class districts such as this.

Halting on the pavement outside, while Harry took his time lighting a cigarette, they carefully took in the façade of the premises. Behind double glass doors, closed and locked at this time of the day, they could see a small foyer and pay desk. On one side of the entrance pasted on the brickwork was a poster announcing that the main evening's entertainment this week was being provided by the renowned comedy duo of 'Teddy Turnbull and his partner – Daisy Dolman, the Dainty Comedienne'. Beside the locked doors was a board directing customers to 'Queue Here'. Painted over the door frame in small neat letters were the words 'Licensed for music, singing, and dancing, and for the sale of intoxicating liquor on the premises. Manager Sylvester Hardesty.'

'Looks like we're having an evening at the theatre. My treat,' murmured Will.

Never a great lover of music hall, Will found the two hours spent in the crowded auditorium a trial. After an hour watching a team of Spanish jugglers, whom he judged – having overheard a couple of their shouted instructions –probably originated nearer Glasgow than Madrid, followed by Dainty Daisy the delightful debutante, who exchanged witty quips with members of the audience, both he and Harry were bored stiff. Sitting on one of the hard seats at the end of the back row, for the second time in as many minutes Will consulted his watch. The evening's star turn, 'Happy Harry Turnbull', had just concluded his monologue parodying a high-class butler attempting to negotiate a series of calamities created by an inept employer, and was taking his final bow.

Harry quietly stood up. 'I'll line us up a couple of pints,' he whispered.

As the final curtain came down a general movement began towards the bar, where most of the audience would spend the remainder of the evening before drifting home. It was the usual Friday night out: an evening in the music hall, followed by an hour or so drinking with friends and neighbours, before making their way, slightly worse for wear, to their beds.

The plan that Will and Harry had devised was very simple. As the place was closing for the night they would make their way down to the toilets and hide until the staff had locked up and gone home. Then they would search the manager's office, to see if there was anything that would tie him or the theatre to Kempin. If something turned up, the next morning they would return and speak to Sylvester Hardesty in person.

At a quarter past eleven, as the barman began to throw the towels over the beer pumps, they slipped out of the bar and back into the theatre. It was pitch black. The silence was oppressive and eerie, the atmosphere laden with stale tobacco smoke and beer fumes.

Harry checked the luminous dial of his wristwatch: it was half past midnight. He and Will had hidden in the cramped and smelly gents' toilet for over an hour before making their way back into the stalls. They stood still, patiently waiting for their eyes to adjust to the darkness and listening intently for any sounds.

As they were about to feel their way forward along the deserted centre aisle, a scrabbling noise on the far side of the hall, followed by the sound of a large animal shaking itself into wakefulness, stopped them in their tracks. Exchanging looks of consternation, they quickly retreated through the curtain into the passageway from which they had just emerged. The guard dog padded back and forth across the board floor between the rows of seats, snuffling around and trying to pick up their scent. Will hoped it would take the animal a minute or so to locate the source of the noise that had woken it. If they were lucky, the heavy curtain behind which they were hiding would prevent it from picking up their scent long enough for them to find somewhere safer.

Harry touched the sleeve of Will's jacket and pointed in the dim light to a half-open door further along the passage to their right. Diving in, they just had time to push the door closed and latch it before the sound of the prowling dog was clearly heard outside. Instinctively the two men, hardly daring to breathe, put their backs against the door and waited. After a few seconds of casting around the animal came to a halt, and began to pay purposeful attention to the base of the door. Putting a finger to his lips, without moving, Will quickly looked round. They were in a medium-sized storeroom full of stage props and artistes' costumes. The light from a street lamp immediately outside, shining in through the single grubby window, provided a ghostly illumination. From the other side of the door came a deep-throated growl as the dog began to scratch at the wooden panel.

Racks of ladies' crinolines were stacked alongside cavaliers' plumed hats and thigh length boots in an untidy jumble in the centre of the room. The walls were crammed with scenery boards and posters of bygone attractions, along with the details of popular acts that had graced the boards in the distant past. Beneath the window, leaning precariously against a wardrobe manager's table, a large painted board proclaimed the previously unseen magical skills of 'The Great Marcini and his Beautiful Young Assistant, Sophia, appearing for the first time in Europe outside his native Italy'. The board gave Will an idea. Whispering hurriedly to his companion, he crept over to one of the racks and took down a voluminous magician's cape. From the nearest rail he pulled a long, flowing Chinese robe. Tossing this to Harry, Will took a deep breath, positioned himself in the middle of the room and gave a quick nod.

Grasping the gown in his right hand, Harry cautiously lifted the latch and eased the door ajar. The dog, using its muzzle, forced the door open sufficiently to push its way into the room.

Standing perfectly still, Will held the cape open in front of him like a matador. Beads of sweat stood out on his face as he saw that the guard dog was a huge, brindled, short-haired beast with small pointed ears that were laid flat back against its head. Lips drawn back, it growled menacingly, padded into the centre of the room and stopped to assess its prey. Watching Will intently, the dog sensed the man by the door and for a few seconds was unsure what to do. A thin drool of saliva flecked its mouth and hung suspended as it decided which intruder to deal with first.

Harry spun the Chinese gown in a circular movement so that it spread out and flew over the dog, dropping across its back and head, temporarily blinding it. Enraged, the animal spun around to locate its attacker, giving Will the opportunity to step forward and completely envelop the huge head in the magician's cloak. Completely disorientated, the dog dropped its head and began to claw frantically at the garments. Dashing past, Will and Harry threw themselves into the safety of the corridor, slamming the door shut behind them. Seconds later the infuriated hound hit the wooden door panels with the force of a battering ram.

They made their way back into the theatre, and paused to catch their breath. Will hoped that the sounds of the dog's furious barking would not attract the attention of a passing policeman.

'This is the last time I ever go to the theatre with you, mister,' hissed Harry, leaning against the wall, his heart racing.

'Not a problem – I was always good with dogs,' responded Will. Relief at their narrow escape flooding through them, they grinned at each other in the darkness like a pair of mischievous schoolboys.

Using a small electric pocket torch that Will had brought with him, they soon discovered a narrow staircase leading from the back of the bar to the first floor. The first room they looked into was another store, full of junk and piles of old theatre programmes, similar to the one they had found in Charlotte Groves's wardrobe. The second was a small kitchen, which obviously served as a staff rest-room. The third door, at the end of the corridor, was locked, but it took Will less than five minutes using a small pick lock to open the flimsy mortise. They found themselves in a cramped office: a filing cabinet, roll-top desk and office chair occupied most of the floor space. Using a much smaller pick lock from his set, Will quickly opened the desk. Inside was an untidy pile of correspondence and recently opened mail, including a letter from the licensing magistrates informing Mr Sylvester Hardesty 'that an inspection by a duly appointed officer from Commercial Road Police Station will be made in the near future to ascertain if his theatre licence should be renewed'. It was signed 'Chapman Absolom, Det. Insp.'. In a recess at the back was an unlocked steel cashbox which, according to the slip of paper on top of the evening's takings, contained £53 6s in change, and two crisp white £5 notes. Will began leafing through the pile of documents in the top drawer. Among bills for such mundane items as liquor supplied to the bar and cleaning materials was a small notebook that contained a list of names and addresses. Some were those of theatrical agents, while others appeared to be suppliers in various parts of the country. At the back, written in a small neat hand, was a list of dates, each accompanied by an entry reading 'BG. Post Office. Post Ord. £2'.

Harry was engrossed in an account for the services of 'Wee Willy Samson, Scotland's Strongest Man', and Will slipped the notebook into his pocket before turning to him. 'Wee Willy Samson. Never heard of him,' he murmured.

'Neither have I,' whispered Harry, 'but somebody has. At two hundred pounds for five nights' appearance he should be as famous as Harry Houdini. This place must be taking a fortune if they can afford to pay these prices.'

'Or this is all a front,' replied Will thoughtfully, 'and the accounts are being doctored. It'll be interesting to see how much Willy Samson's agent says he's being paid – if he exists at all.' He slipped the bill into his pocket with the notebook.

From the street outside came the dull clunk of a padlock being turned and the chinking of a metal chain as the beat man checked a factory gate. Will switched off his torch, and the two men waited, listening as the plodding footsteps of the policeman passed by.

'I think we've been here long enough.' There was an edge of concern to Harry's whisper. The sound of the dog's frenzied barking was echoing through the deserted building: very soon it would attract the patrolman's attention.

'Clean out the cash box and we'll get moving.' A momentary frown creased Harry's brow. 'Unless you want to let the dog out and tidy that storeroom up, there's no way we can conceal the fact that there's been a break-in. Burglars steal money, so that's what we do. When we get back I'll shove it in the Salvation Army box, or give it to the suffragettes to fund their next hunger strike.'

The cool night air was welcome as they emerged cautiously into the deserted street. A thin damp fog was beginning to descend, shrouding the narrow roadway in an eerie gloom. Checking his watch, Will was surprised to find that it was only a quarter to two. 'Right,' he said cheerfully, 'let's find a taxi cab and get back to the hotel before some of the locals hear you chinking down the street and relieve you of your ill-gotten gains.'

Chapter Twenty-Five

Over breakfast in the small commercial hotel that they had booked into in a side street off Finsbury Circus, Will and Harry reviewed the previous night's events and discussed their next course of action.

'It's a pity that we got nothing more worthwhile out of the office,' said Will, forking a piece of bacon into his mouth. 'Once the cleaning staff discover the break-in they'll get hold of Hardesty, and with any luck he should be there when we arrive.'

'If the burglary's been reported there'll probably be someone there from Commercial Street,' suggested Harry. 'That should be interesting.' He sipped at a cup of coffee and waiting patiently to light his second cigarette of the day. Harry was not a breakfast man, and at this time of the morning preferred to stick with caffeine and nicotine.

Will considered briefly. 'In that case we tell them we arrived last night and decided to take a look at the theatre this morning on the way to presenting ourselves at Commercial Street. Play down the post office and concentrate on the programme in Lottie's room.'

At a quarter to ten they strolled into Needlegate, and saw that one of the glass front doors into the Tivoli was ajar. In the foyer a thin woman in her late fifties with a rat trap face was mopping the black and white tiled floor. Touching the brim of his bowler hat politely, Will said, 'Is Mr Hardesty about, please?'

The woman straightened up and gave him a sour look. 'Oo's arskin'?' The flat Cockney accent carried a mixture of suspicion and disinterest.

'Precisely. Who's asking?' A large middle-aged man in a dark suit had appeared in the doorway that led into the theatre. Like the two Kelsford detectives he wore a bowler hat, which immediately identified him as being from the local police station.

Will gave him an appraising stare and a friendly smile. 'Detective Superintendent Mardlin, Kelsford Borough.'

The other man's features remained impassive. 'Detective Inspector Absolom. Bit off your area, aren't you?'

It was no less a reception than Will had expected. The man's florid face bore little trace of welcome. The blue veins lacing his bulbous nose and the tiny red trails of broken capillaries in the corners of his eyes were the legacy of a lifetime's heavy drinking. 'We came to see you, actually.' The easy smile still played across Will's lips. 'You did an enquiry for me recently about some money orders that had been bought from a post office in Brushfield Street.'

Absolom gave the slightest of nods. 'Yes, I did.'

'We've just turned up a connection between this place and a woman who was murdered. Thought we'd run down here and see if you could help out.'

'What sort of connection?'

'A prostitute by the name of Charlotte Groves was stabbed to death a while back, and we've just found a theatre programme in her property. It was for the Tivoli Palace. My inspector and I were coming down on a job across the other side of town and decided to take a morning out to have a look at this place. Thought perhaps the manager might know the woman. We picked up his name on the board outside – Sylvester Hardesty, isn't it?'

'You'd have done better to have cabled me.' The other man appeared to have made a decision, and allowed his features to relax into an amiable smile. 'He's not here. Left last week. New man's not taken over yet.'

'Any ideas where I might find him?' Will already knew the answer, despite the fact that the notice of inspection addressed personally to Hardesty, signed by Absolom and lying on the desk upstairs, bore the previous day's date.

The inspector shook his head. 'No. He simply gave in his notice and took off. There's been a break-in here during the night. Offices entered, cash box taken.' His eyes did not leave Mardlin's face, Detective Inspector Absolom did not like coincidences. He was well aware that the two Kelsford officers had paid a visit to Bishopsgate post office the previous day, and their arrival here on the heels of the burglary was ringing all sorts of alarm bells.

Will looked around, as if taking in his surroundings for the first time. 'These places are always risky. They need to get a guard dog.'

Absolom's face closed down again, certainty in his eyes. 'If you want to talk to me I'll be back in my office around lunch time.'

Will's smile was genuine this time. 'No, Inspector. Thank you, but if Mr Hardesty has gone away I think we'll leave it at that.'

At the end of the road Will and Harry turned right into Duke Street and paused in a shop doorway out of sight of the music hall entrance. From their vantage point they had a clear view of the stage door, which opened onto the alley at the side of the premises.

'Bit risky letting him know it was us who screwed the place, wasn't it?'

Harry eased his position to obtain a better view.

'I wanted to see his reaction,' replied Will, watching the door intently. 'We need to provoke him . . .' He was prevented from saying anything further by the sudden opening of the stage door, to reveal a portly man in his sixties wearing a broad-brimmed soft grey hat and long astrakhan overcoat. Glancing briefly up and down the road, he turned left and started to walk quickly along Needlegate in their direction.

'Well, here comes Hardesty,' breathed Harry.

Pressing back into the doorway, they waited as he passed within feet of them, head down and deep in his own thoughts.

Dropping in a safe distance behind their quarry, the two detectives followed the portly figure as he made his way through a maze of streets and alleyways, leading them deeper into the slums of Whitechapel. Although it was the middle of the morning and there were a lot of people about, it was fairly easy to keep track of the felt hat with its wide silk band as it bobbed along.

After about a quarter of an hour they found themselves in Wentworth Street, and watched as Hardesty disappeared into the bar of a large run-down pub on the corner of Commercial Street.

Stopping on the opposite corner, the two detectives took their time before crossing over. There was little point going in after the man if he was only having a quick drink before continuing on his way – and if he was aware that he was being followed he might already have dodged out through a back door.

The pub was typical of those built during the mid-Victorian era, when architects were never quite certain whether they were designing a public house or an hotel. It was three storeys high, and the huge ground-floor windows, now in sore need of a coat of paint, reached up fifteen feet from the tiled lower brickwork. It was a mausoleum of a place. At first-floor level two tall peeling signboards proclaimed the hostelry to be the Princess Alice.

Five minutes later they crossed over and, avoiding the open trap door to the beer cellar in the pavement, made their way inside. Despite the early hour the place was busy. Men in cloth caps and collarless shirts open at the neck, most wearing the heavy boots of costermongers and market traders, thronged the bar. While some were drinking pints, there were others who had come in for a break from work and were sipping at small glasses of spirits.

As Will passed a glass of rum to Harry, the man in the grey fedora came over to stand by them. At first they thought he was waiting to be served, but instead, speaking in the deep sonorous tones of a thespian, he said, 'You've been following me, gentlemen.'

Will wondered if he was managing a back street flea pit because his own career on the boards had been less than successful. If the empty whisky glass in his hand were an indication this was probably so. What was obvious to both him and Harry was that they had been led into a trap.

'We wanted to speak to you, Mr Hardesty,' said Will quietly.

Harry had already turned to survey the bar.

Hardesty's mouth twitched in an empty smile. 'You're strangers here, gentlemen, and following people into unknown territory is a dangerous occupation. A lesson that you're about to learn.'

As Hardesty turned to walk away from the bar, a heavy fist closed around Will's forearm, holding it in a grip of iron. A beefy man in his thirties, wearing the sleeveless leather jerkin of a market porter, had moved in from the side. At a table near Harry another man, slightly shorter and with a broken nose and the missing front teeth of an habitual brawler. was standing up.

It had been too easy: they knew that now. Hardesty leaving by the stage door in full view and leading them here. That they were policemen was obvious to everyone gathered in the bar, and there was not a single friendly face.

'What's your problem?' Will kept his voice even, judging his opponent. The man holding his arm was half a head taller than him and slightly heavier.

'You're the one with the problem.' The big man had sour breath and a drooping eye. 'The word is that you're dicks come down from the country, poking your noses into things that don't concern you.'

Absolom! This was his way of showing the provincial officers that he was master in his own manor.

Harry edged a pace to his right so that he and Will stood back to back. Facing down the second man, he drew his right hand slowly from his trouser pocket, a handkerchief balled in his palm providing a pad for the three penny pieces inserted between his fingers, edges facing out of his fist. It was an old trick. The knuckleduster that it made would cut a man's face open, but the user had nothing more sinister in his possession than a pocket full of loose change and his handkerchief. He eyed the man's broken nose speculatively.

Without taking his eyes off the man in the jerkin, Will was aware that all activity in the room had ceased. A thin and wiry market trader had stationed himself by the door to block off their escape. A grin of anticipation spread across the big man's face, and Will felt an almost imperceptible loosening of the grip on his arm as he prepared to strike. Spinning on his heel, Will grabbed the lapel of the open jerkin with his free hand and pulled the man in towards him. The move was unexpected and caught the porter off balance, causing him to release his grip. Will kneed his opponent hard in the groin, registering with satisfaction the feel of testicles crushing under the impact. As the man doubled over, Will grabbed at the back of his coat, and hauled it up over his head, dragging him into the middle of the room. Crippled with pain and blinded, the porter was disorientated and helpless. Taking a pace back, Will kicked him full in the face, hurling him senseless into one of the iron-legged tables, smashing glasses and sending drinks flying across the room.

At the same moment that Will made his move, Harry swung his clenched fist into the face in front of him. His aim was perfect: he sliced into the man's upper lip between his mouth and nose, splitting it wide open. Grabbing both of the bruiser's lapels, Harry forced his jacket back over his shoulders, pinning his arms by his sides, before pulling him in close and headbutting him full in the face. Blood spurted from the man's split eyebrow, as Harry, using all his strength, heaved him sideways into another table. In a continuous movement, Harry snatched up an empty stout bottle from the bar and smashed it on the polished handrail. Turning to face the room, he half-crouched, the smashed bottle held out in front of him. By his side Will also faced the room, fists close to his body, waiting.

For a moment no one moved, then from a nearby table three men slowly got to their feet. Two more on the opposite side did likewise, and they all began to move in purposefully. One of them, middle aged and, like the unconscious man on the floor wearing a sleeveless leather top, reached into the back of his belt and produced a short-bladed sheath knife. Harry turned to face him, arm extended, the jagged bottle gleaming wickedly in his hand.

Without warning, an arm encircled Will's neck from behind as the barman, leaning over, dragged him backwards across the counter. His feet off the ground, Will lashed out wildly at other hands that were attempting to grab his legs. A fist driven into his exposed stomach drove the wind from his body as one of the assailants weighed in to help the barman. In the middle of the floor Harry was still facing the man with the knife when the leg of a stool slammed into the middle of his back just above his kidneys, dropping him to the floor like a sack of potatoes. Only half conscious, he rolled to his right to avoid a second crippling blow to his kidneys, and a hob-nailed boot caught him a numbing blow to the side of the face.

Will reached blindly behind him and located the barman's face. Pressing against the back of his head and finding his nose, he tore at the nostrils. The head was pulled back to avoid his clawing fingers, which eased the vice-like grip on Will's neck sufficiently for him to lever the arm away from his throat and sink his teeth into his assailant's wrist. With a scream of pain the barman released his grip.

The sudden crash of a pistol shot brought the room to an instant halt. In the ensuing silence everyone's gaze turned towards the two figures standing just inside the open street door. The market trader who had been standing there was lying on the floor unconscious. In the still room dust and plaster gently drifted down from the hole in the ceiling made by the bullet which the taller of the two men had fired.

The newcomers were swarthy and heavily set. Even without the revolvers in their hands, it would have been apparent to anyone that they were not locals. A third man now appeared in the doorway. Dressed in a light business suit and Royal Engineers tie, Ralph Gresham somehow contrived not to look out of place even in these surroundings. 'I think it's time for you to leave, gentlemen.' His voice, along with the armed men flanking him, carried an authority that was not to be challenged.

A movement to one side caught his eye as the man behind the bar began to edge towards the safety of the cellar door. With casual grace Gresham's right hand came up, and in one fluid movement he put two shots into the line of spirits bottles inches from the man's head. He froze.

Will, his feet back on the sawdust floor, shook his head, trying to grasp this latest development. Harry, lying prone beneath an upturned table, groaned, and made an unsuccessful attempt to get to his feet. The younger of Gresham's two men moved over to Harry, covered by his companion, and pulled him into a standing position. Beginning to react once more, Will slipped an arm round his colleague's waist and helped drag him towards the door.

Behind him he heard Ralph Gresham, speaking in a slow clear voice. 'If anyone steps out of this door in the five minutes after we leave he'll be shot from across the street.'

They were bundled into the back of a waiting taxi. It remained stationary long enough for them to be joined by Gresham before roaring off towards Whitechapel High Street. Settling back in his seat, their escort turned his attention to a slowly recovering Harry North.

'Near thing, gentlemen,' he said absently, raising Harry's left eyelid and peering closely at the pupil.

'Please don't think I'm not eternally grateful, but what the bloody hell are you doing here?' asked Will.

Ignoring the question, Gresham leaned over and touched the driver on the shoulder. 'You can go a bit steady now, Percy. I don't want to attract any attention.' The fingers on the wheel lifted in acknowledgement as the driver brought his speed down to a sedate twenty miles an hour.

'In answer to your question, Will . . . some associates of mine felt that this little foray of yours to London might stir up a few muddy puddles, so we decided to keep an eye on you. Just as well, as it happens. It would have been better if this fracas hadn't occurred, but I have no doubt that we've given Inspector Absolom something to think about. You'd done rather well up to now, but I'm surprised you allowed yourself to be led into such an obvious trap.'

Will raised an eyebrow, and wondered exactly what was meant by 'you had done rather well up to now . . .'.

The remainder of the journey passed in silence as the cab left the crowded streets of central London and passed into the more affluent West End. After about twenty minutes they drew up outside a large Georgian house in a residential part of Kensington. Once he had parked, the driver got out and strolled a short way back up the road, pausing by a lamp standard to light a cigarette. After a couple of minutes he flicked away the half-smoked Woodbine and returned to the vehicle. As he bent forward to speak to Gresham through the window, Will caught sight of the butt of a service revolver inside his jacket. 'All clear, sir,' he announced softly.

Inside the house, standing in the hallway, Will was impressed by the grandeur of his surroundings. To their left there was a broad staircase, the wall hung with portraits of men in blue and white uniforms that he did not recognise as being British. The landing was dominated by a huge depiction in oils of a battle, with men on horseback being fired upon by heavy cannon as they picked their way over the bodies of fallen comrades. The ornate glass chandelier hanging from the ceiling was, Will guessed, probably worth more than he would earn in his entire career. It was, he felt, more like an embassy than a private house.

An elderly butler dressed in a dark morning suit murmured a polite greeting before leading them towards the staircase. He was, Will noted, of the same sharp-featured appearance as the two men who had rescued them from the fight in the Princess Alice. Noticing the small black yarmulke on the butler's head, he realised that the hawkish features and dark eyes were Semitic rather than Mediterranean. Whoever these people were, their origins were Jewish.

Clearing his throat, Harry, now almost fully recovered, spoke for the first time since they had left the taxi. 'What the hell's going on here?' he whispered as they reached the head of the stairs.

Before Will could answer, the manservant paused before tall double doors and tapped lightly. Without waiting for a response, he pushed the doors open and ushered them in.

It was not the opulence of the room that surprised Will so much as the tranquillity that it seemed to generate. As they entered, his feet sank into the soft pile of a richly patterned Indian carpet, which served to absorb the murmur of conversation coming from the two men seated on one of the long silk-covered couches that flanked a low glass-topped coffee table in the centre of the room. Intricate hand-woven tapestries covered in strange geometric patterns adorned the walls, and the sound of trickling water somewhere in the background emphasised the restful atmosphere.

Will's eye strayed to a large oil painting set in a deep gilt frame which formed the centrepiece of one wall. It depicted an East European market-place peopled by men and women in flowing clothing. Among the figures picking over an infinite variety of items on the stalls and laid out on the ground was a group of soldiers wearing the long black Cherkeska tunics and tall fur hats of Russian Cossacks. One of them, crossed cartridge belts over his chest, was bargaining with a stallholder for a beautifully detailed copper samovar.

'Fascinating picture, Mr Mardlin. Russia, Unghvar at the foot of the Carpathian Mountains, painted in about 1880. It doesn't matter where you look, you always see something you hadn't noticed before.'

At the sound of the voice Will turned his attention to the occupants of the couch. It was the older of the two who was addressing him. Immaculately dressed, clean shaven and with well-barbered silver hair, he was, Will supposed, in his middle to late sixties.

The second, younger and in his thirties, stood up and, with a friendly nod to Ralph Gresham, extended a hand. 'Please, take a seat.' He inclined his head to Harry. 'You look as if you've been in the wars, Mr North.' Returning to his place, the man gave the newcomers an amiable smile. 'We haven't met before, gentlemen, so allow me to introduce myself. My name is Edward Bayliss. I'm part of the intelligence gathering section of His Majesty's Armed Forces. Colonel Gresham – whom you already know – and I have an interest in the research work that's being conducted at the Old Watermill in Kelsford.' Indicating the silver haired man he continued, 'This is Mr Lionel Cohen, through whose good offices you were extricated from your recent unfortunate dilemma. Ralph, perhaps you would care to explain matters to our guests.' Producing a packet of Passing Cloud, Bayliss proffered them to Gresham and a grateful Harry, whose own cigarettes had been ruined in the fracas.

Gresham paused momentarily, as if reaching a decision before beginning. 'I need to be perfectly frank with you, which means I need an assurance that anything discussed here will never go beyond the five of us.' He glanced across at the silver-haired man, who gave an almost imperceptible inclination of his head.

Harry's good eye held a hard, suspicious glint. 'By intelligence gathering I presume you mean you're spies?'

'A rose by any other name,' replied Gresham with a non-committal smile.

The conversation was interrupted by the arrival of a young man carrying a tray of black tea and tiny pastries. Placing it on the coffee table, he shot an enquiring glance at Cohen, who murmured something in Yiddish. With a deferential half-bow the youth retreated, closing the door behind him. Mardlin was struck once more by the serenity of their surroundings.

'You've had a near miss today, and I have to say that the presence of myself and my friend's associates wasn't entirely accidental.' Gresham helped himself to a cup of tea before continuing. 'First, let me explain that the research being carried out at Kelsford has far greater implications than I led you to believe Will.' Again the disarming smile. 'The truth of the matter is that the research is of national importance. Dr Duggan and Paul Kändler have successfully developed a nerve gas designated MD19, which has the potential of altering the course of the war. In brief, a small amount of the stuff that they've come up with is capable of taking out an entire sector of the battlefield in a matter of minutes.' He paused to sip at his tea.

'Or a small town,' said Will, his face grim.

Gresham held his hand up. 'Believe me, its use will mean that very soon conventional warfare will become history. I'm sorry this has landed on your patch, Will, but there were good reasons for siting Project 19 in Kelsford.'

Will sat back and exchanged a glance with Harry. Both men were troubled at this latest revelation.

'Please allow me to continue. The fact that you're here now is because we've reached a crucial stage in our operation. One of the reasons for siting the project at the Watermill was that it's being financed through a substantial donation made by the Kosminski jewellery empire.' He hurried on before the detectives could ask any questions. 'That's why Samuel Norton was put in charge of the day-to-day running of the site. At first he wasn't aware of the true nature of the research. The unfortunate accident with the beer lorry changed that.'

'Does Irene know what's going on?' asked Will flatly.

Gresham took another sip of the tea before giving an emphatic shake of his head. 'No. She doesn't know anything that might compromise you.' The implication of the carefully chosen words were not lost on Will. 'What's become a matter of concern is the recent series of murders which you're investigating. Initially I thought they were of no concern to us, but now I'm not so sure. Charlotte Groves and Ivor Rees were involved in the swindle at Kelsford War Hospital that you seem to be presuming Byron Carstairs set up. I'm by no means certain that this is so. Carstairs was certainly a key figure, but I think that whoever's responsible for the murders was probably the prime instigator of the fraud.' He caught the looks of consternation on the policemen's faces. 'I'm sorry if you thought that no one else was privy to that information. I can assure you that we won't interfere with your enquiry in any way. The death of Kathleen Doyle is obviously murder – and I'd be interested in knowing what progress you make,' he added. 'As I said, until recently I assumed that the killings weren't connected with Project 19, but two developments have made me reconsider. First, we've discovered that a German spy whom we know only as Nemesis is leaking information about the project to High Command in Berlin. It's certain that Nemesis is based somewhere in the Kelsford area. Second, James Simmonds has been spying on the activities at the mill.'

Will frowned. 'James?'

Gresham nodded thoughtfully. 'He's been spotted recently by patrols on the outer perimeter, hiding in woodland with binoculars. So, you see, things are beginning to overlap. Simmonds is involved in the war hospital – which means he would have known about Rees, who was a contractor, and he was also associated with Doyle. Now he's showing an interest in the research site. Furthermore, your interest in the Tivoli theatre has drawn a connection between certain events. A while ago a routine bank report to the Treasury showed that large sums of money are being laundered through the Tivoli. At present we've been unable to trace the origins of that money.' Seeing the enquiring look on Will's face, Gresham explained. 'It's fairly common knowledge in financial circles that all the clearing banks are monitoring their larger client accounts. Any unusual transactions are flagged up and reported back to Ted's people.' He waved a hand in Bayliss's direction. 'It's a basic wartime counter-intelligence measure, and while there are a lot who find the system irksome, it does help to keep track of money laundering.'

Harry leaned forward, wincing at the pain lancing across the back of his eyes as he stubbed out his cigarette in a cut-glass ash tray. 'That explains why they're paying 'Scotland's Strongest Man' forty pounds a night. He gets a tenner and the books show two hundred for the week's appearance.'

'Precisely. Considerable amounts of cash are being processed. On paper money is paid out to non-existent acts, agents, advertising companies. We would very much like to know where that money's coming from and going to.

Is it simply going into a crooks retirement fund? Is it coming from Germany? From the events of the weekend the chances are that the place is being used to process the money siphoned off from your war hospital. Give us time and we'll trace it, but unfortunately time is short.'

'The money's going back and forth between here and Kelsford,' said Will thoughtfully. Gresham raised an eyebrow. 'Lottie Groves found out where the money was going, and came down here not long before she was killed – presumably to confirm her suspicions. She had a programme from the theatre in her possession that whoever killed her didn't know about. And we now think that there were two people involved in her murder.'

It was Bayliss's and Gresham's turn to exchange glances. 'If,' said Bayliss, 'the money's from Kelsford, then it's to our mutual advantage to work together. I have to say, though, we're most unhappy about Simmonds, who I presume you're aware makes regular business trips to London.'

Will nodded pensively. 'Yes – but let's keep that to ourselves for the time being, shall we?'

'It would have been better to have had this conversation earlier, rather than you watching us, waiting to see where we led you.' Harry's voice held a challenge.

'Quite right, Harry, but unfortunately it was necessary.' Gresham turned to address himself to the inspector. 'Once we realised that your enquiries unwittingly cut across ours, we enlisted the help of our friend here to keep an eye on you, purely for your own safety.' Ralph held out a hand, indicating that the older man should take up the briefing.

'First, let me say that I'm not part of any government department.' The tones were soft and cultured, with just a trace of an accent in the background. He was probably a little older than Will had first thought, and the suit was unquestionably Saville Row. 'I represent an organisation that has a vested interest in ensuring the welfare of certain persons, both here and abroad. Over time my work has resulted in my forming a certain sphere of interest that coincides with that of Commander Bayliss, and it was he who asked me to ensure that while you were in London no harm befell you.'

'And to monitor any progress that we might make,' interjected Will grimly.

In the ensuing silence, Gresham reflected that it was not only Mardlin who wanted to know who the mysterious 'Mr Cohen' was. Ted Bayliss, responsible for arranging the surveillance placed on the two detectives from the moment they left the train at St Pancras, had been reluctant to disclose anything about the organisation that Cohen controlled. Until now his explanation had been that his contact was an extremely wealthy criminal who ran a smuggling enterprise between England and the Continent. That this was patently untrue was obvious.

In a perverse way Gresham reflected, things had turned out to his advantage. He was under no illusion that had the two detectives not precipitated matters, this meeting would never have taken place. He and Bayliss would have talked with Mardlin and North in some discreet club, or probably an apartment in the West End rented by Room 40 as a safe house, and no one other than his naval counterpart would ever have know of Mr Cohen's existence. In the intelligence world there was only one absolute truth – knowledge is power. Now that he was aware of Cohen's existence, it would only be a matter of time before he discovered the man's true identity, and then he could discuss the small matter of power sharing with Bayliss.'

Cohen smoothly acknowledged Will's statement. 'That would be part of the remit. We were a little concerned about your nefarious activities last night, but you seemed to resolve the matter of the guard dog satisfactorily. This morning was not quite such a resounding success. Your instincts not to trust in the good offices of Chapman Absolom were absolutely sound. It's a sad fact of life that there are certain officers in the Metropolitan Police who aren't entirely reliable, and he's one of them. He has a vested interest in your not talking to the theatre manager. Sylvester Hardesty, as I'm sure you've worked out, was told to purchase a postal order for two pounds every week, and send it to the address in Leicester where your man Kempin was living. I've no doubt that his instructions were to use a different post office each week in order to obscure matters. Fortunately for us, human nature being what it is, Hardesty couldn't see the point when he could simply pop into the one around the corner every week. Once he left the public house this morning, after the disturbance, my men lost track of him. I suspect he's been safely spirited away by Absolom for the time being. Whoever the owners of the Tivoli are, they've covered themselves very efficiently, and it's going to take us a while to identify them. When we do, please rest assured that the information will be passed to you.'

In the ensuing silence Will looked at Gresham enquiringly. 'All right, Ralph. Now that we know where we stand, what exactly do you want from us?'

Gresham considered for a moment. It was exactly the question he had been asking himself. 'It's still possible that we're barking up the wrong tree – that your search for a killer and ours for a spy are going to go off in different directions. If you get anything at all on Simmonds, or any results in relation to the murder enquiries, I'd appreciate being included. Simmonds, I feel, is deliberately giving the impression of an interfering, flag-waving buffoon. My instinct is that we all need to look more closely at him.' Pursing his lips, he decided to give Will a piece of information that was of passing interest to Bayliss and himself, and see if it came back to him later. It would be a good way of judging how discreet the superintendent was in his dealings with his mistress. 'A minor matter, but worth mentioning . . . the French are now showing an interest in what we're doing.'

The silver-haired man looked sharply first at Gresham and then at Bayliss. Bayliss reassured him with the merest flicker of an eye: he was well aware what his partner was doing.

Picking up the exchange, Gresham experienced a definite feeling of satisfaction. So Cohen was not privy to everything, which meant he really was an outsider and not, as he had begun to wonder, Ted Bayliss's controller. 'French military intelligence has cottoned on to the Kosminski involvement. It's bad luck really, but given that Kosminski's is essentially a French company I suppose it was inevitable: they were bound to pick up on the substantial financial donation to HM Government. They've pulled a fellow by the name of André Tessier – an intelligence officer in the Chasseurs at Ypres with Samuel Norton – out of the field, and set about infiltrating him into the French end of things. Major Norton got a letter from Tessier a couple of days ago with the cover story that he'd been badly wounded at Ypres, invalided out of the army and needs a job. He asked Norton if he'd give him a letter of introduction to his mother, with a view to finding employment with Kosminski's in Paris.'

Will absorbed the information in stony silence. If this was a test to see how much he gave away to Irene in pillow talk, then Ralph was going to be disappointed.

The purpose of the meeting achieved, Gresham began to wind things up. He took a deep breath, and the twitch caught briefly at the corner of his mouth. 'Whatever happens, Project 19 will be concluded within a month or two and the Kelsford connection will be closed down before the end of the summer. In the meantime it's essential that we nail this bastard Nemesis and close down his activities.'

Will gave a slow nod of agreement. The nerve gas that was the prime concern of the two men sitting across the table would be used on the battlefield in the coming summer campaign – but perhaps by joining forces he might be able to bring to a conclusion his own murder enquiries.

On the train back to Kelsford Harry broke the silence. 'They think they hold all the cards, but I'm not so sure.'

Will, preoccupied by the fact that Gresham obviously knew about himself and Irene, grunted absently, and continued to wrestle with the problem that had been exercising him ever since they had left the house in Kensington. Who, he asked himself for the hundredth time, other than Harry and Béatrice Palmaerts, knew about them?

Giving up for the time being, he turned his attention to his travelling companion. 'What are you thinking of?'

Harry pushed an empty Player's packet into the parcel rack under the window strap and fished a new one from his pocket. 'Gresham and Bayliss are certainly clever – and they know one or two things they're not supposed to – but they're also running scared.' He found a box of Swan Vestas in another pocket and applied a match to the end of a fresh cigarette. 'They gave away very little about this spy. That's what they're really worried about. Obviously their MD19 gas has got to be ready for the summer offensive, and they're pulling out all the stops out to find him before he shags them. And it's obviously upset them that the French are rattling their cage. The so-called Mr Cohen seemed particularly put out about it – as if it was something he'd have expected to have been told about. We need to use whatever they know to push along our end of things. I'll be interested to see if the Pipeline comes up with who owns the Tivoli.'

Will raised an eyebrow. 'The Pipeline?'

Harry grinned back. 'I'm fed up with being treated like some sort of yokel, just off the farm. Years ago – I'm talking about 1888, just before Tom and Ruth Norton pulled stumps and went to live in France – there was a big furore over a necklace stolen from Russia. We never knew the truth, although I suspect Tom Norton knew a lot more about it than anyone else. The story was that the necklace had been brought to England by a secret Jewish organisation called the Pipeline, set up to bring Jewish émigrés out of Tsarist Russia. To fund their activities they dealt in jewellery as well. A lot of people never believed that the Pipeline existed – claimed it was a myth.' Harry took a pull at his cigarette and stared quietly out of the window. 'Until now, that is.'

Will returned his gaze, waiting for him to continue.

'Cohen. Thirty years ago he was dark haired, good looking and very wealthy. He was a banker by the name of Manfred Issitt. Lived with his wife and family in Leaminster Gardens, not far from where Weldon went into the river. He was a prominent member of the Jewish community. If he's now number one man in a secret organisation that's backing the British Secret Service, then it has to be the Pipeline. So that answers the speculation – all those years ago the organisation did exist, and it still exists today.'

'You crafty old sod ... is there anything you don't know?' Will's admiration for his friend's depth of knowledge and powers of recall pushed the matter of his own liaison to the back of his mind.

'Not much,' replied Harry smugly.

Will's thoughts turned to the notebook that he had slipped into his pocket in the Tivoli. When they got back to Kelsford he would show it to Harry, and they could make a start on contacting the people named in it, to investigate their involvement with the theatre.

Throwing his cigarette out of the window, Harry settled back in his seat and, closing his eyes, began to doze. Will looked out at the countryside, and passed the time wondering how Simmonds fitted in.

His cogitation was interrupted by a sleepy voice. 'Still got that notebook, have you?'

In the dimly lit snug of the pub in Gray's Inn Road, Ralph Gresham and Edward Bayliss sipped at their beer and discussed in muted tones the events of the morning. 'You've taken a chance bringing them in, Ralph.' Bayliss pensively twisted his signet ring.

Gresham replaced his pint pot on the table and drew a circle with his forefinger on the damp surface. 'Calculated risk, Ted. Nemesis has been operating for too long. Time's running out for us: we've got to eliminate him, and do it quickly. Those two might just find him for us. Neither of them's a fool – far from it – and if the wheels come off they'll provide us with a bit of cover.'

Bayliss nodded thoughtfully. We all have to take risks, he mused, like letting Ralph Gresham get a look at Manfred Issitt. In the circumstances that had become unavoidable after the débâcle in the Princess Alice.

It had been necessary to convince Mardlin and his companion of the urgency of the situation before removing them from London, and the further attentions of the Metropolitan Police. Fortunately, Inspector Absolom's sphere of influence extended no further than the boundaries of Whitechapel. Bayliss had led Gresham to believe that his surveillance of the two Kelsford detectives was being undertaken by a small group of local criminals, paid daily – but after the morning's activities this fiction could no longer be maintained. What Military Intelligence must not be allowed to discover was that Manfred Issitt, alias Lionel Cohen, was the head of the Pipeline; or that, through Naval Intelligence and under the codename Zeus, he was responsible for brokering the financial arrangements with the War Office on behalf of Kosminski's.

Chapter Twenty-Six

Clinging onto the cold steel rim of the U39's conning tower, Siegfried Keppler was feeling decidedly seasick as the submarine pitched and wallowed in the choppy North Sea waters. It was four in the morning, and Captain Diessbacher was anxious to deposit him on the deserted beach before daylight prevented his escape into deep waters.

Keppler was returning to Whitby from a briefing in Berlin concerning Operation Nemesis with his senior controller, Colonel Liesendahl. While the outward trip to Hamburg had been relatively pleasant, the unpredictable North Sea, lashed by a late spring gale that blew up the day after the U39 set off on its return journey, had made the last two days a nightmare for him. Never a good sailor, in the confined atmosphere of the Unterseeboot he had spent most of the voyage alternately hanging over the edge of his bunk vomiting or lying perfectly still, attempting to quell his churning stomach.

The fact that his meeting with Liesendahl had gone well did little to ease Keppler's situation. A new summer offensive was being planned, and his report that Nemesis was absolutely certain the Allies would not be in a position to employ their MD 19 gas operationally for another six to eight weeks had been received with jubilation. Although research at the Kelsford scientific unit was on schedule, Nemesis's information was that further field trials were not planned until early June. How the gas would be trialled was not yet decided, or if it had been the arrangements were so secret that the agent had not yet been able to discover any details. The main thing was that the progress of the war was swinging in the favour of Germany. Churchill's ill-conceived campaign in the Dardanelles had collapsed, and the way was now clear for a renewed attack on the Western Front.

Early the previous evening a coded signal from the *Viking Tun*, to the effect that the trawler had developed engine trouble and could not rendezvous with the submarine to take Keppler off, had caused a great deal of consternation, and much against his better judgement Klaus Diessbacher was forced to come close enough to the coast for his passenger to be rowed ashore. After a hurried discussion it had been decided to bring the U39 into the shallow waters just off the tiny village of Staithes, a few miles up the coast from Whitby. Some time before Keppler had acquired, through Ludwig Heitmann, a small fishing boat of the type used by inshore fishermen. He kept the coble either in harbour at Whitby or on the beach near Staithes, and having learned to sail it proficiently he spent much of his time fishing in the calmer inshore waters between the two places. It allowed him to come in and out of Whitby without attracting attention, while the catches of mackerel that he sold on the fish dock provided him with a visible income.

Bereft of any forward motion, the U39 pitched and rolled in the heavy swell. Struggling in the pre-dawn light to maintain his balance on the tiny bridge, Keppler fought against the embarrassment of being sick over the side in front of the two sailors who were with him.

Franz-Georg Heinig scanned the dark silhouette of the coastline, balanced against the guard rail and with a pair of Zeiss glasses glued to his eyes. 'No sign of any activity, Herr Kapitän.'

Diessbacher nodded, and signalled to the men on the deck below. Bosun Grönemeyer issued quiet orders, and the boat's inflatable dinghy slid with a barely perceptible splash into the black waters. At the end of a short painter, it bumped and yawed against the submarine's ballast tank.

Heinig tucked his chin into the upturned collar of his reefer and turned his face away, grinning to himself. The Oberleutnant had the sailor's inherent disdain of landsmen, and he found it amusing to watch Keppler's mixture of apprehension and nausea as he swung over the edge of the bridge and began to climb down the conning tower ladder. There was, though, more to it than that: Heinig considered that carrying a non-sailor served only to increase the dangers of submarine life. Whether their passenger was a soldier or a civilian he was not sure. The one thing that he and the rest of the crew knew very well was that he was a spy, and it was because of him that the U39 was standing out to sea day after day, week after week, hiding from the Royal Navy patrol boats. As a serving officer of the Kaiser's Imperial Navy, Heinig regarded the activities of men such as this with contempt. It was, in his opinion, those like Keppler who prolonged the war and increased the dangers for him and the crew of the U39.

Next to him, Klaus Diessbacher allowed himself a low chuckle as Keppler, grabbing at Grönemyer's outstretched hand, lost his footing and sprawled headlong into the dinghy.

'Fotze,' muttered Heinig, bringing the glasses back up to his eyes, this time examining the horizon to the east, where a pale pink tinge was beginning to light the sky.

'Genau,' replied the captain. 'Exactly, but there's nothing we can do about it. Until he's done whatever it is that he's doing we're stuck here.' Klaus

Diessbacher knew little more about the intelligence officer's mission than his crew. His orders were to stand by, well out to sea and keep a constant radio monitor on the channel that Keppler's radio, hidden under the floorboards of the house in Mission Yard, was tuned to. Once or twice a month a signal would come in for the U39 to rendezvous with the *Viking Tun*, and Keppler would be transferred aboard. They would then set sail for Hamburg, where the agent would disembark and be whisked off in a waiting staff car to Berlin. Three or four days later he would reappear at the dockside and, refuelled and freshly provisioned, they would return to meet the *Viking Tun* and transfer their passenger before taking up station once more. It was a boring but hazardous existence, and Diessbacher wondered how much longer it would carry on. While the Mediterranean had been a dangerous and busy posting, the warm climate and accommodating Spanish women had made it infinitely preferable.

Later that morning, gazing idly out of the taproom window at the Nelson's Flag, Siegfried Keppler turned over in his mind the events of the last few days. Nemesis was proving to be a priceless asset to the German intelligence network. When the agent was slipped quietly into place the potential value of his presence in Kelsford could never have been remotely imagined by Rudolf Liesendahl, or anyone else involved in the war against Britain. Very soon now the research work at the Old Watermill would be completed, and the second phase of the operation made ready for implementation. It would be Nemesis's responsibility to somehow acquire a quantity of the chemical from the laboratories in Kelsford and deliver it to Keppler. The plan outlined in his recent meeting with the German Intelligence staff officer was that Keppler should take a phial of MD 19 to London. There, in a similar manner to that employed by the British in Northumbria to kill the prisoners of war, he would leave the chemical in a location where it could do the most damage. After some discussion it was decided to place it in a litter bin on St Pancras railway station during the early evening, attached to an alarm clock detonator that was set to explode an hour later. This would give Keppler time to escape by train and be well on his way north before the phial delivered its deadly contents into the London atmosphere. The following day, along with Nemesis and some further samples of MD 19, he would be taken off by U39 and returned safely to Germany.

A well-built middle-aged woman in a crisp white apron cleared away his empty plate and poured a mug of fresh coffee from the tall jug in her hand. 'Everything all right, my dear?' she asked.

Keppler returned her smile and nodded pleasantly. It had taken him some time to become accustomed to the British habit of eating huge amounts of fried eggs and bacon along with slabs of bread and cooked tomatoes first thing in the morning. Now, however, tired and bleary after being dropped from the submarine and braving the choppy inshore waters to bring the tiny coble round the coast into the estuary, he found the hot greasy food enjoyable and comforting.

The *Viking Tun* was due in any time to allow repairs to its engine, and Keppler decided that after quickly speaking to the skipper he would wander down the road to his lodgings and a good morning's sleep. Since taking up residence in Whitby, Keppler had moved three times, only visiting the room in Mission Yard briefly to use the radio before slipping away through the back alleys.

During the last month or so, crewing the *Viking Tun* on a temporary basis as part of his cover, Keppler had got to know Captain Tam and his two crewmen quite well. Tam, half Irish, was no lover of the King of England, and was more than happy to receive the cash stipend that was paid discreetly into the bank in Dublin by a Dutch import firm, before being transferred to an Edinburgh account.

Other than disrupting the arrangements for his return to Whitby, the fact that the *Viking Tun* had developed engine trouble did not particularly bother Keppler. Tam had signalled that he would make his way into Whitby this morning and, once the engine was fixed, return to the fishing grounds around the Firth of Forth. If there were a message for him, Keppler could deliver it to the boat at the dockside.

Three men strolling up Pier Road from the direction of the customs dock caught his eye. As one of them was the harbourmaster, Keppler presumed at first that they were making their way to the harbour office further along, near the lifeboat station. However, when they stopped, the harbourmaster shading his eyes and looking up the estuary towards the battery at the river mouth, he revised his opinion. The two men accompanying the harbourmaster were bowler hatted and wearing suits: all his instincts told Keppler that these were policemen. They were peering intently at the *Viking Tun* as it picked its way through the fishing boats towards the jetty.

Apparently absorbed in reading his newspaper, Siegfried Keppler watched closely as one of the crewmen, having jumped ashore to tie up the forward mooring line, was approached by the men. A moment later Tam's head appeared over the edge of the dock as he climbed the metal ladder up to the jetty.

Two uniformed constables stepped from a nearby doorway and walked briskly over to join the group. At a word from the stouter of the two policemen they took up positions on the quayside by the ladder, while the harbourmaster and his companions descended out of sight onto the deck of the boat. Half an hour later, looking frustrated and angry, they reappeared, and made their way towards the harbourmaster's office accompanied by Tam, who with a glance at the window of the Nelson's Flag gave Keppler a slight shrug.

Keppler remained at his table and politely asked for more coffee. He did now know what had gone wrong. Perhaps Tam had become careless and drawn attention to himself, or his presence so regularly in these waters had aroused suspicion. What was clear was that all contact with the fishing boat had to be discontinued. He hoped that Tam would produce documents to satisfy the police that his activities were completely legitimate. That captain and crew had not been arrested clearly indicated that the authorities did not have any evidence against them. Keppler experienced a feeling of unease. Could one of the reasons for the officers' apparent discontent be that they had not found an extra crewman on board?

Finishing his coffee, he abandoned any idea of sleep and made his way down to where the thirty foot coble was beached. Pulling a fishing net towards him, he settled down to mend a hole in the mesh while waiting to see what happened aboard the *Viking Tun*.

Tam was at the harbour office for almost an hour, and Keppler's sense of unease deepened at the sight of the man's angry face as he strode back along the harbour.

It was early evening before the engineer who had boarded the trawler shortly after ten in the morning wiped his oily hands on his overalls, threw his tool box onto the jetty and disappeared into the failing light.

As soon as it was dark, Keppler made his way to the house in Mission Yard and let himself in after checking to ensure that he was not observed. Removing the boards under the bed, he withdrew the radio set and placed it carefully on the bedcovers. Next he took the Luger and laid it on the table. There was still thirty-five minutes to go before the pre-arranged time at which he was to send a signal to the U39. Taking down a rag and a can of gun oil from the shelf near to the door, Keppler unwrapped the pistol and, with practised hands, deftly stripped it down and began to clean it.

'Make a signal . . . radio defective . . . heave to . . . I have urgent documents for you.'

Klaus Diessbacher waited patiently as the seaman beside him on the bridge worked the clattering shutter of his signal lamp. It was midday, and the U39 had been trailing the *Viking Tun* at periscope depth for the last two hours, waiting for the Royal Navy M Class destroyer sitting five miles off their starboard bow and on the same heading as the trawler to overtake it and continue its leisurely patrol.

Following Keppler's transmission the previous night, U39 had picked up the fishing boat soon after ten o'clock that morning, ten miles east of Holy Island. Waiting on the surface was fraught with dangers, and to Diessbacher's annoyance the lookout had spotted the Royal Navy destroyer in the distance moments after sighting the trawler. Cursing his luck, the German captain gave the order for battle stations and submerged to periscope depth. The M Class destroyer, which had replaced the older slower Tribal Class eighteen months earlier, was a swift and dangerous enemy. Its twenty-seven and a half thousand horsepower engines could drive the sleek hull through the water at speeds of up to thirty-six knots, and if it caught an enemy submarine on the surface the destroyer's four inch guns and twenty-one inch torpedoes could destroy the U-boat within minutes.

Watching the sleek greyhound ploughing through the grey waters, throwing up a creaming bow wave – despite the fact that its skipper was running with the engines at half speed to conserve fuel – Klaus Diessbacher considered a rumour that was presently current. On his recent berthing at the North Sea submarine pens there had been talk that the British were developing an underwater bomb known as a depth charge. Until now, when chased by a destroyer, if through its greater manoeuvrability a U-boat could evade being sunk by the enemy's guns the submarine captain, given sufficient time to dive was relatively safe. Within about forty-five seconds, the U-boat would be under the surface of the water and able to slip away. Now, however, if the rumours were true, the Engländers were using a bomb with the fuse set to explode at a certain depth, which vastly altered the balance of the chase.

It was now twenty minutes since the navy vessel had disappeared from view, and Diessbacher was confident that the *Viking Tun* and the U39 were alone in the vast stretch of ocean. Even so, he had no intention of remaining on the surface in broad daylight a moment longer than was necessary. A speck of light from a hand-held lamp on the wooden bridge of the fishing boat blinked out an acknowledgement, and the trawler grew rapidly larger as the submarine closed on it. Diessbacher could make out the figure of the captain in the wheelhouse, bringing his boat around broadside to await the approaching submarine. Two other figures came up from the galley. The distance between the two vessels narrowed to a little over two hundred yards as, diesels closed down, barely holding her head against the swell, U39 nudged forward at less than walking pace.

Klaus Diessbacher took a final look at the radio signal in his hand, then gave a brief nod to his second officer. Heinig unclipped the voice pipe and spoke quietly and clearly into the mouthpiece. 'Fire port torpedo.'

The horror-stricken men on the trawler suddenly saw the silver trail heading towards them. Tam attempted vainly to open the throttle, while spinning the wheel hard to starboard, in a doomed attempt to evade the missile that was hurtling across the narrow stretch of water towards them.

In a blinding flash of light the trawler exploded as it was hit full amidships, the torpedo ripping through the hull and igniting its laden fuel tanks. The heat from the blast blew across the deck of the U39, as if for a split second the door of some mighty furnace had been thrown open. Dazzled by the detonation, it took several seconds for the men on the bridge of the submarine to recover their vision properly. All that was left of the *Viking Tun* was a slowly spreading patch of oil and some debris floating lazily on the surface of the water.

Heinig signalled down from the bridge to Erwin Fahr. Fahr raised a hand in acknowledgement and spoke to Lothar Krüger and Günter Schmidt, who set about securing the heavy machine gun. It would not be required. After the explosion of the fuel tanks there were no survivors.

Chapter Twenty-Seven

James Simmonds hefted the heavy canvas bag into a more comfortable position as he strode along the path that led through the woods between the Old Watermill and the road to the town locks. From the locks it was a five minute walk to his office in the High Street. On one hand, he reflected, things were going extremely well. The theatre in London was in the process of being closed down, along with any traces that might lead back to himself, and given another fortnight he would have removed all traces of his financial activities. Next, with each of his former partners in crime dead, he could tidy up the proceeds of the war hospital swindle, which he estimated had netted him in excess of fifty thousand pounds – currently distributed between half a dozen banks up and down the country in a variety of false names.

On the other hand, the Watermill and the covert project that was being conducted there bothered him considerably. A man of complex morals, James Simmonds was if nothing else a patriot. The belief that during the last few weeks he had uncovered not only an enemy spy at work but also strongly suspected that he knew his identity weighed heavily upon him. What he was going to do about it he was not certain. He had to wait until his own affairs were all neat and tidy, but after that he would talk to Mardlin.

Pausing to adjust the strap of his bag once more, Simmonds was startled by the sound of a twig snapping in the undergrowth. Holding his breath, he remained perfectly still. Further rustling in the early morning quiet confirmed that he was not alone. Half turning, he peered into the dark shadows between the trees. Nothing moved. Sharp and clear, another sound came to his ears – one he had not heard since his return from France and which made his blood run cold. The click of a gun being cocked.

Instinctively he dropped flat onto the soft leaves of the woodland floor. As he rolled to one side the crack of a pistol shot was followed by a strip of bark tearing from the tree next to which he had been standing. Lying prone beneath a bush, Simmonds searched the undergrowth for signs of movement.

Over to his left a dark shadow darted between two saplings and was lost in the trees. Unarmed, he knew that unless he escaped quickly it would only be a matter of time before the would-be assassin got back in position.

Taking a chance, he got carefully to his knees, then grabbed the canvas bag and ran at a fast crouch towards a tall elm tree five yards away. Immediately two more shots whistled past his head in rapid succession, but now he was running full pelt, zigzagging towards the narrow stream that cut through between the woodland and the road back into town. Splashing across the water, he knew that if he were going to be picked off it would be out here in the open. Dashing over the road, Simmonds threw himself into the shallow ditch on the opposite side and waited. It afforded little protection, but in order to get another shot at him his attacker would have to come out into the open.

Nothing happened, and after ten minutes he heard the sound of a heavy truck coming along the forest path. He realised that the shots had attracted the attention of the Watermill sentries, and a detachment of soldiers had been sent out to investigate. Safe for the moment, he made his way cautiously along the ditch until, deeming it clear to emerge, he climbed out onto the road. Wet and dishevelled, he began to make his way back towards Kelsford. Constantly checking around for signs of his attacker James was relieved to find that the only others using the way into town at this early hour of the morning were a military dispatch rider and an old tramp dozing beside a farm gate.

Alone in his office, Harry North replaced the telephone earpiece on its rest and drummed his fingers on the top of his desk. He had hoped that the captain at the Salvation Army hostel in Salmon Lane would be able to help him, but he was unlucky. Captain Dawson had not seen Tuppenny Rice since the previous week. His eyes strayed back to the scrap of paper on his desk, reading again the small neat writing of the pencilled message: 'Need to speak, very urgent, if you want to know the time ask a policeman, teddy bears had a picnic.'

Harry's day had been busy and frustrating. In the morning, as he was having his breakfast of coffee and a cigarette, Laura Percival, who they both fondly believed to the majority of the outside world was simply his landlady, had presented him with the folded piece of paper which had been slipped through the letterbox. That it was from Saul Meakin he had no doubt. How the little man knew where he lived was something he would pursue at a later date. While the meaning of the note completely eluded him, it was obvious that Meakin had some information that he needed to impart as a matter of urgency.

On his way to work, Harry checked the yard at the rear of the Flag and Unicorn, where he and Meakin had first met. It was empty, and Harry continued towards Long Street. He had hardly had time to take off his coat when Eric Broughton poked his head round the office door and announced that Mr Simmonds was asking to see either Mr Mardlin or himself.

That James Simmonds was rattled was apparent. Seated in the detective inspector's office, he explained that he had wanted to speak to Will, but in his absence was sure that Harry could be of assistance.

Glancing through the office window, Harry momentarily caught sight of a diminutive figure hurrying along the pavement towards the High Street carrying two cardboard boxes. It was fairly obvious that Tuppenny Rice was hoping to spot him, as he usually avoided the vicinity of the police station in his meanderings around town. For a moment he considered sending a uniformed constable after Meakin, then decided against it. Turning back to his visitor, Harry explained that Will was away in Sheffield with the chief constable and would not be coming in until late afternoon.

'I've been shot at, down in the woods near the Old Watermill.' Harry raised his eyebrows and waited for the solicitor to continue. 'This morning I went out for an early walk. I haven't been sleeping well. I was in Hundred Acre Woods when someone took pot shots at me.'

'What time was this?'

'About six-thirty.'

Harry paused thoughtfully, his mind busy. 'Strictly speaking, the woods are subject to military restrictions and off-limits to civilians. You shouldn't have been there at all. You may have been fired at by an over-enthusiastic sentry.'

'I don't think so.' Simmonds drew a deep breath. 'I've been under fire before. A sentry uses a Lee Enfield 303 rifle. This was someone with a hand gun, and he was following me.'

For the next twenty minutes the inspector questioned Simmonds closely about his movements that morning before and after the incident. An experienced court room advocate, Simmonds answered the detective's queries astutely and concisely, sticking to his story that he was merely out for a morning stroll in the woods.

'I'll speak to Major Norton at the Old Mill and see if he can shed any light on what might have happened,' said Harry, as he awkwardly shook James's left hand and bade him goodbye on the police station steps.

Shortly after Simmonds left, Harry slipped on his jacket and took a turn around the town to find Meakin. It was a fine sunny morning. That the little man was nowhere to be found, despite the urgency of his note, was beginning to bother him.

The pile of cigarette stubs in his ashtray grew higher as Harry read and re-read the note, trying to work out its meaning. He was about to give up when a thought occurred to him. Something that the little man said when they first met in the pub yard. When Harry asked him if he knew anything about the murder of Charlotte Groves, Meakin had merely started humming a tune: 'if you want to know the time ask a policeman'. The significance of this had not registered with him at the time, but now he suddenly realised what it was that the vagrant was telling him. Saul Meakin was in Devonshire Gardens when Charlotte Groves was murdered, and he saw the policeman – Tom Weldon – there. Which meant that he had also seen the killer.

The second part of the message still eluded him: ' the teddy bears had a picnic' When Will came in he would ask if it meant anything to him.

Ringing the bell on his desk, Harry summoned Eric Broughton from his little cubby hole down the corridor and, feeling in his pocket for some money, told him to go down the road to the tobacconist's for more cigarettes.

With a cheerful 'Yes, sir,' the lad disappeared into the passage, humming a tune to himself. Harry's bellow halted the startled youth in his tracks, and he reappeared in the doorway looking distinctly nervous.

'What's that song you're singing?'

The office boy had spotted the phrase on the piece of paper on the inspector's desk as he fished in his pockets for the cigarette money. 'It . . . it's a music hall song, sir,' he stammered.

'Tell me the words,' said Harry softly.

When Eric Broughton, having done as he was bidden, left to complete his errand, Harry sat back in his chair, his mind reeling. 'If you go down in the woods today, you're sure of a big surprise. If you go down in the woods today, you'd better go in disguise . . .' Saul Meakin had been in the woods this morning, and had seen for the second time the person who killed Charlotte Groves. Being the inquisitive little weasel he was, this time he had followed him and now knew his identity.

Harry pursed his lips and took off his steel-rimmed reading glasses, dropping them into a drawer. Heaving a deep sigh of frustration he sat back in the chair and putting his head back, closed his eyes. He remained like that for several minutes, turning over in his mind all of the possibilities.

The one thing that was crystal clear to him was that Weasel Meakin was in mortal danger. If the murderer realised that he had been followed, Meakin's life was not worth a shilling.

Having scoured the streets all afternoon, Harry returned to his office to phone the local Salvation Army citadel. It had been his last remaining chance, and it failed.

Suddenly, as if on springs, his eyes flew open, and he sat forward in his chair, a look of deep satisfaction on his face. The ends of his heavy walrus moustache lifted as an enigmatic smile played across his lips.

Glancing out of the window, he saw that the afternoon light was fading. He had two choices: leave it until early tomorrow morning, or go now and risk the fact that it would be almost dark when he got there. Making a decision, he went to the door and peered through into the detective office. To his annoyance it was empty, which meant that he would have to go alone.

The only person in the charge office was the duty sergeant, Dugard Findlay, and his cell man, an elderly constable named Challis Underwood. North spoke briefly to Findlay, who took a single brass key from the desk drawer and followed the detective inspector into the small room at the end of the cell block passage. Let into the back wall was the six foot high door of the station strong room.

'What's cracking off, Harry?' Findlay asked, inserting the key into one of its two Chubb locks.

Harry inserted the key that he took from his waistcoat pocket into the second lock, and the sergeant pushed down the polished brass handle with a dull clang and swung the heavy steel door open. 'Just a quick job,' Harry replied vaguely as they walked into the musty atmosphere.

'Who's authorising it?'

'I am.' Harry's voice was muffled, as in the gloom he pulled down a box from one of the shelves bolted to the wall.

'You can't do that.' Findlay's voice was concerned. 'You can authorise ranks below you to draw a firearm, but you can't authorise yourself to. It's got to be the detective superintendent or the chief constable.'

Ignoring him, Harry pulled the lid from the box and checked the .38 Smith and Wesson revolver lying in oiled paper along with ten rounds of ammunition. Load five rounds, leave the chamber under the hammer empty for safety and put the other five in your pocket. Harry shook his head irritably: he didn't want a pocket full of loose ammunition rattling around.

'Harry, you daft sod, inspector or not, are you listening to me?' Findlay was nervous. Wherever Harry was going that he needed a gun, the issuing of it would be the charge sergeant's responsibility.

North replaced the weapon and pulled down another box. Giving a satisfied grunt, he pulled out a brand new American Colt M1911 semi-automatic pistol. It would fit in his overcoat pocket much better than a bulky revolver. He and Will, along with Webster Pemberton, had spent a morning down at the firing range at Sevastopol Barracks the previous month trying out new weapons. The civil servants in London were paranoid about the possibility of a German invasion, and had made an allowance to police forces for the purchase of firearms. Sydney Hall-Johnson had invested thirty pounds in half a dozen army rifles, and with the money that was left over had bought three of these brand new automatics.

'Don't worry, Doog.' Straightening up, Harry gave the sergeant a reassuring smile. 'Superintendent Mardlin authorised it. Give me your pen.' With his back to Findlay, he signed the issues book, writing his own name in the space for the name of the authorising officer. If this went wrong there was no point in compromising Will. Slipping a clip of ammunition into the butt of the pistol and another into his pocket, Harry closed the ledger and turned to face the sergeant. 'Come on, you miserable old bugger , let's get moving before your tea gets cold.' A distinctly unhappy Dugard Findlay found himself being led back into the charge office.

With the onset of evening the warmth of the late May day had been replaced by a cold dampness that was beginning to envelop Dakin Street. It was littered with debris, remnants of household possessions and furniture that had been strewn around by people carelessly moving away from an area that was in the process of being demolished. Picking his way down the middle of the road, Harry felt his spirits drop. As a young man he had worked the beat around here, and had known the shopkeepers and occupants of the little terraced houses that made up the narrow dingy streets. Alois Frenberger's barber shop on the corner of Courtyard C, two doors away from the shell of the Nautical William, was now derelict, the front door hanging off its broken hinges. At one time there was a pub on every corner, and an off-licence between them where the old women had quart bottles filled up with cheap cooking sherry to see them through the morning. It used to be, he reflected, a good place for a keen young policeman to work. Downe Street was where most of the criminal elements in Kelsford based their activities, with bent pawnbrokers, dingy beer houses and brothels among the cheap lodging houses.

Now it was derelict. A reforming corporation was busily pulling down the slums as fast as money became available, although for the time being the war had put a stop to wholesale demolition and rehousing. Empty properties were providing a safe haven for life's flotsam. Vagrants who were moving from town to town, allowed to spend only the statutory three consecutive nights at the workhouse, passed the intervening time drifting about the abandoned buildings. Alcoholics, soaked with cheap gin and rum, slept their days away on dirty rag mattresses before going out at night to ambush an unwary passer-by and steal a few pence for a drink. Even the occasional prostitute still walked her client back to the deserted front room of a tumble-down property, for a few minutes of fumbling and groping.

Most of the house numbers in Dakin Street were gone, wrenched off by itinerant rag and bone men for the meagre value of the metal. Counting along from the main road, Harry paused outside what he calculated to be number fifty-four. It was, he knew, a long shot. This was the house where thirty years earlier Meakin had lived with Queenie Bartholemew. The front door was boarded over with rough planks to prevent unauthorised entry, as were the ground-floor windows. Prising one of the boards back a few inches, he peered into the gloomy interior of what had been a front parlour. There was little to see: as he expected the room was devoid of any furniture. What remained of the floor, some of which had been ripped up to provide firewood, was littered with broken glass from discarded bottles and smashed windows.

Replacing the board, the detective took a careful look round. He had absolutely no doubt that his arrival in the apparently deserted street had not gone unnoticed. Turning to face the broken windows on the opposite side of the road, he fished in the pocket of his jacket and pulled out his whistle. Allowing it to swing ostentatiously on its silver chain for the benefit of any unseen watcher, Harry glared stonily up and down the street, then pushed it into his top pocket and hooked the chain over his tie. It was a signal to anyone who might have designs upon him that he was a policeman, and that to follow him would be ill advised.

The entry that separated numbers fifty-two and fifty-four was a foot high in builders' rubble and split joists, and Harry's suit trousers were covered in brick dust by the time he reached the gate at the end. This was jammed half open, allowing him just enough room to squeeze through into the filthy back yard. Immediately on his right was a grimy window, which appeared to be the only piece of glass in the house that was still intact. The kitchen door was swinging on a single rusty hinge.

Stepping through the doorway, Harry moved from the kitchen into the back parlour and stood perfectly still, listening. The rank odour of urine and faeces mixed with the stink of unwashed humanity assailed his nostrils. The house was being used by someone. Was the occupant the person for whom he was searching, and, more importantly, was he there?

Harry slipped the automatic from his pocket, eased off the safety catch with his thumb and reached down with his left hand to rack a cartridge into the breech. With the gun cocked he held his breath, listening carefully. There was not a sound other than his own heart beating.

Stealthily, he made his way up the staircase that led through a doorway directly off the back room, moving guardedly on the uncarpeted treads. At the top the last few stairs had been removed, as had about eight feet of floorboards from the landing that led towards the front of the house. Turning right from the stair head, Harry worked his way along the narrow passageway towards the back bedroom, which he judged would be directly over the kitchen. In the failing light he had to tread carefully. There was no sound of anyone attempting to climb out of the back window onto the sloping tiled roof. The smell was much stronger. At the far end of the landing the door to the back bedroom was closed tight. Covering the last ten feet at a run, Harry kicked the door back on its hinges with a resounding crash, charged into the room and spun round, his back to the wall, pistol held out double-handed in front of him.

On the far side was a bed made up of old rugs and newspapers. That the room was in use was apparent from the rubbish and scraps of food lying around. Other than that, it was empty. Harry allowed his adrenalin to dissipate a little before making a closer examination of his squalid surroundings. Ripping down the newspaper from the broken window, which was intended, he presumed, to keep out the weather in some small way, he reviewed the situation.

It was getting dark now, and he needed to leave as soon as possible. That he was breaking the rules which applied to himself as well as to any uniformed beat constable, Harry was well aware. Entry into the demolition area was, by instruction of the head constable, to be undertaken only in pairs. Many of the properties were structurally dangerous, and if an officer was injured or attacked while on his own he might not be found for weeks – if at all. Harry was conscious that no one knew where he was. With night coming on he was vulnerable.

Making his way back down the staircase, a thought occurred to him. If the man he was looking for had heard him in the entry, there was still one place where he could be hiding. Harry cast around in the dim light of the kitchen, and quickly spotted what he was looking for. Incongruously a dark green chenille curtain was still covering the entrance to the cellar. Pulling the door wide open, he stood at the top of the worn stone steps and peered down into the blackness. From the left-hand pocket of his overcoat he withdrew a small flashlight.

The dank steps were slippery and dangerous. Fixed to the wall by nails knocked into the brickwork was an old clothes line in place of a hand rail. At the bottom Harry switched off the torch and allowed his eyes to adjust to the dim light. The cellar ran to the front of the house. A patch of light at the far end was coming from a grating in the pavement, through which bags of slack once had been tipped from the coalman's wagon. Although there was no longer any coal in the cellar the atmosphere was chokingly oppressive, and the stink of unwashed humanity was stronger than ever. His movements stirred up the dust on the floor, making it difficult to breath in the stale atmosphere.

Switching the torch back on, Harry started to move forward. The butt of the automatic in his right hand was slippery with sweat. Old boxes were stacked from the floor up to the low ceiling. Along the left-hand wall he saw that the last occupant of the house had put up some shelves, on which flat fish boxes containing kindling and paper in readiness to light the kitchen range were still neatly stacked.

A sudden movement startled Harry as a mouse that had taken refuge in one of the boxes at the sound of his approach leapt across his sleeve. The jolt caused him to drop the torch onto the concrete floor, plunging the cellar into darkness. He stood still, heart pounding and silently cursing. Ten feet away the sound of a slight movement near the back cellar wall caught his attention. Tightening his grip on the gun, he peered intently into the far corner. Save for the tiny patch of light from the grating, the cellar was completely dark. Harry moved forward a pace, his eyes beginning once more to adjust to the gloom, and he made out the figure of a man, legs outstretched, his back propped comfortably against the wall, sitting on the floor and watching him.

It was Tuppenny Rice. He had removed his balaclava, and Harry saw that, lips drawn back over his toothless gums, he was grinning widely at the policeman's apparent fright. Recovering his composure, Harry relaxed a little. 'You've given me quite a time finding you,' he said softly. 'You must have been frightened shitless when you heard me searching the house.'

The seated figure made no reply. The only acknowledgement that he was listening was a slight movement of his left hand, which was resting on the floor by his side.

Once more in control of the situation, his pounding heart beginning to slow down, Harry gathered his thoughts. He needed to work quickly to convince the little man that it was all right to leave his hiding place.

'Don't worry: you're safe now. You can leave here with me before it gets completely dark. Once we're out of here I'll get you a square meal and a comfy night's sleep.'

Moving close enough to get a proper view of the man's face, Harry could see why he had not replied. There was a large empty hole where his left eye should have been. The side of what had once been his face was a mass of blood, having been sliced open by the sharp instrument that had cut his throat and almost decapitated him. In the dim light the detective could see that the once whitewashed wall against which the corpse was propped had been spattered with blood and brains when his attacker had repeatedly slashed at him.

As Harry bent forward to check if the body was still warm, the rat that had been busily gnawing the fingers of the vagrant's left hand turned baleful amber eyes up at him, before silently disappearing into the darkness. Later, he could only attribute it to a sixth sense. Almost too late he became aware that he and the corpse were not alone. Spinning round, he caught a flash of steel as the trench knife arced down towards him.

The explosion of the Colt .45, as with a reflex action Harry pulled the trigger, was deafening. The muzzle flash blinded both him and his attacker, and the knife's blade struck the brickwork of the cellar wall with a dull metallic sound. Stumbling backwards, Harry's feet slipped in the congealing blood and became entangled with the corpse's legs. He lost his balance and fell backwards. As he hit the ground he rolled to one side and fired again, but knew that he had missed. The shadowy figure of his assailant was already halfway up the stone steps.

From his prone position on the floor Harry fired two more shots towards the stairs, but he knew that it was too late. The man had gone.

'His name is – or rather was – Saul Meakin.' Harry was still badly shaken by his recent experience, and the fact that his key witness was now lying on a mortuary slab awaiting Arthur Mallard's ministrations did not help.

'What the hell possessed you to go there alone?' Will's anger was more than mixed with a feeling of relief that Harry was all right. 'For Christ's sake, you know better than to go there on . . .'

'On my own?' Harry's face showed deep regret. 'I needed to find him. He was my informant and he trusted me. Because I was too stupid to understand what he was telling me he's dead now.'

Will made a conciliatory gesture and sat down wearily behind his desk. He was appalled at the risk that Harry had taken. Slumped in the office chair, his suit torn and dirty, his colleague looked worn out, and every bit his fifty-odd years.

'All right, but it was a near miss.' Clarrie Greasley lit a cigarette and passed it to him. Bert Conway held out a half-full tumbler of whisky. Harry accepted both gratefully.

'What's the story,' Will asked quietly.

As he recovered his composure, Harry explained how at New Year he had worked out who Meakin was, and the vagrant's connection with the present events. 'I didn't put it together soon enough. He saw Lottie Groves's killer, but didn't know who he was. Then later he saw James Simmonds and whoever took a shot at him in the woods. One of them he recognised as Groves's killer. He followed him and found out who he was. For my money it's Simmonds.'

The other three waited expectantly. 'Go on,' said Will.

'Just after Simmonds arrived at my office this morning I spotted Weasel scuttling off down the road, looking over his shoulder. I think he was trying to catch my eye and saw Simmonds come into the nick. I also think that Simmonds saw him in Devonshire Gardens on the day of the murder, but dismissed him as being of no account. He must have seen him again in the woods, then later outside here, and the alarm bells started to ring. Weasel probably hung around hoping to get to speak to me after Simmonds left – which was a big mistake. Simmonds picked him up somewhere and followed him, until eventually he led him away from the town centre and up to Dakin Street. I got there a few minutes too late to save Meakin, but before Simmonds had a chance to leave the cellar. Once I started to search the house he had to stay where he was, and got a chance to have a go at me as well.' Emptying his glass in one swallow, he held it out for a refill.

Chapter Twenty-Eight

Climbing down from the railway carriage, James Simmonds picked up his overnight bag and began to walk slowly along the platform, deep in thought. The trip to London had been successful. Winding up his interests in the Tivoli Palace was long overdue. The theatre had provided a perfect conduit through which to redistribute the money that he and his associates had systematically siphoned off from the war hospital project during the last fourteen months, but the fact that Mardlin had found a lead back to the music hall through Hardesty's carelessness meant that the venture was now decidedly unsafe. On his instructions Absolom was in the process of selling the music hall to a consortium of businessmen who owned several other theatres in the East End. The policeman would receive a handsome pay-off, and Sylvester Hardesty was safely hidden away somewhere with sufficient cash each week to enable him to drink himself to death. After today Simmonds's only association with Absolom would be when he made the monthly journey to collect his supply of morphine.

Next he would unobtrusively wind up the matter of the war hospital. It had been Carstairs's idea originally. He overestimated the ordering of supplies and materials, and showed features in his plans that were never incorporated into the building. It was necessary from the outset for the principal carter, Ivor Rees, to be involved, along with himself as the project treasurer. After the hospital began to receive patients, Kathleen Doyle – already his mistress – played an integral part in falsifying the records of the number of staff employed on the site. Originally the plan was to run the swindle until the end of the war, then dispose of the premises through a bogus company set up through Byron Carstairs, which would ensure that the buildings were pulled down for development, thus permanently removing any trace of their activities and allowing them to realise a handsome profit. With Carstairs dead and the police conducting an investigation, that was no longer possible.

To close things down now, Simmonds was aware, would require some highly creative accountancy – and a scapegoat – which was where the Belgian, Palmaerts, came in. The morality of what he was doing did not bother him. War changed so many things. Before losing his hand, Simmonds had been an officer and a gentleman, with a promising military future ahead of him and a comfortable civilian occupation to return to afterwards. Now he had one good hand, a life of pain and discomfort, and a small box with a medal inside. No, Simmonds had no compunctions about reconsidering his priorities. His sole regret was the death of Kath Doyle. She had been a good friend and an enthusiastic partner in bed. Unfortunately, like Rees, she knew too much.

As he passed the station news-stand, Simmonds spotted the figure of a smartly dressed, dark-haired woman in a dove grey travelling suit on the next platform, about to board a waiting train. Watching his cousin climbing up into the carriage, he wondered how long she and Mardlin expected to keep their affair secret. He wondered if her priggish brother was still unaware: other people, he reflected, were not quite so stupid. As Irene disappeared through the carriage door Simmonds paused, deep in thought. She was still a beautiful woman, though. He hefted the overnight bag in his hand, and he made his way towards the ticket barrier.

Summer sunshine made a dappled pattern across the papers scattered over Will Mardlin's desk, and glinted on the polished wire in-tray. He pushed the offending item to one side irritably. Glaring towards the source of the timorous knock that had attracted his attention, he saw the figure of Eric Broughton standing patiently in the doorway. 'Gentleman at the front desk to see you sir. Mr Simmonds – the solicitor,' he added nervously.

Mr Mardlin, Eric was well aware, was in an extremely bad mood, and had been for some days. Earlier this morning, when the boy could not find some files that the superintendent wanted urgently, he had been sent down into the station basement with instructions that unless he found them, not to bother to come back. The effects of his ill-humour, like the ripples on a pond, seemed to be affecting those next door in the detective office. Even Mr North was becoming tetchy and irritable. Yesterday Eric had overheard Sergeant Conway commenting to Clarrie Greasley that 'Foxy's walking about with a face like a dropped pie'.

'You'd better bring him up then,' the superintendent growled. The lad turned and scuttled off.

In Will's present mood, a visit from James Simmonds was the last thing he wanted. Despite their suspicions concerning both his involvement in the War Hospital fraud and the strong likelihood that he was the killer they were looking for, there was still no evidence to arrest him. They had nothing that would convince a judge and jury. However, Will had a gut instinct that things were rapidly coming to a head.

The real cause of his bad humour, as those working with him were well aware, lay in the deterioration of his relationship with Irene Deladier. Recently she had been making more visits to London than before, which meant he was seeing less of her. On average she was now spending two or three days a week at her charitable committees, and he was beginning to wonder if she was seeing someone else. Deep down he knew that the newly widowed Irene had been drawn to him for all manner of reasons, none of them permanent. They needed to talk, he decided.

The figure of James Simmonds looming in the doorway brought him back to the present. 'James, please take a seat.' Automatically holding his hand out, Will immediately cursed his ineptitude. The solicitor, however, by now used to this error on the part of others, deftly reversed his left hand and offered it, palm outwards. Not for the first time Will was surprised by how easy it was to shake hands in this manner.

'What can I do for you?' Will forced a smile.

'Couple of things, actually. Firstly, this business at the war hospital. I think I may have found something out.'

Will raised an eyebrow, his interest aroused, and waited for the other man to continue. This could be exactly what he had been waiting for.

Simmonds glanced over his shoulder to check that they were alone. 'I think I may have come across something useful. As treasurer of the project management committee, I recently asked for all of the original receipts and pay sheets and have been going through them closely. The figures for staff payments – nurses, domestics and suchlike – were all signed and approved by Kathy Doyle as hospital matron and Matthias Palmaerts as the accounts clerk. If anyone in the hospital knew exactly how many staff were employed it would have been Kath. I've checked for myself, and without a shadow of doubt there are five nurses being paid who don't exist. As for domestics, they're shown as casual labour, so God knows how many of them are fiction.'

Will steepled his fingers under his chin and remained thoughtful for a while. 'So what you're saying is that Kathy Doyle and Palmaerts were working a fiddle by manufacturing false staffing levels?'

'Precisely. It would have been so easy. Kath validated the worksheets and Palmaerts authorised the payments.'

'And this would probably tie in with a much wider swindle involving the falsification of building work and materials delivered to the site, which would have to involve the architect and Ivor Rees,' Will suggested slowly.

'I think so.' Simmonds nodded in agreement.

'Apart from the pay sheets and receipts, do you have anything else to support your theory?'

Simmonds held his hands up. 'Not yet. I thought if we worked towards the same goal we might just come up with something.'

Will studied the desktop before replying. 'I think you might be onto something. Logically if your theory's correct, and Charlotte Groves discovered what was happening, she was blackmailing Doyle, which would provide a perfect motive for killing her.'

In his best courtroom manner Simmonds gave a nod of approbation. 'You're ahead of me ,Will, but yes, it would be entirely logical.'

'You said there were two things you wanted to talk about.'

'Yes . . .' Simmonds hesitated. 'I think that something's going on at the Old Watermill.'

Will kept his face impassive. 'Go on.'

'It's fairly obvious to everyone that some sort of clandestine research is being conducted.' Simmonds paused, but the detective did not offer a reply. 'I think that whatever's going on has serious implications. They are, I'm certain, working on something to do with gas.'

Will remained quite still. 'Why do you think that?' he asked very quietly.

'I have to tell you that I've been secretly keeping watch on the place for some months now. A regular convoy of trucks moves back and forth between the railway station and the old mill during the week. On occasions I've seen, through gaps in the canvas sides of the lorries, things such as carboys of chemicals and steel canisters being moved in and out. Anyone who doesn't think we're working on perfecting better gas techniques than the Germans is very naïve.'

'If you're correct, James, then I must sincerely advise caution in this matter.' Will chose his words carefully. This time it was his turn to glance towards the closed door, ensuring that they were not overheard. 'I'm not privy to what the military are doing, but as you say it would be sensible to acknowledge that research is necessary, whether it is being conducted here or elsewhere.'

Simmonds nodded animatedly. 'Yes, I thoroughly understand that, but the point is I think there's a security leak. Clearly, if the old mill's being used for research work then there has to be someone in charge of the security aspect, most likely from Military Intelligence. It's not going to be that idiot cousin of mine, he's not bright enough: he's merely worked himself a comfy billet back here in Blighty. No, the security officer will be Gresham.'

He hesitated, waiting for a response. Chin still resting on his fingers, Will replied with an air of finality. 'You're on dangerous ground. I think you should cease these observations that you appear to be making, and leave well alone.'

'You don't understand, Will. I think there's a spy at work. If you have any contact with Colonel Gresham he needs to be told. Until I have more evidence it would be wrong for me to speculate further, or to name names, but I can tell you that I think information is being passed out of the mill to a third party.'

Despite Will's best efforts, his visitor refused to enlarge on his statement, insisting that he needed to check several things before putting him fully in the picture. Eventually Will gave up and the solicitor left, promising that he would contact him later.

Following Eric Broughton down the stairs to the main enquiry office and the way out into Long Street, James Simmonds felt a mixture of elation and uncertainty: elated that putting into place the first stage of his plan to disentangle himself from the war hospital fraud had been so easy, and unsure concerning his suspicions over the Old Watermill project.

What if he was wrong? Will's reaction to what he had said was inconclusive. Simmonds decided he would have to redouble his efforts.

A recent report in the *Daily Telegraph* concerning a Scottish fishing boat that had been sunk off the east coast interested him greatly. The skipper and crew of the vessel, the *Viking Tun,* had apparently been interviewed by police in Whitby over suspected espionage activities. Not long after their release from custody they had set sail, ostensibly to return to their home port in Scotland, and the boat had mysteriously disappeared. It was being broadly hinted that the boat had either been sunk by an enemy submarine or by one of the British naval ships patrolling the inshore waters around Rosyth.

Simmonds decided that, with the coming weekend being a bank holiday he would pay a visit to the fishing port and make a few enquiries.

In his office Will sat lost in thought. His instincts were right. Simmonds was starting to panic. Will was now certain that he was responsible for killing Charlotte Groves. Charlotte Groves had led them to the Tivoli Palace, so logically there must be a connection between Simmonds and the Tivoli Palace. It would have been a simple matter for the solicitor to plant the trench knife that had led them on a false trail to Frank Kempin. Simmonds's present efforts to throw suspicion on Matthias Palmaerts as Kathleen Doyle's partner in crime were at best clumsy. If they could find what it was that Groves had hidden he was certain they would close the circle.

Simmonds's assertions concerning a security leak at the Old Watermill were a different matter. How, Will wondered, had he stumbled on that? The only conclusion that he could draw was that someone, somewhere had slipped up, and the solicitor had seen something that only he knew about. Reaching for the telephone, he asked the switchboard operator to connect him with Colonel Gresham's extension in London.

'All set for tomorrow, love?' Bernard Ashe asked in a low voice, checking quickly to ensure that they were not being overheard. He need not have worried: the taproom of the Pack Horse, crowded with early evening drinkers, was too noisy for his question to have been picked up by anyone else.

'Shh . . . you'll get me the sack.' Connie glanced around nervously. 'I've told my mum that I'm going to Whitby for the weekend with Emmie Dykes. See you in the morning at the station.'

Ashe watched with a feeling of deep excitement as Connie moved away to serve a florid commercial traveller further along the bar. He and Connie had been going out with each other for over a year now and had been sleeping together for the last six months. This weekend would be the first time they had gone away together.

The coming Whitsuntide weekend presented an ideal opportunity for them. Whitby was the local seaside resort for Kelsford, being just under two hours away on the train. As a child Bernard had spent almost every summer holiday there and knew the place well. Connie, who came from Market Harborough, a small town about sixty miles away, had never been to the resort, having spent her early holidays at Skegness. As Connie's parents did not live in Kelsford it was easy for the two of them to arrange the weekend. Her mother and father thought she was going away with a girlfriend, while her landlady was under the impression that she was going home. The weather was forecast to be warm and sunny, and Ashe knew they would enjoy the journey up to York, where they would change trains for Pickering and Whitby. He had booked a double room at the Black Horse in Church Street under the name Mr and Mrs Ashton.

Still serving the commercial traveller, Connie turned to the shelf behind her and reached up for a packet of Black Cat cigarettes. The movement stretched her dress tight across her back, revealing a small patch of sweat beneath her armpit. Bernard felt a sudden stirring as he thought about her naked. Catching his eye, Connie gave him an enquiring smile and continued to serve the florid man. Bernard picked up the three pints of mild and made his way across the crowded room to the corner table where Clarrie Greasley and Bert Conway were waiting.

'Took you long enough,' grunted Conway.

Ashe smiled non-committally. 'Busy at the bar.'

Greasley shot him a glance, then in a low voice continued his conversation. 'Foxy's right. We need to be finding whatever that pawn ticket related to. The sooner Mardlin gets back on track the sooner we can nail this bastard.'

Bert Conway picked up his pint and, holding it up to the light, scrutinised its contents. Among the regulars it was known as the Pack Horse salute. 'Josh has been putting fucking slops in this again,' he muttered dourly. Joshua Littleton, the long-suffering landlord of the Pack Horse Hotel, was glaring across the room in the direction of their table. Conway glared back at him.

'Shall I take it back?' asked Ashe resignedly. The weekend with Connie was becoming more attractive by the minute.

'No, leave it: this is my last anyway.' There was, Ashe knew, nothing wrong with the beer. 'He's right actually: it's too soon.' Conway returned to the subject that he and Greasley had been discussing. 'I just wish that Mardlin would get himself sorted out with the Countess of Kingsbury Lane, and we could all get back to what we're supposed to be doing.'

Ashe sighed inwardly. The fact that Mardlin's affair with Mme Deladier was common knowledge in the detective office would have appalled the superintendent had he known. Even Inspector North, he suspected, didn't realise that the secret was out. It was, the young man reflected, virtually impossible to keep anything confidential in a police station.

'I think we should go back to that boiler room and turn over every brick in there. If Doyle didn't top herself – which we know she didn't – then why was she there? She was looking for something. The same thing we're looking for.' Conway took a sip at his beer and pushed a packet of Gold Flake across to the other sergeant. 'Bernard, tomorrow first thing you and I will go down there and make a proper search.'

This was the moment he had been dreading. 'I'm sorry, Bert, but I'm not here tomorrow. I've got some leave over the weekend.'

Bert Conway put his glass down, and gave what Ashe could only describe as a stunned look.

'What do you mean you've got some leave? We're in the middle of a murder enquiry and you're going off on bloody leave?'

'Mr North authorised it.' The words came out in a rush. Ashe had known all day that Conway would be awkward. 'It's Whit bank holiday, and I've arranged to go up to Whitby for a couple of days. I'll be back for Tuesday evening.'

'And who might you be going to Whitby with?' Clarrie Greasley's voice carried a note of interest.

'I've arranged to see some of the lads from the cricket team there,' Ashe replied lamely.

Greasley gave a raucous laugh and directed his gaze to the bar, where Connie, oblivious to their conversation, was pulling pints. 'She'll have your middle wicket out, bales and all,' he said loudly.

'I'm going with a couple of mates,' retorted Ashe, the colour rising in his cheeks as he wished that Greasley would keep his voice down.

'You're off shagging,' rumbled Bert Conway, entering into the fun.

'You'd do better to go B and B.' Greasley guffawed loudly at his joke.

Bert Conway and Bernard Ashe both glared at him.

Chapter Twenty-Nine

Walking hand in hand over the swing-bridge across the river Esk, Bernard and Connie paused to lean on the parapet's iron railing and gaze up the estuary, taking in the huge variety of boats either moored up against the harbour walls or plying back and forth along the river. Half a mile away the afternoon sunshine glinted on the shiny steel mirror of water where the river flowed into the ocean near the battery. Earlier in the day they had climbed the steps away to their left known as the Khyber Pass, up to the headland over West Cliff Sands, and sat on the top along with all the other holidaymakers, enjoying the warm weather and watching the families on the beach below them. Connie could not get over the old-fashioned mobile bathing huts, a relic of bygone years that still dotted the sands, along with the carefully clad prospective bathers who emerged from time to time, picking their way carefully down to the gently lapping water.

'What do you want to do, love? Go down along the other side or back up to the room?'

'Why would I want to go back to the room on such a lovely afternoon as this?' she asked archly.

'Because there's a nice chilled bottle of wine in the overnight jug, and some cold chicken sandwiches to see us through till dinner this evening. And I thought you might want to take your stays off and have a little rest.'

Grinning back, she took Bernard's hand and they walked on over the bridge towards Church Street.

As the couple were passing a tiny alley that bore the name Benson's Yard, Bernard spotted a man a few yards in front of them, fitting a heavy key into the door of a tiny fisherman's cottage almost opposite the Black Horse, where they were staying. About to follow Connie through the pub's door, Bernard paused in puzzled surprise. The man, who had not noticed him, disappeared into the front room of the cottage, closing the door behind him.

'Are you all right, love?' asked Connie.

'Yes, perfectly,' he murmured absently. Ushering the girl through into the narrow passageway, he followed her upstairs, deep in thought. What the hell was *he* doing here, he wondered.

'Come away from that window and get back into bed.'

Connie Armitage was getting annoyed. At twenty-three she was a few years younger than Bernard, and this weekend was the greatest adventure of her life. They had the remainder of today and all Monday before she would have to catch the train home and go back to work at the Pack Horse. In the meantime she intended to enjoy every minute at the seaside. Sunshine, sea and sand. Good food, and sex at least three times a day with a man who cared for her. The question was, she reflected, how much did she care for him? Quite a lot, she decided. Bernard was clever and kind, and he had a good job. He was certainly a good lover, and did not seem to mind that he was not her first. Connie was sure that he was not far off asking her to marry him, and when he did she was going to say yes. Pushing the covers aside she got out of bed and joined him at the half-open window.

'Con, for heaven's sake, the first person who looks up from the street will see you!'

'If they know quality they'll appreciate it,' she replied unperturbed. 'What are we looking for anyway?'

Bernard pulled her to one side behind the curtain and kissed her hard on the mouth. Seeing her naked, gazing down on passers-by only feet from them, suddenly excited him – and within seconds they were making love again.

'You still never told me what you were looking for this afternoon.'

Dinner was over, and after an evening stroll the couple were back in their room again. Bernard pulled aside the curtains. It was dark outside and the street below was quiet. 'There's a man in that cottage over there.' He nodded into the darkness. 'I know him, and he shouldn't be here.' A gas mantle was turned up in the bedroom opposite and the dim outline of a figure appeared, moving around the room. He was putting on a jacket, pulling a cap down over his eyes.

'Listen, I'm going out for a few minutes,' Bernard said quickly, grabbing his own jacket from the back of the dressing table chair. 'I won't be long.' Before Connie had time to protest he was gone.

The man was quite tall, over middle height, and wearing a heavy pea jacket despite the warmth of the evening. Following at a discreet distance, Bernard was busy trying to work out what he should do next. He badly needed to give Mardlin his new-found knowledge, but that would have to wait. For the moment he needed to know where the man was going and why.

He suddenly realised his quarry was no longer in sight. Turning sharply into a tiny market square, he saw the man a few yards ahead of him, looking in the window of a bookshop. Breaking his stride slightly, Bernard continued past the jacketed figure and turned left at the far side of the square. Immediately round the corner he dropped into the shadows of a deep entry between two cottages. Cursing his carelessness, Bernard wondered if the man was really looking at the display in the shop window or checking the reflection in the glass to see if he was being followed.

A shadow passed the mouth of the entry, and the policeman slipped back out into the street.

Fifteen minutes later, having been led down into the town centre, where amongst the late evening holidaymakers the pursuit was much easier, Bernard found himself back in Church Street. He had, he decided, wasted his time. The man was simply taking a stroll before going to bed. He was surprised, therefore, when instead of going back into his cottage, the man continued up the street and turned left, towards Tate Hill Pier, which at this time of night was deserted.

Bernard waited a full minute before going down onto the flagstoned jetty. It was the furthest of the landing places from the town, and a cool breeze was coming in from the sea. Although it was dark he could see in the moonlight the silhouettes of boxes and barrels piled up along the quay, in readiness for the next morning's catch.

Stealthily he picked his way past the stacks of boxes until he reached the end. Gentle waves lapped against the stonework below, mingling with the sounds of rigging creaking and a ship's bell tinkling on the other side of the harbour as the fishing fleet swayed back and forth at its moorings. Bernard cursed under his breath. The pier was deserted: he was alone with nothing in front of him but the North Sea. Wherever the man in the pea jacket was, he had not come down onto the jetty.

The sound of a light footfall caused Bernard to turn abruptly, but he was too late to avoid the crushing blow from the timber shaft that knocked him senseless and pitched him over the stone wall into the grey waters below. In one swift movement the man hurled the boat hook far out into the estuary. Without a backward glance he turned and strode quickly towards the gas-lit street at the other end of the quayside. Pausing to make sure that there was no one about, he strolled off towards Church Street.

From behind one of the herring barrels another figure emerged, and stared thoughtfully at the place where moments before the young detective had been standing. Pulling up the collar of his jacket, he slipped away silently into the shadows.

Harry North placed the telegram on his desk and picked up the telephone handset.

It was Bank Holiday Monday, and he had been planning to have a day out. The inspector had a hobby that very few of the people with whom he worked knew about. He was a keen motorcyclist, and his most recent acquisition, a brand new 1915 six horsepower Rudge complete with sidecar, for which he had paid the princely sum of £78, was standing in the front garden at Tennyson Street, ready to take him and Laura to the Peak District for the day. It had been his intention to set off after breakfast on the forty mile journey to Castleton, arriving in time for a couple of pints in the tiny pub in the village square, then to climb the steep winding path up to the medieval ruins of the castle and eat the picnic that Laura had prepared for them.

His plans were brought to an abrupt halt by the arrival at the front door of Eric Broughton with the telegram now lying on his desk. As it was holiday time, it occurred to him that he should ask if the office boy was ever given a day off.

'Damnation.' It was not so much an expletive as an expression of something much more profound. He put his reading glasses on and read the telegram once more:

> MON 5th JUNE 1916
> FOR ATTENTION OF OFFICER IN CHARGE
> DETECTIVE DEPARTMENT KELSFORD BOROUGH
> POLICE STOP
> ORIGINATOR SGT 3 WALPOLE WHITBY
> DIVISION STOP
> BODY FOUND 0600 HOURS TODAY HAGGERLYTHE
> WHITBY STOP
> IDENTIFIED AS BERNARD ASHE KELSFORD
> CONSTABULARY STOP
> PLEASE CONTACT THIS OFFICE SOONEST STOP

Harry had already spoken on the telephone to Sergeant Walpole. It appeared that Bernard had been reported missing by a young woman named Constance Armitage the night before, when he had failed to return to the room they were sharing at a local pub. His body was found at low tide on the sands near a fish jetty. Walpole said that the cause of death had been certified by the local police surgeon, who was of the opinion that the young man had been walking on the pier when for some reason he had fallen into the water, striking his head on the stonework and knocking himself out before hitting the water.

Constance Armitage. That would be Connie from the Pack Horse, mused Harry. He would talk to her later. First he needed to inform Will Mardlin and Bernard's parents.

Siegfried Keppler smiled over the lip of his coffee cup at Ludwig Heitmann. 'You're sure that the signal went safely?'

Taking a quick look around to ensure that they were not overheard, Heitmann nodded quickly. 'Ja, bestimmt.'

'Good. Very good indeed.' The coffee house was busy with holidaymakers young and old enjoying the last day of the Whitsuntide bank holiday before catching their trains home. Outside the weather was still warm and sunny, women carrying parasols strolling along Pier Road arm in arm with straw-boatered escorts, most of them discussing the main news of the day – the body of the young man found on the sands near to Tate Hill Pier.

'When did you send it?'

'Yesterday afternoon.'

'And what was Diessbacher's position?'

'We're in huge luck.' The French polisher was bursting with excitement. 'The High Seas Fleet has recently been in battle with the British Grand Fleet at Jutland. Submarines have been stationed all across the North Sea to pick off damaged ships returning to home ports. U39, along with the others, went up into the area north of Scotland. He signalled that he was twelve hours steaming from the Orkneys.'

Keppler grimaced at the phrase. Typical sailor's jargon. How could a vessel powered by a combination of diesel and electric engines conceivably steam anywhere? He was extremely annoyed that U39 had been redeployed, however temporarily. Diessbacher should not have been involved in some stupid naval engagement when the entire Nemesis affair was so close to a conclusion. As it was, he decided, no harm was done, and chance had placed the submarine exactly where it needed to be. Sipping his coffee, he stared out across the river to the ruins of the abbey on the hill opposite, the smile still playing around his lips. 'To Russian Intelligence,' he murmured, tilting the cup in salutation towards his companion.

Both men were smiling broadly, although as far as Keppler was concerned the dapper little man opposite knew only half of the story, and it would always remain so.

The British government, courting the Russian military machine which was holding back the Germans on the Eastern Front, was desperate to discuss tactics with the Russian leaders, as well as such matters as the supply of munitions, which were needed for them to pursue their latest initiative against the German armies in Poland. Since the beginning of the year it had been planned that a British envoy should go to Russia. What Keppler could not believe was that the man chosen was none other than Field Marshal Lord Kitchener. Kitchener, although becoming less popular in government circles by the day, was still the driving force behind the British Army, and to risk sending him on the lengthy and dangerous sea voyage through submarine-infested waters was, in Keppler's opinion, the height of folly – and an opportunity not to be missed. Matters had been made easy by a complete lack of security on the part of the Russians. With their poor use of code ciphers, and with the Tsarist court being a hotbed of gossip and rumour, it had been simple for Berlin to keep a close watch on the unfolding arrangements from the beginning of May.

The previous day Lord Kitchener had caught the overnight train from London to Edinburgh, travelling on to Thurso and by destroyer over the Pentland Firth to Scapa Flow. There he had transferred to the armoured cruiser HMS *Hampshire* for the voyage to Archangel.

Keppler consulted his pocket watch. 'Another five hours, and if all goes to plan *Hampshire* will set sail along with her escorts.'

Heitmann's close-cropped head bobbed up and down in assent. 'What I'm not clear about, mein Herr, is why U39 has been ordered to attack the rearmost destroyer, the one that's holding back out of sight of the main flotilla.'

It was Keppler's turn to make sure that they were not overheard before explaining. 'Quite simple. The *Hampshire* will be escorted by two destroyers. They're heading north towards latitude six twenty north, where there's a submarine pack waiting for them. The sea lanes through which the British ships are passing have been laid with mines. There's no way that Kitchener will ever get to Archangel. When his vessel is sunk it'll be the biggest loss to British prestige of the entire war. The Engländer are aware of the risks, and the third destroyer is following at a discreet distance so that it can rush in and take off any survivors – meaning of course, the field marshal – if *Hampshire* is hit by either a mine or torpedo. Diessbacher's job is to eliminate the rescue ship.'

He watched as Heitmann processed this information, before grinning broadly at him. 'Ausgezeichnet!' he breathed. 'It'll turn the Allied High Command upside down at a stroke.'

The intelligence officer smiled back good-humouredly. It was, of course, a lie. The third destroyer was staying out of sight because neither Kitchener nor Captain Savill, the commander of the *Hampshire*, knew of its existence. Apart from British Intelligence and Nemesis, no one was aware of its presence in the North Sea. According to Nemesis, the complex process of producing MD19 was now in its final stages, and a trial under battlefield conditions was the only thing required before it could be let loose on the trenches in France. The fact that a British mission was being sent to Russia provided the perfect opportunity to ship a consignment of the nerve gas to the Eastern Front, where it could be tested out.

To have attempted to infiltrate the field marshal's ship or one of the official escorts would have been folly, so Naval Intelligence along with Room 40 had arranged for a destroyer to be detached from the fleet now limping back home from Jutland. The previous morning HMS *Dunfermline* had departed from Thurso to take up station just off the west coast of Hoy. Aboard was a consignment of MD19 under the care of Herbert Duggan, who was to supervise the field trials on the Russian Front, along with a member of the Intelligence Services.

There was no way that High Command in Berlin would allow a nerve gas to be released against German troops on the Eastern Front. Klaus Diessbacher's orders were to allow *Hampshire* and her destroyer escort to pass, then torpedo *Dunfermline*. If *Hampshire* did not strike one of the carefully laid mines floating in the waters of the channel, it would inevitably be sunk by one of the waiting submarines. The beauty of the plan was that with the trials disrupted and Kitchener dead, Nemesis would be able to steal away quietly to Germany with the formula for MD19.

'Just five hours,' whispered Heitmann.

Keppler nodded in silence, his mind busy. He had deliberately ensured that the radio signal to U39 went out from Flowergate. Recent events made him very uneasy, and any transmissions were now going to be made by the French polisher. He intended to move away from Whitby and find a safer base as soon as possible.

Harry North stubbed out his cigarette and stretched his arms above his head. The atmosphere at the table in Phipps's coffee house was sombre. Harry felt tired and, for the first time in a long while, old. Bernard Ashe was just twenty-seven, and he was dead. Death was part of Harry's stock in trade, but this had affected him badly. Bert Conway and Clarrie Greasley had said very little when they were told, but he knew they were upset. They had taken a special interest in the lad, teaching him the little tricks of their trade that made the difference between failure and success.

His conversation earlier in the day with Connie Armitage at her lodgings worried him deeply.

'Do we know any more about the attempt to shoot Simmonds?'

North's attention was drawn back to the present conversation. Will looked as tired as he felt, while Ralph Gresham, as ever, was immaculately attired in suit and Royal Engineers tie.

In a familiar gesture Will rubbed a hand across his jaw, 'Yes, I think we may do, Ralph. Simmonds was up by the mill in Hundred Acre Woods when someone took a shot at him. We know from you that it definitely wasn't the sentries, so someone other than us has latched onto his amateur espionage game and wants him stopped. Second, we think that Tuppenny Rice was out there at the same time, and later the same day he was murdered in the cellar at Dakin Street. We can rule out coincidences, so it was either Simmonds or the person responsible for the shooting who killed him. Because of the injuries we all suspect, I think that it's Simmonds. His motive was that he suspected the vagrant could identify him as having murdered Charlotte Groves. The question we're asking is if the shooting in Hundred Acre Woods is connected to Nemesis.'

'I think it's got to be.' Gresham toyed thoughtfully with the spoon in the saucer of his coffee cup. 'I think that if we hold our breath just a little longer we're not far from blowing this thing wide open. People are losing their nerve. Simmonds is trying to implicate Palmaerts in the war hospital job, which means he's moving to extricate himself. The attempt to frame Kempin was a disastrous failure and led us almost to his front door, and now a third party has been provoked into action in an attempt to protect Nemesis.'

Harry studied the other two for a moment. 'The key is Bernard's death. Hands up everyone who thinks that Bernard simply went out in the dark and walked off the end of a jetty.' Gresham and Mardlin watched him intently. 'I talked to Connie Armitage this morning. The girl is beside herself. She was very fond of Bernard. I think they were looking at getting married. Once she knew I wasn't about to tell her landlady what they were up to over the weekend she calmed down a bit, and I got her to talk sensibly. Apparently Bernard didn't just go out for a stroll last night. During the day he saw someone whom he recognised – that's all she knows – but Bernard was very interested. He spotted him again from the window of their room. She says he just grabbed his coat, went off to follow the man and never came back.'

'Any description or indication who he was?' Will knew the question was a waste of time.

Harry shook his head. 'No. She's a bright girl. If she knew anything she'd have told me. Once more, there's no such thing as coincidence in our game. Your man's controller is in Whitby, Ralph. One of our men who was in Whitby identified and followed someone, and wound up dead. For my money our killer at this end is running scared and so's your spymaster – and Bernard found a link between them. We're very close to both of them now.'

Gresham tapped his spoon on the edge of the saucer. From his perspective things were going quite smoothly, and he agreed with Harry that the net was tightening on Nemesis and his controller.

Originally it had been agreed that he and Ted Bayliss should go to Russia to oversee the trials of MD19. Following the incident in the woods they had taken a decision that Ralph should remain and, in the certain knowledge that the incident was connected to Nemesis, work with the two policemen to try to track down the person responsible. A further change of plan was that, at Herbert Duggan's insistence, Paul Kändler was included at the last minute in the party travelling with the nerve gas. Ralph had a shrewd suspicion that, with the research so close to a conclusion, Duggan was having a crisis of confidence and needed the Belgian with him. Whatever his reasons, it was academic now, as along with Bayliss the two scientists were safely aboard HMS *Dunfermline*, standing off the Orkneys and waiting for Kitchener's flotilla to pass by.

'All roads appear to lead to Whitby, gentlemen,' he said decisively. 'I think it's time that I made my way there.'

Despite it being June, the weather off the Scottish coast was abysmal. Patrolling back and forth off the southern tip of Hoy, HMS *Dunfermline* was pitching and tossing in the grey waters of the Pentland Firth like a child's toy.

'I don't care what the Admiralty orders say. If these seas get any worse, I'm heading for the nearest safe harbour until this has blown itself out!' Hanging onto the bridge rail as the destroyer corkscrewed sickeningly into the trough of a thirty foot wave, Edward Bayliss was momentarily unable to reply to the captain's shouted words, bellowed in his ear from a distance of no more than five feet.

They both breathed an audible sigh of relief as, bringing her bows out of the mass of water threatening to engulf her, *Dunfermline* righted herself, before riding on upwards into the next massive sea.

Bayliss signalled an acknowledgement. His head was aching and he felt violently sick, as, he suspected, did the other men on the bridge. The two helmsmen who had been tied to the wheel were battling to keep the vessel's head into the oncoming waves. He had never seen weather like this. The gale that had been blowing earlier from the north-east had forced the convoy to change its route: rather than sailing to the east of Ronaldsay and up past the Orkneys, it would pass to the west of Hoy and out along the mercantile sea lanes for Murmansk and Archangel. This course, only decided late that afternoon by Admiral Jellicoe, seemed sensible. It was only when the cruiser and its escorts set off that the wind unexpectedly veered round into the opposite direction, battering the ships with the force of a cyclone.

Down below, prostrate in the first officer's quarters, Herbert Duggan and Paul Kändler were attempting, between bouts of intense sickness to remain in their bunks. Bayliss wondered ruefully whether, in view of the cargo they had brought on board the destroyer, some form of divine justice was not being wreaked upon them.

Gripping the rail as another column of spray burst over the ship's bows and doused the bridge windows, Ted Bayliss wished, not for the first time, that, in accordance with the original plan, Ralph Gresham were there with him to share the discomfort. More logically, he hoped that the canisters down in the ship's hold would withstand the punishment that the ship was taking – otherwise the storm was going to be the least of their worries.

Captain Ford put his mouth against Bayliss's ear. 'I'm turning back!' The man clinging to the rail beside him might be wearing the uniform of a naval officer, but Jarvis Ford did not like him or the civilians with him. It was obvious from the sealed orders handed to him by the commander when he came aboard, and the mysterious packing case that was so carefully stowed in the ship's hold, that the man was an intelligence officer – which meant that he and his companions were up to no good.

The orders to follow *Hampshire* as an additional escort might at any other time have been plausible, except for the fact that Captain Savill aboard the *Hampshire* knew nothing of their presence – which made a nonsense of the story. Whatever they were doing, it was the flotilla of warships that had steamed past on the horizon an hour ago which was providing cover for *Dunfermline* – not the other way round.

Ted Bayliss knew that the captain was right: they were barely making ten knots. The destroyer had neither the weight nor engine power to maintain headway in the prevailing conditions. The only consolation was that *Unity* and *Victor*, HMS *Hampshire*'s escorts, were older than *Dunfermline* and would be in a similar if not worse position, forcing the heavy cruiser either to throttle back to their speed or steam on ahead and leave them behind. Bayliss knew that very soon, like *Dunfermline*, the other two destroyers would also have to turn back.

A deluge of ice-cold water poured down over Franz-Georg Heinig as he forced open the hatch of U39 before climbing up onto the conning tower bridge. Behind him Klaus Diessbacher suppressed a grin. Captain's privilege to go second, he thought. Up on top, the tiny bridge offered neither of them any protection from the raging elements. The conditions were as they expected from the buffeting U39 took as she neared the surface. The seas were too high and visibility too poor for them to see anything at periscope depth. The choice was to surface and take a look around or remain submerged until the weather abated.

Following the first officer's example, Diessbacher clipped a line to his belt before swinging his glasses in a hundred and eighty degree arc. Through the lashing rain he could see nothing except the towering waves. That they could not remain on the surface was obvious: they would be swamped in minutes.

'Jesus Christ!' Heinig's arm extended towards the port bow, pointing frantically at the massive stern of a destroyer looming above them less than fifty metres away. 'Alarm! Alarm! Dive, dive, dive!'

With a speed born of desperation they unclipped their lifelines and hurled themselves back onto the control room ladder, Diessbacher slamming the hatch behind them and twirling the securing nuts before sliding down behind Heinig. The bows of the submarine were already tilting downwards.

'Twenty metres, then hold!' the captain bellowed. 'Fucking hell, Franzie, that was close!'

Pale and visibly shaken, the first officer nodded in speechless silence. They had been shadowing *Dunfermline* at a safe distance for more than two hours. Just before the storm blew up they had sighted *Hampshire* and her escorts as they steamed through the Pentland Firth and on past Hoy. Half an hour later, exactly on schedule, their quarry came over the horizon.

Despite the fact that they had narrowly avoided a collision, Klaus Diessbacher could not believe their luck. Getting close enough to torpedo *Dunfermline* might not be as risky as he had first thought. In these seas it would still be hazardous, as he would have to get dangerously near to ensure that a pattern would sink the British warship, but on the other hand all the advantages that the British torpedo-boat destroyers normally held over a submarine would be negated. At over a thousand tons displacement, the M Class destroyers were capable of speeds in excess of thirty knots, earning them the nickname Greyhounds. For once, however, the capricious sea had given the advantage to the U-boat commander. *Dunfermline* could not, Diessbacher estimated, be making more than ten knots in these seas, and even if she sighted U39 would not be able to manoeuvre fast enough to bring her guns to bear. If he could get in close enough the destroyer's fate was sealed.

Heinig, his equilibrium recovered, was busy checking the depth gauges.

'Zwanzig Meters, Herr Kapitän.' His stomach was still churning at the memory of the massive stern towering above them. The gale must have blown the warship off course, which, combined with its loss of speed, meant that the gap between them had reduced disastrously.

Klaus Diessbacher became aware of eyes on him. All the crew were standing by at action stations. Erwin Fahr was watching both him and the first officer, wondering if some explanation would be forthcoming. Bosun Grönemeyer, his bovine features impassive, was awaiting instructions, along with the steersman. 'Kramski, take us round to starboard onto a course of three one five degrees. Bosun, make the forward torpedoes ready to fire, if you please. We have a British warship in our sights.' As the submarine began to turn onto its new heading he saw that Heinig was looking at him with a quizzical expression. 'She was turning, Franz. The weather's too much for them. They're turning to go home.'

Understanding dawned on the first lieutenant's face. The warship was making an anti-clockwise turn to head back to port. In the present conditions, U39 could turn the opposite way faster and in a tighter circle underwater. If they got it right, by the time U39 came onto its new bearing *HMS Dunfermline* would be cutting straight across them.

It took some minutes for the U-boat to complete the turn, during which time tension in the hull mounted. Everyone held their breath, not making a sound, waiting for the thud of diesels overhead and the pounding of screws – indicating that Diessbacher had got it wrong and they were about to be run down by the destroyer.

As soon as the gyros pointed to 315 the order was given to return to periscope depth. Seconds later the small boat, once more buffeted by the huge seas into which they were emerging, poked above the surface. Grey water filled the periscope lens, then, just discernible through the waves, two hundred metres dead ahead was the warship – broadside on.

The captain made a sweeping hand signal to Fahr.

'Fire torpedoes!' The lieutenant's voice echoed down the voice pipe.

All the men on board felt a slight tremor as the salvo was launched from the forward tubes. With bated breath, each of them silently began to count the seconds. After what seemed an eternity the dull crump of a direct hit, followed almost immediately by a second, came to their ears. A cheer rang through the steel hull as sailors' faces cracked into huge grins and the pent-up tension evaporated.

'The others are going to have to turn back as well. *Hampshire* should be all right, but *Victor* and *Unity* won't be able to hold up in these seas.' Captain Ford had his face close to Bayliss's, shouting in his ear to make himself heard. However good his reasons for turning back – based on thirty years at sea – Ford knew that when all of this was over he would be taken to task for failing to obey the Admiralty orders that the commander had given him.

Bayliss nodded in agreement, concentrating on maintaining a footing on the slippery deck of the bridge. Water was pouring in through the smashed armoured glass of the window on the starboard side where the seas were now heaviest, and everyone was soaked. The captain was right: to attempt to go on was foolhardy. The entire expedition should have been put off for at least twenty-four hours until the weather cleared. That the two older destroyers would also have to put back was inevitable. He wondered if Kitchener, aboard the heavier cruiser, would insist on continuing without an escort. He suspected that he would. That was ill-advised. Intelligence reports showed that at least ten and probably more German U-boats were patrolling in the seas around Orkney, and it was possible that two of their new mine-laying submarines had been busy mining the sea lanes towards Cape Wrath. If *Hampshire*, sailing on alone, hit a mine or was torpedoed, in this weather it would go down with all hands.

He was about to reply to the captain when something hit *Dunfermline* amidships, like a mighty fist. The ship seemed first to stagger, then suddenly lose way, when a second blow followed by a huge explosion hit the stern. 'Torpedoes!' yelled Bayliss at the top of his voice.

Captain Ford was picking himself up from the deck where he had been thrown by the force of the explosions. The navigation officer, a young lieutenant, was groping for the voice pipe to speak to the engine room as smoke began to fill the bridge, when a series of detonations deep in the bowels of the ship told him that at least one of the boilers had exploded. Without further warning the destroyer heeled over sharply and began to settle in the water.

Down below, Paul Kändler picked himself up from the floor of the cabin, where he had been thrown by the initial explosion. Herbert Duggan, caught in the process of making his way to the heads at the end of the passageway, lay unconscious in the doorway. To his horror Kändler saw that water was rushing along the companionway outside. Finding that by some miracle his glasses were still on his nose and undamaged, the Belgian checked quickly around him. The cabin was at an angle of forty-five degrees. Books and clothing, the possessions of the first lieutenant whose quarters they were occupying, were strewn about and beginning to float in the sea water that was pouring over the cabin step.

Grabbing Duggan by the back of his shirt, Kändler hauled him over onto his back. A quick examination of the deep gash on the older man's forehead, and the unnatural way in which his right leg was bent, told him all that he needed to know. It was obvious that the ship had either hit a mine or been torpedoed. He needed to escape from the lower decks before they became a floating coffin – and he was not going to be able to haul Duggan up with him. Stepping into the companionway, he moved as fast as was possible, but the sea water gushing around his legs was almost up to his knees. With relief he found the ladder leading up to the safety of the main deck. Thick acrid fumes were beginning to fill the between decks and he realised that he was alone: the nimbler and well-trained sailors must have been up the ladders within seconds of the vessel being hit. Gripping the rungs above his head, Paul Kändler began to scramble up.

From the bridge Ted Bayliss could see that the situation was hopeless. Ford had already given the order to abandon ship, but both of them knew that in these seas this was suicidal. *Dunfermline* was settling fast by the stern, where the second explosion had torn away a huge section, including the steering gear. On the deck below them sailors were frantically attempting to launch the ship's lifeboats. He watched as two were swung out on the davits, only to be smashed to matchwood against the ship's side – killing in an instant the men in them.

Another group was trying with little success to cut free a life raft. As he watched, the short figure of Paul Kändler emerged onto the deck from one of the hatchways and lurched, slipping and sliding, towards the men working at releasing the raft. Bayliss's view was momentarily obscured when a wall of water poured over the side. As the deluge subsided and flowed back into the boiling sea he saw that the deck was empty. All that was left was the raft swinging from its one remaining lashing in the sheeting rain. He would, he calmly decided, remain on the bridge with Captain Ford.

Eyes glued to the periscope, Diessbacher watched with a mixture of horror and fascination as the scene unfolded. His emotions were mixed: the thrill of watching an enemy vessel sinking, along with the seaman's revulsion at what he was doing – sending other mariners to their doom in the icy waters.

The destroyer was settling fast by the stern when the sky was suddenly lit up by the glow of a massive explosion. Poor bastards, he thought. That was either the magazine or the main boiler going up.

At that moment another monstrous swell hit U39, throwing her upwards then hurling her down again into the trough. Clinging to the periscope, Diessbacher gave the order to submerge before he in turn was sunk by the massive waves. Swinging the viewer round one final time, he saw that the sea was empty.

Chapter Thirty

I t was not Béatrice Palmaerts but a small plump housemaid who answered the door of 26 Kingsbury Lane to Will Mardlin's impatient jangling of the bell pull. Mardlin was still in a foul mood, and the warm summer weather was doing little to improve his disposition.

Things were, he was aware, deteriorating rapidly between Irene and himself. He had always known that their affair could not continue indefinitely, but over the months he had become very comfortable with the arrangement. Seeing her two or three times a week, along with the secrecy with which they had surrounded themselves, lent a decided frisson to the relationship, and deep down he also knew that, with her outlook on life, Susan would not have disapproved.

'Madame is not here, sir. She is gone to Whitby for a few days, sir.' The girl pronounced the name 'Weetbee', which for some reason irritated Will intensely. Another lame dog Belgian refugee for whom she had found some employment, he decided uncharitably.

'It is not Madame that we came to see,' he said, speaking very slowly to ensure that the girl understood. Will was perfectly well aware that Madame had 'gone to Weetbee'. That she had sent a peremptory note telling him that she was going away for a couple of days irked him: he felt that at least he warranted a phone call. It was her absence, combined with his continuing ill humour, that had prompted this visit. It was, as he told Harry, time to rattle a few cages and see once and for all if the Belgian was actually involved in any way in the war hospital fraud.

Harry, on the other hand, took the view that the visit was Will's way of getting back at Irene. Anyone involved in the enquiry could see that Matthias Palmaerts was not involved in anything criminal – and very soon Harry himself was going to lose his temper.

'We've come to see Monsieur Palmaerts, if you please.'

'Please wait in the drawing room. I shall go and find him,' she said, with some relief. Monsieur Palmaerts would know what the gentlemen wanted and how to deal with them.

'No. We'll go upstairs and speak to him.'

The maid was confused. She was sure that Monsieur Palmaerts would not wish them to go up to his and Madame's private apartments. Brushing her aside, Will made for the stairs.

With a perfunctory 'Police', Harry North cut short any protest and followed the superintendent across the hallway.

Béatrice Palmaerts answered the door of their second-floor living room to Will's single knock. A quick look of concern passed across her face as she admitted the two men. After almost two years of living as outsiders, she and her family were well used to feeling apprehension when the weight of authority was brought to bear on their lives. A visit from the police while Madame was away – even if one of them was her lover – did not bode well.

Her husband was dressed in his customary style, dark hair and beard carefully trimmed, moustache waxed. Like his wife, he appeared to have put on a little weight: the waistcoat that had previously hung loosely on his frame had once again filled out, and fitted as it was intended to. A neatly folded newspaper was on the recently vacated armchair. It was, Will noted, turned to the financial page.

'Monsieur Palmaerts, we have a few questions that we would like you to answer.' Will's tone was formal and unfriendly.

Béatrice shot her husband an apprehensive look.

'Please, gentlemen, be seated.' Harry noticed that the Belgian's English was now almost flawless. Indicating the dining room table, Matthias sat down and waited while the two detectives took places opposite to him. 'I had expected you to come to see me earlier, Mr Mardlin,' he said politely.

'Why would that be?'

'Because in the light of what has happened recently, I am certain that you must view me as a possible suspect in relation to the thefts from the war hospital. I am an accountant. I was – and still am – responsible for the administration of the hospital accounts. Your Mr Ashe has spent a considerable amount of time with me here going through the receipts and invoices. That I should be regarded as a suspect is inevitable.'

'Does that worry you?' Will's tone was slightly less formal. The man appeared to be willing to talk, and he needed to keep things going.

'No. And the reason for that is very simple. I am not a thief, and I have done absolutely nothing wrong. I have found during the time that I have lived in this country that the police are not to be feared as they were in my homeland. You, Monsieur, I think are an honest man, otherwise Madame Deladier would not have trusted you as she has done.'

The oblique reference to his relationship with Irene threw Will slightly, and, sensing this, Harry picked up the thread. Either Palmaerts was an honest man or a clever one, he decided.

'You know that Mr Ashe is dead?'

Palmaerts nodded. 'Yes. I understand that he had an accident and fell from a quayside.'

'Where have you been this weekend, Monsieur?' Harry's tone was hard.

Matthias Palmaerts stared at him, a look of comprehension slowly dawning in his eyes. 'Ah,' he said quietly, 'maintenant je comprend.' This is not simply about the thefts. You think that I am involved in these other terrible things. I was stupid not to think of that. The people who have been killed were all involved, and you think that I may have been responsible.' He looked visibly shaken. 'I am sorry about Monsieur Ashe,' he said softly. 'He was a nice young man.'

'Where have you been this weekend, Monsieur Palmaerts?' repeated Harry.

Palmaerts held the policeman's gaze steadily, looking him straight in the eyes. 'I have been here in Kelsford all weekend, Mr North. Since the government introduced this latest tax on people's income I have had one or two local businessmen ask me to sort out their affairs. I spent all day Saturday and the morning on Sunday at Dr Mallard's house, auditing his accounts.'

Will and Harry exchanged glances. Harry's imperceptible nod confirmed Will's own instincts. Matthias Palmaerts was telling the truth.

'Who do you think is responsible for the war hospital thefts, Monsieur Palmaerts?' Will asked.

Matthias Palmaerts took a deep breath, aware of the decision that the detectives had reached. 'It can only be James Simmonds,' he said flatly.

'I agree,' said Will. 'I also think that we can prove it, but I need your expertise as an accountant.'

For the next half hour Will discussed with Palmaerts what he knew or suspected of the connection between Simmonds and the Tivoli Palace. The Belgian listened attentively, occasionally scribbling notes on a sheet of paper. With the atmosphere now more relaxed, Béatrice made coffee and brought in some tiny sweet pastries.

Eventually the accountant sat back in his chair and looked up at the ceiling. 'It is easy for me to prove through the hospital invoices and time sheets shown to me by Monsieur Ashe that Madame Doyle was claiming for staff and provisions that did not exist. Those documents never came to me – had they done so I would have identified immediately that they were fraudulent. The matron submitted those direct to James Simmonds, who as treasurer authorised payment, and merely informed me what the overall sum of money to be paid out was. It is obvious that the architect fabricated grossly inflated estimates for building materials and labour. Ivor Rees was the main haulage contractor, so he would have been aware that the goods on the invoices did not match the quantities that his men delivered. These things I can prove as an accountant.'

'But how were they going to get away with it?' queried Will. 'Someone was eventually going to look at the hospital and realise that the work had never been done, and that the staff did not exist.'

Matthias Palmaerts smiled slowly. 'Do you think that I have not been asking myself the very same question Superintendent? I think that the answer is brilliantly simple. The key to the entire equation is the building. As soon as the war is ended the premises will be sold off to a development company – no doubt set up by Simmonds from the proceeds of the fraud. The company convinces the local authority – through Simmonds – that with the war over the town does not need such a huge undertaking, and would benefit from a housing development as part of the post-war building programme. He might even offer to build a smaller hospital for the town on another site. What he has to do is ensure that this particular building is razed to the ground. Once that is done there is nothing left for anyone to question. No evidence, nothing, rien.'

Harry looked thoughtful. 'Yes, it works,' he mused. 'So far as the staff are concerned they're all transient in effect. Royal Army Medical Corps orderlies will be discharged from the army at the end of the war. Nurses and doctors are here for a while, then sent off to France. Voluntary Aid workers are organised on a temporary basis – yet again by Simmonds – and the majority of the domestic staff are refugees who'll want to return home at the first opportunity.'

Will handed Matthias Palmaerts the notebook taken from Sylvester Hardesty's office. The accountant adjusted his spectacles and studied the pages. Looking up, he said, 'There are three addresses here that I recognise. In London, 54 Driscoll Street and 17 Hadderley Court are both according to my books builders' merchants; and the address in Leeds is a firm that has supplied electric light fittings to the hospital.'

Will and Harry beamed at each other. 'That's the link we needed. We've got him, Harry,' Will's voice was filled with excitement. 'Thank you, Matthias. You're a genius.'

Standing up, Harry stretched his legs and eased his back. At last they were in a position to bring it all together: the hospital fraud and the murders. Finally they were ready to arrest James Simmonds. Picking up his empty coffee cup he placed it on the silver tray. As he did so he noticed, gazing sadly down at him from a shelf on the dresser, the porcelain figure of a Madonna and child. Over the years Harry had developed an interest in porcelain, and the figurine was, he thought, very nice. Standing about twelve inches high, the deep colours and unblemished finish made it an attractive and valuable piece. Idly he wondered how the Palmaerts family had, in their flight from Belgium, managed to bring it unscathed across war-torn Europe.

A nervous voice at his side said, 'Elle est belle, n'est-ce pas, Monsieur?' Béatrice, still very unsure of the policemen in her home, smiled at him gently.

'Yes it is, Madame. I was wondering how you managed to get it here safely from your home in Belgium.' Harry was at his most charming. He wanted to put the woman at her ease and allay her nervousness, but he was also genuinely interested in the ornament.

Her reply startled him, and brought Will onto his feet beside them. 'Ah, non, Monsieur: it was a gift. You remember when we lived in those terrible rooms at Devonshire Gardens, the lady who was murdered – Madame Groves – she gave it to us as a present.'

Very deliberately, Harry asked, 'When exactly did she do that?'

'Oh, it was a few days before she died. She came down to our sitting room and said that she had seen a lovely Madonna in Monsieur Feinemann's shop in Thomas Street. She said that as we were Catholics and we had been through so much she wanted to get it for us as a present. It didn't matter what we said, she insisted, and she gave Philippe half a sovereign to go and buy it. Everyone says that she was a bad woman, but she was very kind to us.'

Harry turned the ornament upside down, knowing what he would find. In the base was a small hole less than half an inch in diameter. Taking a pencil from his pocket, he inserted it into the aperture and felt around. Will watched him in silence. After a moment Harry glanced up and nodded. 'There's something inside. Feels like rolled up paper.'

'I'm afraid, Madame, that we're going to have to break this,' Will said to the bemused woman. 'Whatever's inside holds the answer to why Charlotte Groves was murdered.' Outwardly calm, Will was tense with excitement.

Matthias Palmaerts held out his hand in a gesture of agreement. 'Ça va. Il faut nécessaire.'

Spreading Matthias's newspaper on the dining room table, Will laid the Madonna on its side and struck it a sharp blow with the steel poker Matthias handed him from the fireplace. The figurine shattered into a dozen pieces, to reveal a tightly rolled bundle of papers held together by a fine cotton round the middle.

There were five sheets of paper, each referring to Captain James Simmonds, Kelsford Yeomanry. The first related to Simmonds's treatment after he had been wounded. Signed by Colonel Walter Trethowan RAMC, it was a record of his admission to the casualty clearing hospital at St Omer. It showed that he had been admitted on 24 August 1914 with shrapnel wounds received in action at Nimy Bridge, near to the Mons Canal. The injuries required the amputation of his right hand at the wrist. The operation was carried out by Colonel Trethowan on 25 August, after which Simmonds was transferred to Calais for repatriation to England.

Turning to the second and third sheets, Will saw that they were a record of Captain Simmonds's treatment at Ampthill Hospital in Bedfordshire, where he was sent by convoy train from Dover in the last week of August. At Ampthill a post-operative problem developed with the nerves in his severed wrist, necessitating the arm being put into plaster. Looking at the treatment sheet attached, Will noted that one of the doctors who was treating him was concerned at the high levels of morphine that the patient required to control his pain.

The final two sheets began with Simmonds's arrival at the 5th Northern General Hospital in Leicester, where he remained until his discharge from both the hospital and the army on 18 December 1914. It was this record that brought mixed expressions of both understanding and concern to the faces of the two detectives. During the period that James Simmonds was a patient at the 5th Northern General two other doctors expressed concern at the high level of intra-muscular injections of morphine that the patient was receiving, and noted that, in their opinion, Captain Simmonds was addicted to the drug. Will tapped several entries on the 5th Northern General records with his forefinger, and Harry grunted an acknowledgement. Almost daily the signature of the nurse administering Simmonds's drugs was Charlotte Groves.

Back at Long Street in Will's office the two men sat facing each other across Will's desk. 'So now we know. It was James Simmonds that Charlotte Groves was blackmailing – not Kath Doyle.' Will's face bore an expression familiar to both of them: it was a mixture of triumph at discovering a long-sought solution, and indecision over what their next step should be.

'Simmonds is a morphine addict and Charlotte Groves was his nurse. When she got the sack from 5th Northern General she stole the record sheets relating to his case and hotfooted it here to his home town. From there it was easy. Where we made a mistake was in assuming that she was involved in the war hospital fraud. I doubt she even knew about it.'

'First she got a job at the hospital as a nurse and started to blackmail James over his addiction – war hero, prominent local figure, he'd have been a gift to her. No doubt she was his supplier at first, but because of her own addiction stealing enough for the two of them must have attracted attention, and Doyle had to dismiss her. From that point she really put the screws on James in order to fund her own needs, and she went on the game. If we really dig deep I think that we'll find that she isn't the only nurse at the hospital who was making a little bit of cash on the side nicking drugs.'

'But she didn't know about Kathy Doyle.' Harry turned the argument over in his mind.

'No. Because Kath was having an affair with James, she must have known about his problem and she started to supply him. Once he'd replaced Groves with the matron, James was in a position to remove Lottie altogether.'

'How he convinced Kath to help him we can only surmise. They say that love's blind. Kath Doyle certainly didn't kill Charlotte. She merely went to Devonshire Gardens and knocked on the door. When Groves answered, Kathy must have told her some story to gain entry, probably that because of staff shortages at the hospital she could reinstate her and all was forgiven. When Lottie turned to go back up the hallway, Doyle slipped the latch on the front door so that Simmonds could nip in, hide in the kitchen until she left and then go up and kill Lottie.'

Harry lit a cigarette, then studied the glowing end.

'Tom Weldon saw Simmonds, and from that point on Simmonds exchanged one blackmailer for another. Ironically neither of them realised Tuppenny was in the street. He was just an old tramp who blended into the background. Public opinion was already fixed on 'the soldier', so why not strike while the iron was hot and eliminate Ivor Rees as well? Kath Doyle had already set up Kempin on the basis that his hospital record at the clap clinic tied him in to Lottie Groves. Dropping a trench knife on the tram was amateur, though, and, if you'll pardon the pun, overkill – it simply alerted us to the fact that someone was trying to frame Kempin. Whether or not they discussed Rees's murder before it happened, she certainly must have known afterwards that it was James who'd done it, and that tied her in even tighter. What are your thoughts on Weldon, Harry?' Will sat back in his chair.

'I've been turning it over, and this is just a guess. I think that most likely he only saw Simmonds going into the house. Consequently he didn't know that Kathleen Doyle was involved. Once Weldon started to put the bite on our man the happy couple decided that he'd have to be the next to go. This is pure speculation, but I think that Kathy put herself in Weldon's way and gave him the come-on. We know what he was like, he'd shag anything with a pulse, so that wouldn't be difficult. I think she arranged to meet him while he was on nights – the bridge is between his beat and her flat – and it wouldn't have taken much to persuade him to walk back there with her on a promise. Once they got on the bridge she told him she couldn't wait and pulled him into a close embrace, giving James the opportunity to creep up behind and hit him over the head. I think that when we search his house we'll find that James has more than one prosthesis, and that he has a false hand with a hook – that's what the hospital usually sends out. That would account for the blow to the head that Ducky Mallard identified as being inflicted before death, and for the tear in Weldon's greatcoat when they heaved him over the parapet.'

Will gathered his thoughts. 'All along we've assumed that the killer was right handed because in each case the injuries were inflicted from the right. That was why we thought Simmonds couldn't be our man. As you say, he's probably got more than one hand. What's to stop him having one with a blade on it? He goes to London a lot, so it would be easy for a technician there to make him something on the quiet that would fit the bill. When he's going to use it he carries it in his briefcase, and simply fits it on in place of his glove.'

Harry nodded. 'And that's how Weldon died: the flat of the hook to stun him, then over the side. The inspector stubbed out his cigarette and took another from the packet of Players on the desk. 'And that's probably when James went completely round the twist and decided to eliminate Kath Doyle as well.'

Will shrugged. 'I think he was already completely mad by then. Even with Groves, Rees and Weldon removed there were still two weak links in his chain. 'One, to him the most important, was that he couldn't find the stolen medical records that Groves had removed from the files at Leicester.

Until he recovered them he'd never be safe. Second was Kathleen Doyle. She could scupper him at any time. She'd have known how to access the proceeds of the swindle, and she also knew where all the bodies were buried. It would have been reasonably easy for him to get her down into the boiler room. All he had to do was share with her the bright idea that as Lottie worked at the hospital the basement would be a perfect place to secrete the papers. He probably even told her to check at the back of the pipes. Even if Kath spotted him coming into the room she wouldn't have been suspicious. There's no doubt in my mind that it was also his intention that Frank Kempin should turn up dead, and then the matter would be conveniently closed.'

Harry realised he was desperately tired. 'I need a drink. You?'

'Good idea.'

A couple of minutes later the inspector returned with a bottle of Old Dublin Irish whiskey and two glasses from his office. He poured them each a generous measure. 'It all started to go wrong with Tuppenny Rice, didn't it?'

Aware that the inspector still blamed himself for the little man's death, a thoughtful expression clouded Will's face. ' I'm not sure when it all began to unravel. Once neither Groves nor Doyle were available to supply him, James would have had a problem. Arthur Mallard's his GP, and I doubt he was prescribing for him. So the recent trips to London must have been dual purpose: to sort out the Tivoli and to source a new supplier.'

Harry pulled a face. 'Enter that double-dyed bastard Absolom.'

Will nodded. 'Without a doubt. Tuppenny Rice didn't know who James Simmonds was when he saw him leaving Lottie's, but when he saw him again at Hundred Acre Woods he followed him back either to his house or his office, then tried to tell you. James must have seen him that time, remembered seeing him before in Devonshire Gardens and realised that he was a danger.'

Harry took a slow sip at his whiskey. 'What about this thing on Sunday morning when someone took a couple of shots at Simmonds?'

Gazing out of the window, Will watched a young policeman in the street below talking to the driver of a hansom. 'I might be inclined to say that it was a fabrication to throw us off the scent in case we suspected him, but he's too arrogant for that to occur to him. I think there are several things here. We know that, mad as he may be, Simmonds is a rabid patriot. Being knocked out of the war and cheated of his glory is almost certainly what tipped him over the edge in the first place. We also know that he's been spending a lot of time watching the Watermill. What if he somehow stumbled across something to do with Nemesis? Possibly even suspected his identity?

'According to Gresham, Nemesis's controller is based somewhere in the Whitby area. That makes sense: it's on the coast and a relatively short distance from Kelsford. What if James has worked out the Whitby connection and went up there to do a spot of sleuthing, saw Nemesis and was following him when Bernard Ashe came into the picture?'

He paused, the cab driver flicked his reins across the horse's back and clopped sedately off towards the High Street. 'Question is, do we bring Simmonds in now, or let him run for just a day or two longer and risk him killing again in the hope that he'll lead us to Nemesis?'

Harry placed his empty glass on the desktop and stubbed out his cigarette in the ashtray. 'We bring him in right now. So far as Nemesis is concerned . . . I know who he is.'

Will stared at him. 'Go on,' he said slowly.

'Crosswords . . . you don't do them, do you?' The question was rhetorical. Will gave a slight shake of his head.

'I realised when we smashed the ornament. Should have worked it out a long while ago really. It was quite a valuable porcelain that's been made in the town of Meissen near Dresden since about 1710, and as the experts say it's eponymous – takes its name from the town. Nemesis is an anagram of Meissen. Meissen's master modeller, responsible for creating all of the company's new designs between 1730 and 1770, was a man named Joachim Kändler. Do I need to go further?'

Standing at the front door of the large house in Stanway Road, Will checked to left and right to ensure that everything was in place. A hundred yards away, near the junction with Dolman Lane, two constables were posted out of sight of the house. Bert Conway and Clarence Greasley should, he estimated, now be in position at the rear.

Before setting off from Long Street he had made two telephone calls. The first, to Sam Norton, had left him frustrated and annoyed. Never good, his relationship with Irene's brother had deteriorated considerably since the young man had worked out that his sister was having an affair with the policeman. At first he had refused point blank to discuss Paul Kändler with the superintendent, claiming that Kändler's whereabouts and activities were matters of national security. It was only when Will abruptly cut through the young major's irritating pomposity and informed him forcefully that he was acting directly on behalf of Colonel Gresham that he grudgingly told the detective that Kändler, along with Herbert Duggan, was away on government work at an undisclosed location.

In truth, Sam had not the remotest idea where the two scientists were. He had long ago ceased asking what was going on at the Old Watermill, accepting that his position was merely that of a figurehead whose real purpose was to ensure the continuing security of the Kosminski investment. The discovery that Will Mardlin was now involved in some clandestine association with the intelligence officer only served to deepen his resentment.

Will's second call was to Ralph Gresham, at the hotel in Whitby that he had booked into the previous evening. Gresham received the information concerning the identity of Nemesis in silence, then with a brief 'thank you' hung up. At least thought Will, that was one responsibility he could now divest himself of.

Slipping his hand into his jacket pocket, he felt the reassuring cold metal of the Smith and Wesson. He gave the doorbell a sharp tug and waited, a knot tightening in his stomach as he wondered what the next minutes would bring. He wondered if, should the need arise, he would actually use the gun. As a young boy, the son of a senior NCO and brought up in army camps across India, Will had been familiar from an early age with both pistols and rifles. Target and game shooting were one thing; this was another.

A strange feeling came over him as he found himself wishing that his father was standing there beside him. Not the elderly licensee who had to find his spectacles before he could read a newspaper, but the tall sunburnt figure in red tunic and helmet of his childhood. In those seconds, unbidden, the answer to the question that had plagued him all his adult life became blindingly clearly to him. Thirty years ago, at the Collett's Lane Siege, his father would have had no compunction at all about shooting to kill. Along with that realisation came the knowledge of what he himself would do if things went wrong in the next few minutes.

Closing his hand around the butt of the pistol, he drew it from his pocket and pulled the hammer back, holding it unobtrusively under his jacket. He risked a quick look at Harry standing a yard to his left next to the door frame, covering him. His face impassive, he had the Colt .45 in his hand, safety catch off, pointing into the doorway. Impatiently Will tugged again at the bell pull.

The door was opened by a young girl in the uniform of a maid. 'I'm sorry, sir, Mr Simmonds is not at home . . .'

She got no further, as with a curt 'Police' the two detectives thrust her to one side and moved quickly into the hallway. Will moving to the right and Harry to the left, they stood stock still, listening, pistols held out. Other than the maidservant's startled intake of breath everything was silent.

Harry pushed open the first door to the left and looked quickly into the library. It was empty, as was the front drawing room which Will checked. It took them just minutes to confirm that other than the bewildered young girl the house was empty. Her master was, she explained, away on business overnight.

The main bedroom yielded nothing more than a wardrobe containing James Simmonds's clothes and an immaculately pressed uniform with the two lines of braid and three stars of a captain on the cuffs of the tunic. The cap, which was wrapped in tissue paper and stored in a hat box, carried the distinctive interwoven silver badge of the Kelsford Yeomanry.

'Is there a cellar?' asked Harry.

'Yes, sir.' The girl bobbed nervously up and down. She was, surmised Will, no more than about fifteen, and was frightened out of her wits.

Leading them through the kitchen into the scullery, where they were joined by Greasley and Conway, she showed them a heavy door which was securely locked. It was obvious that the original flimsy internal door had been replaced by one fitted with a mortise lock.

'Presumably you don't have a key?' the superintendent asked.

The maid shook her head dumbly, wondering how on earth she was going to explain these goings on to her master when he returned home.

Harry inspected the lock and stood back. 'It'll go,' he said to Will. 'He's done what they all do. Beefed up the door and lock without strengthening the frame.' He gave a brief nod to Conway, who stepped forward and kicked at the door as hard as possible, just below the lock. At the third kick the frame gave way, and with a splintering crash the door flew open.

Just inside was an electric light switch, which Harry flicked on – to reveal neatly whitewashed walls and a narrow stairway disappearing into the darkness below. Acutely aware of his last experience, he slipped the safety catch off the automatic before descending the narrow brick steps.

'What is it with you and cellars?' demanded Will in a low voice from behind him as they made their way cautiously down.

A second light switch at the bottom bathed the room in bright light.

'Fucking hell!' exclaimed Clarrie Greasley as their eyes roamed around the display of militaria on display.

Moving around, careful not to touch anything that might later be evidence, they examined the items that constituted James Simmonds's private museum. Along one wall, hanging from individual pegs, was a collection of about twenty rifles, ranging from two Martini Henry mark II single action breech loaders dating, Will judged, from around 1870, to such modern weapons as a French Lebel, German Mannlichers and a Short Magazine Lee Enfield .303 service rifle. On a facing wall was a collection of swords from around the world: Japanese samurai blades, which Will surmised were worth a small fortune, and European officers' dress swords, with ornate scabbards and regimental insignia on the hilts. At the back of the cellar, on the far wall, was an assortment of wicked-looking trench knives and bayonets, some with spiked knuckledusters on the hand guards, others with the standard rifle fixing. A final selection had been shortened to about six inches for carrying in a belt scabbard. This particular display, of three rows each made up of four knives, was missing one item at the bottom right-hand corner.

'We know where that one is, don't we, Harry?' said Conway, gazing in deep thought at the empty space.

'It's in your office drawer, with a nice "FK" cut into the haft.'

In the centre of the floor stood a table covered in a purple cloth. On it was an assortment of regimental cap badges, all, so far as they could see, relating to the British Army. A second table, set to one side, carried an assortment of service pistols, among them two .445 Webleys, a Mauser revolver and a Russian Nagant. The focus of this display was a small glass case in which, laid out on snow-white silk, hanging from its crimson and blue ribbon, was a Distinguished Service Order. The Imperial Crown set in laurel leaves gleamed dully in its gold and white enamelled centre.

Pulling open the drawer of the table, Will saw that it contained an assortment of maps and plans. He laid them out carefully in front of him.

They were detailed troop movements on the Western Front, along with annotations of displacements.

'He's been copying down everything in the newspapers and plotting his own campaign,' muttered Greasley.

Will nodded. 'He must have spent hours doing it,' he acknowledged, delving further down into the pile of papers. Suddenly he stopped, and pulled out a sheet of heavy paper that appeared to have been cut from an artist's sketchbook. It was a plan of the Old Watermill and the surrounding woods. James must, he realised, have traced the drawing from an Ordnance Survey map of the area. The drawing was overlaid in meticulous detail with the locations of all of the buildings and the perimeter fence. Simmonds was, he reflected, more organised than he and Gresham had given him credit for.

A sharp intake of breath from Bert Conway broke his concentration. Along with the other three he found himself looking at another drawing that Bert and Clarrie had found rolled up at the back of the drawer. It was of an artificial limb, obviously intended to be attached to the right wrist and forearm, the prosthesis being in the form of a short-bladed trench knife.

Unlike the others on display this was in the form of a double-bladed dagger, the last three inches of the upper edge serrated into saw teeth capable of ripping through bone, or causing a massive injury to flesh as the weapon was withdrawn from a wound. At the end of the knife haft was a metal cup designed to sit snugly on the stump of an amputated wrist. Attached to this cup was a length of carefully moulded steel, with straps to fit round the wearer's arm and give it strength and stability.

They were, they all knew, looking at the blueprint of the weapon that had been used to murder Charlotte Groves and Ivor Rees. What was bothering Will was the fact that the actual weapon was nowhere to be seen.

'Wherever he is, he's got that with him,' said Harry quietly.

Leaving the two detective sergeants to await the arrival of someone from Saunt's to take photographs of the grim exhibition, Will and Harry returned to the scullery where the maid was waiting apprehensively for them.

'Where is Mr Simmonds?' asked Will.

'I don't know, sir.' The girl burst into tears, and Will realised that she was absolutely terrified of them. 'Please, sir, I truly don't know.'

Sitting her down at the large kitchen table Mardlin said gently, 'Listen to me. You're not in any trouble. Neither with us, nor Mr Simmonds when he returns home. Please think, when did he go away?'

'This morning, sir. He had a suitcase with his overnight clothes and his briefcase – that was all.'

'Think carefully. Did he leave you any address or telephone number to contact him?'

She shook her head. 'No, sir. He said he'd be back tomorrow.'

'Did he make any telephone calls this morning, lass?'

At Harry's question she brightened up slightly, able at last to help. 'He did make a telephone call this morning, sir. About half past eight, before he went out.'

Closing the scullery door, Harry went into the hallway to where the telephone sat on a small table. Five minutes later he was back. 'We need to go,' he said tersely. 'I suggest we leave Clarrie and Bert here to tidy up.'

Without questioning him in front of the girl, Will went off down the cellar steps, reappearing a minute later with Greasley. 'Take a statement from this young lady, Clarrie, then search the rest of the house thoroughly, including the loft. Make sure that Saunt's man gets everything in the cellar. See that someone stays with him while he does the developing, and brings all of the pictures and the glass negatives back to you or Bert personally.'

Out on the street he said to Harry, 'What have we got?'

'I've spoken to the woman who's the switchboard supervisor at the telephone exchange. There are only four girls on the switchboard, and they keep a written log of the numbers that they obtain for subscribers so their bills can be worked out. Simmonds made a call to this number at twenty-nine minutes past eight this morning.' He handed the superintendent a slip of paper torn from his notebook. On it was written the telephone number of Kelsford railway station. 'The operator heard him asking the booking clerk for the time of the next train to Whitby. Thing is, why's he going to Whitby now?'

'I'll tell you why,' replied Will, an expression of deep concern on his face. 'Because Irene Deladier is there.'

'Why would he want to kill her as well?'

Will shook his head. 'He doesn't need a reason. Could be as simple as the fact that she's involved with me. The bastard's as mad as a brush and he's gone right over the top now. What I do know is that we need to get to Whitby as soon as possible.'

Chapter Thirty-One

Siegfried Keppler considered the news of the sinking of *HMS Dunfermline* in stony silence. Getting up, he inched aside the curtain and studied the square of hard-baked ground leading out into Mission Square. It was, he decided, no use crying over spilt milk, as the British were so fond of saying. With the death of Paul Kändler, the entire operation to subvert Project 19 was ended. The arrangement had originally been that Duggan would go to Russia on the *Dunfermline* along with the consignment of MD19, while Kändler remained safely tucked away at the Old Watermill. Once the *Dunfermline* had been consigned to the deep, with Duggan aboard, Kändler would be the only person in the world who held the secret of the newly developed nerve gas. The fact that Germany had stolen British research to obtain the weapon was, he felt, a wonderful touch of irony. Had things gone to plan, he could have arranged for the scientist's disappearance from Kelsford and had him back in Germany before the stupid Engländers even realised that he was gone.

The last minute decision to put both of the scientists on the destroyer was something that Keppler could not have anticipated. Briefly he turned over the situation. Had Paul Kändler known of the arrangements to sink the ship he might conceivably have been able to avoid travelling on it. As it was, all of the research was lost, and he doubted if the British would now be in a position to restart the project. A major factor in the war was lost – but it was lost to both sides, so the overall balance had not been altered.

Outside a small girl of about nine wearing a scruffy apron and frock was playing in the dirt, and Keppler moved back out of sight. The child belonged to the ferret-featured woman from the lodgings above. In this area no one took much notice of, and made even less comment, about the activities of a neighbour, but there was no point in drawing unnecessary attention to himself. Reaching under the bed, he drew out the radio transmitter and set it up. Another five minutes to the agreed time, between 1455 and 1505 hours, which constituted the window for contacting the submarine. Too early or too late and Diessbacher would presume that something was wrong.

It was time, Keppler decided, to pull out and head for home. Apart from anything else he was worried about the length of the signal sent to the U-boat ordering the sinking of *Dunfermline*. Any listening radio unit in the area could have triangulated on the transmission and even now be watching the French polisher's shop. Since the signal had been sent, Keppler had not returned to Flowergate or made any contact with Heitmann.

He checked the time and began to send a message. Using a short pre-arranged code, he asked to be picked up the next day from Staithes.

In his room at the Marine Hotel, James Simmonds sat quietly staring out of the half-open sash window at the back wall of a shop twenty feet away. It had taken him almost two hours to locate the hotel where Irene Deladier was staying. The clerk on duty at the desk had been surprised when the tall and distinguished gentleman with the cavalry moustache and briefcase declined the room facing out onto the harbour in favour of one round the side, overlooking the kitchen yard. The gentleman, with an embarrassed smile, explained that in common with Hans Christian Anderson he had a phobia about being trapped in a hotel fire. Unlike the renowned writer of fairy stories he did not go to the extreme of carrying a rope ladder with him, but he always insisted on a room with an adjacent fire escape. With an indulgent smile, the clerk conducted him to a first-floor room over the kitchens which, he would readily have conceded, was probably the poorest in the hotel.

Simonds got up from the chair and, having first checked that the door was locked, opened the old leather briefcase on the side table and took out his beloved trench knife. The tempered steel blade gleamed brightly in the afternoon sun as he carried it over to his armchair by the bed. Rolling up his shirt sleeve, left handed and using his teeth, he undid the straps holding his gloved fist in place and laid it on the bed. He had been very careful during the last few days, and his stump, he was pleased to see, was clean and hard. With infinite care he strapped on the lethal blade, ensuring that his wrist sat comfortably in the cup and that the straps which bound it to his forearm, giving it the strength to thrust and slash without coming adrift, were secure.

Reaching over to the bed, Simmonds picked up a hypodermic syringe and a tiny glass phial. A humourless smile twisted his mouth: money, he told himself, could buy you anything. One telephone call to Chapman Absolom followed by a trip to London had ensured his morphine supply indefinitely. Placing the phial between his knees, he pushed the needle into the sealed rubber top.

Mistily, as the morphine coursing round his body began to take effect, the blade became first an extension of his arm, then of his body, replacing the missing hand and filling his entire vision. Hovering dreamily just beyond the tip of the now circling blade, Irene Deladier drifted into his view, lips parted in invitation, the clear blue eyes and dark features framed by waves of flowing midnight-black hair. Slowly, deliberately, as he watched she slid the light silk robe that she was wearing from her shoulders and allowed it to drop away, leaving her naked in front of him. As she watched in silent fascination, he moved to caress her. The steel hand gently moved across her breast leaving a thin trail of scarlet blood, marring its snowy whiteness, trickling down across her belly. The vision started to blur, fading as the white body became redder and redder, the blood a torrent now, flowing over her flanks and down her legs. Within minutes she receded into an enveloping darkness, and Simmonds drifted off into a deep pain-free sleep.

It was almost six o'clock when he awoke. His head was pounding and his mouth dry. Removing the knife from his wrist, he sluiced his face in the water left by the chambermaid in a white china jug on the nightstand, allowing some of it to slake his thirst. Taking his Gillette safety razor from its case, he poured more water and carefully shaved. He examined his face in the dressing table mirror, and was pleased to see that there was not a single nick on his dark blue jawline. Shaving in cold water was an acquired knack that had to be mastered if one were to survive in the army. After more than a decade serving in the Territorial Force, attending training camp every year, he had perfected the art. He smiled cheerfully at the image that gazed back out of the mirror at him. Captain James Simmonds, DSO., Kelsford Yeomanry.

Consulting his watch, he saw that it was now twenty-five to seven. Dinner would not be served for an hour and a half: ample time to take a turn round the town, check the coastal defences on the battery at the harbour mouth, then return for dinner with his victim – and a satisfactory conclusion to the evening.

Downstairs in the lobby, Simmonds checked the keys behind the reception desk. Number thirty-four's was hanging on its hook, bearing mute witness to the fact that Madame Deladier was out. He raised his hat politely to a lady coming in through the swing door, and passed unnoticed into the street.

Purely by chance, he had only gone a short distance from the Marine Hotel when, walking purposefully up Pier Road towards him from the direction of the drinking fountain, he spotted his cousin. 'Irene, what a pleasant surprise!' The bushy moustache lifted in a greeting.

'Jamie! What on earth are you doing here?' Taken unawares, it was difficult for Irene to keep the annoyance out of her voice.

Ignoring her tone, he dropped in beside her and turned back to retrace his steps. 'Took a few days off to enjoy the summer weather, my dear. Haven't been up here since I was a lad. I used to come up with Mother and Uncle Tom, before she married Reuben.'

After the initial shock, Irene made an effort to recover some of her good will and, with a forced smile, asked politely, 'Where are you staying?'

To her further chagrin, she discovered that by an unfortunate chance he was booked in at the same hotel as herself. Some time ago, she suspected, her cousin had worked out what was happening between her and Will. He was not alone in this, she well knew, and she did not really care. Her brother had started asking some very pointed questions that she had quite easily deflected, leaving him under no illusions that it did not concern him. Jamie presented a slightly different problem. Although he had been very attentive when she had arrived in Kelsford newly widowed, Irene had quickly realised that his interest was more than casual – and that given the slightest encouragement he had the potential to be a nuisance. Since she had become involved with Will, her cousin's attitude was definitely cooler. Perhaps the seaside air today had served to mellow him.

Half listening to his stream of conversation as they strolled back to the hotel, Irene was lost in her own thoughts. The affair with Will could not continue indefinitely. Her brother was right: the social gap between them was too wide, and before long she would have to find a way to end the affair.

'. . . for dinner?'

She looked sharply at Jamie. 'I'm sorry, what were you saying?'

'I thought that as we're staying at the same hotel perhaps you'd like to join me for dinner.'

Inwardly Irene groaned. 'Yes, thank you, that would be very nice.' Tomorrow, she decided, she would have to do something about her cousin – who seemed to be pursuing her once more.

As the station clock struck half past seven, Harry and Will descended from the train and, stretching their aching limbs, walked purposefully towards the Angel Hotel, where Gresham was waiting on the steps for them. 'I've already booked you in adjacent rooms,' he said, as he escorted them past the reception clerk and up to his own room.

Gratefully, they slumped down in the two easy chairs in Gresham's large first-floor double. A plate of ham sandwiches each and a bottle of beer soon revived them, while they outlined the course of recent events that had brought them there.

Pacing up and down, Gresham brought them up to date with the sinking of the *Dunfermline*. 'The fact that we've identified Nemesis puts a totally new slant on what's going on here. Potsdam are going to be most unhappy with Nemesis's controller. Having gone to so much trouble to remove Duggan from the equation, he's also eliminated his own agent – who, most importantly, was also the key to them being able to produce MD19 themselves.' The irony of it was beautiful, he thought: he could not have arranged it better himself.

'It was a brilliantly simple plan. Only Duggan and Paul Kändler could together or independently produce the nerve gas. With Duggan and the existing samples of MD19 aboard *Dunfermline* removed from the equation, the only person who could manufacture the stuff was his own man. Spirit Kändler away from Kelsford to the Fatherland, and in a month's time the Germans would be able to flood the trenches with a new weapon that could destroy the entire British Army in France.' Gresham paused, a look of regret crossing his dark features. 'Unfortunately, Ted Bayliss was aboard the *Dunfermline* when it went down. Plans were changed at the last minute. Herbert Duggan, as the senior scientist, decided on the morning of his departure that he needed his colleague Kändler along with him. He felt that the field trials would be conducted more efficiently if they were both involved. At that time we didn't know that Kändler was Nemesis, and he didn't know that arrangements were in place to sink the destroyer they were travelling on.'

Ralph picked up a packet of Passing Cloud from the night table, and offered one to Harry. During the time he had spent with Ted Bayliss he had developed a taste for the oval, loosely packed cigarettes. 'Actually,' he continued, 'there was another change to the plans. I was supposed to go with them on the destroyer. The intention was that *Dunfermline* would shadow Kitchener's vessels, and, so far as Jellicoe and the Admiralty were concerned, be there as an added security measure set up by Naval Intelligence. However, just after the convoy sailed we received information of a lengthy radio intercept by Room 40 which, because the operator remained on the air too long, we were able to trace fairly accurately to a small area here in Whitby.'

Gresham paused to gather his thoughts, the familiar twitch grabbing at the side of his mouth. He was not certain how much more he should disclose to the two policemen. Without Ted Bayliss to partner him, however, he was very isolated, and they might provide him with back-up if he needed it. True, he had a team of men watching the shop in Flowergate, but they knew very little about what was going on. They had simply been told a German agent was hiding in the premises, and to maintain surveillance until they received further instructions.

Reaching a decision he continued. 'Let me explain the intelligence situation here. In August 1914 a German cruiser, the *Magdeburg*, was sunk by the Russians in the Gulf of Finland. Before the vessel went down the captain ordered a signalman to take the ship's codebook, row out to deep water and throw it in. Fortunately for us the signalman was killed in the process and the Russkies captured the codes, which they subsequently handed over to us. Since then we have been highly successful in decoding German naval signals.' This was, he knew, the royal 'we', as Leigh-Hunt had not yet managed to take control of the cryptographers in Room 40. 'From the beginning of this year we've been reading the directional signals beamed out to the U-boats stationed in the North Sea. But there's one set of signals that so far we've not cracked. They're going to a U-boat patrolling between Scapa and the Wash. From our inability to decode these particular transmissions we assume that the boat's of particular interest, and we're fairly certain it's being used by Nemesis's controller. What we've been able to do is trace this recent signal to Whitby, and specifically to the Flowergate district. There's one strong suspect: a French polisher who has a shop there. He's a German immigrant by the name of Ludwig Heitmann.'

Crushing out his cigarette, he lit another. 'The stupidity of it is that from all the intercepts that are being decoded, Naval Intelligence knew before Kitchener's flotilla set off that eighteen German submarines were stationed along the route that *Hampshire* and her escorts were taking. Jellicoe, or his staff – we'll never be sure who – messed up badly. The information either didn't reach the admiral, or it was ignored. At least five mine-laying subs are out there right now. Kitchener was sailing into a death trap.' As, he added silently to himself, was Ted Bayliss.

'We've only seen what was in the papers,' put in Harry. 'What really happened?'

'Jellicoe didn't just foul the intelligence reports,' said Gresham bitterly. 'The meteorological forecasts were for a storm of almost cyclone force that was going to hit Kitchener's ships head on. In fairness I suppose it would have taken a brave man to tell Horatio Kitchener that he wasn't going just yet, but the sailing should have been put off for twenty-four hours until the storm abated. As it was, two of the escort destroyers put back to port because of the weather, and so far as we can see *Hampshire* probably hit a mine and sank with heavy loss of life. The few men who survived are being interviewed now. Kitchener and his staff all went down with the ship.' Pausing, he reflected that in reality there would be more than a few at Westminster – including his own master – heaving a small sigh of relief at what would be publicly declared a national tragedy. Over recent months the overbearing field marshal's autocratic conduct of the war had made him many enemies in Parliament.

'I'm sorry about Bayliss.' Will spoke quietly, not quite certain what to say to the colonel. 'Do we know what happened to *Dunfermline*?'

Gresham's expression did not change. 'Not for certain. She put out a mayday call at 1902 hours yesterday. The message said she was holed both amidships and in the stern, and was sinking fast. That's consistent with being torpedoed. That fact, and the presence on board of the scientists with their cargo of MD19, cannot be a coincidence. For a U-boat to be working in those conditions would be very risky: it had to have been detailed to take out a specific target, namely *Dunfermline*.' Changing the subject, he continued. 'I appreciate you're here to arrest Simmonds – and I'll give you whatever help I can. Meantime, we're not certain where he fits in with the Nemesis operation – if at all. He was becoming paranoid about Nemesis' activities, and as we're aware he somehow worked out his identity, possibly even the identity of his controller. That could be why he's here. On the other hand, we also know that he's a psychopath, and he could be here simply to kill Irene Deladier. Does he know about your relationship with her, Will?'

The detective returned his gaze steadily: this was not the time to play games. 'Very possibly. I suppose that by now one or two people have worked things out, and he's more than likely one of them.'

'Would he deem that sufficient reason to kill her?'

Will nodded slowly. 'We know he needs little or no reason to murder anyone who gets in his way or whom he suspects may represent a threat. He definitely had designs on Irene at one time, so if he's jealous he'd consider that ample justification to kill her.'

Harry got up and began to pace back and forth. 'It's nearly eight o'clock. Our guess is that he intends to return home tomorrow, so it's a safe bet that he knows where she is – and intends to do the job tonight.' He turned enquiringly to Will, who gave a cursory nod.

'Agreed. You and I should make a start on checking hotels. We need to know where she is, and get to her before he does.'

'We could work faster separately,' Harry suggested.

Will shook his head. 'No. We stay together. When we find her it'll take both of us to give her adequate protection.'

'What about the local police?' asked Gresham.

Again Will shook his head. 'It would take too long to explain. They'd have to contact their chief constable – and by the time we'd convinced them that the man's a psychopathic maniac it would be too late.'

Gresham smiled. 'If we're lucky, my friends, by the time tonight's over we'll have wrapped everything up. You'll have Simmonds under lock and key, and I'll have my hands on Kändler's controller.' Tucking a .38 service revolver into the back of his belt, he pulled his jacket on and led the way to the door.

Irene wondered for a moment where she was. Her head ached intolerably, and it was several seconds before she realised that she was sitting on an upright chair with her hands tied behind her back. The curtains were still open and it was dark outside. Gathering her thoughts, she attempted to ignore the pain in her temples and to work out what had happened to her. The last thing she remembered was having dinner in the restaurant of the Marine Hotel with her cousin. After that everything was blank. No, not quite. She forced her aching mind to function. As they finished the meal she had begun to feel unwell. The room had begun to spin and she had felt very faint. Dimly she recollected Jamie helping her up the stairs. He had said something to the hotel clerk about her having had too much sunshine.

A movement brought her attention back to the room. It was almost a carbon copy of her own: a double bed in front of her and a plain deal nightstand next to the window. As an evening breeze caused the curtains to stir slightly, James Simmonds emerged into her line of vision. 'You're awake, my dear,' he said solicitously. 'I was beginning to think that I'd have to wait all night for you.'

Irene stared at him in fascination. He was wearing dark trousers and a navy blue military-style tunic buttoned up to the neck. Other than the colour, she recognised it as the sort of top that a surgeon would wear while working in an operating theatre. But it was not the tunic that held her attention. Attached to the stump of his right wrist was a long-bladed knife, one edge of which was serrated halfway along.

'It's called a trench knife,' he said, in a voice that was little more than a whisper. 'Would you like to touch it? The blade's very sharp.'

James moved his right arm, bringing the point of the knife up until it was touching her left breast. Through the fabric of her dress she could feel the edge of the fine blade. Beads of perspiration broke out on her forehead.

'Don't worry. You won't feel a thing.' He allowed the blade to slice into the dress, with a tiny movement. As if it were happening to someone else, Irene watched as a thin trickle of blood began to stain the material. Dully she realised that he was right; she had not felt any pain.

James lifted the blade away an inch or so, snatches of his recent dream running through his brain in a confused kaleidoscope. 'You've been a silly girl, haven't you?' The question was posed in a distant voice that neither sought nor required an answer. 'You betrayed me, Irene, and traitors have to die. Your policeman lover can't help you now, can he?'

Irene watched as he moved back a pace, mesmerised by the thin cut that he had made on her body. He appeared to be in a world of his own: talking, then retreating into his mind. A sudden anger filled her. 'I knew that you were dangerous,' she said bitterly. 'I didn't realise just how dangerous, though. It was you who murdered the others, wasn't it? The woman at Devonshire Gardens, and the man in the candle factory. Did you kill Kath Doyle as well?'

A light seemed to glow in James Simmonds eyes as his attention returned to what she was saying. 'We were lovers, you know.' He gazed longingly for a second at the woman tied to the chair before the blank expression clouded his features once more. 'I wanted you – but you became involved with the policeman. He was married, but that didn't bother you, did it? He betrayed his wife for you. But it was you who were the real traitor, my lovely Irene – and traitors have to die, don't they?'

She knew that as soon as he stopped talking the blade would come back and slice into her flesh, and that once he started slicing he would not stop until she was dead. 'Why did you kill Kathy?'

'Kathleen was very good, but she knew too much. She helped me sort out Charlotte Groves and the policeman – Weldon. They were both blackmailers, but even that isn't as bad as being a traitor, is it, Irene?' His eyes suddenly lit up and an expression of serenity came into his face. 'Now it's your turn – then him. You know who I mean, don't you?'

The sound of a light footfall outside in the corridor followed by a tap on the door brought him to an abrupt halt. Holding the tip of the blade to Irene's throat he held the forefinger of his good hand up to his lips, indicating that she was to remain silent. Once again there was a tap on the door, and a timorous voice said, 'Mr Simmonds . . . are you there, sir?' The blade pressed against her throat as the door handle was gently turned. 'Mr Simmonds, sir, room service.'

Simmonds recognised the reception clerk, his voice cracking with nervousness. Almost imperceptibly the door handle continued to turn. Spinning away from the woman, in two swift strides he was at the open window. He threw his leg over the sill and climbed awkwardly out onto the fire escape.

From behind him came Irene's frantic screams for help and the rending sound of the doorlock being kicked off, followed by the deafening crash of a gunshot. Splinters of wood flew past his ear as a .45 calibre bullet splintered the window frame inches from his head.

Harry fired a second shot from the window at the figure disappearing down the fire escape before diving out of the window after him. Will ran to the woman in the chair and tugged at the cords that tied her wrists. 'Are you all right?' he gasped, as the length of clothes-line that Simmonds had run around Irene's ankles, after securing her wrists, fell away.

Nodding dumbly, she brought her hands round in front of her and began to massage the circulation back into them.

Will took her in his arms and held her. 'Dear God, I thought we were too late. We checked half the hotels in the town before we found you. The clerk said that after dinner you were unwell and James took you back up to your room. When you weren't there we knew he had to have you in here.'

'I'm all right,' she said, finally finding her voice. 'Get after Harry. I'm all right now.'

Nodding quickly, Will went to the window and, revolver in hand, made his way down the escape. At the foot of the steps he found Harry's crumpled form: it was obvious that instead of immediately running away, Simmonds had waited in the dark and ambushed his pursuer. From the graze across his head it looked as if Harry had been caught a glancing blow by the flat edge of the trench knife. It was a mistake on Simmonds's part, thought Will grimly. He had little doubt that the blow was intended to have been fatal.

Harry groaned and sat up. 'Bastard was waiting for me,' he muttered shakily.

'Don't worry. Get yourself together and we'll start looking for him.' Will picked up the heavy automatic from the ground and thrust it back into his partner's hand, before they climbed the fire escape again. Having checked Simmonds's room for any clues about where he might be heading, and finding nothing, they reassured themselves again that Irene was unharmed. After they had escorted her to the Angel, where she was instructed to lock herself in Will's room, they set off to find their quarry.

At the bottom of St Ann's Staith the detectives paused to take stock. On their left lay the River Esk and, over the bridge, the far side of town. To the right was the railway station. It was now past midnight and there were few people about. The station was a terminus and at this time of night there would be no trains arriving or leaving, so it was doubtful that Simmonds would go there – but they would have to check. It was more likely that he would try to hide out in the town and then, in the morning, mingle with the holidaymakers and attempt to jump on a train as it was about to leave.

The sound of approaching footsteps caught Will's attention and, swinging round, he brought up the Smith and Wesson. A few seconds later a small group of men led by Ralph Gresham appeared. In the middle, securely handcuffed, was the figure of Ludwig Heitmann.

Briefly Will and Harry filled Gresham in on what had happened.

When they had finished, Gresham said in a low voice, 'Put him in the van, Percy, and get off back to York. I'll join you tomorrow.' Detailing three of the men to remain with him, he waited until the German was locked safely in the back of the anonymous black delivery van that was parked by the kerb, and as it drove off he said quietly to Will, 'I suggest that we work in twos and start to make a search. The area's small enough that at this time of night we can attract each others' attention easily.'

Will nodded in agreement. 'You and your men stay this side of the river; Harry and I will do the other. Check the railway station. If we spot him we'll have to play it by ear. It's 12.40 now. Meet back here in an hour.'

As they split up, Will thought gratefully that as it was a small town there would probably only be one beat officer allocated at this time of night, and he might be somewhere on the outskirts. The last thing he wanted was for an unsuspecting constable to encounter James Simmonds.

Without any further conversation they split up, Gresham and his men making their way cautiously towards the railway station, Will and Harry, one either side of the road, crossing the ornate metal swing-bridge. Once across the river they moved stealthily along Sandgate and into the market-place. After a quick conversation they decided to work independently, checking doorways and alleys but staying within sight of each other. For the next fifty minutes they quartered the tiny narrow streets on the east side of the river. The town was deserted, and Will realised that the night duty policeman was indeed safely out of their way. He checked his watch, saw that it was just over ten minutes before the rendezvous time with Ralph's men, and signalled Harry that they should make their way back to the bridge.

Deciding to take one last look along the bottom end of Church Street, Will turned back into Grape Lane. Looking round, he realised that Harry had missed seeing him turn back, and was now nowhere in sight. This was always a danger when searching an area in the dark, and he decided that he would pick him up again at the meeting point.

A slight movement in the deep shadows of a narrow alley stopped him in his tracks. Freezing with his back to the wall he waited, hardly breathing. For a full minute nothing happened. In the reflected light of the gas lamp over a nearby shop he saw a board fixed to the wall bearing the name Tin Ghaut. At the end of the alley a pale patch of moonlight glinted on the gently rippling waters of the Esk. He could just make out the bar of sand below, with a fishing coble pulled up high, out of the reach of the tide. Next to the wall at the side of some stone steps was a man, standing perfectly still. Will felt a cold sweat break out on his body and, tensing, he gently pulled back the hammer on the revolver.

'Will.' The voice was barely a whisper. 'It's all right. It's me – Harry.' The shadow pulled back out of sight into the doorway of one of the tiny cottages flanking the Ghaut.

Breathing a sigh of relief, Will dropped the hammer of the gun back down and eased his way along the cobbled surface. 'What have you seen?' His own voice was almost inaudible on the night air.

'Shhhh . . .' There was no movement from the doorway.

Will was only feet away when the realisation rushed into his head that in all the time they had worked together Harry had never called him Will.

Simmonds was on him before he could use his gun. The blade arched brightly in the moonlight, slashing through the air at the point where, seconds before, his head had been. A shower of sparks briefly burst through the darkness as the steel skimmed along the brickwork, followed by a deafening shock as Will fired two shots at him. He knew immediately that he had missed. Simmonds was moving even as he swung the blow that was intended to decapitate Will. Barging into him, his attacker aimed a second blow with the weapon that Will managed to deflect, but the swing was followed up by a well-timed kick in the stomach that left him retching on the ground.

When Will dragged himself to his feet he found himself alone in the Ghaut. When he staggered back into Grape Street it was deserted, as he expected, with the sound of running feet disappearing into the night. Will took off towards the broad bridge over the estuary, desperately hoping that his quarry was running into the arms of either Harry North or Ralph Gresham.

As he began to cross the bridge, Will thought at first that he was wrong and that Simmonds had not come that way. There was no sign of the others.

Then, at the far end of the bridge, on the west side near the drinking fountain, he saw him bending down in the shadows. Simmonds had the front panel off one of the lights that were used in winter months to illuminate the bridge. Will hesitated for a moment, puzzled. There seemed to be some sort of control panel at the base of the lamp.

Suddenly the decking beneath his feet began to move sideways, and he remembered reading somewhere that the bridge swung open from the middle in order to allow tall ships to pass along the estuary from their moorings and out to sea. He realised that the lamp standard housed the control mechanism that operated it.

From behind him came the sound of pounding feet, and he knew that somehow both Harry and Gresham were on the wrong side of the bridge. Probably Simmonds had watched as Gresham and his men, alerted by the gunshot, had run across the bridge to the east side. Safe from his pursuers, Simmonds could open the bridge and disable the controls. The gap in the centre was increasing, leaving an inky void of cold river. At its narrowest point the chasm was already five feet wide.

Will Mardlin was a bulky man, neither built for nor given to running, but in one supreme effort he launched himself full tilt into the air. If anyone had asked him to repeat the feat and offered him a large sum of money to do so, he would have refused point blank to have even considered it. As it was, when he crashed down onto the moving surface he completely lost his balance and fell with a sickening force, which for the second time in as many minutes drove the air from his body and left him in a helpless heap. Instinctively he knew that James Simmonds was not going to jump back onto the safety of the road. He was going to try to kill him.

Rolling to one side, Will made a grab for the wrought iron of the bridge's side and hauled himself to his feet. He was only just in time. A second later Simmonds was grappling with him. His left hand clutching Will's jacket, he aimed the blade on his extended right arm in a downward slash. Avoiding the blow, Will pulled back and aimed a kick at Simmonds's crotch. He was too high and Simmonds took it on the thigh. Knocked off balance, he reeled backwards. Will dived at him, and the two men fell, locked in a deadly embrace. Under normal circumstances Will would have been able to win from this position as he was a strong man, but he realised very quickly that he had made an error. These were not normal circumstances: his opponent was completely deranged, and had that peculiar strength which is given to madmen.

Within seconds Will was fighting for his life. As they rolled over, he tried to maintain some sort of advantage while battling to keep Simmonds from using his right arm and the knife. Momentarily he saw Harry and Gresham, helpless spectators, twenty yards away on the other side of the bridge. He felt the solid surface of the bridge vanish from beneath his back as his head was pushed back into space. The struggle had taken them to the edge of the bridge, and Will was being forced over the void into the icy waters below.

James's left hand was now around Will's throat, squeezing his windpipe. As he fought for breath he felt consciousness slipping away. His grip slackened, and suddenly he no longer held the trench knife at arm's length: it was free and poised above his face. In a last desperate effort he clawed at the other man's eyes. Simmonds threw his head back and to one side, while Will's nails tore deep lacerations down his cheek.

Blood welled from the wounds, but there was a light now in Simmonds's eyes. It was the same light that had shone as he prepared to strike at Irene. It was the same light that had shone while he was carrying Sergeant Auld away from the bridge at Mons.

As if from a distance, Will saw the straps attaching the blade to his wrist, a tight buckle cutting deep into the man's flesh, and the support that ran up his arm giving it strength. Slowly a smile crossed Simmonds's face as his arm started to descend in a practised motion; then there was an immense explosion in Will's head and, like a light being switched off, the eyes looking down at him became blank. As the grip on his throat relaxed, Will became aware that Simmonds was staring at him with an expression of uncomprehending curiosity.

A second explosion rent the air, and Will was aware of being spattered with blood and brains as the heavy calibre bullet passed through the back of Simmonds's head and exited through the front of his skull, blowing away most of his face. The third shot lodged in his neck, severing his spinal column. Unable to move, Will watched horrified as more bullets ripped through Simmonds back and into his chest. Uncannily, amid the bellow of the gunfire he was aware of the metallic tinkling of ejected cartridge shells bouncing off the wooden decking, inches away from him.

As if by some pre-arranged signal the firing stopped, and as if aware that the ordeal was over James Simmonds's dead body slid sideways, to rest against the bridge's ironwork. Standing less than a foot away from him, a smoking Luger pistol still pointing at the dead man, stood Irene Deladier. Will heard two sharp clicks as, the magazine empty, she pulled the trigger twice more.

Chapter Thirty-Two

'It was in his briefcase.' Irene's voice was dull and tired. Will watched as the detective inspector took down her statement. The local police were – not unreasonably, he thought – less than happy with them. Police officers from a different area conducting a murder enquiry in the town without telling them was a bad enough breach of procedure, but the shooting of the prime suspect by one of the witnesses required a deal of explanation.

Will checked the clock on the wall. Twenty-five minutes past three. The office was a carbon copy of a hundred others that he had sat in over the years. Whitewashed walls, half a dozen desks piled high with paperwork and files. The thought crossed his mind that the number of holidaymakers passing through at this time of year would greatly increase their workload.

'Why did you take the gun out with you, Madame Deladier?' The detective inspector's name was Travis Ryder. He was a small, slightly built man of about the same age as Will. He appeared competent enough and was asking all the right questions. Will hoped that he would not stumble across something he was not supposed to – for instance the fact that he and Harry had arrived in Whitby armed to the teeth, prepared, had Irene not done so, to kill Simmonds themselves. After a hurried discussion before the arrival of the local police, Harry had gone back to Tin Ghaut with his flashlight and recovered Will's gun from where he had dropped it when he first disturbed Simmonds. Both Will's revolver and Harry's automatic were now safely locked away in Harry's room at the Angel.

Another thing that might have given Ryder further cause for displeasure was the fact that earlier in the night British Intelligence agents had quietly entered a shop in Flowergate and taken away a German agent, probably Nemesis's controller, without anyone being the wiser – and were now en route with him for the military headquarters at York.

'After Will – Superintendent Mardlin – untied me, he and Inspector North took me back to the Angel and left me in Superintendent Mardlin's room. They also left Jamie's briefcase with me for safe keeping. It seemed pretty obvious that it might contain important evidence, so I had a look and there at the bottom was the gun. I waited and waited, but Superintendent Mardlin didn't come back, so eventually I became worried and decided to go and look for him. I took the gun with me to give to him. I thought he might need it.'

Ryder resumed writing in a neat cursive hand.

'Simmonds had a thing about weapons and militaria,' Will explained. 'When we raided his home we found a whole armoury downstairs in the cellar.' He glanced across at Harry for confirmation. Harry had a blank expression. The message to his senior officer was plain: when you're in a hole stop digging.

Travis Ryder laid down his pen. 'Thank you, Madame Deladier.' He gave Will a long hard stare. 'You three seem to know each other very well,' he said pointedly.

'Yes we do,' replied Will. He hoped that he sounded convincing. 'Over the last year Inspector North and I have been investigating a series of murders. Kelsford, like Whitby, is a small town. Madame Deladier has been involved in various aspects of our enquiries, and over time we've become fairly well acquainted.'

At least the last part is true, thought Harry.

'Obviously, Mr Mardlin, you'll appreciate my position.' Inspector Ryder was an unhappy man. Irene Deladier had virtually committed a murder, and in any other circumstances none of those present would have been going anywhere other than before a magistrate the following morning. 'Because of the circumstances and the fact that you were in direct pursuit of the dead man in relation to your own murder enquiries, I'm going to release the lady into your custody on the understanding that you'll be responsible for her return here to attend the coroner's inquest. 'In the meantime,' he continued coldly, 'your actions tonight have created what I can only describe as an embarrassing situation. Had you and Inspector North contacted me at the outset, what has happened could have been avoided, and I think that's something our mutual chief constables will be discussing. Tomorrow, or rather after breakfast this morning, you'll oblige me by catching the earliest available train back to Kelsford.'

Seated opposite each other in the railway carriage, the two men were lost in their own thoughts. The clatter of the metal wheels as they ate up the miles of bleak moorland provided a muted background for their reflections. It was almost an hour since either of them had spoken.

As the train pulled into York station Will broke the silence. 'I need to make a telephone call.' His voice was flat and expressionless.

Harry nodded slowly, as if it was something that he had been expecting.

Threading his way through the crowd that thronged the busy platform, Will made his way to the stationmaster's office. Production of his warrant card and the declaration that he was on urgent police business quickly obtained for him the use of the station's only telephone.

Sidney Gresham was standing by the reception desk at the Angel, paying his bill, when the clerk politely handed the telephone to him. For five minutes he listened intently, before a brusque 'Thank you. I'll deal with it.' He hung the speaking trumpet back on its rest and handed the instrument back to the clerk.

Standing on the platform, Harry watched Will as he walked quickly back along the train to their open carriage door. He threw away his half-smoked cigarette and climbed back into the compartment behind him.

As the train pulled out of the station, Will sat staring moodily into space. Eventually, seeming to have reached a decision, without meeting Harry's eyes he said quietly, 'It wasn't his gun.'

Harry said nothing, sadly watching the man who over recent months he had come to regard as his closest friend. He knew exactly what Will was going to say. He had known since the previous night.

'A Luger's an automatic, and he didn't have any automatics in his collection, did he?' Harry made no response, silently waiting. 'You like that Colt automatic, don't you?'

'Yes, Will. I do.'

Neither of them registered the fact that he had used his friend's first name. The other man continued speaking as if he had not heard the reply. 'When we tried those hand guns out at the barracks that was when we tested it.' Will gave a tired smile. 'We had reservations. It was a good heavy calibre weapon. Even at long range it would stop a man dead, quite literally – but don't you remember, Fletcher Pemberton couldn't use it because he's left handed. The expended shells are ejected by the magazine gases to the right-hand side of the gun, so every time he fired the empty cartridge case flew out across his body, hitting him in the face or catching his clothing. It's the same with the Luger: it ejects to the right, and the safety catch, which is on the left-hand side of the butt, has to be worked with the thumb of the right hand. James Simmonds hadn't got a right hand.'

'And if the pistol wasn't his . . .' Harry ventured, knowing the answer. He had known since last night.

'It had to be hers. She brought it with her.'

'James Simmonds was a psychopathic killer, but he wasn't a traitor. Somewhere along the line he worked out that Irene was involved in betraying Project 19 – that she was Nemesis's courier. Perhaps it was the weekly dinner parties. With the benefit of hindsight that was obviously when Kändler was slipping her the information. All those trips to London were a lie. She never went to London at all: she was coming up to Whitby to meet the controller. We thought Simmonds followed her up here this weekend because he was jealous. We were wrong. He came up here to kill her because he knew she was a spy. Our arrival altered things. We might have saved Irene's life, but we also gave her the perfect opportunity to remove him.'

'What are you going to do?'

For the first time since he had begun speaking, Will met Harry's gaze. 'It's done,' he replied, with an air of finality.

'When this is over I'll find a way to kill you, Stefan, however long it takes.' Irene's voice was devoid of all emotion: it was a statement of fact.

'You'll have to be rather more successful than you were in your initial efforts to kill your cousin James, ma chère Irene.' Stefan Capewell gave her a long appreciative stare. It seemed like only yesterday that they had ridden out together from her parents' château, or hiked along the mountain paths high above the Loire. His mind dwelt on the occasions they had lain in an affectionate embrace, concealed in the bales of an haystack, or snuggled under the blankets of a narrow bed in some hunting lodge, caressing and fondling each other. In those days he had merely been the son of the estate manager to the high and mighty Norton family. No longer: now he was Siegfried Keppler, a senior intelligence officer in the army of Kaiser Wilhelm II.

'In the woods I was trying to frighten him off, not kill him. He saw Paul handing me the weekly package after one of the Sunday night dinner parties, and became suspicious. It wasn't until last night that I realised how dangerous he was. He really intended to kill me. Kept telling me that I was a traitor and that I must die.' Irene's mind flicked back to the hotel room, James taunting her with how clever he was. 'Last week at the railway station in Kelsford he saw me getting on the train to come up here. I pretended that I hadn't seen him – I was supposed to be going down to London – but he became suspicious. Then he read about *Viking Tun* being sunk and really started to wonder. He decided to have a look for himself. After that it just got more complicated. He couldn't believe it when he almost bumped into that young detective dashing out through the pub doorway, and then saw that he was trailing you. Like Ashe, he recognised you immediately from the photograph of the picnic party for Sam's twenty-first, and everything dropped into place: Paul stealing the information from the Old Watermill, handing it to me every Sunday evening, and then when I was supposed to be in London doing war work I was up here.'

'You were doing war work, my dear – for the Kaiser.' A cold smile flitted across Keppler's angular features.

'This mess is your fault,' she said bitterly. 'Letting James see you push that poor lad Ashe off the quay. He was totally unbalanced, and after that he became obsessed with killing me. Then he said he was coming after you.'

'No,' Keppler corrected. 'This present mess, as you choose to call it, is entirely down to you leaving a family photograph on full view in your house. James visited regularly, and Ashe saw the picture every time he came to work on the war hospital accounts with your man Palmaerts. It was pure misfortune that when Ashe came here he recognised me.'

'You didn't have to kill him.'

'Be your age, Irene – he recognised me. What I couldn't have foreseen was that your maniac cousin James would be following both of us, and also recognised me.'

Keppler sighed. 'That, of course, was when Simmonds really put it all together: that if I was here then you had to be my contact in Kelsford. As you so correctly say, he'd already seen Kändler slipping his weekly envelope to you at one of your Sunday evening soirées. He simply needed to watch you and wait, and follow you up here next time you made contact.'

'You're a bastard, Stefan, and I repeat – one day I'll find a way to kill you.' An angry flush suffused the young woman's dark features.

'Stop calling me Stefan. My name's Siegfried Keppler. You've no idea how useful this war's been to me. All the while I was at university I worked for the Kaiser. Did you really think that I wanted to go back to your parents' château, and just like my parents know my place, and touch my forelock every time your wealthy mother or her husband passed by? "When you've graduated from university you'll take over the management of the estate . . . One day you'll be our devoted servant, Stefan . . ." Do you think I didn't detest every inch of that estate, and you, and your parents, and your priggish brother? I was always just good enough to accompany you on your rides and outings, hold the horses and carry the packs. You were always a teaser. "Just there, Stefan, faster Stefan . . ." Now, my dear, it's my turn.'

The flush extended down Irene's neck and disappeared into the collar of her dress. It was difficult to tell whether it was anger or embarrassment at her recollection of teenage indiscretions. 'What about Jean-Claude?' Her voice was harsh with emotion.

'Ah . . . Jean-Claude. The last time I heard he was well, and writing you another of his interminable letters.'

'Where is it – the letter?'

'Safe somewhere in Germany. Truly, Irene, it was no different to the dozens of others that he spends his days composing. How much he loves you, please be careful, please get him out of prison.'

'Where is he, you bastard? Our agreement was that if I did as you asked he'd be released and allowed to go to Switzerland.'

Keppler appeared to give the matter some consideration. 'You're not in a strong position, ma chère. Officially your husband is dead – killed in action. I now have the information that I needed in relation to Project 19. You really need to calm down and be a little patient. For the time being I think he's better served in the officers' camp in Prussia – where we can keep an eye on him.'

There was, he realised, no point in allowing her to know that he was leaving aboard the U39 that night. It would take the British several days to come to the conclusion that Ludwig Heitmann was not the man they were looking for, by which time he would be safely back in Berlin. Despite recent events, the information that Paul Kändler had passed back was sufficient for their own scientists to begin work on producing a version of the gas, but, he admitted ruefully, without Kändler it was going to be at least two years before a finished product could be achieved.

The capture of Jean-Claude Deladier so early in the war, combined with Keppler's knowledge of the Norton family, had proved invaluable to German Intelligence. Swapping Deladier's papers for those of an officer killed in August 1914 was an easy matter to arrange. Not long after her arrival in Kelsford – soon after her affair with Will began – Irene had been contacted by a German agent during one of her trips to the War Charities Commission, who told her that Jean-Claude was a prisoner of war, and explaining what she had to do to keep him alive and unharmed.

A look of dismay came into the woman's eyes. 'You promised . . . you said that if I helped you to get the details of the nerve gas Jean-Claude would be released!'

'There remains one last job that I need you to do,' continued Keppler smoothly. 'It's possible that Kändler left some research papers at the Old Watermill. I need you to persuade your brother to let you see them. It shouldn't be difficult, brotherly trust and all that sort of thing. After all, Sam isn't the sharpest knife in the box, is he? Once you've done that I'll arrange for someone to contact you, and we can review your husband's situation.'

The wheels of the locomotive were slowly beginning to turn when Irene Deladier looked up in startled surprise as the door of her first-class compartment was suddenly jerked open. A briefcase was thrust through it, followed by the slim figure of Ralph Gresham attired in a dark business suit and grey homburg hat. Thrown off balance by the jolting train as it gathered speed, Gresham dropped into the seat beside her.

'Ralph, this is most unexpected. I thought you were returning to London.' She was confused by his sudden appearance in the reserved compartment.

'Change of plan, my dear,' he replied, patting her hand in a friendly manner.

Irene just had time to register the involuntary twitch at the corner of her travelling companion's mouth, before the hand on her arm tightened into a vice-like grip. Twisting his body, with his free hand Gresham deftly pushed a handkerchief soaked in chloroform across her mouth and nose.

As soon as he was satisfied that Irene was unconscious, Gresham removed his jacket and took from his briefcase a tiny glass phial. With infinite care he broke the seal and exposed the splinter of sharpened bamboo, no thicker than a sewing needle, tipped with curare. Drawing the compartment blinds, he lay the unconscious woman in a prone position on the bench seat and set to work. Ten minutes later, adjusting Irene's disarranged clothing, he hauled the inert body back up into a sitting position in the corner by the window.

His task finished, Ralph realised that he was sweating both from exertion and the heat of the day. Consulting his watch, he saw that they were due to arrive at York in thirty minutes. Not that time was critical, he thought, arranging Irene's hands in her lap and depositing her hat neatly beside her. She would be dead well before the train steamed into the station. Stepping back, he took a careful look around him and gave a small grunt of satisfaction. To all intents she looked exactly like any other passenger who, lulled into drowsiness by the motion of the train, had simply dozed off.

Walking into the street outside York station, Ralph Gresham folded his newspaper and, tucking it under his arm, raised a hand to the driver of the waiting staff car.

Tomorrow's *Times*, he anticipated, would doubtless carry a brief obituary to the wealthy young widow who, following the unprecedented traumas of her experience at the hands of a madman in Whitby, had succumbed to the sudden and unforeseeable effects of a heart attack. In the unlikely event of a post-mortem being conducted, it was an almost foregone conclusion that the heart attack diagnosis would be confirmed. The beauty of the South American poison was that, having suffocated the victim, it left no traces in the body and perfectly mimicked the effects of a cardiac arrest. It would take a very observant and diligent physician to find the tiny puncture mark deep in her crotch.

Settling back into the seat next to the driver, he said quietly, 'Percy, when you've dropped me at headquarters get yourself over to Kelsford. On the sideboard in the drawing room of Irene Deladier's house in Kingsbury Lane is a silver-framed family photograph. I want it.'